ANNE was suddenly reminded of how useless it would be to ask anyone about Michael. Besides, more and more she was aware of a certain curious conspiracy, a kind of web of silence woven around him. "He does not exist." That's what the Prince had said. "Poison," Carl had called him. "Where he is, there's trouble." Who had said that? But tonight's threat had surely been against him. Or her? When the maid said goodnight and left, she did not need to remind Anne to put the chains on her doors.

Fawcett Crest Books
by Jane Aiken Hodge:

LAST ACT

Jane Aiken Hodge

FAWCETT CREST • NEW YORK

Despite any superficial resemblances, Lissenberg is neither Liechtenstein nor Luxembourg, nor is its royal family in any way based on theirs. It is, of course, Ruritania.

LAST ACT

Published by Fawcett Crest Books, a unit of CBS Publications, the Consumer Publishing Division of CBS Inc., by arrangement with Coward, McCann & Geoghegan

ISBN: 0-449-24379-6

Printed in the United States of America

First Fawcett Crest Printing: March 1981

10   9   8   7   6   5   4   3   2   1

For Alan

From the *Lissenberger Zeitung:*

BEETHOVEN OPERA DISCOVERED

The palace archivist today confirmed rumours that he had found an unknown opera by Ludwig van Beethoven among the papers of the Hereditary Prince Heinz Gustaf the Second. Beethoven's own notes suggest that the opera, *Regulus,* was written for performance at the Congress of Vienna. The project must have been abandoned when the Congress broke up in disorder after Napoleon's escape from Elba. Prince Heinz Gustaf, of course, was in Vienna at the time, representing Lissenberg at the Congress. A musician himself, he very likely knew Beethoven and bought the opera from him in the panic and chaos before Waterloo. He must have hoped to have *Regulus* performed here in Lissenberg, but died very suddenly in the summer of 1815. The score of Beethoven's lost opera has lain among his private papers ever since, and we must congratulate Herr Valst, the archivist, on his find, and on the patient care with which he has checked on its authenticity.

For a discussion of the significance of this spectacular musical discovery, and the prospects of performance of *Regulus,* please see our Centre Arts Pages.

1

"How long does he say?" asked Anne Paget.

The doctor looked down at the letter on his desk, and then straight at her for the first time. "Six months; something like that? If he'd only had the X rays when he saw you. These wretched delays...What with the post and the technicians' strike. That's why he wants to do the exploratory operation the minute he gets back. If you'll just agree to that we'll have a better idea. X rays don't necessarily tell the whole story. And these—well, you know how things have been with this strike on. It's a miracle we got them done at all."

"You mean." She grasped at it. "There's some doubt? They're not clear?"

"Clear enough, I'm afraid. With the other symptoms. That's why I sent you straight to the top. It's a pity about that conference he's had to go to, but just another week's delay...He's still the best man." He looked back at the letter on his desk. "He says, after the operation we'll know where we stand."

"And it might cure me?" She asked the straight, vital question.

"He doesn't say that. Oh, it might, I suppose. Miracles do happen, but I most certainly would not feel justified in suggesting...in holding out hopes..."

"I thought not. It might just give me a little longer?" She could not take her eyes off the letter on his desk, her death warrant.

Even on this, he was not prepared to commit himself. "It might. But it's been too long already. You should have come to us sooner."

She nearly screamed at him, "But I did, and you said it was 'nerves'." What was the use? He had been busy. He was always busy. Even now, facing death across his desk, she was aware of the queue in the waiting room outside.

He was writing. A prescription. More tranquillisers? "Some pain-killers for you." He handed it to her. "You'll need them, I'm afraid. I do suggest that you reconsider and have

8

the operation. Consult your husband, your family... **Ring** when you've made up your mind, and we'll put things in **train** right away. He'll be back on Monday week. You **shouldn't** leave it longer." He was folding up the consultant's **letter**, putting it neatly in her file. The interview was over.

She went on sitting there for a moment, trying to take it in. Surely there was something more that she should ask? That he should say?

Apparently not. He rose courteously to his feet, and as he did so, pushed her folder to one side and picked up the next patient's notes. "I'm sorry," he said.

"Not nearly so sorry as I am." Anger got her to the door and out through the crowded waiting room into a street where the sun still shone. She would not ring up. Why should she expose herself once more to those cold, impersonal hands? For dying, six months were enough. Too much.

She passed the building where she worked, and headed blindly for the Green, quiet at this time of day, with children at school and dogs walked for the morning. An empty bench with a view of trees. One of them an elm: dying. Talk to your husband. The unconscious irony of it had left her speechless. But why should this doctor have known? It must be pages back in his files. Another tired man, in another town, had given her all those tranquillisers and sleeping pills after Robin crashed the car, killing himself and the unknown girl with him. She had wanted to die then: Robin gone; her faith in him gone; everything gone. She had been angry with the doctor for giving her those tempting, lethal pills; she had thrown them at last into the river and made her sleepless, automaton's way through the scandal and misery of the inquest and newspaper sensation. "Young Pianist in Death Riddle" had been one of the headlines; "Date with Death" another that seemed grimly appropriate now. Robin and the girl must have been blind drunk, according to the official figures. Robin who never drank because it made his hands shake on the keys.

And the girl—four months pregnant,—had never been identified: an illegal immigrant, the police thought; a musician, perhaps, encountered on the concert tour Robin had made alone because of Anne's pupils. He had not wanted her to take them, any more than he had been prepared to let her go on with her own brilliantly promising career after they married. The career, in the first glow of the honeymoon, she had sacrificed almost gladly. How could she tour with Glyndebourne or Kent Opera parts when Robin needed her at home to protect his practice from intrusions? But the pupils, presenting themselves a year later, had been something else. By then, Robin had managed to alienate all her old friends. She must be all his, he had said, and said it again when she wanted to come off the pill. Lonely then, and a little frightened, she had insisted on taking the pupils when they offered themselves. They had quarrelled about it, seriously, for the first time, and he had gone on the German tour without her. So—all her fault? The drink; the girl; the death? If only she had gone on that tour—of course that was when the affair had begun. No. She looked down at her ringless engagement finger. It had begun long before. When she sang *Che faro* from Gluck's *Orpheus* at the summer concert and met the brilliant young pianist making his own debut with a taxing Beethoven sonata. Brilliant, a genius, Robin had a genius' total self-absorption. Fathoms deep in first love, she had ignored the danger signals, married in haste and only gradually begun to see how completely she had been taken over.

All past. All done with and best forgotten. She rose slowly to her feet, aware that the sun had gone in and she was shivering. As if it mattered—*I have caught an everlasting cold*. She moved instinctively towards the safety of her bed-sitter. With Robin's death, everything had gone; all the possessions she had lovingly collected for their first home, the convenient cottage so handy for London. All sold, swallowed in the great morass of Robin's debts and unpaid tax. Two people might or might not live more cheaply than one. Two households most certainly could not.

And with all the rest, unbelievably worst of all, her voice had gone. And so—because of that? because of the scandal?— had the pupils. In a way, it had been liberating. That was when she had packed her old college suitcase with what was incontrovertibly hers, taken off her wedding ring and moved to London, to a bleak hostel, to the blessed anonymity of her maiden style, Miss Paget, and at last to a job. Lucky to get it, they had said at the employment exchange. Arts graduates were two a penny, and her singing experience useless now her voice was gone. In the end, her small savings exhausted, she had preferred the wretched job in the back-street plastic assembly works to the grudging dole allowed to a widow who had been self-employed. Sweated labour, and the smell of it never left you, but by working all the overtime she could, she had managed the move to the glorious privacy of a bed-sitter.

Her key in the front door lock, she remembered what palatial luxury it had seemed. Still did. Glancing at the hall table where residents' mail was left, she was surprised to find two letters for her. One a buff envelope. Not more taxes? Send my demand to the graveyard. Take it out of my death benefit if you can. So far, she had not cried. Now, she could feel hysteria, a coil of snakes in her chest, rising, rising...

Upstairs, quick. The other key: her own room. The door slammed behind her. Over to the window; the high view of suburban gardens; trees in early leaf; a prunus flowering. She swallowed with an effort, then stood still, making herself do the breathing exercises Carl Meyer had taught her. Carl. Her mind was steadying. She had a friend. Had had a friend? Dear Carl, so furious when she gave up her singing career that he had actually come to the house and made a scene with Robin. Or tried to make a scene. Robin did not indulge in scenes, he sulked. She had begged Carl to go, and he had gone.

She had not heard from him since. Not a word, even, when Robin's death made headlines. So—not a friend? But memory of him was warming, just the same, helped to hold down that angry knot of hysteria in her breast. Carl, an untidy contrast to Robin's careful elegance; unpressed trousers, shaggy hair, hands and teeth stained from his perpetual cigars. If he was here, she might almost tell him that she was dying.

Dying. She took ten more deep breaths and moved across the room to plug in her electric kettle. Just enough water for a cup of instant coffee, and she needed it. What does one do about dying? It is time that I made my will. With all my worldly goods I thee endow. She looked round the shabby room and loved it, suddenly. The Japanese print she had bought at college; the blue vase with the chip at the back where it could not be seen.

The kettle boiled and she made the coffee, black, strong and milkless. Sipping it, she picked up the letters, which had been forwarded from the old address. Now she looked at it properly, the buff envelope was the wrong shape for a tax demand. The postmark: Lytham St Anne's. She had forgotten all about those ten premium bonds. Twenty-five pounds, perhaps? But the form said it was a thousand. She gazed at it blankly. A thousand pounds. *Now I can die in some comfort.* She opened the other letter, noticing for the first time the flimsy, foreign-looking paper and unusual stamps.

Typed. Two pages. "My dearest Anne." Dearest? She

11

turned to the second page and saw the scrawled black signature: "As always, Carl." And, below, neatly typed by some efficient secretarial hand, "Carl Meyer, Director."

Director? Of what, dear, shaggy Carl? She sat back, relaxed for the first time, actually tasted the strong coffee, and read the letter:

"My dearest Anne,

"I only heard the other day. What can I say? How can I bear not to have been there for you, in so much trouble? What must you have thought of me? What a selfish brute I am to worry about that, but I do.

"I also know that you will have been very brave, perhaps too brave for yourself. I do not like what I hear, and we will not talk about it, ever, if you do not wish to, but I hope you are singing again. Your poet Milton said something about a talent that must not be hidden. Yours is one of those, and you know it. You will be happier, dear Anne, if you use it. But it will be difficult, I know, for you to get back into things, and that is why I dare make my proposition.

"I am sure you will have read about the lost Beethoven opera that was found here last year. It has fallen to my country to have the honour of mounting the first production of *Regulus* in our new opera house, which is to be opened when the international peace conference is held here next month. What could be more fitting? Beethoven wrote *Regulus,* as I am sure you know, for performance at the 1814 Congress of Vienna. When Napoleon escaped from Elba the project was abandoned and the score lost. It is magnificent, Anne. It is Beethoven, the master, at his strongest and, although it is a tragedy, at his happiest. It is a profound statement of the value of the individual. I find it more moving, even, than *Fidelio.* What more can I say?"

She turned the page. "Dear Anne," the letter went on, "if I am boring on about this, it is with a purpose. I have the infinite happiness of acting as producer/director. We are keeping our costs down as much as we can, for various reasons. But it should be a great event, just the same. And there is a part in it just right for your extraordinary voice. Marcus, page to Regulus. Do you know your Horace, English barbarian? Or shall I tell you the story? I wish I could be with you, over a bottle of wine at Luigi's, to tell it properly and see those big brown eyes of yours fill with tears at the ending. Regulus was a Roman general, ignorant Englishwoman, who fought against the Carthaginians in the first Punic war, was captured, held prisoner for some years and finally sent back to Rome on parole to urge an ignominious peace. Instead, he warned the Romans roundly of the dangers they faced from Carthage, then insisted on keeping his word and returning to Carthage, to face torture and death. Quite a story?

"And Marcus, his page, a character supplied by the librettist, goes back too, although he has fallen in love with Regulus' daughter. Not a huge part; but vital. His parting duet with the girl, Livia, is only matched by his last one with Regulus. I wish I could offer you the part itself, dear Anne, but that goes to one of our own Lissenberg singers, who will do it well. The only understudy we have found is a disaster, in voice, looks and manner. She has a contract, unfortunately, but I am sure, if you come, I can find some means of getting rid of her. Of course I thought of you in the first place, but thought you—unavailable. We were talking of it the other day and someone mentioned your husband's tragic death. So, I am writing to you, to urge you, to beg you to come. It is the chance of a new start for you, and of a change, both of which I think you must need. The pay will be small, I fear, and I must warn you that Lissenberg is even more expensive than Switzerland, but you will be housed and fed in the singers' hostel, adjacent to the opera house itself.

"It is only three weeks to the opening night. The whole of Europe will be there. If anything should happen to Alix, who sings Marcus, we would be a laughing-stock. Imagine the disgrace to Lissenberg, the ill omen for this important conference and—to be selfish—the effect on my career. It is not a long part. I know how fast you learn. I promise you could do it. Dear Anne, telephone me, any night, between six and seven, reverse the charges. I'll pay. Just say you will come. I need you." And then, the familiar, scrawled, "Carl."

The letter fell to the floor. The first tears were streaming down her cheeks. Carl needed her. Offered her the chance she needed. And—she could not help him, could not take it. The chance, of course, was neither here nor there. In six months she would be dead, beyond all chances. But—what a chance it was. Even in the shocked aftermath of Robin's death she had been aware of the furore when Beethoven's forgotten opera was found. And now it was to be produced in connection with the great international peace conference. At the new opera house in Lissenberg. She had forgotten Carl was born there. She now remembered him describing it; a tiny country, somewhere in central Europe. Dear Carl. Even

13

to understudy on such an occasion would be a chance indeed. But there was more than that. There was something in Carl's letter; a note almost of desperation. "If anything should happen to Alix." Why should anything happen to Alix? Of course, things did happen; sore throats; infectious diseases; motor accidents. The snakes were writhing in her breast again. She made herself get up and move over to the open window to do her breathing exercises. Ten times, deep and slow, as Carl always made her begin her lesson, and then the arpeggios.

She was singing them. The notes rang out, round and true, and, outside a blackbird stopped singing. She was shaking. With shock—with joy—with excitement. One more great, delicious breath of spring air and she was fully launched into *Che faro. I have lost my Euridice...* They had sung it in English at her school, where she caused a sensation as Orpheus, but the Italian came out, as always, rounder, more satisfying. When she had finished she stood for a while, leaning against the window frame, breathing quietly, taking in the full miracle of it.

A knock at the door roused her. Opening it, she was confronted by fat Mrs Briggs who owned the house. "I'm sorry I'm sure to have to speak," said Mrs Briggs, "but I did say, when you moved in, Miss Paget, no loud gramophone or radio in the daytime. You know Briggs and I work at home."

"I'm sorry. I quite forgot."

But Mrs Briggs was darting sharp, suspicious glances round the room. "I don't understand," she said. "We quite thought, Briggs and I, it was that Kathleen Ferrier on a record we didn't know. 'Pity to turn it off, really,' Mr Briggs said. Quite a connosser he is, in his quiet way. But rules is rules. Only"—she came to the point,—"Where have you got the gramophone?"

"I'm sorry," said Anne meekly once again. "It was me. I won't do it again."

"Christ almighty!" said Mrs Briggs.

Three weeks from six months leaves something like a hundred and sixty days. Suddenly hungry, Anne opened a tin of sardines and ate them, prowling around the room, thinking, calculating... The doctor had not been definite. Say four months then, to be on the safe side. It still left a hundred days. The season at Lissenberg was to be short, she was sure, a couple of weeks or so. What exactly had the doctor said? Pain increasing towards the end. Well, of course; it was in-

14

creasing already. Except, oddly enough, that she had hardly felt it since she opened the two letters. Reminded of them, she filled in the premium bond form, put it into its envelope and hurried down to catch the afternoon post at the box on the corner. A thousand pounds. It had been her annual income once, before Robin persuaded her to sell her inherited investments. Now, it should last her very pleasantly for six months, however high the cost of living in Lissenberg.

Was she really planning to go? She seemed to be. Was she mad? Very likely. Suppose she spent all her money and then took more than six months to die? Well, she would just have to cross that bridge, like all the others, when she came to it. She walked the two long blocks to the plastics factory to give in her notice. It was unpleasant, but easier than she had expected. Would dying perhaps be the same?

She went on to the public library, to look for an atlas. "Liss...Lissatinning...Lisselton..." There it was: "Lissenberg. Page 34." Central Europe. A physical map, she was glad to see, with green valleys and brown mountains, and Lissenberg, when she found it at last, a green patch fringed with brown, with the town of Lissenberg marked, and the river Liss flowing west through the valley to join the Rhine before it plunged into Lake Constance. How large? She measured with a thumb and decided the whole country must be something like ten miles by eight. Smaller than London. Extraordinary.

There was no mention of Lissenberg in the library's subject index, but the girl at the desk suggested she try under Austria or Switzerland, and she found it at last in a battered old 1970 guide to Switzerland, with a whole page to itself, but not a great deal of information. An independent principality since 1780...tourism...ski-ing. The capital also called Lissenberg...total population 30,000. German spoken. Currency: the Lissmark. Three hotels in the town of Lissenberg itself, which lay between the Liss and the mountains, and two more higher up with ski-ing facilities.

The travel agent in the High Street was helpful. He had indeed heard of Lissenberg; was amused that she should doubt it. "It's a tax haven, you know, like Liechtenstein. People go there to set up offices, hold conferences. The hotels are quite good, I believe. One or two of the coach tours are beginning to stop off there, just for lunch and a bit of shopping. And now, of course, there's the new conference centre and the opera house and the big new hotel that goes with them. Booked solid for the opera season. I had an enquiry the other day, turned down flat. Expensive, too." He had summed up her frugal appearance with a professional eye.

"I've got the chance of a job there," she explained. "Living in. It's just a question of getting there."

"Oh, I see. No problem. You fly to Zurich, get the local train there. Or train all the way of course—cheaper." He had her placed, she thought, as a nanny or au pair.

"Oh, I'd fly. Can you look me up the connection?"

"A pleasure." He delved through time-tables, found a morning plane to Zurich; then an hour on the international express. "To Schennen. Then it's a local bus, I'm afraid. I couldn't book you on that."

"No. Naturally." She had written down the times as he looked them up. "I'll let you know in the morning what day. There won't be any problem about the flight, will there?"

"Not for a week or two. They're pretty heavily booked later on, what with the conference and the opera."

"Yes. I'll come in first thing in the morning. Thanks." Leaving the shop, she felt the familiar onset of pain and stood quite still, making herself breathe quietly, pretending to gaze at the tour advertisements in the window. Crazy to be planning this. But she had decided. She was going. There was something very liberating, she began to think, about having only six months to live. And—something else had decided itself—she was not going to tell Carl anything. It was odd to be so sure of her voice, but she was, and as to the other thing, that was, simply, her own affair. The travel agent had confirmed that *Regulus* was only running for two weeks. She had never been incapacitated by the pain yet. She would go. She would plunge back into her old, lost world. She would make the most of it, and then, when it was over, she would begin to think of a refuge, a hole where she could crawl and die with as little fuss as possible.

Shops were closing now, the pavements crowded. Time to go home for a cup of tea and get ready to telephone Carl at six. Reminded, she stopped at the sub post office on the corner and got a pound's worth of change. Thanks to that blessed premium bond there was no need to behave like a pauper and go through the inconvenience of reversed charges. Her small savings would last her until the cheque came through from Lytham St Anne's. She must ask Mrs Briggs to forward it. A blessing that the premium bonds, bought with her first earnings, were in her maiden name.

16

Lissenberg could be dialled direct. The public telephone was in the corner of the ground floor hall, with no pretence of privacy, but she did not need it. She piled her ten-and two-penny pieces beside it, dialled the long code, waited for the ringing tone and pressed a cautious tenpence into the slot. "Opera," said an unmistakably German female voice.

Robin had been almost as fluent in German as in English, and had been impatient with Anne's attempts at it, so that hers remained largely operatic, but she had prepared for this: "*Herr Meyer, bitte,*" she said, and went on, in carefully studied phrases. "I am calling from England. He expects the call." She pressed more money into the slot.

"Ah." The girl obviously knew about the call and put her through at once. "Hallo." Carl's cross voice might have been from round the corner. "I told you I'd pay for the call, extravagant hussy."

"Darling Carl." Amazing to hear the laughter in her own voice. "I'm a rich woman. For the moment. Do you really want me?"

"*Want you!* When can you come? Tomorrow?"

"The next day." Pips sounded. "Hell!" She pushed in more tenpenny pieces. "Four thirty at the bus stop in Lissenberg?"

"Always so capable." Now Carl was laughing at her. "I should have told you that. So—yes. I'll meet you there."

"What do I bring?"

"Your voice." The pips again. "Till then, *liebchen*?"

"Till then, dear Carl." She put down the receiver slowly, puzzled. That German endearment had been so unlike the Carl she knew. But then, much can happen in two years. He was back home in his native principality, where they spoke German. A pity she did not know it better.

Mrs Briggs was hovering. Mrs Briggs very often did hover when one telephoned, as if one might have some fiendish way of doing it without paying. "Off for a trip?" she asked coyly.

"Yes." This was an expected bridge. "I'm sorry, Mrs Briggs. I've been offered a job abroad. I'll pay you a week's rent, of course."

"From Saturday." Mrs Briggs was mollified. "What about your things, dearie? You can't take all that stuff abroad."

"No." This had been bothering her. What does a dying woman need with "things"? And yet, if she did come back to England to die, she would like that Japanese print with her.

"I tell you." Mrs Briggs had thought about it too. "There's

a cupboard at the end of the hall. See?" She opened its door and showed a cavernous depth. "Anything goes in there, we'll look after, Briggs and I, pound a week. Right?"

"Fifty pence."

"Seventy-five. You can afford it, ducks. Anyone who can sing like that—we don't know what you're doing here, Briggs and I, and that's for sure."

"Thanks." She meant it. "It's a bargain, Mrs Briggs, and if anything should happen to me abroad, you keep the things."

"Thank *you*, I'm sure. But you'll be back, Miss Paget. We look to hear you at Covent Garden, Briggs and I. On the telly, that is. Can't afford their prices, not these days. But we do fancy an opera on the telly. Sandwiches and beer for us, when they do one. Would you be singing one of those what-d'you-call-'em parts miss? Boy's clothes and all that? You've the figure for them, that's one thing. We watched one the other night; girl with a face like a horse and legs like a kitchen table, all done up in breeches and a fancy wig, and the ladies falling over themselves for the 'boy'. Clean spoiled it for Briggs and I. We wished we'd listened on the radio 'stead of watching. Now, you'd be something else again...Tell you what." She loomed nearer, smelling of beer and fried onions. "You want to practice, between now and when you go, go right ahead. It'll be a pleasure."

"Thanks." Escaping at last to her room, Anne felt warmed by the unexpected encouragement. She swung open the door of her tiny closet and looked herself over gravely in its long narrow strip of cracked glass. Touching of Carl not to ask whether she still looked the part—suppose she had been one of those women who grow fat on disaster. But in fact, she had lost weight. Twenty-three, five foot four, a hundred and twelve pounds. Short dark hair, brown eyes, a face that, amazingly, smiled at her from the glass. Yes, she thought, I'll do. I won't disappoint Carl. Of course, nothing will happen to Alix, but I will be singing again. She moved to the window and began.

2

Somebody, somewhere, was going slow. The departure lounge at Heathrow was packed with people, and the boards showed flight after flight as "delayed." When Anne arrived, breathless from her early start, just at checking-in time, the flight indicator for Zurich showed only a blank. She wished now that she had had the strength of mind to join the queue at the airport bank and get herself some foreign currency before she came through passport control. Too late now, and, if her plane was much delayed, no time at Zurich either. Her suburban bank had produced traveller's cheques readily enough to the extent of her small savings, but had been able to supply neither Lissmarks nor Swiss francs at such short notice.

Paying the fare on the bus from Schennen to Lissenberg was going to be a problem. If she caught it. An hour and a half had seemed ample time to get from Zurich airport to the station. But was it? And how did one do it? Anyway, she was not going to have an hour and a half. The figures on the board flickered and changed, now showing a half-hour delay on her flight. Would a Zurich taxi-driver take English money? And was her German good enough to ask him?

Reminded, she went over to the bookstall to buy herself a German phrase book, and notice, as usual, how few books there were that she felt like buying. But here was a paperback she did want, *The Birds Fall Down,* by Rebecca West. She bought it, the *Guardian,* and the phrase book and went back for another look at the board.

At least there was no further delay on her flight, though some had been indefinitely postponed and others cancelled. The lounge was more crowded than ever—children were crying, voices were rising—but she found a patch of floor where she could get her back against the wall, sat down and unfolded the *Guardian*. Headlines much as usual: a strike; a police confrontation, and, on the far right, a long ribbon of text headed *Outlook Good for Conference*. A quick look assured her that it was indeed the peace conference at Lissenberg, and she folded the paper back to read in more comfort.

Things really did seem promising for the conference. Even the guarded *Guardian* sounded hopeful as it described the preliminary work that had already been done on a wide range of subjects. The American President had made an extremely positive statement of intent, and the Russians sounded unusually cooperative, though they had not actually named their representative as the Chinese had. The British Foreign Secretary was going, and the Queen would be represented at the gala opening of *Regulus*. Cautiously optimistic, the writer seemed to think there was a real chance of an arms limitation agreement and some kind of charter of human rights. A final paragraph described the preparations in Lissenberg itself. The Hereditary Prince, Heinz Rudolf, would welcome his distinguished guests in person. Not, surely, at the bus stop? No—Anne read on—there was a helicopter landing strip on top of the opera house. Guests would be flown there from Zurich.

Landing on top of the opera house? She let the paper lie in her lap and thought about sound-proofing. Horrible to imagine a helicopter landing just as some unlucky singer was launching into a solo. But the architect must have thought of this. She wished, now, that she had not economised on newspapers since Robin's death. It was absurd to know so little about the Lissenberg enterprise. The travel agent, yesterday, had mentioned the architect's name and said something respectful about the project, comparing it, in some way, to the Sydney Opera House, but she had been too preoccupied to take it in. Oh well, if her plane ever took off, she would know all about it tonight.

And now, at last, her flight was called. She tucked the paper beside the books in her big tapestry shoulder-bag, checked that her boarding pass was safe in the outside pocket of her smaller purse and rose to her feet, shaking down the skirt of the lightweight Jaeger suit that had been part of her trousseau. The topcoat over her arm was lightweight too, and she had been cold leaving home. Had she been foolish to assume it would be warmer in Lissenberg?

There was a queue already at the departure gate, and as she stood in it, the two bags surprisingly heavy on her shoulder, the pain struck for the first time that day, and hard. The worst yet. She put down the tapestry bag and leaned against the corridor wall for a moment, eyes closed. What had Aunt Susan always said? *Listening to the pain helps.*

"Excuse me, you are not well?" She opened her eyes at the friendly, foreign voice and saw that the queue was beginning to shuffle forward and that the man behind her had leaned forward to pick up her big bag. "Let me help you with this?" He was middle-aged, city-suited, carrying the flat brief-case of the professional traveller. "Mine is nothing." His smile was kind. "But, are you sure you are well enough...Let me call a stewardess."

"Oh, no, thank you. It's nothing. I got up too early." She managed the pretence of a smile. "No breakfast." It was true, so far as it went.

"Foolish. A traveller, like an army, marches on his or"—
he smiled again—"her stomach. You will let me carry this
for you until we are on the plane, and perhaps do me the
honour of sitting with me and letting me buy you a brandy.
I am a reliable person." He reached, one-handed, into his
breast pocket, produced a card and showed it to her. "Wilhelm
Schann of Zurich. I shoot trouble in computers. Or they shoot
me." It was obviously a joke he had made many times. "Ah.
We move again. Let me take your arm."

She was glad to. The print on the card had dazzled in front
of her eyes. "Rest," the doctor had said. "Regular meals. A
sensible life." What was sensible about this enterprise? Nothing. She could still turn back. The queue was shuffling forward only slowly as people at the front were searched.

"Are you sure you should go?" He might have read her
mind. "If it is just a holiday? You look, if you will forgive
me, very far from well, Miss—"

"Paget," she supplied it.

"Miss Paget. I could help you back with the bag. Really,
I think it would be wise."

It was said with a kind of fatherly emphasis that she
found, for some reason, irritating. "But my luggage," she
objected. "It will be on the plane by now."

"True. I had not thought of that. But if you told
them...explained...They would get it back for you. They
are not entirely incompetent, the airlines."

"It doesn't matter." The pain was easing at last. "I must
go. It's not a holiday," she went on to explain. "It's a job. I
can't possibly let them down."

"Oh, in that case." He picked up the tapestry bag as the
queue moved forward once more. "You must just let me help
you on to the plane."

She was very glad to agree, and more grateful still when,
having settled her at last in a window seat, he rang for a
stewardess and asked for a glass of water for her. "The lady
is not well," he explained. "I suppose you cannot find anything stronger?"

"Not until we are airborne, but I'll remember then. I'm
afraid it may be some time."

"Oh?"

"We've not got clearance yet. The way things are, goodness
knows when we will." She glanced anxiously at Anne, quiet
in her corner. "I'll fetch that water right away."

Sipping it, Anne felt better. Idiotic to have gone without

21

breakfast, but there had been no time. If only she had known about the delay. She looked at her watch. "Are we going to be very late, do you think?"

"I am afraid we may be. For me, it is no matter. I am merely going home. But you... you have a connection perhaps?"

"Yes. I'm going to Lissenberg. I have to catch the express. Tell me." She had been wanting to ask the question. "Is it far from Zurich airport to the station?"

"The bus takes half an hour. They run every five minutes. Or, if you are lucky, there are taxis. Ah..." The captain had come through on the intercom to announce their imminent departure.

"Good," said Herr Schann. "What time is your train?"

"One thirty."

He looked at his watch. "You should do it easily. I, too, go to the station for my local train home. I will see you to your train; that way there will be no delay—no strangeness, no questions."

"You're very kind." She smiled at him gratefully. "I only wish my German was as good as your English."

"It will come with practice. Here we go."

Anne leant back and closed her eyes. She had never much liked the moment of take-off, and was glad when they were airborne at last and she could look down at reservoirs, and neat green fields and then, inevitably, cloud.

"This will do you good." She turned when Herr Schann spoke, and saw the stewardess holding out a small glass half full of brown liquid.

"Strictly for medicinal purposes." His English *was* good. He let down her table for her. "Take it slowly," he warned.

Brandy. On an empty stomach. Sheer madness, but the most heart-warming kind. Stomach-warming. She felt the pain ease as she took a further sip. "I needed that. Thank you so much." She smiled at him warmly.

"Now, rest," he advised. "I will wake you when they bring our meal, whatever they call it. Breakfast for you, foolish child."

"Yes. Thank you." She closed her eyes and let herself drift into the light-headed tranquillity of the air. She was free...she was on her way. Herr Schann, kind Herr Schann, would see her safe to her train; Carl would meet her at Lissenberg...The pain ebbed and vanished. It had only been so bad because of yesterday's exhaustion and today's early start. In future, she would have more sense. An understudy's life need not be too exacting...And she would be singing...She would be better when she was singing.

"Miss Paget." Herr Schann's voice woke her. "Our lunch is here."

"Oh." She came dizzily awake to the stir and movement in the plane as the loaded trolley edged down the aisle. "Thank you." Taking her tray from the stewardess, she saw that Schann had moved over into the vacant third seat on the aisle. On the table between them stood two plastic glasses and two bottles.

"I took the liberty of ordering." He poured champagne carefully. "With food, it will do you good. In fact, you look better. You have slept for almost half an hour."

"Goodness." She was wrestling with the close-fitting top of her lunch tray. "Have I really? I'm starving!"

"No wonder. Here, let me." He reached over as she began the next struggle, to get plastic utensils out of their sealed polythene bag. "It is not only computers I can manage." He produced a small penknife, slit the bag neatly and handed it back to her. "And your roll?"

"Oh, thank you!" The fresh but lifeless bread was just what she wanted. Washed down with her first sip of champagne it seemed the best food she had ever tasted. Presently, letting him refill her mug, she protested. "I shall fall asleep again."

"It will do you good. I'll wake you when we get there. Besides"—he refilled his own mug—"I am a selfish brute. You will not get nearly your share."

Cold paté, coleslaw, cold chicken...She ate them all, gratefully, even gnawing the chicken bone. "*Cold, cold, my girl*..." But she was feeling better by the minute, what with the food and the champagne. I, who am dying, am alive at last, she thought. I shall make the most of it. Oh, God, how I will sing. Oh, Carl, how grateful I am.

Schann was pouring a last trickle into her mug. She voiced a vague protest. "Are you sure you had more than half?"

"See how much better you feel. You do not like the sweet? No, nor do I." He reached over to take her tray. "One could do better with cement, I always think. Now, finish your drink and sleep again. I promise I will rouse you when we are near Zurich."

"Thank you." She would have liked some coffee, which was now being brought down the aisle, but it seemed ungra-

cious to object, and, besides, it was extraordinarily restful to
let herself go with his kindness. Her head, like the plane,
hummed faintly, pleasantly... Once again she slept.

The airport bus was as swift and efficient as Herr Schann
had promised, but just the same it was twenty past one when
they reached Zurich station. "You have your ticket?" Herr
Schann picked up her suitcase.

"Yes. But—your luggage?"

"I'll see you to your train and come back for it. You most
certainly should not be carrying this."

"You are *kind.*" She fell into step beside him and they
made their way through the crowded station to the departure
board.

"Track 8," he said. "This way. You will need to be at the
front of the train." He hurried her through the gate and down
the long platform, where people stood expectantly, luggage
ready, awaiting the train's arrival.

"There." He put down her bag. "This should be just right.
Will you promise to ask someone to get it up the step for
you?" A quick glance at his watch. "I could just catch my
local."

"Of course. I don't know how to thank you."

"It's been a pleasure." He hurried away down the long
platform and she found herself ungratefully glad to be alone
at last, free to anticipate her adventure, to imagine Lissenberg.

"Liechtenstein?" A loud, enquiring English voice a little
further down the platform. "We are right for Liechtenstein?"

"*Ja, ja,*" said a uniformed official, then burst into a flood
of German of which Anne, suddenly alert, picked out only
one word, "Sargans."

But that was all wrong. She remembered the travel agent
explaining that she needed the express that went along the
north side of the lake, for her stop at Schennen where she
caught the bus up the Lissenberg valley—not the southern
route by Sargans. The uniformed official was making his
dignified way along the platform towards her. *"Mein Herr?"*
And then, quickly, as he paused, her German entirely de-
serting her, "For Lissenberg, here?"

"Aber nein!" He looked down at her anxious face, then at
the station clock. "Quick!" He picked up her bag and set off
at a round pace along the platform, while she almost ran
behind him. At the gate, he shouted something in the direction of track 4 and turned that way without a pause. Follow-

24

ing him breathlessly, she saw a train already standing there, doors closed, platform empty, poised, as it were, for flight.

But they were expected. That shouted appeal had had its effect. An official stood with the nearest door open. She was almost thrown up into the train, her suitcase pushed up after her. She had only time for a heartfelt "*Vielen danke*" before the train moved off. Breathing fast, she pushed her suitcase into the open carriage, saw with relief that it was almost empty, and subsided on a hard seat. Then, anxious again, she leaned forward to ask the young man sitting opposite: "For Schennen?"

"*Ja*." He returned to his newspaper.

Gazing out the window at the featureless suburbs that might have belonged to any European town, Anne sighed with relief at the narrow escape, and bafflement at how it had happened. Herr Schann had been so kind, so reliable... A horrid doubt struck her. Lissenberg... Liechtenstein. The names so alike. Could she possibly have said Liechtenstein instead of Lissenberg? After his first question, they had not discussed her journey further. An easy—a nearly disastrous misunderstanding. Idiot that she was, champagne-filled fool, not to have rechecked with him before they set out on that rush across the station.

But at least, by a miracle, and the kindness of that Swiss official, here she was, regaining her breath slowly, on the right train. She sighed, settled more comfortably in her corner and picked up her bag, noting as she did so that the catch had slipped open as it often, maddeningly, did. If there had been time, she would have bought a new one. Reaching for her comb—she must look as shaggy as she felt—she stopped, horror-struck. Where was her purse?

It must be there. Though the catch did slip, the bag was so designed that things did not fall out. Or—never had yet. Searching feverishly through its three compartments, refusing to believe what was already obvious, she racked her brains to think when she had last had the purse. On the plane? No. Herr Schann had insisted on paying for their drinks. But, surely, she would have noticed its absence when she tidied up before they landed? Her baggage check had been with her ticket in the front compartment of the bag and there, thank God, the ticket folder still was, along with her traveller's cheques. But the purse—she had to face it—the purse was gone, and with it all her cash, her bank card, Carl's telephone number, carefully written down on a piece of paper, just in case, and the covering note for her traveller's cheques.

She remembered now. She had opened her bag at Zurich airport, expecting to need the baggage check, but as usual the luggage had been cheerfully handed over without query. If the bag had been open ever since, some thieving hand had had its chance. What in the world should she do? For the moment, nothing, except curse her own carelessness and wonder what size station Schennen had. Would there be anyone there who would help? It was, after all, an international junction of sorts. Perhaps there would be an English-speaking station master to whom she could appeal. She got out the travel-folder again and checked that there was a half hour's wait for the bus. The station might be in the centre of the town. She consulted her phrase book and found the phrase for "Where is the police station?" But would she understand the answer?

The guard came down the aisle, inspecting tickets. "Do you speak English?" she asked, as he handed hers back.

"*English*?" He shook his head and hurried through into the next compartment before she had time to try him in French. So much for that. She looked at her watch. Almost an hour before the train reached Schennen. It was out of the town now, running along the side of the lake. Water, cool grey under a grey sky, and on the far side, mountains. Bright green pastures, at first, then the dark of pine trees and beyond and above—in the far distance—bleak, brown-grey escarpments rising to the gleam of snow.

She shivered. It had been cold in Zurich. It was cold on this train. Idiotic to have thought Lissenberg would be warmer than England, to have expected the sun to shine. But by now this whole enterprise seemed idiotic, doomed to disaster. Her voice would go again; she would become inconveniently, unconcealably ill; Carl would be furious with her, and would have a right to be. Unpardonable to have come here without telling him the truth. She had not even taken out travel insurance. It seemed a waste of time—it never covered illnesses you had already. And naturally there had not been time to get the official form that would have entitled her to free medical care in Lissenberg. Fool...fool, and fool again. She blinked back tears of pure anger and gazed unseeingly at a gabled beerhouse by the lake.

A tinkling bell announced a refreshment trolly. The champagne had left her parched with thirst, and it was small comfort to think that even if she had not lost her purse, her English money would be useless here.

"Fräulein?" The young man on the seat opposite leaned towards her as the trolly approached. "You will let me have the pleasure of buying you a beer?" He spoke in German, but slowly and carefully, so that she could understand.

"Oh, thank you!" It was just what she needed. "I mean," she paused. "*Danke schön.*"

"Ah, so you do speak German?" He leaned out into the aisle and bought two squat dark bottles of lager and two paper cups.

"No, alas." Her headshake underlined the words.

He shrugged, pantomiming disappointment, and poured the fizzing lager carefully into her cup. It was curious and heart-warming, she thought, accepting it with a smile of thanks, to have men going out of their way to be courteous to her again. It had not happened, somehow, for a long time.

The train had left the lake now, and was running up a valley. Brilliant green pastures on either side had mild, beige cows grazing, and an occasional ox-cart. Higher up, more pastures were defined by dark woods, with here and there a wooden chalet. The road ran along beside the railway line here, both of them hugging the floor of the valley, and she was surprised to see a long convoy of military lorries. But of course the Swiss took their neutrality very seriously indeed. She leant back in her seat. If the peace conference was a success, the world might breathe a little more easily. It would be good to be taking however tiny a part in trying to make it succeed. She felt better again, calmer, ready to face the problems of Schennen and her lost purse.

With a sudden, black rush, the train was in a tunnel. Lights came on belatedly and she saw the young man opposite beginning to gather himself together. She looked at her watch. Not time for Schennen yet, and she was sorry to see him go, when the train emerged from the tunnel into a small town running up the hillside to its surprising onion-domed church. On a further crag, the ruins of a castle straight out of Walter Scott served as a reminder that this must always have been one of the ways war would threaten the peaceful Swiss valleys.

She smiled goodbye to the young man. Less than half an hour now before they reached Schennen. She got out her phrase book and soon found herself wishing she had bought a dictionary. It was amazing how phrase books always con-

27

trived not quite to provide the phrase one needed. And people in opera seemed to encounter such different kinds of problems. In the end, "Do you speak English" seemed still her best bet. Surely someone at Schennen station must do so?

But when she saw it, her heart sank. The station building itself was just a large chalet beside the line, and the town she had expected seemed to consist merely of a row of cottages stretching away down a country road. She had pushed her suitcase to the carriage door and was relieved to see an elderly man waiting to get on. With the best smile she could muster, and a kind of multilingual apology, she handed him down her suitcase and followed it as he pushed past her without a word.

Well, no wonder. It was pouring with rain in Schennen. If this was Schennen and not merely its station, stuck, for convenience, out in the deep countryside. Even the chalet-style station, set by the track, looked formidably far away, since she had been at the very back of the train, which was now rolling away, cleared by an official who returned to shelter without so much as a glance in her direction.

Rain was beginning to soak her hair and penetrate her thin coat. Her suitcase was standing in a puddle. Picking it up, she saw that down near the station another alighting passenger had been met by a uniformed man who was picking up first-class-looking luggage. For Lissenberg? Probably. She tried to hurry, the suitcase a ton weight. "Excuse me..." They took no notice, moving towards the station. "*Bitte!*" This time it came out louder, but won her merely a glance and a shrug from the chauffeur.

Useless. She bit back tears and paused at the welcome shelter of a kind of shed which turned out to be the bus stop. At least it had a time-table which confirmed that the last bus of the day for Lissenberg left in half an hour, and a little open waiting room with a bench, a view of the mountains, and nothing else. She pushed her suitcase into an inconspicuous corner, pulled a headscarf out of her bag for her already drenched hair, emerged from the shelter and prepared to run for the station, and possible help, then drew back just in time as a car roared up the turning from the road and pulled to a skidding stop outside the shelter, missing her by inches.

3

"Verzeihung!" He was out of the car in a hurried tangle of long, jean-clad legs and waving arms. *"Fräulein, ich bin..."*

"You nearly killed me," she interrupted angrily. "And I don't speak German."

"I sure did!" His lapse into Anglo-American amazed and relieved her. "Next time you bound out of a hole like a chipmunk, look both ways, huh? How was I to know you were hiding in there like a—like a—"

"Chipmunk," she said coldly.

But he had turned away to survey the deserted, rain-drenched platform. "Late again!" He looked ruefully at a huge watch on his wrist. "And cut out again by the look of it. Did anyone else get off the train, Niobe?"

"How d'you mean, Niobe?" She sounded as cross as she felt.

"You're wet enough," he explained.

"Of course I'm wet!" Aware of rain seeping through her coat, she backed into the shelter, nearly tripping against a standpipe with a tap and mug. "Yes, someone did get off."

"And was met?" He clicked his heels, pulled himself ramrod straight and touched an imaginary cap. His teeshirt, already dark with rain, said "Oxford" in huge letters. His long, curling dark hair was beginning to stick to his skull. "It's raining," he said, as if making a great discovery. "And I've missed another job. You're not"—he looked her up and down, without hope—"you're not by any happy chance wanting a taxi to Lissenberg?"

"I certainly am." It was too good to be true. Well, of course it was. "But I've no money."

"My luck." He shrugged ruefully. "But I've missed my fare—I've got to go back just the same, so, what the hell! Besides, the bus is late today. You'll die of cold waiting here. Did no one tell you we wear raincoats in Lissenberg?"

"You don't seem to."

"Oh, I'm..." He hesitated. "Immune. This your bag?" He moved past her into the shelter to pick it up. "Diogenes! Have you been carrying this?"

"As little as possible. But," she protested again as he

opened the boot, "I really mean it. I've got no money at all. I lost my purse."

"Careless." He swung the suitcase into the boot. "And all the more reason why you need a lift into town. The bus takes hours anyway. Stops at every cowshed and cabbage patch. You're much better with Uncle Michael. I'm more reliable than I look. *And* I drive better. You'd best sit in the front. I don't make passes much, and if we turn the heater on you might be almost dry by the time we get there."

"Lovely!" But once again she hesitated as he held open the rather battered car door for her. "Only, someone's meeting the bus."

"Then OK." He put a firm brown hand under her elbow and pushed her in. "So we meet the bus too and someone will know to meet his friends here another time. He might even pay me."

"I expect he will." She subsided gratefully on to the car's seat, grateful to be taken over by this surprisingly positive young man.

"Better than she looks, eh?" He slid in on his side and started the engine. "You should see the opposition. Shines like a hearse and runs like one. Just the same..." He let in the clutch, and the car moved silently forward. "The boss is going to be furious with me for missing Signor Falinieri. Time-keeping never was my long suit."

"Falinieri? The conductor?"

"Right. You know him?" He swept the surprisingly powerful car left into a rain-drenched village street, then turned to look her over. "What are you, anyway? High brass, middle brass, secretary? We have the lot in Lissenberg right now."

"I sing." She felt the welcome warmth of the heater begin to creep around her knees.

"Ah!" He gave a brief, friendly toot of the horn, swung out to pass a donkey buried under a huge load, and turned to smile at her. "*Natürlich.* The mysterious understudy. The unknown British beauty. And Herr Meyer left you to die of cold at Schennen. I'm surprised at him. And Alix with a sore throat too."

"Alix?"

He laughed. "Forgot my manners, did I? We don't go much for dignity and surnames and all that in Lissenberg. We're all cousins, more or less. The sooner you learn that, the better you'll get on. The others never seem to, but you look as if you might have some sense, when you're dry and got your wits about you."

"Thanks!" She must not quarrel with this useful source of information. "What do you mean 'the others'?" she asked.

"Why—all of them. The foreigners our Rudolf has let loose on us."

"Rudolf? Who's he?"

This time his laugh rang a little harsh. "Our lord and master. The Hereditary Prince Heinz Rudolf of Lissenberg. I'll spare you the rest of his names, not to mention his titles and honours. They take several lines in the guide book. He wrote it himself, when he still thought Lissenberg would make it as a tourist attraction."

"And won't it?"

"He thinks not. Or—only on the grand scale. Not just tourists, but International Tourists, in capital letters, and a damn great international hotel to match. Our beer houses aren't good enough for them. No, ma'am. Got your passport, or did you lose that too?" He slowed the car at a corner and she saw a straight stretch of road leading to a bridge with a barrier across it. "Customs. Such as they are. Anything to declare except the beginnings of a cold?"

"Not a thing."

"No. You don't look like international drug smuggling, though I suppose that might just be the secret of your success." He stopped the car and leaned out to carry on a friendly German conversation with two guards who appeared simultaneously from opposite sides of the barrier, one in grey Swiss uniform, the other immaculate in dark green breeches and high brown boots. "Would you like your passport stamped?" Michael turned to ask her.

"Not if I don't have to."

"It costs five Lissmarks. The tourists all go for it." He was laughing as he let in the clutch and the car moved forward on to the bridge. "They gave poor Signor Falinieri the full treatment," he told her. "That will teach him to take the wrong taxi. All his silk shirts out in the rain, and nothing to show for it except a few filthy pictures, and we don't mind them in Lissenberg. I expect we'll catch them up on the road. This car may rattle but she goes."

"I don't understand." She was looking down at the wide, swiftly flowing river, grey, with here and there white water showing.

"The Liss." He waved a hand. "Welcome to Lissenberg,

Niobe. About Falinieri?" he asked. "Being searched? Because he had a foreign taxi driver. We're not mad about foreigners taking our jobs in Lissenberg, whatever our Rudolf may say. They knew at the border that I was meeting him; they saw what had happened; so, of course..." He laughed again. "They congratulated me, by the way. Thought I'd done better than the opposition after all. Pity you don't understand German. You'd have enjoyed it. If you do that to Kurt Weigel with your hair wet and your lipstick smudged, I can't wait to see you clean and dry."

"It's not smudged!"

"Want to bet?"

"You speak English very well." She got the mirror out of her bag and saw, crossly, that he was right about the lipstick.

"It says Oxford, doesn't it? Positively no deception."

"You mean you *went* there? Then what on earth are you doing driving a taxi?"

"Snob!" But his tone was friendly. "I'm dropping out, of course. Besides, what do you do in Lissenberg with a degree in philosophy, politics and economics? No, don't tell me now." He took a hand off the wheel to pat hers where it lay in her lap. "You may have notice of that question and answer it when you've been in Lissenberg a day or so."

"Thanks."

"Anyway," he went on cheerfully as he took a great swoop round a group of green-overalled schoolchildren. "If friend Meyer won't pay me, I reckon I won't be a taxi driver much longer. Uncle Adolf seems to think time-keeping is important. And he does hate to be scooped by those black cabs from the hotel. Well, so do I. Except this time. Compliment."

"Thank you. And I'm sure Herr Meyer will pay you."

"Sure. But that won't mean I was on time, will it? I was just lucky. Uncle Adolf doesn't go much for luck. He prefers judgment, he says."

"Is he really your uncle?"

"I told you. We're all cousins in Lissenberg. Well, look!" Mountains rose steeply on each side of the river beside which the road ran. "Before Napoleon built this road, the only way into Lissenberg was at the other end, over the mountains, and hard work every step of the way. The Liss and its branches come down from Austria in a series of waterfalls. Oh, there's a road now, since the last war, zig-zag, zag-zig and pray your brakes hold. But in the good old days Lissenberg was cut off all winter. Nothing much to do but go to bed

with a cousin. And very nice too. They call this progress!"
The valley was widening and he pointed to a long, low building set into the side of the mountain. "Industry," he said.
"That was our Rudolf's first idea when he took over. Light,
of course. Ball-bearings; spare parts for computers; bits of
digital clocks for export to Switzerland. All tucked away, tidy
as can be, where you only run into them by accident. More
and more people working in them, and less and less land for
farming. Do you know, up till the last war, Lissenberg was
self-sufficient. What we needed, we grew. What we didn't
grow, mostly, we did without. Salt beef in the winter and
veal in the spring. Goat cheese and barley bread, and a
damned healthy population. Now we have white bread for
the tourists, deep freezes all round, microwave ovens, and
any minute we'll have our first case of scurvy. Maybe that's
what's the matter with Alix."

"You said, a sore throat?" She had been wanting to ask
more about this. "She is the one who is singing Marcus?"

"Page to Regulus." She had stopped being surprised at
how much he knew. "Yes, that's Alix. Quite a voice. Well,
you must know—presumably you've got one like it. Bad luck
for her if she can't sing the part. *Regulus* was her idea in the
first place. A natural, of course, all things considered, and
once they had decided to push on with the opera house and
open it for the peace conference. Do you know the part?"

"No, but I learn fast." Please God she still did. "Anyway,
I'm only understudying the understudy."

"That's what Meyer told you? Crafty devil. He must
know—everyone does—that Lotte's set to walk out when you
walk in."

"Lotte?"

"The understudy. She's been a disaster from the start."
He slowed the car as a spur of the mountain came down to
lean over the road where it ran close beside the river.

"She's not a cousin?"

"Quick, aren't you? Well, in a way she is. The wrong kind."

"And Alix?"

"Oh, Alix is much more than a cousin. Alix is—*Gott*!" He
stamped on the brake and brought the taxi to a skidding halt
as they rounded a blind corner and saw the big black car half
across the road. "You all right?" He turned to her, white-
faced.

"Yes." She uncurled herself slowly. She had thought so

33

often of car accidents since Robin's that head on to knees was a reflex action when, as now, there was no safety belt.

"Value your life, don't you?"

"Yes, I do." And how odd that was. But he was already out of the car and running forward to where two men stood angrily arguing in the road, one the chauffeur she had seen at Schennen, the other, of course, his passenger, whose elegant raincoat already showed dark wet patches.

She sat where she was, digesting shock and listening to the furious, incomprehensible voices. The black car had one flat tire, and must have swerved when it blew, so that it now blocked both traffic lanes.

"Can you lend a hand?" Michael had come back to lean in at her window. "Get back round the corner and stop the traffic while we get this hearse off the road? I don't want my car wrecked too."

"Can you manage?"

"Oh, I think so. Signor Falinieri has graciously consented to steer while we push. Pushing wouldn't suit his dignity."

"Nor his clothes." She accepted the huge scarlet and white striped handkerchief Michael produced from his sleeve and went back round the corner. Nothing in sight, luckily, and a clear stretch of road so that she was bound to see and be seen if something did come. They had seen very little traffic so far except ox-carts, mules and donkeys. She turned to look over the guard-rail at the fast-running river. The driver of the car in front had been lucky—or skilful—to have checked his skid in time. Otherwise the heavy car might easily have been through the flimsy railing and into the current which rounded the corner close to the bank, deep-looking, fast and dangerous.

A noise from down the valley brought her quickly back to her post as a motorbike came in sight, going fast. Stepping out into the centre of the road and waving the red handkerchief, she recognised the green uniform of the Lissenberg customs officer. She ought to have been thinking of useful phrases, but had left her bag with the phrase book in the car. As usual, she ran quickly through her German operatic tags and came up with one that might actually do, from the first scene of *The Magic Flute*. "*Zu hilfe*," cried the prince, pursued by his papier-mâché dragon. "Help!" What could be better?

"Fräulein?" Pulling up beside her, the customs officer recognised her and broke into fluent English. "What's the matter?"

34

"There's been an accident. A car across the road. Just round the corner. A flat tire." It was beginning to rain again, hard.

"So! And our Michael has put you on guard duty. Good. Continue, I beg, Fräulein, for the moment." He stood his motorbike across the road as a barricade behind her, then, as an afterthought, reached into the saddle-bag, produced a green mackintosh cape and draped it round her shoulders. "Michael's my good friend," he said, "but he thinks everyone's made of iron like himself. We must take care of our understudy. In the mean time, thank you, Fräulein Paget."

'You know about me?"

'Natürlich. In Lissenberg the police know everything." A broad smile, gleaming with white teeth, robbed the remark of any possible sinister emphasis. "All twenty of us. And now, I'll be as quick as possible. You're shivering."

"Thanks." But it still seemed a surprisingly long time before Michael appeared with the news that the road was clear.

"Sorry it took so long..." He walked beside her, wheeling the policeman's motorbike. "Rock splinters and oil all over the road. Surprising. We had to clear it up before it was safe to let anyone through. Herr Brech was lucky he didn't puncture two tires and go straight into the river."

"Herr Brech?" She noticed the unusual use of a surname, instead of the friendly "cousin."

"The rival enterprise. Brech's luxurious limousines. If you'd seen what his spare tire looked like, you'd have wondered about the luxury. Ah, he's got it changed." They rounded the corner to see the black car moving sedately away and the policeman taking a last careful look at the road surface. "All clear?" Michael asked him.

'I think so." Kurt Weigel put one last jagged piece of rock into a bulging polythene bag.

'You're keeping the rock?" Anne asked, surprised.

'Funny sort of landslide," said Weigel.

'Right." Michael had been inspecting the damp overhang of cliff. "Not a sign of where it came from."

"Off a lorry, maybe?" said Weigel. "There's oil, too. Proper death trap. Lucky Brech's a good driver. And those heavy cars he runs hold the road like tanks. Now, if it had been you..."

'Yes," Michael said. "I'd thought of that." He broke suddenly into a language that sounded even less intelligible than

35

German, then, after a brisk exchange with Weigel, turned to Anne. "By the way, here's your chance to report that lost purse of yours. I'd meant to take you round by police headquarters on the way to the bus station. We won't have time now. But here's your policeman."

"Why, of course. Thanks!" She explained what had happened as briefly as possible, admitted, with shame, to ignorance of her bank card number, and thanked Herr Weigel warmly when he promised to report its loss for her at the same time as checking with the Zurich police in case the purse had been recovered.

"What a nice man," she said as he rode away on his motorbike. "And what on earth were you two talking? It surely wasn't German."

"Got a quick ear, haven't you? That was Liss, the local language. German with a dash of French and just a touch of Italian. The result of those long winters when no one could get in or out. Napoleon banned it when he took over here. All for European union, was Boney—with him for boss, of course. But I sometimes think it was a pity he didn't make it. We might be in less trouble now. All the fault of you pig-headed British. Boney incorporated Lissenberg in Bavaria, you know. Or rather, I bet you don't. It was the Congress of Vienna that gave us back our independence. Such as it is."

"What do you mean?"

"Well—" He pointed at another long, low, obviously industrial building half-screened by young trees. "Now we've got industry, we've got world finance. It was one thing when we just acted as a tax haven, and charged through the nose for it. Now we're in the export line we're getting more and more dependent on international big business. And when you come right down to it, who pays, rules. Myself, I liked us better the way we were. Salt beef, barley bread, goat's milk and all. Sorry! Lecture ended. Look!" He pointed ahead. "Schloss Lissenberg itself."

"Not Lissenberg." She drew in a deep, delighted breath. "Ruritania." It stood on a spur of the mountain, among green pastures and against a frame of dark pines, the original fairy-tale castle. Silver-grey battlements were crowned by grey turrets and one round, central red-roofed tower much higher than the rest.

"Eligible family residence, isn't it?" Michael's tone was dry. "Forty bedrooms, usual offices—I forget how many recep. Strictly private, you understand: viewed only from here. In

36

the good old days it was open to the public. Justice liberally dispensed in the great hall. The Diet used to sit here well into the nineteenth century. The first Prince only bought the place in the 1780s. No doubt he thought he'd better keep in with the natives."

"Bought?"

"Sure." He pulled the car into a lay-by obviously intended for people who wanted to gaze their fill at the castle. "He was a minor aristocrat in Hanover whose family nose had been put out of joint when the ruling Prince went off to England to be George I. They applied their minds to making money, and made a lot. The one who bought Lissenberg had sold his army to George III for use in the United States—beg pardon, the revolting colonies. Funny thing, none of them ever came back. The ones who didn't get killed or die of disease and starvation and homesickness just settled in the United States. I met one of their descendants at Harvard: Liss, he was called. By what he said, he seemed to own most of Texas."

"I thought you went to Oxford."

"I did a year at the Harvard Business School. Afterwards. You could call me a rolling academic stone. And not much moss to show for it." His tone was wry. "Now, young Cousin Liss was learning to manage the family millions."

"Cousin?"

"I told you, we're all cousins here in Lissenberg. And plenty of Lisses, too. The first one, Heinz Gustaf, who bought Lissenberg because it went so well with his family name, had practically stocked his army with his bastards, they say. One answer to the population problem."

"Have you one?"

"I'd say. End of World War II we had 20,000. Just right for the valley. Fed ourselves—I told you. Then, tax haven and all that, it began to grow. You can imagine how. Old people who thought their pensions would go further. Well, they soon learned their mistake. Not with our cost of living, they don't. Then: tax dodgers. Statutory residence of six months a year. Food from Fortnums, wine from France, clothes from Italy. Much use they are to Lissenberg. That's when our Rudolf up there"—he pointed to the castle—"put his mind to tourism. *And* light industry. So what do we get? The scaff and raff from miles around. Half of them wanting jobs in the factories and the chance of our social security. It's good, by the way. The other half—and I mind them more— wanting Steak Diane and egg and chips. Oh, and souvenirs, of course. You just wait till you see the souvenirs on sale here in Lissenberg. They've created a whole new industry—or we have for them—and it's meant more immigrants. We're craftsmen, we Lissenbergers; what we make, we make well. To make the—what's your British word?—to make the old tat the tourists want, we have to import tatty labour. One way and another our population's up to 36,000 now, and not all of them people I want to call cousin. And that's not racism either." He turned on her, almost angrily. "D'you know what happened here when the war was over?"

"No."

"Remember your history? Remember Churchill promising at Yalta that the Russians should have all their beloved sons back? And how they killed themselves rather than go? Or got killed when they arrived?"

"Yes. Horrible."

"We didn't send ours. Little Lissenberg hung on like Liechtenstein. Most of our Russians were Russian Jews. Some of them were Polish. Everyone knew what would have happened to them. They'd got in, mostly, over the mountains from Austria, helped by our people. The kind of dangerous journey no one forgets. Well, it came up to the Diet—that's our House of Commons. There are twelve men in it. Six of them then were mountain guides; the other six were...oh well, call it war rich. The vote was even. So Michael Josef cast his; and they stayed."

"Michael Josef?"

"You want people here to like you, don't ask that question here, not in that tone of voice. Michael Josef was the Hereditary Prince then; he had the casting vote in the Diet. They threw him out ten years ago."

"Who did?"

"The Diet. Four of the six guides had died, see, and been replaced. By business men. Michael Josef was standing in the way of progress, they said. He didn't want light industry, and tourism on the grand scale and Steak Diane. He wanted Lissenberg to stay Lissenberg."

"What happened to him?"

"Nothing. Unless you call a broken heart something. He has a very nice modern flat. Oh, they offered him rooms in the castle, but he had more sense than that. He got a job and a flat that went with it."

"A job?"

He laughed. "He's not that old. He was twenty when he

gave that casting vote. Not an old man now exactly. But not a happy one either. You'll see. You'll meet him." He glanced up at his rear view mirror. "Here comes your bus. Let's go! Stand by for your first view of Lissenberg."

4

The town was a remarkable mixture of old stone gable-ended buildings, many with ornate wooden balconies, and drab concrete modern offices. "A muddle, isn't it?" Michael slowed the car and pointed to a mounted statue in a small flower-filled garden. "That's the first Hereditary Prince, Heinz Gustaf. He'd turn in his grave if he saw his town now. He'd planned it as a kind of *rus in urbe*. Country in town," he translated for her.

"I know," she said. "Girls get educated in England, too. But how exactly did he plan his country-town?"

"Every house was to have its plot of ground, for vegetables and vines. We make very good wine here in Lissenberg—you must try it. The self-supporting bit was his idea, and a very good one. It worked for years. Until after the last war, when the banks came along, bought up the vineyards, and—see!" He turned the car into a park at the bottom of a fair-sized square and pointed to a handsome gabled building at the upper end. "That's the third Heinz Gustaf's Rathaus—council chamber to you. He built it in the local stone and style when he got tired of having the Diet troop up to the castle for their meetings. And facing it we have the brain-child of the Tenth National Bank of Nebraska."

"Ouch," she said.

"Precisely. And I'm afraid the bus station's not much better." He took her arm to guide her across the square. "We'll leave your bag in the car. You never know your luck. Herr Meyer may need a cab to take you up to the hostel."

"Up?" In her first quick panoramic view of the town, she had looked in vain for the opera house and the new hotel.

"Yes. It's up between the town and the castle. Now, that was ingenious of our Rudolf—you have to give it him. We've got conservationists now, you understand. There won't be horrors like that bank again." He pointed up and beyond the ugly four-storey building to where the castle loomed high above them. "You wouldn't think it, but there's a valley runs sideways between us and the schloss. The whole opera complex is tucked away in there. The only place you can see it from is the castle itself, and, as our Rudolf says, if he doesn't mind, who else could?"

"Except his descendants, perhaps? Has he any?"

"Hereditary Princelings and Princesses? Indeed he has. But here we are, and there's the bus." He guided her into the courtyard of a plain, arcaded building tucked away behind the Rathaus, and there, indeed, was a small green bus discharging its passengers, and standing a little to one side, scanning them anxiously, Carl Meyer. He looked younger than she remembered, and amazingly neat, the once-shaggy dark hair cut short above an elegant grey gabardine raincoat.

She looked down anxiously at her own damp and crumpled clothes. "I look a wreck."

"Well, no wonder, left out in the rain." She was grateful to him for not denying it. "Now he's beginning to sweat," Michael went on, "and serve him right." The last passenger had alighted and Carl Meyer had climbed in to speak to the driver.

"Watch it!" Michael's firm hand held her back as a car zoomed past. "You look left here, remember, if you want to stay alive."

"Which I do." How odd, she had said it again. "Carl!" she called as Meyer emerged from the bus, his brown face wrinkled with worry. "Here I am!"

"Anne!" He came hurrying across to them, arms outstretched. "Dearest Anne!" He kissed her warmly on both cheeks. "You got here, thank God. But how?" And then, seeing Michael, "You?" Something in his tone: dislike? distrust? Or something more complex, less easily identifiable?

"Exactly." Michael sounded amused. "I missed Signor Falinieri, alas, and found Miss Paget drowning in a bus shelter, for which I trust you are grateful."

"I certainly am. It was crazy not to meet you at Schennen, Anne. You must forgive me. But I've had such a time...Such a time! You've no idea. Lord, it's good to see you! Dearest Anne!" Any minute now he would be kissing her again. Had they really been on such warm terms?

"How is Alix's throat?" she asked. And then, "I'm afraid I don't know her other name."

40

"She's not working today. We ran through with Lotte— the understudy. A disaster! What Signor Falinieri will say! But where's your luggage? Why are we standing here?"

"The luggage is in my taxi," said Michael. "And we are waiting to see if you would like me to run you up to the hostel."

"The rehearsal room," corrected Carl. "Signor Falinieri should be there by now. He wants a run through of principals at once. God knows what he'll say when he hears Lotte Moser. I must have Anne there."

"She's wet through and worn out. I'll drop you at the rehearsal room and take her on to the hostel."

"No, thanks a lot." Anne shivered. "I'll be fine. Your splendid heater has dried me off and I'm longing to get to work. Only, would it be a bore to take my case to the hostel for me? And, Carl, I'm terribly sorry; I lost my purse at Zurich. Can you pay Michael for me?"

"Pay Michael?" His bushy dark eyebrows drew together in something between surprise and anger.

"I drive a taxi, remember." Michael sounded merely amused. "But I'll drop your case at the hostel for free, Anne, and gladly." He turned to lead the way back to where he had parked the taxi, and Carl took Anne's arm to follow.

"You *are* wet," he said. "I'm a brute, Annchen." He spoke English with more of an accent than she remembered. "Would you really rather go to the hostel and rest?"

"Of course not. Only, I'm afraid I look a mess. Will you mind? Does it matter?"

"Not a bit! You're going to save our lives—or our opera, which is as important. Besides—in a way, perhaps it's tactful. Lotte's a fashion-plate. Well—you'll see. And Alix is..." A quick glance to where Michael was walking a little in front. "Alix is Alix. With all the problems that involves. You're what we need right now."

"I do hope I don't let you down." But in the face of his obvious state of nerves, she was glad she had not worried him with her own trouble.

Back in the taxi, Anne sat well forward, eagerly peering out of the window at the little town with its curious mixture of ancient and modern: an old brown beer house cheek by jowl with a garish café that advertised "Homburgers and Snaks," tourist gift shops side by side with ironmongers and all the basic supplies of a market town. It was raining again, and a few obvious tourists prowled disconsolately about, peer-

41

ing into shop windows which tended to display umbrellas and raincoats prominently among the inevitable souvenirs—the "tat" Michael had described.

The car was held up for a moment at the only traffic lights Anne had seen, then Michael swung out on to the main road and, surprisingly, turned away from where Anne, now peering backwards, could still see the castle, perched high above the town. "It's a long way round to the castle," Michael turned to explain to her. "By road, that is. The steps are quicker, but hard work." Once again he had to stop and wait his chance to swing the car across the traffic on to a road that angled back and up across the hill, through vineyards.

"We're out of town!" Anne had not expected the transition to be so quick.

"Such as it is," said Carl. "But, Annchen, tell me, quick, your voice? It's the same as ever? What have you been *doing*? I've looked for your name so often..."

"You know Robin didn't like me to sing," she said. And that, like everything else she had told him, was true so far as it went. "You are going to find I need practice. But, after all, what else does an understudy get? It's ideal for me; I'm so grateful, Carl."

"Grateful! It's we who should be. You don't understand. Understudy! It will be a miracle if you don't sing Marcus." He cast a quick, anxious glance forwards to where Michael sat, shoulders hunched, concentrated on his driving along the now steeply zig–zagging mountain road. Alpine meadows below, dark green forest above; if only Carl would leave her alone to enjoy this breath–taking view. But he was talking again, leaning towards her. "It's Alix, don't you see? How can we be sure her father won't forbid her appearing at the last moment? It's the chance we took from the start, but then, she was so sure it would be all right. We should have known better. That mother of hers." He was almost whispering. "And now, there's so much publicity for the peace conference; it's all different—he doesn't like it, he has doubts."

"Doubts? I don't understand." But she was distracted. "Oh!" she breathed. Michael had nursed the car gently round one last hairpin bend and parked it in a lay-by just before a high-arched bridge. "Come on!" He jumped out to open her door. "What do you think of it, Niobe?"

"Don't call me that!" But she forgot her irritation in a gasp of pleasure as she gazed up the valley they had just entered. High ahead, dominant, spectacular, on a further

42

range of mountains stood the castle, even more fairy-tale romantic than it had looked from the town, seeming to grow from the dark green of the high forest. Below it, nearer, to left and right, cream-coloured buildings curved down the sides of an Alpine meadow rich with the whites and yellows of spring. The road, dividing on the far side of the bridge, ran up either side of the valley, below shelving flights of steps that led to the buildings. Straight ahead, at the top of the valley, a classic pillared portico joined the two curving wings. And below it, a stream came plunging out of a dark crevice under the road, to flash and sparkle down the centre of the meadow and then vanish again under the bridge beside them.

"It's extraordinary." Anne was taking deep, reviving breaths of pine-scented air.

"Extraordinary good or extraordinary bad?" Michael asked, as Carl came round the car to join them.

"Do you know, I'm not quite sure. It's...too much, somehow? Too good to be true?"

"A stage set," said Michael, pleased with her. "For *The Tempest* perhaps. Or maybe for tragedy."

"You're talking a great deal of nonsense," Carl said impatiently. "For God's sake let's get on up to the rehearsal room."

"Sorry I'm sure." Michael sketched a mock salute. "I just thought Niobe here ought to get a look at what she's in for."

"Why Niobe anyway?" Carl put a protective arm round Anne's shoulders.

"She was so wet when I found her. I'm sorry." He meant it. "I'd forgotten it was tears. I'd meant a water nymph; a nereid; you know; Sabrina fair, something like that. Forgive me, Miss Paget?"

"Oh, call me Anne, and forget it. I was close enough to tears, goodness knows, when you rescued me." But there had been something disconcerting, just the same, about his choice of name. Had he somehow felt her state of despair? She changed the subject. "Is it really all there? The whole opera complex?"

"Yes, ma'am. The opera house is in the centre, behind that fine, fake portico. It's cut deep into the mountain. Very hard rock we have here in Lissenberg. Administrative buildings, your hostel, all that kind of thing on the left." He waved a hand towards a cloister where she could see people moving to and fro. "And, over there, on the right, the conference centre and the international hotel—when it's finished. Note

43

how much better the road is that side. We're expecting every Rolls and Bentley in Europe in three weeks' time."

"Will it be ready?" Trucks and scaffolding in the cloisters of the hotel and conference centre suggested that work was still in progress there.

"Oh, I think so. Our Rudolf pays well. Has to"—Michael's voice was sharp—"to keep the trade unions out." He turned to Carl. "Have you asked Miss Paget yet?"

"Of course I haven't." He might as well have said, "Mind your own business."

Anne turned to Carl. "Asked me?"

"You don't belong to anything, do you?"

"Belong?" And then, understanding. "Oh, you mean Equity? No, I wish I did."

"Lucky you don't," said Michael. "No trade unions in Lissenberg, Miss Paget, by order of our ruler. 'We are all brothers working for the same cause.'" He dropped his voice to a deep rumble on the words and struck a heroic pose. "The only snag is," he went on in his own voice, "that some brothers seem to get paid a lot better than others. And as to the sisters...well, maybe we won't go into that now." He opened the door of the front passenger seat for her and she felt Carl's arm stiffen on her shoulders. But it would be rude and ungrateful not to sit beside her rescuer for this short last lap of the journey and she climbed in, ignoring a kind of strangled grunt from Carl.

"Trouble-making young sod," he said at last when Michael had dropped them at the foot of the steps just to the left of the central portico. "I *am* sorry I didn't meet you at Schennen, Annchen. That young man's poison here in Lissenberg and don't you forget it."

"Poison? But why? What's the matter with him?"

"Everything." He took her arm and led her up the steps. "Where he is, there's trouble. And no wonder. I can't think why Prince Rudolf let him come back."

"Back?"

"From abroad. I wish I knew who'd sent for him. Full of crazy ideas. Stirring things up. Well, you heard him about trades unions."

"I happened to agree with him." Anne paused at the top of the steps and looked back to see Michael swiftly reversing the car down hill to leave her bag at the hostel. "And I never thanked him properly either; you dragged me away so quick. What's got into you, Carl?"

"I'm mad with worry." He turned to face her, his arm still firm on hers so that he spoke almost uncomfortably close. "This opera is my great chance, and right now it looks headed for disaster. Everything's gone wrong—everything. Alix's throat. Lotte Moser. And now Falinieri's been in some accident and turned up in a filthy mood. It was a miracle I got away to meet your bus. We must go *in*, Anne. We've wasted too much time already sight-seeing with that damned dropout. Falinieri was going straight up to the rehearsal room. Said he wanted to know the worst. And—" here he came to the heart of the matter—"said he'd never heard of you. Well, not surprising. You've kept so quiet. If only Alix could sing today, but she's got this throat...If he hears Lotte first, I'm afraid he's capable of going back to Italy, the mood he's in, and then we're in real trouble. I can't do it all, Anne; I absolutely can't."

"Of course not. It would be crazy to try. But hadn't we better go in, if you're so worried?"

"Yes. No. Do you know any of the music?"

"How should I?"

"No. I'm stupid with worry. But you always did sight-read like an angel." He looked her up and down, and she was very much aware of her shabby appearance. "Tell you what." He let go of her arm and she felt an odd stab of relief. "I've got a better idea. We'll *let* him hear Lotte first. Slip in the side way, sit at the back—give you time to do something about your hair, at least—and listen to Lotte. While he does." He pushed open swing doors and led her across a lobby and down a corridor. "Shh." Finger on lip, he opened another door and a great burst of disastrous sound hit her. A full, rough soprano was making desperate attempts to get her voice down the necessary register to the contralto part.

The rehearsal room, dimly lit, was a miniature theatre with an almost full-sized stage but a truncated auditorium where a few people were scattered, half visible on the banked seats. "We worked like hell on the acoustics," Carl whispered as they slipped into two seats at the back.

"Much good they're doing her!" Onstage, a luxurious golden-haired Valkyrie in a low cut model dress was baying incomprehensibly in something between German and, Anne thought, the local dialect.

"*No, Fräulein Moser. No, and no, and no!*" Signor Falinieri, jacket off, sleeves rolled up, was almost incoherent with rage. "*E impossible...*" He looked furiously round and

45

changed languages. "It's nuts; it's crazy; it's an insult; I won't do it. Where's this Alix? And for Christ's sake where's Herr Meyer?"

"Here." Carl stood up and moved forward to climb onto the stage. "And I've brought the new understudy."

"Oh you have?" Lotte turned on him. "Your precious 'unknown.' I may not have Italian trills and shakes to please the signor here, but what of my friends in Lissenberg? What will they say if a foreigner gets yet another part? Our great local opera, and hardly a Lissenberger in it. And who is this unknown singer? Can she sing? Has she proved it anywhere?" She burst at this point into fluent, furious and entirely incomprehensible Liss.

It was obvious that it was Anne's own presumed character, antecedents and capacities that were being so vividly described, and it was restful not to understand a word of it. At last, after a quick check that her lipstick was back on and her short hair just curly from its wetting, Anne stood up. "Were you, perhaps, talking about me?" She let her deep voice make the most of the hall's admirable acoustics as she moved slowly forward towards the stage, and felt a little hush among the people seated in the twilit auditorium.

"Yes!" Carl Meyer came over to meet her on the flight of steps at the right hand side of the stage. "Signor Falinieri," he said as he helped her up onto the stage. "May I present Miss Paget, who has gallantly agreed to come to our rescue."

"But can she do it?" Ignoring Fräulein Moser, Falinieri surveyed Anne without enthusiasm. "You know the part?" he asked.

"Not a word of it!" It was marvellous to be onstage again. "But it's my register and I'm a quick learner. Besides, just to understudy an understudy." She turned to Lotte Moser. "It's just the pleasure of singing it," she tried to explain.

"Pleasure!" spat Lotte. "If that's your idea of pleasure, you're welcome!" She had been singing from a score and now thrust it angrily into Anne's hands, then turned back to Carl Meyer. "They've offered me a job at the hotel," she said. "Two spots a night. I told them I'd have to think it over. Well! I've thought! I'd rather sing in a beer cellar than be shouted at by that bastard son of an Italian-American Jew."

"That will do," said Carl Meyer. "You're fired, Fräulein Moser. Signor Falinieri, I apologise."

"No need, I think, as between you and me. But perhaps we had better hear this understudy of yours before we decide

46

just how much trouble we are in. The speaking voice is perfect, I admit, but what does that prove? If you don't know Marcus, Miss Paget, what can you sing for us?"

"Orpheus' first lament," suggested Meyer, moving over to the piano where the accompanist had sat all the time, looking miserable on his stool. "You know it, Kurt?"

"Not well, I regret." He spread apologetic hands.

"No matter. I do." Carl sat down and played a few introductory notes as Anne moved forward to the centre of the stage. To sing, here on a stage, where she belonged, was to be alive again, and, singing, it was easy to ignore the slow, threatening bite of pain. Carried by the full tide of the music, she went straight on from Orpheus' lament for Euridice to his passionate cry for reunion or death, and, silent at last, almost expected to hear the dramatic intervention of Amor, the God of Love, who would make all right. Instead, there was a little, breathing hush, and then a sudden burst of clapping from the back of the hall.

"*Brava*," cried a new voice, and silence fell again as a tall man moved forward out of the shadows, vaulted lightly onto the stage and stood revealed as considerably older than his movements had suggested. Grey hair, a Hapsburg-type nose, an unmistakable air of command. Even if she had not seen Carl jump to his feet and join the others in something between a bob and a full bow Anne thought she would have recognised the Hereditary Prince, Heinz Rudolf.

Curtseying is difficult in a straight skirt, but she did her best, only to be gallantly raised and to find her hand kissed by dry aristocratic elderly lips. "No, no," said the Hereditary Prince, "rank bows to the artist. You said you had found us an understudy, Herr Meyer, you did not warn us that she would steal the show. Alix will retire. We must rewrite our advertising."

"But, Your Highness..." Anne paused.

"No buts. Alix will retire." He said it again with some emphasis. "You know the part?"

"No, Your Highness."

"But you can learn it, or you would not have come." He looked at his watch. "Three weeks until we open. A suite of apartments at the castle, I think. That way there can be no disturbance of any kind. What kind of piano do you prefer, Miss Paget? We must find you an accompanist all of your own. For your practice. It will be sensational." He was striding up and down the stage as he talked. "Not just the lost

47

Beethoven opera, but a new star born the same night. I suppose..." He turned now to Carl Meyer and Falinieri, who were standing side by side, a little as if struck by lightning. "I suppose we could not write in a little more music for Marcus?"

"Your Highness." Falinieri sounded understandably appalled. "It is not possible."

And, "Your Highness," said Meyer, "it will not be necessary."

"You're right! And it would mean more for her to learn." He had turned back to Anne and was looking her over with a curiously professional eye. "New clothes." He summed up his findings. "A whole new wardrobe. And not a word—not one word—before the opening. Or, maybe an appearance at the Sunday reception for the foreign ministers? The day before the opening. With a hint to the press? Let me see, gold brocade for that, I think."

"Good God, no," said Anne. "Forgive me, Your Highness, but I am quite an ordinary person. Gold brocade is for royalty. And anyway, I can't afford a whole new wardrobe." She could feel Meyer and Falinieri stiffening with fright, and thought, with amusement, how liberating it was to have only six months to live. But enough was enough. She smiled up at the bristling potentate. "Forgive me, Your Highness," she said again. "And bear with me? I am not rich. I will accept two outfits, gratefully, for publicity purposes. But, please may I live in the artists' hostel? I have been—out of touch a little— I am starved for the company of musicians. It will do me more good than anything." And as she said it, felt again the twinge of pain, the harbinger of death. She stood a little straighter, fighting it, breathing slowly, but luckily the Prince had turned, with a quick nod for her proposition, to plunge into a highly professional discussion with Meyer and Falinieri as to how they should make the most of her surprise debut. No-one was taking the slightest notice of her. She moved across the stage to an upright wooden chair, sat down, closed her eyes and let the talk wash over her. The main question seemed to be whether all the advance publicity should be scrapped and her name substituted for Alix's. If she had felt better, she would have protested but then heard with relief Carl's emphatic insistence that it was too late to make such a change. "Besides, you know well, Your Highness, what a draw the name will be. As if we needed one...But a change now, at this late date, might cause doubts, lead to cancellations..."

"You're right." Prince Rudolf was a man of quick decisions. "After all, it is not just this year's season we must think of, but next, and the one after...And that reminds me: Miss Paget's contract. It must be drawn up at once. We are giving you a great opportunity, Miss Paget." He looked round at her. "Perhaps a clause undertaking to sing for us next year?"

Next year. If she let herself laugh, it would become hysteria. The pain was devouring her now. If she tried to speak, she might cry. She sat there, looking up at them, helpless, silent, aware of the Prince's gathering frown. When he speaks, she thought, people jump.

"We're monsters," Carl hurried to her side. "The poor girl's been travelling all day, Your Highness. She's worn out, aren't you Annchen? A good sleep and she will be ready to discuss the contract, which will be generous, I know, as is everything Your Highness does."

The Prince looked at his watch again. "Quite right. Too late for business today. Take Miss Paget to the hostel, Meyer. I rely on you to see that she has everything of the best. The star's suite, of course. Rest...quiet...meals in her room if she wishes. You'll tell the custodian..."

"Yes, Your Highness."

Anne sighed with relief as the two of them turned away from her to discuss the terms of her contract. She ought to be listening, but it was hard enough work just not to let the pain show.

"You're very tired." It was Falinieri, sounding quite different, human..."Let me take you to the hostel, Miss Paget." An eloquent shrug suggested that Meyer was going to be tied up for some time.

"Oh, thank you! It's been a long day."

"A long day!" He took her arm, sketched an explanatory gesture at Meyer and led her offstage. "If you sing like that when you are tired, I look forward to hearing you in the morning. Oh, there were some roughnesses, of course—a lack of practice? But what I do not understand is why I have not heard of you before."

"I haven't sung for a while."

"Ah! And the voice has grown in idleness. It surprised you, too, did it not?"

"Why, yes. Clever of you to notice."

"I notice everything," said Signor Falinieri, alarming her,

49

but then went on. "And if I were you, I would notice my contract quite carefully tomorrow." He pushed open a door and they were out once more in the cool grey of the cloisters. "This way. It's only a step to the hostel. Wise girl, weren't you, to say no to that apartment in the castle. Now there *would* have been a complication."

"Oh?" She neither liked nor understood his tone.

"You don't know the Hereditary Prince's reputation? Then I admire your instinct. But can you think of any other explanation for that disastrous Fräulein Moser?" He laughed. "Clever of the old fox to arrange for the offer from the hotel. Here we are." He pushed open a heavy bronze door at the back of the cloister and ushered her up a shallow flight of steps to what looked like the foyer of a small hotel. Behind a high desk, a white-haired old man sat reading a newspaper, the *Herald Tribune*, Anne noticed with surprise. At the sight of them, he looked up, smiled with extraordinary charm, and broke into fluent Italian, of which Anne could catch only the high points, the good evening and the welcomes. Italian opera, like the German, seemed to lend itself more to high drama than to everyday moments like hotel greetings.

But Falinieri had noticed her blank look. "English, *mein Herr*, if possible. Miss Paget is tired. His Highness says she is to have the star's suite; everything she needs; supper in bed if she wants it."

"His Highness does, does he?" The hostel keeper's English was Oxford as against Falinieri's American. "Well, he'll just have to think again, won't he? Do you see me throwing Regulus out at this hour of the night?"

"Oh, please." Anne put out a pleading hand. "Just a room, Herr..." she paused.

"Just call me Josef," he told her. "You *do* look tired, Miss Paget. I've had a fire lit in the guest suite. Michael told me about you. Your bag's up there already. It's nicer than the star's, in fact. You get the view of the castle." He reached behind him and took a key from a rack. "Thank you for bringing her, Signor Falinieri. You know your way to the hotel?" It was courteous enough and yet a surprisingly firm dismissal, and Anne thought Falinieri looked slightly miffed as he took his leave.

"He'll get used to me," said Josef, reading her thoughts as he led the way through the lobby to a shining modern lift. "I have my privileges, and one of them is to tell you that you're not to stir from your room again tonight, my child.

I've had Lisel unpack for you. She'll bring you dinner at eight. I'd get into bed if I were you. Shall I switch off the telephone?"

"Telephone? What kind of a hostel is this?"

"You're in the guest suite, remember." The lift had stopped at the first floor and he led the way down a long corridor. "Chorus and such use that." He pointed to a phone booth set in an angle of the hall. "You're hardly chorus." He fitted his key in the end door and flung it open. "Guest suite," he said.

"Oh!" She moved forward, speechless, almost breathless, through a little hall towards the view revealed by uncurtained windows. The floodlit castle was poised as if in the air, high above her.

"I thought you'd like it," said Josef with satisfaction, switching on sidelights. "Michael said you weren't quite in the ordinary way. Those are from him, by the way." He pointed at red roses in what looked oddly like a silver vase.

"Bless him!" And then, "I suppose he's your cousin?"

"No. As a matter of fact, he's my nephew."

"Stupid of me." She laughed. "It's just, he said you were all cousins in Lissenberg."

"And so we are," he said. "I hope. Sleep well, Miss Paget. Pleasant dreams."

"Thank you." But, alone, she shivered, remembering nightmares.

5

As she drowned in sleep, Anne's last impression was of a vast mountain silence with just a thread of sound through it that must come from the stream in the valley. Water, and trees, and quiet. I shall sleep here, I shall rest, she thought. I shall not dream of Robin. And woke to the gleam of sunshine round the edges of heavy curtains.

A soft tapping at the door heralded the girl, Lisel, with a loaded breakfast tray. Coffee in a huge vacuum flask, croussants and rolls, butter in a cool container, black cherry jam. "It's enough?" Lisel's English was merely adequate. "Josef says eggs, bacon if you want?"

51

"Oh, no." She pulled herself up in bed. *"Nein, danke schön."*

"Sehr gut." Putting the tray beside Anne on the big double bed, Lisel moved over to draw the curtains and let in a flood of sunshine. "Today better." Her smile was friendly. "You sleep?"

"Marvellously." Anne was taking in the morning view of the castle, outlined dark against the sunlight. "It's beautiful!" She searched for a phrase and settled for *"wunderbar,"* which seemed to please the girl.

"Josef say, 'Eat well, then see this.'" She pointed to a folded note on the tray. "And not..." She paused, groping for the word Josef must have taught her, "Not to horry."

"Please thank him." Pouring coffee, Anne smiled a grateful dismissal, then fell to with a will on freshly baked croissants. Last night she had been almost too tired to eat; now, with that extraordinary healing sleep behind her, she felt ready for anything. When had she last slept through without nightmare or pain?

She poured more coffee and unfolded the note, which proved to be a succinct time-table for the day. It began, she saw with relief, and a quick glance at her watch, at eleven. An appointment with Carl and the Prince's lawyer. The contract, of course. Then, rehearsal until lunch. "Dining room: 13 to 14 hours," ran the message, "Your room: any time. After lunch, rest." No doubt about it, Josef had composed this missive. At three she had another rehearsal and at five an appointment with the wardrobe mistress. Her heart sank as she reached the last item: "Twenty hours, cocktails and dinner at the castle. The car will fetch you at 19:40."

It was obviously a royal command, and must be obeyed. She finished her breakfast and got out of bed to pad over to the wardrobe where Lisel had hung her clothes. A pity about that gold brocade, she thought wryly, looking at the one evening dress she had not sold at the local second-hand shop. Brown velvet; low cut; and she had no jewels. Oh, well. She found herself smiling suddenly. The last thing she wanted was to attract His Promiscuous Highness. And smiled a little wryly, remembering the contract she was presumably going to sign, undertaking to sing at next year's opera festival. It was not so much, she thought, that being about to die concentrated the mind, it seemed to free it wonderfully. So many things that should have been problems were simply immaterial, trivial... She dressed quickly in Jaeger skirt and pull-

52

over and was just reaching for her lipstick when the telephone rang by the bed.

She lifted it nervously. "Yes?"

"Good morning, Miss Paget." Josef's friendly Oxonian voice. "I hope you slept well."

"Like an angel, thank you. It's all so heavenly... And the delicious breakfast... I feel like a queen!"

It got her a dry laugh. "With a view of the castle. But, to business. Herr Meyer and the lawyer are here; they apologise for being a little early and have no wish in the world to hurry you."

It was her turn to laugh. "You mean, they want to see me at once. Tell them I'll be right down."

"No need. If you are ready they will join you in your sitting-room."

"My—"

"—Sitting-room. The door facing the one to the bathroom, Miss Paget. I can see you were too tired last night to explore. I hope the piano meets with your approval. The room is soundproofed, by the way."

"Goodness! I feel like a princess in a fairy tale." She used the lipstick, ran a comb through her hair, and, feeling a little like Bluebeard's wife, ventured to open the panelled door that faced the one into her bathroom. In so far as she had noticed it, she had assumed that it would be locked, allowing access to the next bedroom when necessary. Now she discovered her mistake. If her bedroom had a view of the castle, this corner room almost seemed to contain it. A bay window, with cushioned seats, had been designed so that the castle hung outside, like some magnificent stage set. Valhalla, perhaps? Not altogether a cheerful omen.

But there at the far side of the room was the piano. A Bechstein baby grand, it made her realise just how large the room was. I shall never live up to this, she thought, and then, Well, I won't be trying for long. And pulled herself up short at a knocking on the door that must lead to the passage. "Come in," she called. Here, presumably, were the Nibelungs bearing their disastrous gold.

Carl Meyer was spruce this morning in sharply tailored light grey, and again she was surprised at the conscious change he had made in his appearance. But that of the lawyer who accompanied him did something to explain this. He was almost absurd in formal morning dress, and looked hot with it, she thought sympathetically.

53

Their good mornings said, he put an elegant flat dispatch case down on the table by the bay window, apologised briefly for troubling her so early, and produced the contract and a golden ballpoint pen. "If you would just sign here," he said.

"I beg your pardon?" The acoustics of this room were good, too, and she was pleased with the emphatic way it came out.

Carl Meyer, she noticed, was sweating lightly. The lawyer, whose name she had failed to catch, looked mildly impatient. "Quite right," he said. "I never expect the ladies to bother with reading the small print, but you are absolutely right, Miss Paget. Do, pray, read it at your leisure." He looked ostentatiously at his watch and handed her the surprisingly long document.

It was, at first sight, a fairly standard contract—printed, with spaces left for various facts and figures to be filled in. It certainly all looked reasonable enough, but she remembered Falinieri's warning, and why was Carl so obviously tense? The salary offered was incredibly high for an understudy, but, equally, low for a principal. She looked at this clause thoughtfully, wondering if it was worth querying, her thumb marking the place. *Money I despise it . . .* But it would be pleasant to have enough money to die in comfort.

"Fräulein Paget"—the lawyer had seen where she had paused—"please, see here." He turned the page to where an extra clause had been typed in, promising what struck her as a quite enormous bonus for each performance at which she actually sang. "We all know you will sing at each one," he said. "It has been discussed . . . The Princess quite understands . . . She agrees . . . She asks me to say that she greatly looks forward to meeting you tonight."

"The Princess?" She looked at him in amazement.

"Princess Alix." He was surprised at her surprise. "You did not know?" He turned to Carl. "You did not tell her?"

"I thought she knew." Carl was still sweating.

"You mean, it's the princess who has the contralto voice."

Anne was working it out slowly. "Her idea, the whole thing." She turned to Carl. "I remember, you said Alix's idea. But you never said she was a princess."

"She prefers to be called Alix," said the lawyer.

"But to give it up now," protested Anne. "Such a chance! Such a part! She can't!"

"She has," said the lawyer. "She talked to her father, and then—she heard your voice. She yields, she says, to the greater singer."

54

"Heard me? But how?"

"We are well equipped here, Annchen." Carl was not enjoying this interview. "You were taped, last night, when you delighted us so."

"Oh, I was, was I?" Odd to be so angry. "Well, before you do it another time you will kindly let me know." She dropped her eyes from his unhappy ones and went on reading the contract, and suddenly, there it was, the point she was supposed to have agreed on without noticing. First, the provision she had expected about keeping herself open for a star part in next year's Lissenberg Festival, and then, an inconspicuous part of the standard printed contract, the unbelievable undertaking: "And I hereby agree that between now and this time next year I will keep myself free of all professional organisations that might in any way guide, control or inhibit my performance." She looked up and met the lawyer's shifting eyes. "This means," she said, "that I would not be able to join Equity if I should get the chance."

"We pride ourselves upon being amateurs here, Fräulein," he said inadequately.

"All very fine for Princess Alix." She reached over and took the gold pen from his hand. "For me, no." She struck out the offending sentence and wrote her initials boldly in the margin, then handed the pen back to the lawyer. "If you will be so good as to do so too," she said. "And you," to Carl, who looked as if he wished the floor would open and swallow him.

"His Highness will not like it," said the lawyer.

"Then His Highness will have to find himself another Marcus, will he not?" Absurd, in a way, to make such a point of this, and yet... "Have all the other singers signed?" she asked.

"That is their affair." The lawyer retrieved the contract and folded it with an angry rustle of stiff paper. "I must consult the Prince about this."

"Perhaps he will let me explain my views to him tonight. It is a matter of principle with me. I am sure he will understand."

"Tonight?" asked the lawyer.

She smiled at him sweetly. "I am dining at the castle," she said.

When the time came, it was the last thing she wanted to do. The day had been an exhausting kaleidoscope of hard work and new faces. The first rehearsal had introduced her

55

to Adolf Stern, who played Regulus and made it very clear that he would rather sing with a Princess than with a British unknown. Incredibly handsome in the best blond Viking manner, he seemed wasted as anything but Siegfried, and made an occasional passing reference to Bayreuth— "But, of course, Lissenberg must come first." He did not explain why, and Anne did not ask him, any more than she asked whether he had signed that anti-union clause in the contract. She thought he very likely had. She was afraid, as he contrived to make her miss her cue for the third time, that she was not going to like Herr Stern very much. She was also very sure that when she knew her words better, she would be able to cope with him, and managed to convey as much to an anxious Carl Meyer in a brief aside as they parted.

Anyway, the music was what mattered, and the music was extraordinary. Carl had been right in his description of it as Beethoven at his best, the music echoing the grandeur of the tragedy, and yet a recurrent C major theme, which she was learning to love, reminding, always, of human dignity. Only Regulus, his daughter, and Marcus were given it, and oddly enough, the Carthaginian leader, just once. But, leafing quickly through the complete score Carl had found for her, Anne saw that it came out strong in the final chorus, sung by the Roman people after Regulus and Marcus had sailed away to the barbarous fate that awaited them.

She looked at her watch. Half past seven. One does not keep royalty waiting. Ten minutes later she was breathlessly applying lipstick when the telephone rang. "The car is here, Miss Paget." Did Josef never go off duty?

She stepped into shabby golden sandals, picked up the bag that matched them, twisted a piece of Woolworth's gold chain round her neck in lieu of her lost jewels, flashed herself a wry grin in the glass and hurried along the hall to the lift. She ought to be worrying about that contract, but, why? So far as she could see, her position was impregnable. I look down on them, she thought, from the unassailable ramparts of death.

Downstairs, Josef was waiting near the lift doors. "Punctuality"—he smiled at her—"is the politeness of princes."

"Or to them. Will I do, Josef?"

"Admirably." Comforting to think he meant it. "The car's outside." He looked as if he might have said more, thought better of it, and escorted her through the lobby in silence. A couple of Roman citizens whom she had met earlier in the

56

day honoured her passing with low whistles, which confirmed her theory that they were Italian. But it was good for morale, and so was the courteous way Josef ushered her out through the heavy door and down the well-lighted portico steps to where a small sports car was waiting. She turned, smiling. "And there was I expecting a pumpkin carriage at the least of it."

"You'll be just as surprised." He led her round the car and opened the front door for her.

"Forgive my not getting out." A girl's voice, warm, deep, friendly and, to the expert ear, unmistakable. "It's such a bind in long skirts."

"Princess Alix!"

"You're quick." A warm hand found hers in the half dark of the car. "I thought it would be easier all round if we met before the battle begins."

"Battle?"

"Well"—Alix had a charming, deep laugh—"you did put the cat among the pigeons this morning, didn't you? Singers aren't supposed to be able to read. Not in Lissenberg, anyway. Brave little thing, aren't you? Half my height and twice my guts. I signed it without a whimper."

"Well," said Anne. "You're a princess."

"God help me. Anyway, what I came to say is, stick to your guns, and I promise it will be all right. I've spent the afternoon soothing Father down. He was biting the carpet when I got home. But I've pointed out to him that a few appearances at Covent Garden would make you even more of a draw next year. Poor Father, he doesn't understand. He thinks because he can ban trade unions here in Lissenberg...And of course Stern's signing didn't help."

"Stern signed?"

"He had his reasons. How are you finding him?"

"Difficult. But I'll manage."

"I bet you will. And Father. Don't worry. He lost his heart to you in a small way yesterday. I could see all the signs. Just play it as cool as possible and you'll have him eating out of your hand. He's quite harmless, really."

"You think so?"

"I hope so. Time to be going." She started the car and drove slowly down the arcaded curve, pausing at the bridge to look back at the opera house. "What do you think of it?"

"Tremendous. And if its acoustics are half as good as the rehearsal room's this is going to be quite an occasion."

"Oh, they're better. You like the opera?"

"*Like it*! How can you bear not to sing Marcus? I can't begin to tell you how happy I am to have the chance to do it."

"And I'm so glad you are. You'll be perfect. As for me...Shall we just say, there were problems. Not just my throat. More than I had expected when I first thought of it. I won't pretend I didn't mind like hell at first. And then, listening to Lotte Moser...But now I've heard you, and met you, it's all right. You'll do, won't you?"

"I'll do my best."

"Fair enough." They had left the valley now and the headlights illuminated a great arc of forest as the Princess swung the car sharply round and they began to climb. Looking back and down, Anne caught a glimpse of what must be the lights of Lissenberg before the black forest engulfed them. "This party," Alix went on. "Nothing formidable. Mother, of course, Signor Falinieri, Carl Meyer, and, I'm afraid, Herr Rummel."

"Rummel?"

"The lawyer. Bit of luck and firmness, you can get all that done with over cocktails." She laughed, but not happily. "You must bear with Mother's American habits."

"Your mother's American?"

"You didn't know? Mother's not just American; she's solid American dollars. What was that song? Eartha Kitt, remember? An old-fashioned millionaire, that's Mother. So, when you're not being patient with Father, just bear with her, there's a dear. She's got plenty of her own to bear. Oh—one thing—her German's terrible so we speak English mostly, which will save you some trouble. And here we are." Huge turreted gates barred their way, with no sign of a guard. "Just watch the miracles of modern science!" Alix played a quick little phrase on her car horn and the gates swung open. "Tune changed every day, of course." She took the car slowly into a large courtyard, waving to a man in the right-hand turret as she passed.

As she parked at the foot of a broad flight of steps, footmen in green livery sprang forward to open the car doors. "Do you mind the back way?" Alix led Anne quickly through a maze of corridors to a lift. "I need to comb my hair." More corridors led to a sumptuous bedroom with a view of lights far below in the valley.

As they stood side by side at a huge glass, Alix spoke. "I wonder how long it will take Adolf Stern to see how much

58

better a foil you'll make for him than I did. I can't tell you what a comfort it is to be back into heels." She laughed. "I'm two inches taller than he is. I had to wear ballet slippers for rehearsals and he still hated it!"

"You'd make a marvellous Orpheus!" It was true. Tall, slender and dark haired, Alix was handsome rather than beautiful, with an air of command which would make her much more suitable to a lead part than to Marcus, the devoted page.

Alix laughed ruefully. "Pity, isn't it? I always wanted to sing Leonora, but I was too convincing by a half as a man." She looked at her watch. "Time to go. Best get your encounter with Father and Rummel over before the others arrive. And whatever happens don't let them bully you. Just remember, I'm not singing, and there's no one else."

"Thanks."

Curtseying low to Prince Rudolf and encountering the full blast of his angry gaze, Anne was grateful for the encouragement.

"So, Miss Paget." He looked her up and down with aristocratic disdain, the lawyer, Rummel, looming behind him. "You do not find our contract good enough for you?"

"Forgive me, Your Highness! For Lissenberg, I am sure, it is admirable, but for an English singer..." She looked up at him pleadingly. "You must realise that it is everyone's ambition to sing at Covent Garden, the National Opera, Glyndebourne...Without Equity membership, we have no hope."

"Oh, you English!" He turned from her impatiently. "You are content to let the trades unions run your country for you. We manage things quite otherwise here in Lissenberg. I trust I can persuade you to think again."

"No. Forgive me, Your Highness, but this is final. It is not just my career." And how true that was. "It's the principle of the thing. Would you betray your position as Hereditary Prince?"

"Of course not." He found the comparison distasteful, and showed it.

"Well, then...I owe a duty to my fellow singers. To myself. I beg you, Your Highness, to bear with me."

He swore, hard, angry, but unintelligible. Then: "Very well, Since it seems we cannot do without you..." He smiled at her grimly, while his eyes did a slow, luxurious traverse of her shoulders. Then he turned to vent his rage elsewhere.

"Herr Rummel, you may go. We shall not need you this evening." He turned away and crossed the wide room to where a range of windows gave onto a terrace.

"There, that's over, and not so bad as I'd feared." Alix's hand was warm on Anne's arm. "Come and meet my mother."

The Hereditary Princess, a plump, artificially blonde lady of uncertain years, was greeting Signor Falinieri and Carl Meyer, who had arrived together. "There you are at last," she addressed Alix petulantly. "I've had messengers looking for you all over."

"I'm sorry, ma'am." The formal address came oddly from daughter to mother. "I thought I told you I was going to fetch Miss Paget myself. And here she is, our new star."

"Oh, that eternal opera!" The Hereditary Princess turned a brusque shoulder to the three people connected with it and looked ostentatiously at her watch. "I can't think what's happened to my cousin and his friends," she said. "They promised to be here for dinner."

"Uncle Jimmy?" Alix sounded surprised rather than pleased. "I didn't know he was about."

"He flew in this morning. That helicopter pad almost makes the whole project worthwhile. He's been down at the works all day. Ah." A footman had been standing at her elbow with a tray of drinks. "Champagne cocktail, Miss Paget?"

It was not Anne's favourite drink, but she took it meekly and noticed that her hostess, exchanging her empty glass, carefully selected one from the back of the tray. "Here they come at last." She took a stiff pull from the new glass and moved forward to greet the little group of men who had just entered the room.

"Oh, hell," said Alix under her breath, and Anne rather shared her feelings when she saw Adolf Stern among them.

Prince Rudolf had been standing a little apart, glowering out the window at the view down the arcaded valley, where hidden lights made strange shadows among the colonnades. Now he came forward with a kind of forced joviality to greet the new arrivals. "James." He shook hands informally with a tall red-faced man. "When did you get here?"

"This afternoon." To Anne's surprise he looked and spoke like a typical upper-class Englishman—a real, old-fashioned lord of creation. "We have to talk, you and I," he told the Prince. "In the morning. I've made a date with that girl you call your secretary. Gloria seems to think she can find me a corner for the night in this schloss of yours." He made it sound as if the castle was some kind of second-class hotel.

"Delighted," said Prince Rudolf without enthusiasm. "And your friends? I don't believe I have had the pleasure..."

"Gloria didn't tell you? My apologies, Your Highness." He contrived to make the title faintly mocking as he waved forward two small men in dark suits who had been hovering rather uncertainly beside the immaculate, Viking figure of Adolf Stern. "My right hand and my left, Your Highness." Once again he contrived to build a sneer into the formal address. "Mr Bland from Manchester and Mr Marks from Birmingham. What they don't know about my business is nobody's business."

"Ah—business," said Prince Rudolf. "And do they propose to honour us with their company tonight too?"

"On second thoughts"—the red face grew redder—"we will all three stay at your hotel. I shall be interested to see what kind of a job your architects have made of that." He did not sound hopeful.

"As you wish. It is not officially open yet, as you know, but, of course, for you—" The Prince turned away. "Herr Meyer, Herr Stern, good evening. Have you met your new colleague, Miss Paget, Herr Stern?"

"Yes." A professional glance assessed the well-worn brown velvet and dismissed the Woolworth chain for what it was. "I have had that pleasure."

"Good." He sounded profoundly uninterested. "Ah, dinner." A footman had thrown open huge double doors at the far end of the extravagantly panelled room. "Gloria, my dear, shall we go?"

"Oh, hell," said Princess Gloria. "I wanted another drink. Find your own way, would you all, while I get one?"

In the general movement that followed, Anne was aware of both Stern and Meyer approaching Alix, who smiled impartially at them and gave her arm to Falinieri. Inevitably, they then both turned to her, but Carl was just the first, and she was glad. Taking his arm, she marvelled again at the change in his appearance. The old Carl had gone everywhere in baggy black trousers and matching polo-necked pullover. This new one was immaculate in white tie and tails. And: "You've given up those dreadful cigars," she said teasingly. "How did you manage?"

"Strength of mind. I'm a very strong character, Annchen,
61

as I hope you know. And it was barbarous, all that cigar smoke around the singers I taught."

She smiled at him. "That's what I always used to say, remember?"

"Of course I do. I remember everything." The pressure on her arm was a trifle firmer. What non-existent past bond between them was he trying to imply?

But the little procession had reached a dining room gleaming with glass and silver against a background of the most ornate heraldic wallpaper Anne had ever seen. Slit windows, high up in the walls, added to the general feeling of gothic claustrophobia. "It's the small dining room," explained Carl, leaning forward to study place cards. "Ah, good, here we are." He must have known they were sitting together. Well, it was logical enough, and so—granted the odd nature of the party—was the fact that she had Prince Rudolf on her other side, with Alix beyond him. Facing her husband across the oval table, Princess Gloria had her cousin James on her right, and Stern on her left, but was talking exclusively to her cousin while Stern looked mulish and replied curtly to overtures from Bland, who sat between him and Carl. Princess Gloria must be fond of her cousin, Anne thought, to let him and his two assistants so totally destroy the balance of her party.

"You like our opera house, Miss Paget?" Prince Rudolf had turned from Alix to do his duty by his guest.

"I've not sung there yet, Your Highness. But Princess Alix says it is even better than the rehearsal room, and I think that's the best place I ever sang in." The champagne cocktail had been strong. She smiled up at the Prince with warm brown eyes. "I cannot tell you how grateful I am for the chance you are giving me."

"You will make the most of it, I am sure." His smile was disconcertingly intimate. "I like a bit of spirit in a woman. There's not many in Lissenberg would stand up to me." There was more meaning in the phrase than she liked, and she was grateful when Alix drew his fire with a question from his other side, and he turned and became involved in an animated conversation with her and Falinieri.

Footmen in a uniform straight out of *Fledermaus* began to pour wine, and Anne turned with surprise at the sound of music from above and behind her. A string quartet in a small musicians' gallery had begun what she diagnosed as someone's selection from light opera.

"And a very good idea, too," said Carl approvingly as they

all started on cold, delicious, unidentifiable soup. "You couldn't call this the easiest party in the world."

"Well, no." A quick glance showed Prince Rudolf still absorbed in talk with Falinieri and Alix. "It is a little ...surprising. I'm quite out of my depth, and that's the truth. I'm so glad to have you, Carl, to explain things a bit." She looked down the table to where Princess Gloria was deep in conversation with her cousin, and spoke quietly as the musicians broke into a lively waltz from *Rosenkavalier*. "The Princess's cousin," she asked. "He's English, surely—I didn't catch his surname—but she's American. And—has he business interests here in Lissenberg?"

"James Frensham." Carl, too, kept his voice low, under the background of music and conversation. "Yes. The Princess's branch of the family went to the States just before the war. He stayed home and made munitions—and money. More money. They've all got it, the Frenshams. And, yes, you could say he has business interests here. He practically owns the place. Well, the opera complex isn't exactly coming cheap, you know."

"I should think not, indeed. But"—she looked round the ornate room—"surely—"

"I quite agree." A note of warning in Carl's voice as the musicians ended their waltz and a little hush fell on the table. "One of the best operas I've ever worked on."

"I know it will be a tremendous success." She followed his lead.

"It had better be," said Prince Rudolf, and she wondered, suddenly, if James Frensham had not perhaps brought him bad news.

"It will." Carl spoke with a confidence Anne admired. "We've got everything going for us, Your Highness." And then, as the Prince turned back to Falinieri and Alix. "But, Annchen, tell me about yourself, what you've been doing all the time since you were my most rewarding pupil. Oh, those days... those happy days..."

Once again she had the curious feeling that he was inventing a past for them that did not exist. "Not much," she answered his question. "Living, you know, and partly living."

"You could never do anything partly, Annchen, not the girl I knew. *Himmel*, do you remember how angry I was when you gave up your career for that husband of yours."

"We will not talk about Robin." It came out more ruthlessly than she had intended, but she was glad to have it

63

said, and glad, too, when the conversation became more general, if still curiously strained, and she was able to devote herself to polite nothings, delicious food and elegant local wine. The mention of Robin had drawn a shadow across the evening. A ghost is walking on my grave, she thought, and, so thinking, felt the first quick stab of pain.

"What's the matter, Annchen?" Carl asked anxiously. "You look as if you had seen a ghost." Then, contrite, "I'm a brute to have reminded you. Forgive me?"

"It's nothing." But it was a relief when Princess Gloria rose abruptly to lead the ladies from the room. In the doorway, she tripped over the hem of her dress and was expertly retrieved by a footman. "I'm bushed," she told Alix and Anne in loud, slurred accents as they followed her through double doors to the salon. "I'm going to hit the hay, and quick, before they bring their quarrel in here." Anne had already noticed her curious habit of using out-of-date American slang.

"Quarrel?" asked Alix.

"I'll say! I don't know what it is, but Jimmy's here to straighten your father out, and thank the lord he's the man to do it. Darling Rudolf's not going to get through Jimmy's money the way he did mine. That damned opera shows a profit, or—" She made an extremely inelegant gesture and left them, staggering a little.

"I'm sorry," said Alix. "Poor Mother, she's had a hell of a time, one way and another. Trouble between Father and Uncle Jimmy would be about the last straw. Though, mind you, I suppose it was inevitable."

"I am so sorry. Should I leave, perhaps?"

"No, please. Do stay. There will be no public quarrel—not with guests. You'll see; it will be all sweetness and light."

"Just like dinner?"

Alix laughed. "Exactly. God you're going to be a comfort, Anne. May I call you Anne, and will you call me Alix?"

"Should I?"

"Can't think why not. You've heard Mother. She's right, I'm afraid. It's not much of a princess whose father is as deep in debt as mine is. I do hope it's not real trouble between him and Uncle Jimmy. We could do without that, right now." She put a warm hand on Anne's. "You see now why this opera has got to succeed. If not, Lissenberg is going to find itself bankrupt. Or part of the Frensham empire."

"What would happen then?"

"I hate to think. If I know Cousin Jimmy, he'd sell us to

the highest bidder. And I don't quite like to think who that might be. We're in what you could call a strategic position. Too strategic by a half. Who wants to end up as a launching pad? And probably for the wrong side at that. Besides—I like us the way we are. Small and beautiful, if you don't think that's too vain. At least, civilised. And—neutral. Like the Swiss. It may not be exactly a position to boast about, but it has its points. Besides, like the Swiss, we contrive to make ourselves useful. And... stick to a few principles."

"I know. Someone told me about the Russians you wouldn't send back. After Yalta. That's something to be proud of."

"And something their bosses won't forget," said Alix. "I wouldn't much like to be sold to them."

"He wouldn't!"

"I'd not like to bet on it. I meant it when I said the highest bidder. Money's Uncle Jimmy's life. If he had to save young James at the expense of his fortune—a kidnapping say—I wouldn't reckon much on James's chances."

"Young James?"

"His son and heir. As formidable as his father, in his own way. His mother was an Italian princess—rich, of course. James went to Harrow like his father. That was before his parents got divorced. Now he lives on his mother's Sicilian estate. Not much love lost between any of them, I'm afraid. Oh dear"—her smile was apologetic— "I'm gossiping. You're a good audience, Anne. Listen! Here they come. Do something for me?"

"Gladly."

"They'll all want to drive you home. Let Meyer, would you?"

"But of course! I'd much rather. We're old friends, you know."

And why did that get her such a strange look from her new friend? Something odd about Alix's tone; about this whole occasion. Or were fatigue and continuing pain making her imagine things? The day was beginning to seem endless, and when the men joined them she seized the earliest opportunity to say she must go, pleading tomorrow's early rehearsal.

"So soon?" But she thought Prince Rudolf was glad enough to have his party break up.

As Alix had predicted, both Stern and Carl stepped forward to offer to drive Anne, but, surprisingly, so did James Frensham, who had come in from dinner ruddier than ever with ill-suppressed anger. "We have work to do,' he explained without grace. "Checking some figures for the morning. There is room in my Bentley."

"It's very kind of you—" Anne began, but Carl interrupted her, a pressing hand on her arm.

"I must plead a stronger claim, sir. Miss Paget and I have things to discuss. With the opening date so near, I feel I must use every minute."

"So I should imagine." Frensham's tone was not hopeful. "Bland, Marks, we have work!" He took an unceremonious leave.

"Come along then, Annchen." A proprietary arm in hers, Carl shepherded her through her farewells as solicitously as if they were old lovers rather than old friends. As he draped her stole tenderly round her shoulders she felt a quick pang of apprehension. If there was one thing she could do without right now, it was an emotional scene. But Carl, helping her into the car and starting the engine, turned at once to a brisk professional discussion of her part, and she got back to the hostel at once relieved and, just faintly, puzzled.

6

Waking Anne with her breakfast next morning, Lisel looked white and shocked. Her hands, putting down the tray on the big bed, shook so badly that the cream spilled. "Forgive me, Fräulein," she said. "It's the news. Horrible!" She spoke in German, but her meaning was clear enough.

"What's happened?" Anne pulled herself up out of deep sleep and was glad to see that the shaken girl understood the tenor of her question.

"*Tot*," she said, and then broke into a jumbled mixture of German and Liss. Anne recognised a few phrases. Herr Frensham. The Princess's cousin. And then again, unmistakable, *tot*. That formidable English tycoon was dead? It seemed impossible. She nodded a dismissal and lifted the telephone by her bed.

"*Ja?*" Josef, too, sounded shaken.

"Josef? It's Anne. What's this about Mr Frensham?"

"He's dead. He drove a couple of his friends home from the castle last night, and they fell off the road. It's a terrible corner." Was he trying to explain to himself, or to her?

"I'm..." What did one say? "I'm so sorry." And then, because she was a professional, "Will it make any difference?" She had not even looked at the note on the breakfast tray that must describe her day's appointments.

"To the opera? None. That has already been settled. The opera, the conference, everything is to go on as planned."

"Yes, of course." Anne remembered her conversation with Alix the night before. "I suppose it must." Ringing off, she opened the day's programme. More rehearsals...Surprisingly, another appointment with the wardrobe mistress for the late afternoon, and a note in Josef's scrawling hand. *Fourteen hours, a car will fetch you to give a statement to the police. Not to worry.*

Alix, telephoning, sounded subdued, but said the same thing. "It's a matter of form, naturally. But—I didn't know you were involved in some kind of accident on your way here from Schennen. The police seem to think this one was like it...a bit too like for comfort. We don't have crime in Lissenberg." Now she sounded angry.

"I'm so sorry. How is your mother?"

"Flat out with shock. She really loved Uncle James." She broke off for a moment, then, "Sorry, Anne, I must go. We're at disaster stations here today. Don't take any lifts from strangers." It was not quite a joke.

The morning's rehearsal was a subdued affair with whispered gossip running through the darkened auditorium so that first Meyer and then Falinieri had to appeal for silence as Stern and Anne ran through their opening duet. At last Falinieri clapped his hands. "Is impossible," he said. "This is an opera house, not a beer garden. You, chorus, go away and chatter outside. For the rest of the day we will concentrate on Regulus and Marcus—oh, and on you, of course, Fräulein Stock." This to the quiet girl who played Regulus' daughter Livia. "We have yet to hear you and Miss Paget. We'll take that after the lunch break."

"I'm so sorry," said Anne. "I can't be here."

"Can't be here? What kind of talk is that?"

"I have to see the police," said Anne, and got the silence they had been wanting all morning. "I'll be back as soon as I can. They are sending a car for me right after lunch."

"I see. Then we will take Fräulein Stock's scene with her

67

father Regulus first, and await you impatiently, Miss Paget. Perhaps you will explain as much to the police."

"I'll try," said Anne dubiously.

She ate lunch in her room, studying her part as she swallowed the hostel's highly seasoned food, and pushing the impending interview with the police to the back of her mind. At ten to two, her telephone rang. "The car is here," said Josef, "but don't hurry."

"You're always saying that, bless you." But she did hurry. The sooner she got there, the sooner it would be over. Besides, why should the police care how she looked? Her lipstick had hidden itself at the bottom of her bag. She muttered a curse, combed her hair and hurried out to the lift.

Emerging on the ground floor, she saw a familiar figure awaiting her. "Still no lipstick, I see." Michael straightened up from where he had been chatting with Josef at the desk.

"I was in a hurry," she said crossly. "If you're my police driver, you're early." But she was surprised at how pleased she was to see him.

"I am, and I am." He was no tidier than he had been when he rescued her from Schennen station, but today his teeshirt read *Votes for Women*. "I thought you'd like it." He had seen her read the message. "And why I'm early is to buy you a drink. Uncle Josef has them all ready in his secret lair. We may as well both tell the same story." He took her arm and guided her behind the desk to a surprisingly elegant little office where two glasses stood on an exquisite marquetry table. "Slivovitz." He passed her a glass. "And if you don't like it, don't let on."

"But I do! It's just what I need, bless you. How do you mean, the same story?"

"About what happened day before yesterday. You've maybe forgotten the order the cars left the castle last night?"

"I'm not sure I ever knew."

"Well." He lifted his glass and drank to her. "It's a funny thing, but once again yours was the car right behind the accident."

"Dear God! But—it's not possible. We didn't see anything."

"Nothing to see," he said soberly. "Not from the road. It was a long way down. The car wasn't spotted till this morning, and the police climbers have still not managed to get down to it. Looks like it's taking all day. Don't worry"—he had seen her shiver—"not a chance but they're dead, poor bastards. Now, drink up, and come and tell all to the police."

"Will it be Herr Weigel?"

"No, the boss. He's not as fierce as he looks—or as stupid." Somewhere between reassurance and warning, it did little to make her feel better. But the slivovitz was cheering, and so was the fact that he had troubled to come early.

"Haven't women got them?" she asked, making conversation as they emerged from behind the desk and crossed the lobby, where as usual several members of the chorus were sitting over coffee.

"Got what?" And then, "Oh, votes! Good God, no. This is Lissenberg. Women know their place here. *Küche, Kirche* and all that." He pushed open the heavy bronze door and led the way down the arcade steps to a smart green car.

"It's a police car!"

"Well, of course it's a police car." He opened the door for her.

"But what about your job? The taxi firm?"

"Oh, I lost that," he said cheerfully. "Driving for the police is much more interesting. How did the rehearsal go?"

"So so." She was grateful for the question. "Herr Stern doesn't much like singing with me. He's making things ...difficult."

"Oh?" He was taking the police car at a good pace down the valley.

"Little things. The wrong cue... It's so easy, and then he's terribly sorry, and then he does it again." She laughed angrily. "He'd rather sing with a princess and doesn't care who knows it."

"Tough." He swung the car round a hairpin bend. "I'd have a word with Meyer if I were you. He'll sort it out for you. It's his job." He looked at his watch. "Time's getting on. Would you like the siren?"

"No, please!" She felt quite conspicuous enough as it was.

"And no need. I can do it in the time without. They're OK, these cars."

"They certainly are. And you don't really need the siren, do you?" She had noticed that motorists and pedestrians alike kept to the side of the road at sight of the approaching green car.

"We respect our police in Lissenberg," said Michael. "I wouldn't want to be the joker responsible for those two accidents."

"Joker?"

"You're right. It's not the word. Has anyone told you just

69

how important a man James Frensham was here in Lissenberg?"

"Princess Alix said something last night. He was—throwing his weight around rather."

"He would. Well—he practically owns—owned the place. What I want to know is what young James is going to do. Someone may have miscalculated badly, if you ask me." He slowed the car for a moment. "And, by God here he comes! Quick, you could call that." A helicopter was hovering over them, its drone audible above the silent-running engine of the car. Michael pressed a button on the dashboard and a disembodied voice spoke from a grille. "Yes, Car 2?"

"Helicopter about to land, sir. Young James Frensham I'll bet. Anyone swept the pad for broken glass?"

The grille emitted a harsh laugh. "Who thinks he's the only brain in Lissenberg?" said the voice. "Come on in, Michael, and step on it. We're waiting for Miss Paget."

"Right." With obvious satisfaction, Michael switched on the siren and took the car through the town at a speed that made Anne close her eyes.

"OK. All over and no lives lost." He drew the car to a decorous halt outside a handsome, flat-fronted house surrounded by flower gardens. "In with you." He was around and opening her door before she could get out of her safety harness. "And remember, the truth, the whole truth, and nothing but the truth."

"That's how we make our stories jibe?"

"Of course."

"Well, then." She summed it up. "Thanks for the drink."

"A pleasure." He was guiding her up steps to where a green-uniformed policeman saluted and then held open big doors.

"This way," he said to Anne. And, to Michael, "The boss wants you to fetch Herr Meyer and Herr Stern."

"They *will* be pleased," said Michael. "Sorry to abandon you but duty calls." His quick smile was heart-warming. "Into the lion's den with you." He pushed shaggy hair back from a high forehead, sketched a half-mocking salute and turned to run lightly back down the steps.

It left her feeling curiously forlorn, but in fact the interview was straightforward enough. Herr Winkler, the huge, calm chief of police took her briskly through the story of her arrival at Schennen and the accident on the road to Lissenberg, then switched to the events of the night before. Here,

70

suddenly, she saw a pitfall she should have anticipated, and was less than grateful, for the first time, for Michael's distraction. Should she tell Herr Winkler about Princess Alix's odd request that she let Meyer drive her home? Every instinct was against it. And yet in the light of what had happened it could be sinister enough. Suppose she had accepted James Frensham's offer of a lift. She shivered. *I am not ready to die yet...*

"What is it?" He was quick, this slow-speaking policeman.

"I just remembered. Mr Frensham offered me a lift. So did Herr Stern," she added.

"But you chose to drive with Herr Meyer? Mr Frensham is a powerful man—was a powerful man."

"I know. But Carl Meyer is an old friend. And I'd had enough."

"Enough?" He raised heavy eyebrows in question.

"Herr Winkler, you must know there's a lot going on behind the scenes at the opera house. Better than I do."

"And at the castle." His smile was friendly. "Yes. I don't think I need your version of all that. Lotte Moser talked to the local press last night. Something tells me they won't be running her story. Well, they'll be busy with the murder."

"Murder?" But she had expected it.

"Or a very odd accident indeed. You were in the next car, Miss Paget. You were—lucky. Between the accident and the time you came by, someone sanded over the oil slick that caused it. Otherwise, we might not be enjoying this conversation."

"Oh! But then—" It dawned on her. "The other time. It can't have been meant for me."

"So it would seem. Or—someone has changed their opinion of your usefulness. And, of course, there is another possibility. Yes!" He lifted the telephone, which had given a sharp, single ring. "Ah, at once." He turned back to Anne. "You will excuse me, Miss Paget. Young James Frensham is here. I must see him at once. If you think of anything out of the way about last night, you will let me know? And I would suggest that you resist any temptation to go for long, lonely mountain walks. Or, for that matter, drives with anyone you don't know."

"That means everyone," she said.

"Much safest." He rose and showed her out.

The lobby was crowded now. Carl Meyer and Adolf Stern were sitting on a bench, deep in agitated and impatient con-

71

versation, while a strikingly handsome young man was looming angrily over the policeman on duty. "Arrangements to make," he was saying, his rich English accent carrying loud in the small lobby. "Standing around here..."

"Now, Mr Frensham," said the policeman soothingly, his eyes lighting up at sight of Anne. "Herr Winkler will see you at once."

"And not before time!" Deep-set dark eyes under a medieval cap of hair dismissed Anne as of no account, but as he turned to make for the office door Adolf Stern intercepted him.

"We were first!" he protested. "We've been waiting I don't know how long! We've work to do." It was an extraordinary confrontation Anne thought, between the blond Viking and the young Englishman who might have stepped straight out of the portrait of one of the more dangerous Medicis. An Italian mother, she remembered. A Sicilian estate...

I am James Frensham." It was obvious enough. He pushed past Stern and stalked into Winkler's office.

Carl left Stern angrily muttering and joined Anne. "How did it go?"

"OK." She found herself smiling. "I liked him."

"Wait for us," he said. "We'll drive you back."

Lifts from friends? Lifts from strangers? "Thanks just the same," she said. "I think I'll walk."

"It's too far. You're forgetting..."

"I am driving Miss Paget back." Michael had emerged from an inconspicuous door in a corner, bringing with him a strong, mixed smell of coffee and beer. "Falinieri will be angry enough already."

"He won't get far without Regulus." But Anne was grateful for the intervention. There was something very comfortable about Michael, even if he did smell strongly of beer and look untidier than ever, black hair tousled as if he had been running his hands through it.

"How did it go?" He opened the door of the green car for her.

"OK," she said. "That's what I told Herr Meyer."

"Quite right. But what are you going to tell Uncle Michael?"

"You're no uncle. Cousin perhaps." And she was not going to tell him about Alix's odd request any more than she had told Herr Winkler. "Tell me." She turned towards him as he started the car. "Who do you think sanded over the oil slick?"

"Winkler told you that? Keep it under your hat, like a wise child. As for who did it? Maybe someone who likes your big brown eyes? Or who wants the opera to succeed? Or just naturally suffers from tidy habits. Three murders might be enough for anyone. If I were you, my songbird, I wouldn't think about it much, and I wouldn't talk about it at all. Except to me, of course."

"I certainly won't," she agreed, noticing with relief that he was taking the car through the town at a reasonable pace.

"What did you think of wonder boy?" He slowed to let a nun cross the road.

"Wonder boy?"

"The heir apparent. Young James Frensham. Whoever killed his father did Lissenberg no service. Old Frensham was a fire-eater, but he knew what opera was. He meant to give *Regulus* a chance. Young James is something else again. I'd be ready for trouble if I were you."

"He'd never cancel it? He couldn't!"

"Probably not. Certainly not if someone can convince him there's money in it. No one's managed to yet." He turned to look at her. "You feeling public-spirited?"

"Me? What do you mean?"

"Got another date with the wardrobe mistress, right?"

"Yes, but how did you know?"

"Oh, I hang about," said Michael vaguely. "Look; she's been told from the top to turn you out, no holds barred, no expense spared. Let her, there's an angel! Don't turn up that nice nose of yours. Don't ask questions, just let her dress you up and make the most of it." He laughed. "What was it someone said about the right thing for the wrong reasons? You sell young James on opera and you're doing us all a good turn."

"But he's just lost his father." It was only one of the many possible protests.

"You think he's weeping anything but crocodile tears? He's the great man, now, right? Who ever minded that? Not James Frensham the second, that's for sure. The question is, what will he do with it?" He pulled the car off the road into a lay-by set into the forest, with tables and benches for picknickers. "Would you like to walk the rest of the way? It doesn't take more than twenty minutes on foot, cutting through the woods, and I reckon it would do you good. You've been at it non-stop since you got here. Falinieri can do with-

73

out you for an extra few minutes. He's got to wait for Stern anyway."

"Yes." Doubtfully. Who was it that had told her not to walk through the woods with strangers?

He gave her hand a quick, approving pat. "Sensible girl. Uncle Winkler warned you to be careful, did he? And quite right, too. But you're safe enough with me. Everyone knows I'm taking you back. I couldn't possibly push you off a cliff and get away with it, even if I wanted to, which I don't. You're too pretty to waste."

"Thanks!" But she was getting out of the car. Sunlight glancing down through beech trees new-green for spring made enticing patches of light on a path that led up through the woods.

"That's the girl." He locked the car and they started up the path side by side. "I have to make you understand," he said. "About James Frensham. He's pretty well the boss here now. If he were to decide the opera wasn't worth the trouble. Well—I don't rightly know what would happen."

"But the peace conference—"

"Exactly. By now, they go together. Trouble is, I just don't know how much young James cares about world peace. I did hear that he wanted to start a small-arms factory here in Lissenberg and our Rudolf wouldn't let him. Like father, like son, and no great stake in peace talks, either of them. But one thing James does care about is his public image. If he thinks the opera's going to be a credit to him—his father put up most of the money, you know—why then he'll go along with it. So, take those clothes you were looking so mulish about; use them; show him you're star quality. Rudolf saw it; James is no fool. Make him see you; make him think opera for everyone's sake; for Lissenberg's."

"But I thought you didn't want the kind of mass tourism the opera's likely to bring." The picture grew more complicated all the time.

"You're right, of course. It's a proper dilemma. But I want tourism a hell of a lot more than I want arms factories. If only they'd stuck to the original plan for the opera house."

"Original?"

"Smaller. Chamber opera. Friendly. Glyndebourne, not Salzburg."

"Pity," she agreed. And then, "Oh, how lovely." The trees had given way to an emerald patch of Alpine meadow. "Cowslips! I haven't seen them for years."

"This is what we want to save," he told her. "No." He read her thoughts. "You can't stop and pick them. That really would be hard on Falinieri." He bent down himself and picked two. "For your buttonhole."

"They smell so good. A kind of orient-flavoured spring." She turned to look back for a moment as they re-entered the woods. "Heavenly place. I must come back here."

"Not by yourself, you mustn't. Aside from anything else, there are bears. You might surprise each other."

She laughed. "How did you guess I was a coward?"

He turned to smile his engaging, lop-sided smile. "I guess you're lots of things, but not a coward. There, you see, it did only take twenty minutes." They had emerged from the wood at the lower end of the opera valley, near the bridge.

"Do you know, I believe you're right." She paused for a moment to look at the arcaded buildings. "It would have been better, smaller."

"Most things are," he told her.

Falinieri was rehearsing the chorus in their welcome to Regulus, but stopped them to greet Anne with enthusiasm. "At last! Now, at least, we can try out your first scene with Livia. Are you there, Fräulein Stock?"

"I certainly am. In fact, I have been here all day. Waiting." Gertrud Stock's tone, like her face, was sullen. A handsome, sallow girl, she spoke with what Anne was beginning to realise was a Lissenberg accent. Was this why she reminded her teasingly of someone? But of whom?

Unlike the rest of the cast, Fräulein Stock knew her part perfectly and made no attempt to conceal her impatience with Anne's inevitably patchy sight-reading. It made the rehearsal even more exhausting than it would have been otherwise, and in the end Anne had to cry for mercy. "I'm out of training, I'm afraid," she apologised.

So I have noticed." But Falinieri's tone was kind. "And also that you learn fast and will make a perfect Marcus. We are lucky to have found you. Now, you will not use your voice again today. You will rest, and study the part."

"Thank you." Anne looked at her watch, saw she was late for her next appointment, and fled for the wardrobe mistress's room. Luckily, this fierce lady was English and had taken a liking to Anne the day before when she had measured her for her page's costume.

"I know." Mrs Riley accepted Anne's breathless apology. "It is the great man, of course. One does not get away from

Paolo Falinieri easily—he's a proper tyrant." She spoke with obvious affection. "Out of your clothes, girl. We've work to do."

"Good gracious!" Struggling out of her pullover, Anne exclaimed in surprise as Mrs Riley opened a cupboard and reached down a long green velvet dress.

"Well, I had your measurements, didn't I? The girls have been at it since word came down first thing this morning. That's right." Anne had stepped out of her skirt and stood obediently while the dress was slipped over her head. "Dead on." Mrs Riley stood back to survey its effect with satisfaction. "Only the hem to do. Here! I hope to God they fit." She opened another cupboard and produced two pairs of shoes and one of gold sandals. "Josef burgled your room," she explained cheerfully. "The sandals are an exact copy; they should be OK. If the shoes don't fit, you'll just have to take them back tomorrow and change them. But they'll do for the time being."

"They'll *do*!" Anne had tried on first a gold sandal, then an elegantly plain high-heel and finally the most comfortable walking shoe she had had for years. "But it's a miracle, Mrs Riley! How on earth...?"

"Shoes are one of their things here in Lissenberg," explained the wardrobe mistress, busily pinning up the dark green hem. "Crafts, you know. They rather go for them. Some escaped Italian prisoners of war stayed on and started a little factory down one of the valleys. You have to admit they're good. I'd be sad to see them go under."

"Go under?"

"If Prince Rudolf gets his way, they'll be making shoddy leather purses for the tourist trade." She sighed and placed the last pin. "Sometimes I wonder if we ought to be working ourselves into the grave trying to make a success of this opera. But you can't help yourself, can you, if it's your job. And then, there's the conference. We don't want anything casting a gloom on that. I wouldn't mind a little peace in our time; I don't know about you." She unzipped the green dress and replaced it with a short one of mixed brown and gold. "How's that?"

"Terrific!" said Anne.

"Thanks!" Once again, she was busy pinning the hem. "There! I'll send it and the green up to the hostel in half an hour. Now, the suit and the skirt and we're done, and you can trot along to Monsieur Charles."

"Monsieur Charles?" This was a new name.

"The hairdresser. He's good, I can tell you. I'd just let him rip if I were you. Proper Cinderella touch, isn't it?" She had Anne in the suit by now, and cocked a considering head. "Chanel with a difference, would you say? I'm not too bad myself. Nice to be doing modern for a change. I'm sick of all those damned togas and tunics. There!" She produced a stripy tweed skirt. "That's for climbing mountains, which, frankly, I wouldn't if I were you. Blouses and pullovers are waiting at the hostel and see you don't let me down, there's a good child."

"Thank you." It seemed entirely inadequate.

"You're welcome. It's a pleasure to dress you, and that's a fact. Wear the long green tonight, and say I made it, if anyone should ask."

"Tonight?"

"Haven't you heard? The Prince is giving a dinner for the cast and the Lissenberg patrons. Business as usual and all that. At the hotel. Well, a kind of preview for the hotel staff too, I suppose. It's not officially open yet, you know. Even the restaurant only opened yesterday."

"Surely a bit off to have a party with Mr Frensham just dead?"

Mrs Riley shrugged. "You might think so. But there's a lot stands or falls on this opera. Anyway, there wasn't much love lost between the Prince and James Frensham senior. I wonder if young Frensham will be there tonight. Princess Gloria won't, I'm sure. She's been in and out of hysterics all day, by what I hear. She really loved that cousin of hers. Remarkable. No! You can't wear that pullover." Back in her own skirt, Anne had reached for the jersey that almost matched it. "It'll wreck your hair, changing. Here!" She opened another cupboard and produced a vyella shirt that would go with both the new skirt and the suit. "Mother Riley thinks of everything." She was pleased with herself. "Now, off with you to Monsieur Charles—two doors down on the right. And have yourself a good dinner, I don't think."

These cryptic words were to be explained when Anne arrived at the hostel. A stranger to herself in a glowing rinse and the green velvet dress, she had rather wished that Michael was still driving a taxi. His reaction to her sea-change would, she thought, have been reassuring. But it was one of the black limousines from the hotel that picked her up, and the dour driver simply shut her in the back and hunched himself over the wheel as if in scorn of people who had cars to take them a mere couple of hundred yards.

Reaching the hotel steps, he blew a resounding blast on his horn and sat tight. Nothing happened. He blew another. Still nothing happened.

"This is ridiculous." Anne opened her door and got out. "What do I owe you, *mein Herr?*"

"Nothing," he said rudely, in German, and drove away.

It was raining again and the steps were damp. Anne lifted velvet skirts lovingly out of the wet and began to climb. As she reached the top, the hotel's big doors flew open and two frantic page-boys came running out to meet her, absurd under huge green umbrellas.

Saving her upswept hair from the umbrella prongs by a miracle, she entered the foyer of the hotel and paused in amazement. If the outside conformed with the classic façade of the opera house, the inside was somebody's dream of gothic splendour. Pointed arches here and there in the walls of the windowless room had lights behind garish stained glass. Even the unoccupied reception desk looked like a cross between a pew and a pulpit.

"You like it?" Carl Meyer came forward to greet her, immaculate in evening dress.

She smiled at him. "Frankly, no."

"Quite. Just don't tell the prince. He designed it." Returning her smile, "I like *you*," he said. "Good to see you looking yourself again. This way—unless you want the powder room?"

"No, thanks. Who's here?"

"Everyone. Except the Princess, of course. Alix is representing her."

"Young Mr Frensham?"

"Yes. Anne, dear, they may ask you to sing. Do you mind?"

"Sing?"

"After dinner. Old-fashioned custom. Something simple? Something young Frensham might understand?"

"Goodness," she said. "What would that be, I wonder?"

"Here's your chance to find out." He steered her into a crowded reception room lit by baroque cut-glass chandeliers. Near the doorway, members of the chorus in rather miscellaneous evening dress were drinking champagne and talking in small groups and muted tones. Beyond them, the floor rose by a step, as if to a dais, and Anne remembered that the whole hotel was built into the slope of the mountains.

78

On the dais a small group stood apparently frozen round the Prince and James Frensham. The Prince had his back half turned, but they got the full benefit of young Frensham's sneer as they approached. "Killer roads, and a twenty-man police force," he said. "An opera no one knows and a cast no one's heard of. Not a star in it. And a black hole of a hotel with steps for the guests to fall over, and you still think you can play host to an international peace conference. No wonder my father said he was pulling out."

"Your Highness." Carl Meyer boldly intervened before the Prince's rage boiled over in reply. "Allow me to present the star we are launching: Miss Paget."

"Ah." The Prince's furious face smoothed into a smile as Anne went down into her deepest curtsey. "I knew it. Trust an old fox like me to know the real thing...the gem when he sees it. And they've not done too badly with the setting, either." He was eating her up with his eyes, and she thought dismally of the payment it would be in his character to expect.

But for the moment he had more pressing business. "No star, you say, James? I think both our conductor and our Regulus will have a bone to pick with you over that. But here, as Herr Meyer rightly observes, is our lead card, our discovery: Miss Paget."

"Hmmm." The dark, deep-set eyes looked Anne over. She might have been a horse, she thought, in a Florentine market, having its points examined.

She put her head a little back and looked up at him with considering eyes. "How do you do, Mr Frensham?" The room, suddenly quiet, echoed to the resonance of her deep voice. "I am so sorry about your father." She made the words almost into recitative.

"Quite something." He was shaking her hand, ignoring the reference to his father. "Pity to put you into boy's clothes, though."

She laughed, and felt a quick, sharp warning of pain. "Not the kind I'll be wearing. The Romans knew a thing or two about dress, and so does our wardrobe mistress. Don't worry. I won't let Lissenberg down—or Beethoven, which is more important." He was actually listening, and she sensed a little breath of relief from the group around them. "I know how lucky I am to be appearing in Beethoven's lost opera. The whole world must be waiting for it. It's going to be the most tremendous draw." She turned to Carl Meyer. "Surely the house must be sold out?"

"Sold out! We've a waiting list as long as the Bible."

"And if it's a disaster?" Frensham turned on him. "And the guests stuck in this hotel with steps everywhere, and no service. My father was right. He told me."

"You should both have stayed at the castle," said the Prince. "I only wish your poor father had." He turned away from the painful subject. "It's true, the hotel's not running quite smoothly yet, but it's not even officially open and there's a whole week to go."

"A week!" The sneer was back. "A month would be better news."

"I should think tourists would love it." Anne felt a twinge of pain and took a deep breath. "There's a great rage for medieval banquets in England. They pack them in."

"England!" said James Frensham in his rich English. "If they like it there, it has to be bad. Just look at them. A strike a minute and shouting for help the next."

Anne took a reviving sip of champagne. "We don't all of us shout," she said. "Quite a few of us work, Mr Frensham."

She had expected an explosion, but the handsome, guarded face broke into a remarkably sweet smile. "I like you," said young Frensham. "You've got something, haven't you? If you can sing too, maybe we've not got such a disaster after all. Can you?"

The pain was devouring her. If she had to stand much longer, she might faint. She tried to make her smile reach her eyes. "I hope so," she said.

And, blessedly, big doors at the side of the dais were thrown open and a green-clad waiter announced that dinner was served.

"I take Miss Paget in." Taking Anne's arm, James Frensham made it a challenge.

"Naturally," said the Prince, without pleasure. "You are our honoured guest and she is our star."

Taking her place between them, Anne looked across the long table at a big dining room that seemed to combine the worst features of the lobby and the reception room. The chandeliers here were even more brilliant than those in the reception room, their colours just slightly at odds with those of illuminated stained glass panels.

"What do you think of it?" The Prince turned to her.

"It's formidable," she said, with truth. And, with equal truth, "I'm sure it will be a huge success."

"I hope so," he said. "I've got a plastics factory down the valley hard at work turning out models to sell to the tourists."

"Just the thing." James Frensham leaned across Anne. "It should make perfect plastic models. The opera house, too, I hope."

"The whole complex." The Prince obviously did not like young Frensham's tone, and Anne did not blame him.

"A bit like a set of false teeth. But no doubt the tourists you expect will buy them. If they come."

"They are already here." Now the Prince sounded angry. "The town is full and this hotel is booked solid from the official opening on."

"Of course, " said James Frensham. "I quite forgot. It's not open yet, your fine hotel. That's why the service is so slow. You'll need to feed the conference delegates faster than this, if they are to get anything done at their great peace meeting."

Like his father, he was a master of inflexions, Anne thought. He had contrived to suggest that the peace meeting would be anything but great. Time to intervene. "When is the official opening of the hotel?" she asked.

"Not for another week," the Prince told her. "And of course the conference delegates won't be arriving until the weekend your opera opens. Almost three weeks still."

"Yes, thank goodness," said Anne with feeling. She looked across the open-sided top table at the crowded dining room, aware of a slackening in the babble of talk. It was true, the service was slow, but here at last came waiters pouring wine.

"You think three weeks long enough to learn an entirely new opera?" asked young James.

"Oh, yes." She smiled at him, grateful for the moral support of hair-do and dress. "I'm a quick learner, and the others have had longer, which helps enormously."

"So you expect a success?" He sounded as if he might be really interested.

"I don't see how we can fail. Beethoven's lost opera—it's the most marvellous music. And Signor Falinieri's an extraordinary conductor. I've never sung with him before. You've no idea how he is making us work. It's not every conductor who will spend three weeks rehearsing. But then this is a special case."

"You enjoy the work?"

"Oh, yes. There's nothing in the world like it."

"And the others?"

81

"But, of course. Or they wouldn't be here. It's a tremendous chance for us all."

"I just hope you won't have to sing to a starving audience," said James Frensham, reaching out for a second roll.

But now, at last, green-clad waiters were beginning to scurry about with plates of melon filled with prawns. "About time." Frensham turned as the plate was put down in front of him and demanded a vodka martini, but the waiter had already hurried away.

"Call it service!" he said. "Opening in a week. They need six. Imagine the world's journalists—who I presume will be covering this opera of yours—enduring this kind of thing. Just think what they will say."

She could, and could think of nothing to say herself. Hunger made the pain worse. For the first time, she actually wished herself back in England. Beside her, the Prince had turned away to carry on a surprisingly animated conversation with Gertrud Stock. Odd that she was next to him rather than Hilde Bernz, the older singer who played Regulus' wife.

James Frensham was clicking his fingers unavailingly at a passing waiter. "I had no lunch," he told her. "What I need is a real drink. And real food." He picked up the menu from its silver container. "It says here we start with Game Soup Lissenberg. This doesn't look much like it. Ladies' food. I just hope we get the Steak Diane."

"So do I." Anne sighed with amazed relief at sight of a long-legged waiter refilling Gertrud Stock's glass. She leaned behind the Prince and breathed a quiet, "Michael."

He finished pouring, swathed the bottle in its napkin, and turned to her, heels clicked, the picture of service. "*Mein Fräulein?*"

"Mr Frensham would like a double martini. Vodka."

"Instantly." He bent forward and whispered. "Chaos in the kitchen—sabotage. Keep them sweet if you can." And was gone, his long white apron flying.

"Capable girl." Frensham was actually looking at her with approval. "What the hell's he doing here, and what did he say?"

"Helping out, I suppose. He does seem to be a jack of all trades."

"You could call him that. But what did he say?"

"Trouble in the kitchen." She left it vague.

"Excuses as usual! They couldn't organise a children's outing in this country, and they try to run an international

82

conference. *And* an opera. Talk about disaster. I just hope your opera goes better than this dinner. Ah." Michael's long arm had put down a large glass beside him. "Michael, what in the world?" But Michael had whisked away.

"You know him?" asked Anne, surprised.

"Well, of course. But what the hell he's doing here? Oh, well." He shrugged and drank. "He always was his own law. And look where it's got him."

"Where?"

But he had taken another heartening pull at his martini and begun on his melon. "It's good," he said, "even if it's not game soup."

"Delicious!" Anne also thought it a very clever choice for a first course, granted the chaos in the kitchen of which Michael had spoken. It took a very long time to eat. Waiters were scurrying about, refilling wine glasses. The tone of the conversation had settled down as people savoured the sauce, or worked to get the right mix of shrimp and melon.

"Someone can cook," said James Frensham. "What's in this sauce, d'you think?"

"Cream," said Anne. "Lemon, of course. Sherry perhaps? Or a touch of bitters?"

"Cook as well as sing, do you? How d'you keep that figure of yours?" He was mellowing with every sip, but his glass was nearly empty, and Anne looked around for Michael. He was ahead of her. Once again his long green arm swooped down to replace the empty glass with a full one. Then, to Anne's surprise, he paused behind the Prince's chair and murmured something in his ear.

The Prince's response was obviously both Liss and un-printable. He turned to Anne. "Miss Paget." The thick brows were drawn together with rage, but he managed a smile for her. "It seems there is a small problem in the kitchen." He was speaking low, obviously hoping that Frensham would not hear. "I had planned to ask you to sing for our guests, later, over coffee. Could you do it now? Would it be asking too much..."

She smiled back at him, grateful that the pain had ebbed with food and wine. "Frankly, if I've got to do it, I'd rather do it now. I never did understand how Victorian young ladies managed to sing after those huge meals they ate. What would you like?"

"Ask Mr Frensham," suggested the Prince. "Then let me know when you are ready."

She turned to her other neighbour. "Heaven help me." She made it an appeal, eyes widened under lashes she had taken trouble with. "The Prince wants me to sing! What would you suggest to keep all these hungry people happy, Mr Frensham?"

"I'm no expert. Nothing too heavy, if you ask me."

"That's just what I was thinking. Not opera at all. It's not the moment for that." She looked around the crowded room. "D'you think everyone understands English?"

"If they don't; tough."

She smiled at him brilliantly. "Thanks! That's just what I needed!" And turned to the Prince. "Ready when you want me."

His short speech was masterly, leaving it in some doubt as to why the singing was to be so early in the meal. As he spoke, waiters were moving briskly round the tables, refilling glasses and supplying more rolls. The panic of the first course had subsided. It may work yet, thought Anne, and rose to her feet. "Ladies and gentlemen, I hope you will bear with me. I am going to sing to you in English, unaccompanied, and at short notice. And before such a group of experts, too! I beg your indulgence." And to a polite little murmur, she took a deep breath and plunged into an old English ballad with an irresistibly lilting rhythm. Down the table, she saw Falinieri lift his head in surprise, then, catching her eye, give a tiny nod of approval.

She went on to some of the pop songs of her own youth, guessing that the Lissenberg element of the audience were older and should recognise them, and then, encouraged by increasing applause, ventured a little further out. "Where have all the flowers gone..." got a surprisingly warm reception, and so did "Greensleeves," but she was getting tired, the pain twitching at her warningly.

"One more." Michael's quiet voice behind her. "And we'll do, God bless you."

"What shall it be?" She turned to Frensham. "You must have a favourite."

"Music?" He shrugged. "No. I'm not like my father. I'm a philistine. And proud of it. But I can see that you do it very well."

"I'm sorry. How boring it must be for you. Well, positively the last." She took a deep breath and began *The Battle Hymn of the Republic*.

Bowing for tumultuous applause at the end, she turned to smile an apology at Frensham. "All over."

"And a success. You are good, I can see, Miss Paget. May I call you Anne? And here, at last, comes food."

It was both delicious, and, to an expert, quite obviously a last-minute improvisation: veal escalopes, lightly cooked in an exquisite sauce, fluffy dry rice and a wide choice of obviously frozen vegetables. Frensham's glass had been exchanged once more while she was singing. He raised it: "To your bright eyes! The opera will succeed, I think. I congratulate you."

Kindness itself. So why did his tone send a cold shiver down her spine? Why in the world did she suddenly find herself thinking of Robin, and all that disaster?

7

"But what on earth went wrong with the dinner?" It had been as much pleasure as surprise to find Michael waiting to drive her back to the hotel, a dark raincoat hiding his green waiter's costume.

"You may well ask." He had cut her neatly out from Frensham, Stern and Meyer, who all thought they should walk her home, and was guiding her down the hotel steps. "Ipecac in the game soup, and lavishly scattered all over the Steak Diane. The way we flavour things here, no-one would have noticed. It's a fierce emetic, you know. Just think of tomorrow morning." He opened the door of a small car parked on the double yellow line. "I thought you'd need a breath of air after all that politeness. And the chef sent you his blessings in broad Liss. Damn clever choice of songs; I congratulate you on that, as well as the singing. Some fool might have got up and let fly with Beethoven."

"Not this fool; not with James Frensham sitting there like a thunderstorm about to break. You saved the situation just as much as I did with those martinis. But how come he knows you?"

"Oh, everyone knows me. Hopeless Michael and his mad ideas." He had taken the car demurely down the curve of the arcade, now put on a burst of speed on the main road and swooped off it again on to an uphill turning she had never noticed. "I'm not kidnapping you." He had read her thoughts. "Just taking you to a favourite pub of mine. Half an hour's compulsory relaxation before bed. Just what the doctor ordered."

"Thanks." She shivered at the unlucky phrase.

"What's the matter?" He was disconcertingly quick, this young dropout. "You ought to be on top of the world, after a success like that, and against such odds, and you sound below zero."

"I'm a little tired," she prevaricated.

"Long, hard evening? You were terrific. Let me be the first to tell you so. And warn you you've got quite a complicated three weeks ahead of you. The waiter sees most of the game, and if James Frensham and our Rudolf haven't both got plans for you, I'm no mind reader. If I were you, I'd send for the doctor in the morning. Tell him you're overtired with all the pressure. Get him to put a ban on nights out. He'll do it, I promise."

"Another of your cousins?" The unconscious irony of his suggestion almost choked her.

"More or less. Ah, here we are." He swung the little car off the road and its headlights lit up a chalet with the usual wide overhanging eaves and a stag's antlers over the front door.

"It looks closed," she objected.

"It is closed. Uncle Hans always closes at ten, and always opens up again for his friends." He played a little tune on the car horn, and lights glowed out from the front of the chalet, illuminating a terraced beer garden with a luxuriance of flowers in boxes, their colours deep and strange in the artificial light. "In with you." The front door had swung open and a huge man stood outlined against the light. "Uncle Hans, this is Miss Paget, who is going to sing us all into history. She wants something to settle her dinner."

"She shall have it." Hans shook hands warmly and beamed down at Anne out of a cheerful, weather-beaten face. "Didn't know you were hungry, did you?"

"No." But it was true.

"Michael—" He paused. "My friends always come up here after the big banquets. They say food eaten under such strain is no use. Now, which shall it be, a hunter's breakfast or some of my dumpling soup?"

"Oh, soup! How lovely," said Anne. And, "Hunter's breakfast," said Michael. "If the guests are hungry, how do you think the waiters feel?"

"You were splendid." Anne let him seat her at a little table in a corner by a blazing fire. "You can't have learned that at Oxford."

"No, that was Harvard. How else do you think I paid for my graduate year there?"

Hans gave something between a cough and a chuckle and vanished through a door at the back of the room, throwing over his shoulder: "I'm cook tonight. You see to the drinks, Michael."

"Sure. What's it to be?" He looked at Anne thoughtfully. "If it wasn't for those dumplings, I'd recommend a glass of milk. How much wine have you had?"

"Only two glasses. And I can't remember them. Could I have a slivovitz?"

"Lovely girl!" He moved behind the well-equipped bar and filled two glasses. "Here's to you."

"And you." But as she raised her glass they heard the sound of another car, and then the emphatic blast of its horn.

"Turn them away, Michael," came Hans' voice from the kitchen. "I'm cooking your eggs."

"Gladly." Michael went out into the darkness, closing the front door behind him. He came back looking grave, but nodded reassuringly to Anne before he vanished into the kitchen where she could hear a quick, anxious conversation, unintelligible in Liss. But she could also hear the car start up and turn away to go back down the hill.

"What was it?" she asked when Michael returned and began professionally setting their table.

"Police." He refilled their glasses. "Food in three minutes. Drink up, like a good girl, it's not the nicest news."

"Not something else?"

"Not exactly. But they got down to old Frensham's car at last. Took them all day. He was the only one in it."

"But he took Bland and Marks home."

"Precisely. Or they took him. It always did seem an odd kind of an accident. It gets odder and odder. Uncle Winkler wants a few words with Messrs Bland and Marks, so the police are out scouring the countryside for them. All twenty-one of us."

"You don't seem to be scouring much."

"I'm seeing you safe home first. And fed. And here it comes."

"Food is good for the nerves." Hans deposited a well-warmed soup bowl and steaming tureen in front of Anne. "Help yourself, my dear, and may it do you good."

"Thank you." How odd to find herself on the verge of tears.

"And as for you." He put a huge platter in front of Michael. "Shall I start a second one for you? It sounds like a long, hard night."

Michael laughed. "No, thanks. I'm getting old, Hans. I can only do one at a time now." He broke the delicately fried egg that topped the heaped dish.

"What on earth is it?" Anne was helping herself to thick soup and fluffy dumplings.

"Hunter's breakfast? Oh, a bit of everything. Uncle Hans' own beans, sausage, bacon, anything else he happens to have lying round. You must try it some time."

"Not till the opera's over. This soup is the best I ever tasted. Thank you." She smiled up at the big man as he produced two green-stemmed glasses and a squat bottle. "Oh, I don't know..."

"Liss wine," he said. "The lightest and, we think, the best in the world. No harm in it, except it won't travel. Don't worry, it will do you good. Not a hangover in it."

"It's delicious." She drank to him, then turned back to Michael. "But—Bland and Marks. What are they?"

"Assistants to James Frensham, deceased. That's all anyone seems to know. Young James didn't work with his father. He had his own affairs in Sicily. He'd never even heard of Bland and Marks. At least that's what he told Winkler. One thing—if the two of them aren't out of the country already, they won't get out now. Winkler's closed the frontier. Tight. Lucky thing tonight's guests were all staying locally."

"But aren't there paths?"

"One. It starts from here and goes clear over the top into Austria. It was the great escape route in the war. Everyone knows about it, but it's not everyone can find it. Still less get through when Uncle Hans closes it."

"Closes?"

"Yes. Don't ask me how, because I don't propose to tell you. Anyway, it's time for your bed, my nightingale. Business as usual in the morning, but don't forget to send for Dr Hirsch. Come to that, you do look kind of tired."

"I feel it," she said with perfect truth. "Who is Dr Hirsch?"

88

"A great man—you'll like him. Russian originally. He had a hard war; prisoner in Germany, came into Lissenberg the tough way, over the mountains."

"You mean he's one of the Russians Lissenberg wouldn't send back?"

He smiled at her warmly. "You do learn, don't you? That's right. And, my goodness, he's paid us back for it. What a man. What an organiser. Clinics...hospitals...he's practically our health service here in Lissenberg. Well, you'll see."

Back at the hostel, Josef greeted them with relief. "I'm about ready to lock up." He looked exhausted, and Anne apologised warmly for keeping him up. "No, no," he protested. "The police have only just left. They're checking all the buildings. Not much use in the dark, I told them, but you can imagine what the pressure's like. Her Highness is building up quite a head of steam, they say. Oh—there's a message for you, Michael." He handed over a folded note.

Michael read it quickly. "Yes," he said. "I'd better be going. Josef, fix for Miss Paget to see Dr Hirsch in the morning?"

"The doctor?" It got Anne a quick, anxious look from dark-circled eyes.

"It's OK," Michael told him. "Just that our prima donna is going to need an alibi after being such a success tonight."

"Hmmm..." said Josef.

Alone in her room at last, Anne drew a deep bath and lay in it a long time, trying to sort out the chaotic images of the day. It was all a jumble, confused, incomprehensible. Why should Bland and Marks have murdered their employer? And how in the world did the murder tie in with that strange business of sabotage in the hotel kitchen? Or, for that matter, with the accident to Brech's car the day she arrived, the accident that might have killed Falinieri and stopped the opera. James Frensham had been a music lover, had put up the money for *Regulus*. Could his murder be a more drastic move against the opera? It was a thought to make one shiver.

And where did Michael fit into it all? Michael, who turned up everywhere, had his finger in everything. Michael, she reminded herself, who disliked what Prince Rudolf was doing in Lissenberg, who seemed to disapprove of the opera complex. What had he said? A stage set? For tragedy? She knew so little about him. Carl Meyer had called him poison; warned her to keep away from him—but then Carl Meyer himself was behaving so strangely. Once again, this evening, urging

89

her to walk home with him from the hotel, he had used the possessive tone almost of an acknowledged lover, and she had seen Michael notice it.

Back to Michael. What an enigma he was. But she liked him, wanted to trust him, indeed did so instinctively. After all, the police seemed to, and Josef, and Hans. She must ask Josef about him in the morning. Absurd not to have done so sooner. But of one thing she was certain without any asking. He loved Lissenberg. So: why all that time away? How long? Oxford, then Harvard... He must be older than he looked. She had thought this once or twice. There was a strength about him that did not go with his casual, dropout exterior. Dropout? Who had called him that? Carl, of course, who disliked him. Or had he said it himself? She rather thought he had. But then, had he meant it? It was often hard to tell whether to take what he said at its face value. Anyway, she would ask Josef about him. Josef would know, she thought, climbing tiredly into bed. Josef would explain... She slept at last, and dreamed of Robin, the old nightmare. But this time Robin had Michael's face.

The doctor's visit was the first item on next morning's programme, and Anne was only just dressed in time to receive him, which meant that she had no chance to prepare a story. But very likely it would not be necessary. She liked him on sight, a spare, dry man with a curiously immobile face.

His greeting was abrupt. "You're overtired, I understand. And no wonder." He reached for her wrist to take her pulse. "I'm to prescribe rest and safe nights at home. Not a bad thing, with a murderer loose in the valley." He looked down at his watch, his hand still on her wrist. "You had an agitating evening yesterday?"

She smiled at him. "You could almost call it that. But is it really murder?" Anything to distract him from this too close attention to her pulse.

"It's murder all right. They found another body at first light. Mr Bland. Looks as if he helped contrive the 'accident' to Mr Frensham and was then disposed of in his turn—by Mr Marks presumably." As he talked, he had put an enquiring hand on her forehead, and turned her gently round to face the morning light from the huge window with its view of the castle. "Only Mr Marks didn't know the habits of our River Liss. He put the body in at the wrong place," he explained, producing a thermometer from his pocket and silencing her with it. "So, of course, it washed up where they always do. Not that we have bodies often, you understand, but anything that goes in above the town, beaches on the big bend below it. Winkler had men there this morning just in case, all ready to receive poor Mr Bland. He was shot in the back. No accident. I've just finished the post mortem." He felt her shudder, and patted her kindly on the shoulder. "Don't mind. I went home and had a bath. After all, the dead are just—dead." He withdrew the thermometer and studied it. "And now, young lady, perhaps you will tell me what is the matter with you? I could find out, of course, but it would take time, which we haven't got, and anyway I rather think you know." He pulled up a chair, comfortingly close to hers, and looked at her steadily. "I am a reliable person," he said. "As, I think, Michael would tell you. I take my hippocratic oath with the greatest seriousness." His smile transformed his face, but looked, oddly, as if it hurt him. "You could say my face was my fortune." He was talking, she knew, to give her time. "The Nazis gave it to me after I was captured—or took it away from me—because I would not do what they wanted. I was young and romantic then, but I think I would do it again, if necessary. So, Miss Paget. A small secret—such as yours must be. You can see, it will be entirely safe with me."

She was crying. She could not have believed she could cry so much. She was on the floor, with her head on his knee, sobbing out her story; the first suspicions; the slow relentless movement of the health machine, and, at last, the verdict of death.

"And then?" He handed her a huge silk handkerchief.

"They wanted to operate. Said it might give me an extra few months."

"And if not?"

"No operation? Six months—something like that?" She looked up at him with tear-drowned eyes. "Dr Hirsch, have I been very wicked? It's only three weeks of rehearsals, and then two weeks of performances. I'll be able to do that, won't I? I couldn't *bear* to let them down!"

His warm hand on hers was extraordinarily reassuring. The other one was stroking her hair, gently, as if she was a child. "Of course you'll not let them down. I was there at dinner last night. I heard you sing. If I hadn't, I don't think I would have come—not even for Michael. I don't much like fake illnesses. Now, it's different. You will let me treat you?"

"Treat me? But there's nothing ... You don't mean ..." She pulled away from him. "Not the operation?"

"No. That was the wisest thing you ever did, I think, running away from that. And—I'm glad you ran here. This is a battle, Miss Paget. A battle for you to fight with your illness. When we send a soldier into battle, we do not begin by mutilating him. We put him into strict physical training; we do our best to fill him with happy, positive thoughts—with the conviction, perhaps, that he is fighting for a glorious cause. Well, you have a glorious cause to fight for. Not just your life, but that voice of yours, that's something else. So—now you have an ally. We are going to fight, you and I. I do not promise—I do not even let myself hope—that we will win, but dear God, we are going to try. And, first, you are going to tell me a great deal more."

"More?"

"Yes. I am a hard man to deceive, Miss Paget. I shall call you Anne." He smiled his painful smile. "Since, I think, Paget is not your name." He reached out and took her left hand, feeling gently where the wedding ring had left its mark. "I want to know what has made you so unhappy," he told her. "Body and soul are two, but what hurts one, hurts the other. So, tell me about yourself."

She had never talked about Robin's death before. She had not believed she could. But when she had finished, still on the floor against his knees, with his comforting arm around her shoulders, she felt amazingly better. "You see how I failed him." She was surprised to hear herself saying it.

"Failed? How can you tell? But better to think so than that he failed you, in my opinion. Either way, now it is time to forget and forgive, both him and yourself. Let the dead past be dead, Anne. You have the future to think of."

"My future? A dying woman's?"

"You're not dead yet." Now he sounded angry. "Can't you fight girl? Do you *want* to be dead?"

"I think, perhaps, I did."

"If it was not so serious, I'd be inclined to say, 'Serve you right.'" But his grip on her shoulder was kind. "I've seen people with so much less to live for than you, Anne Paget, or Anne whatever it is. People with no family, no friends, nothing. Horribly disfigured, wounded ... And fighting still, fighting for dear life. It is dear, you know."

"I've been beginning to think so, since I came here."

"I should hope so, with your voice." He looked at his watch.

"I have been here quite long enough for a doctor who has been bribed to prescribe absolute rest."

"Nobody could bribe you."

"Thank you. But there are bribes and bribes. I care, immensely, for Lissenberg. And for Beethoven. Will you do what I tell you?"

"Yes."

"Good girl. You will take the medicine I send you. I am a homaeopathic crank, did you know?" She shook her head. "No matter. Say it's a tranquilliser, but take it. Tranquillisers are respectable. Work yourself to exhaustion; stay home and sleep; worry about nothing; or, if that is too difficult, worry about Lissenberg, not yourself. You are unimportant compared with Lissenberg. Do you know what will happen if the opera fails?"

"No?"

"Young James Frensham will be delighted. In my position one hears things. There's something, in the mountains, under the opera complex, that he wants. Give him an excuse; he'll tear it down."

"Tear it down! The opera house? What kind of something, Dr Hirsch? It must be very valuable."

"Yes. A mineral of some kind. Szilenite, they call it. I've heard it's the basis for a particularly powerful new nerve gas. Not something the world needs. And most particularly not in the hands of someone like young James Frensham, who thinks purely in terms of money. And, another thing, quite aside from the results, the development involved would be the end of Lissenberg as we know it. It wouldn't be just the opera complex we'd lose, it would be our whole way of life." He stood up. "You will work like the brave girl you are to make the opera a success; you will worry as little as possible, eat sensibly, take the pills I send you, and retire to your room after supper. No more parties; no more wining and dining. Not even at the castle." The uncomfortable smile cracked his face once more, "I might say, particularly not at the castle. And"—he turned back at the door, his face very grave—"I do not think I would go out by myself, if I were you. An accident to you would mean disaster for the opera. If you must walk—you see, I know you English—stay with the other members of the company. Or Michael, of course, but I'm afraid he is going to be busy until they find Mr Marks."

"Has Michael really joined the police?"

"Joined?" He seemed to find this amusing. "Well, yes I suppose you could say he had."

"Not such a dropout after all." Here at last was her chance to ask about him.

"Dropout? Who told you that?"

"Why, Michael himself." She had remembered in the night.

"The best authority. Yes, you could call him that. Or dropped. He's always been his own worst enemy. But I wouldn't go round asking questions about him, Anne. It might make trouble for him. If you must ask—ask him." The telephone rang. "I must go. I've made you late as it is. Tell them it's my fault. You are suffering from nervous strain, and are under my strict orders. Refer anyone to me. I have a certain standing here in Lissenberg."

"Thank you." She smiled a watery farewell and picked up the receiver. "Anne—" Josef's voice. "Falinieri is about to have a fit. You are twenty minutes late."

In some ways, her late arrival made her explanation easier. Falinieri, who had been angrily rehearsing the chorus while he waited for her, accepted it with a brief nod. "So long as you save your strength for your singing." He had not asked what was wrong with her. For him, only the opera mattered. He rapped with his baton for silence. "To work, ladies and gentlemen."

It was good to be working, to let herself think of nothing but the music, and by doing so forget the question that had haunted her since Dr Hirsch had told her about James Frensham and the "something" he wanted from under the opera house. Presumably his father had wanted it too. And been killed for wanting it? So—by whom? Well, by Marks presumably. But who had he been working for? Did Prince Rudolf care enough about Lissenberg? she wondered. But then, the Prince surely knew that young Frensham was an even greater threat to the opera than his father, and the opera was clearly Prince Rudolf's prime consideration. It was all baffling, sinister, frightening.

"Miss Paget!" Falinieri's furious voice roused her. "You have missed your cue again."

"I'm sorry." She made herself concentrate, and was amazed when the lunch break was called. Walking along the arcade to the hostel, she regretted having refused Josef's offer of a tray in her room, yet knew she had been right to do so. Part of the rehearsal process was always offstage, as the members of the cast settled down with each other. To isolate herself would be fatal. She was even beginning to wonder whether it had been wise to agree with the doctor's suggestion about her evenings.

She was distracted by a question from Frau Bernz, the plump, competent Austrian singer who took the part of Regulus' wife. "Oh, I'm all right, thanks." She joined Hilde Bernz in the queue for the light meal that was served for their lunch. "Just a bit tired."

"And no wonder." Hilde Bernz helped herself lavishly to cold meat and salad. "All this drama! Sabotage and murder. I don't like it, Miss Paget. We might all have been deathly ill today. What kind of a joker would try to poison us all?"

"Not exactly poison," said Anne.

"We'd not have got much work done today. Somebody sure has it in for this opera." She spoke amazingly good English, with a strong American accent. "A little bird told me you had some trouble on the way here. Lost your purse; got misdirected? Did it strike you that if you'd not been here for that first audition, Signor Falinieri might have gone straight back to Italy?"

"No." Anne picked up her tray and followed Frau Bernz to a table for four. "I hadn't thought." It was true. So much had happened in the few days since her arrival that she had almost forgotten about the odd business of the wrong train. Could kind Herr Schann, the computer trouble shooter, actually have been part of the plot against the opera? It was true enough that if she had found herself on the wrong train, and without money, it might easily have taken her a couple of fatal extra days to get to Lissenberg. And, now that she was thinking about Herr Schann at last, she remembered how hard he had tried to persuade her that she was not well enough to travel. Having failed in that, had he intentionally given her first brandy and then champagne on an empty stomach, warded off the coffee that might have cleared her head, and then neatly removed her purse and directed her to the wrong train? She looked unhappily at Frau Bernz. "I believe you're right. I'd just assumed it was a series of accidents, but in the light of what has happened since..."

"Precisely," said Hilde Bernz. "I think you're a very sensible girl to be too tired to go out at night. Only, lock your door, eh? There's things go on in this place, too, and that odd character Michael thick as thieves with the old man who

95

runs it. I wouldn't make any late-night dates with *him*, if I were you. We can't spare you, my dear, and don't you forget it. All the rest of us are replaceable. Not you."

"Oh well...There's Lotte, and, surely, Alix?"

"You didn't hear about Lotte?"

"No?"

"Course. You left early last night. When the floor show started, Lotte chose to delight us with a selection of songs from *Regulus*."

"*No!*"

"Yes. Comic, really, when you think how we've been rehearsing behind locked doors, to keep the element of surprise. She didn't get far, I can tell you. Meyer and Falinieri advanced on her like a pair of male Valkyries. I imagine she's over the border by now."

"She'll be lucky," said Anne. "They closed it after Mr Frensham was found."

"Murdered!" Hilde Bernz shivered dramatically. "Honey, sometimes I wish I were safe back in Vienna, singing light opera. I know *Regulus* might make all our names, but what's a name if you're dead? I tell you, you're not the only one who's going to stay home at night. It's so *dark* here in Lissenberg. I wish they'd get the lights fixed along the arcade."

"The lights?"

"Didn't you notice? You *must* have been tired! They blew while we were at dinner last night. Black as pitch coming home, and me in my high-heeled slippers. I asked that sinister old Josef about it on the way in to lunch. They can't find what's wrong, he says. So—stay home, my dear, stay home tonight. Alix's throat is worse, I hear. She's not going out tonight either. Well, what would you do if you were her? Invitations from James Frensham *and* Adolf Stern. So—her throat's worse. Let me get you some coffee—you do look tired. What did the doctor think was the matter?"

"Oh, nothing much. Yes, I'd love some coffee, thanks." Glad to be alone for a moment, Anne resolved to be careful what she said to Frau Bernz, who showed every sign of being the cast's gossip, and a malicious one at that. It was a comfort when Gertrud Stock joined them over coffee and firmly changed the subject from last night's dinner to the absorbing one of the opera, and her part in it. It suited Anne very well, and she sat silent, half listening to the other two, sipping strong coffee and trying not to wonder about Michael.

"—Heard about the opera house?"

She realised that Gertrud's question was addressed to her and pulled herself together. "No? What about it?"

"The lights have gone there, too," Gertrud told her. "No rehearsals there until they're fixed, and it seems to be taking long enough. They've had every electrician in town up there this morning and none of them can find the fault. If we don't start rehearsing in there soon we're going to be in real trouble."

"Yes," agreed Hilde. "For the principals' movements the rehearsal room's fine, but what's going to happen to the chorus? All those comings and goings and only two exits."

"Only two?" asked Anne.

"You've not been in to look?"

Anne laughed. "No time."

"Of course. You weren't here for the first conducted tour. Well—it's built right into the rock, see, like the Felsenreit-schule at Salzburg. Brilliant bit of design, but damned awkward. All your management from above and the side, and only the two exits, right and left. Even principals are going to have to hurry like hell to get off in time. We ought to have been in there from the start. Besides, I'd like to be singing when a helicopter lands on the roof and find out just how good the sound-proofing really is. Mad idea, if you ask me."

"James Frensham's," said Gertrud Stock, as if that explained everything. "But of course the landing strip is above the audience, not the stage."

"So they'll get the noise, if any. Much comfort that would be." She sighed, looked at her watch and finished her coffee. "Back to the treadmill."

Emerging into the arcade, they were confronted by a high double ladder, on which a man in overalls was perched, working on one of the lights. "I'm not going under that," said Hilde. "This opera's had enough jinxes without asking for them." She walked across to the steps below the cloisters.

"Sorry!" The man had heard her and turned to look down and smile at Anne. "I promise I won't drop anything."

"Michael! What in the world?"

"Jack of all trades, that's me. But this is one problem that's going to take a bit of solving. Ask Signor Falinieri not to keep you after dark, there's good girls. There'll be no lights in this arcade tonight, I'm afraid."

"We can ask," said Gertrud, "but will he take any notice?"

"Probably not," he agreed. "Well, then. Wait for me, when he does let you go, and I'll see you home. All of you."

"It's only a few steps," protested Anne.

"A few steps are enough to break a leg." He looked up the arcade. "Falinieri's just gone in. Off with you, ladies, and watch how you go."

Falinieri had heard about the light failure in the opera house and was beside himself with rage. "*Not* the moment," whispered Hilde to Anne, "to make any suggestions about when we stop."

"I should rather think not."

The rehearsal did not go well. Falinieri's bad temper communicated itself to the singers, who were tired anyway, many of them having stayed up late at the hotel the night before. And, behind all this, loomed the fact of the murders. Over and over again Falinieri brought his baton down with a crash to rebuke whisperers at the back of the small auditorium. "Is this an opera we are working on," he asked at last, between gritted teeth, "or a disaster? I can tell you which it will be if you do not pull yourselves together and stop gossiping. We have sixteen days until the opening night; God knows when we will be able to get into the opera house for full rehearsals, and all you can do is chatter and giggle in the back there. You, the chorus, go away, for God's sake, and think about your movements, if you can't make them. I will spend the rest of the afternoon with my principals."

After that, things went better. Adolf Stern still sang Regulus with unfortunate Wagnerian overtones, but at least his attitude to Anne had changed completely. Someone must have spoken to him, she thought. Michael's doing? In any case, now that he was working with instead of against her their scenes together were rapidly taking satisfactory shape.

Hilde, too, behaved like the professional she was, and Gertrud knew her part so well that Anne could not blame her obvious impatience with her own inevitable blunders—though it would have been easier without her ill-suppressed exclamations of annoyance. Still, things were improving. The two weak points in the cast, as, Anne suspected, in the opera, were the Carthaginian and Roman leaders, played by an Englishman, John Fare and an Italian, Claudio Ricci. Throughout the opera, they had a kind of private musical duel, or duet, fighting, like the angels of light and darkness, for Regulus. Interestingly enough, the Carthaginian, who had come to Rome with Regulus, had become his friend, and was always on the brink of urging him not to return to Carthage, and certain death, while the Roman was his ancient enemy and, it was hinted, his wife's lover, with every inducement to get rid of him.

Two very complicated parts, and very difficult musically, and Anne could feel and sympathise with Falinieri's anxiety about them. Claudio Ricci had obviously worked hard at his part and had the voice for it, but somehow, when he came to sing with John Fare something always went wrong. "There," whispered Hilde to Anne as they sat at the back of the auditorium and watched the two men rehearse their first duet. "He's done it again!"

"Done what?"

"Miscued him. Very subtly. Ah!" Falinieri had crashed his baton on his music stand. "He's no fool, thank God. If anyone can make this opera a success, he should."

"You're doubtful?"

"Well, the cards do seem stacked against it, don't they? Talk about jinxes..."

8

When the three women emerged, well after dark, from the rehearsal room where Falinieri was still struggling with Claudio and John, Michael was waiting for them, dressed in jeans and windbreaker. "Still no luck with the lights, I'm afraid." He produced a handful of flashlights from his pocket and gave them out. "Compliments of the management."

"How about the opera house itself?" asked Anne.

"No luck there, either. We think there has to be a connection. The palace has been trying all day to reach the electricians who wired the place. Pity they didn't use local labour. How did the rehearsal go?" Flashlight in one hand, he had taken Anne's arm and was leading the way down the pitch-dark arcade towards the hostel.

"So-so," she told him.

"That John Fare should be pickled in slivovitz," put in Hilde Bernz. "Anyone would think he was trying to wreck the opera. I know he and Claudio are enemies from way back, but that's no excuse for what he's doing."

99

"Which is what?" Michael asked, as they reached the hostel door and paused for a moment outside it.

"Oh, the subtlest kind of sabotage: a missed word, a missed cue; a mistimed movement. I guess Falinieri's sorting him out back there."

"I certainly hope so." Gertrud sounded angry. "This opera's my big chance, but the way things look right now..."

"Oh, come." Michael pushed open the bronze door. "It's early days yet. Come in out of the cold, ladies, and let me buy you a drink."

"Lovely," said Hilde. "Just what we need. Sherry for me, thanks, and something warming for Anne here, who looks tired to death."

Death. Anne shivered, but forced a smile. "A long day," she said. "I'm out of practice. I'll have a slivovitz please, Michael."

"I can't imagine how you could bear to let that voice of yours go so." Malice in Gertrud's tone? How very strange. And then, on a different note. "My usual,—thanks, Michael. *I* don't change my habits." She turned back to Anne. "The way you pick up the part is amazing, Miss Paget."

"Oh, do call me Anne." She resisted the temptation to say, "No thanks to you." There were enough hostile undercurrents already. And how odd to find that Michael and Gertrud were apparently old friends. But then, of course, they were both Lissenbergers...cousins, would Michael say? "Have they caught Mr Marks yet?" she asked as they settled themselves at a table in the hostel bar.

"Not a trace of him." Michael was pulling back a chair for Hilde. "But one of the hotel taxis crossed the border just before it was closed last night. He could have been in it."

"Unless someone local is hiding him," said Anne.

"Why in the world should they? A stranger." Did he sound almost too surprised at the suggestion?

"Well," said Anne, "there do seem to be people round here who don't much like the Frenshams' plans for the country."

It won her a very sharp look indeed as he turned away to order their drinks. Returning with them, he sat down beside her, and was starting a question, when Josef appeared. "Telephone, Anne. Will you take it in your room, or in my office? It's from the palace."

"Then your office, if I may. Mustn't keep the palace waiting." Grateful to him for the warning, she gave herself a moment to get settled in his office before she lifted the receiver, "Miss Paget here." The palace staff must speak English.

She had hoped it would be Alix, but it was the Prince's rich voice that finally greeted her. "I have to thank you, Miss Paget, for your help last night. Without you, the evening would have been a disaster." How often that word kept cropping up. "And now, I hope I am not too late in inviting you to dine with me. Quite informally, at the Golden Cross in town. I cannot tell you what pleasure it would give me, nor how eagerly I look forward to hearing you on our opening night."

"I do *thank* you, Your Highness." Lord, she was grateful to Michael and the doctor. "But, unfortunately, I am under doctor's orders. He has confined me to barracks for the duration."

"Confined? Oh, I see... But, Miss Paget, an early evening like this? A nothing. You shall be safe in bed by eleven, I promise you." And then, as an afterthought. "You are not, in fact, ill, I do hope?"

"Oh, no." It weakened her stand. "A bit of overstrain, that is all. But Dr Hirsch was most definite. I feel I cannot possibly disobey him the very day he gave the orders."

This got her one of the Prince's warm laughs. "I understand, Miss Paget. That Dr Hirsch is a great bully. In a few days, when the order is less immediate, I will try again, and hope for a different answer. In the meantime take the greatest care of yourself."

"Your Highness is too kind. I mean to do just that. Josef has promised me a tray in my room, and I intend to be asleep by ten."

Now why had she said that? she wondered, as she rejoined the now cheerful party in the bar. Corroborative detail, presumably, intended to give substance to an otherwise bald and unconvincing narrative.

"The palace?" Michael had contrived to meet her in the doorway as he was leaving.

"Yes. A dinner invitation."

"Which you refused, I trust."

"Well, of course. Doctor's orders." Was it ungrateful to find herself irritated by the cross-examination? And why had he assumed the invitation was from the Prince? "Good night." She moved over to join the other two women.

"Mysterious young man that," said Hilde Bernz.

"Mysterious?" Gertrud's usually fluent English seemed to fail her.

"More to him than meets the eye, if you ask me. Always about when there's trouble. Want to bet he's at the back of it? Stirring things up. One of those students who think they can change the world, and end up making things worse for everybody. What does he *do* anyway? Aside from failing to fix our lights."

"He used to work for the other taxi firm," said Anne. "Not Brech's, at the hotel."

"Right. And look what happened to them."

"What did?" asked Anne.

"Mortgage suddenly foreclosed. End of business. Funny thing; no one seems to know who held that mortgage. But then, Lissenberg is full of funny things like that. I'll be glad when I get back to Vienna. Let's go and eat. I'm starving."

They had reached the coffee stage when Hilde looked up. "I wonder where Josef is off to in such a hurry."

"Good gracious," said Anne. "I didn't think he ever took time off."

"He doesn't much," said Gertrud. "How should he?" She was facing the door. "Here come the men. Still arguing. I think I will say goodnight."

"And I." Hilde gathered up her furs. "I see Herr Stern has taken himself off. To the palace, no doubt, to make sheep's eyes at the Princess." She laughed. "A blow for him when you turned up, Annchen. He *did* enjoy singing with her. Those fatherly pats on the head—and elsewhere. Oh, he *was* devoted to his page. I'm not entirely sure that didn't have something to do with Princess Alix's sore throat, though she doesn't seem to mind him hanging about the palace. Anyway, I'm glad to see he's stopped taking it out on you." She turned and rose to her feet as Signor Ricci approached their table. "I trust your rehearsal went better after we left you to it."

"A little." He made an expressive face. "May I join you ladies?"

"I'm afraid we are just leaving. Miss Paget is under doctor's orders, you know."

"Alas." He held Anne's chair for her as she rose. "Take good care of yourself, Miss Paget. We cannot do without you."

"I can tell you someone we *could* do without." Hilde was watching John Fare join a group of male chorus members at a large table on the far side of the room. "Well, good night, Claudio. I wish you a peaceful evening."

"Thank you." Another expressive grimace as he settled himself at the unused place. "Good night, ladies. Sleep well."

"A last drink?" suggested Hilde as they paused in the lobby.

"I don't believe so, thanks," said Anne. "I really am a little tired."

"And no wonder. Good night, then." She and Gertrud moved towards the bar as Anne crossed to the desk to pick up her key from the stranger who had taken Josef's place. The man said something incomprehensible to her in Liss as he handed it over.

"I'm afraid I don't understand." It was her best German phrase, but it got her only an uncomprehending shrug. Oh well, whatever it was, Josef would doubtless tell her in the morning. She turned away and climbed the stairs slowly, aware of tiredness in every bone, and of the pain, quietly reminding her of its existence. Opening her bedroom door, she saw that someone had turned on welcoming lights, and blessed Josef before she noticed that the door to the sitting room stood open, revealing lights in there too, and, surely, a whiff of cigar smoke.

The bedroom door had locked itself behind her. She crossed the room, still carrying her coat, and met Prince Rudolf in the doorway. His arms were full of flowers, his expression a compound of triumph and apology. "Since the mountain is not allowed to come to Mahomet"—he held out the flowers—"Mahomet has taken a great liberty, and come to pay a little call on the mountain. I am glad to find I was right in thinking that anyone so alive as you would not really condemn herself to a tray in her bedroom." And having thus neatly underlined the lie she had told him, he held out the exotic sheaf of flowers. "Do please accept these as a token of your forgiveness and my immense admiration."

She curtsied. (*Curtsey while you're thinking, it saves time.*) "Your Highness is too kind." She closed the bedroom door firmly behind her and moved forward into the sitting room, dropping her coat on a convenient chair. A quick glance showed the door into the hall securely locked. She accepted the flowers and held them rather like a barrier between them. "But I must confess to surprise—"

"At finding me here? You must see, Miss Paget, that the Hereditary Prince could hardly exhibit himself hanging round in the lobby downstairs. The man at the desk quite

103

understood my problem. He did not explain to you? I must apologise once more."

"He did say something. In Liss, unfortunately." Josef would not have allowed this to happen.

"Or you would have avoided me? Heartless Miss Paget. You must have seen how I have longed for a chance to tell you what I feel for you. The flowers—do put them down, Miss Paget,—are a mere trifle, a token. Here!" He reached into a pocket and produced a jeweller's box. "Here is something that might just begin to be worthy of our prima donna." And then, impatiently—"Do, please get rid of those damned flowers and sit down." An arm indicated a small table with canapés and a swathed bottle in a silver bucket. "Hostel food is not good enough for our diva. You and I will picnic together. But first—" He took the flowers with one hand, dumped them unceremoniously on a chair, and handed her the leather box.

"A thousand thanks." She handed it back, unopened. "Perhaps when the opera is over—if it is a success—"

"If!" She had succeeded in enraging him and was glad. "Of course it will be a success. How can it not?" He twisted out the cork of the champagne bottle with a professional hand, filled a glass and passed it to her in lieu of the jewel box. "Very well, if you insist." He put the box back in his pocket. "It is an unusual woman who will not even look."

"I hope I *am* an unusual woman." She put all the meaning into it that she could, remembering and regretting, as she spoke, that the suite of rooms was sound-proofed. What an absurd, what a maddening, what an impossible situation. "Do, please, have one of these delicious canapés." She did her best to turn the occasion into an ordinary social one by sitting down on an upright chair and handing him the dish. "And champagne. How thoughtful of you. I really am excessively tired." She took a sip, felt the bubbles fizz comfortingly at the back of her nose and remembered Herr Schann. "We have been rehearsing all day. I hope Your Highness will be pleased with the results."

"I know I shall be pleased with whatever *you* do. Your singing last night, Miss Paget—I shall call you Anne—your singing was a revelation. And not only to me. I think the enemy are beginning to take my opera seriously at last."

"Enemy?" She put down her glass. This was no time to let champagne cloud her judgment.

"Come, Anne. Beautiful Anne." He moved his chair nearer to hers. "Do not pretend to be stupid. It's not possible. You

104

know perfectly well that there is a faction, here in Lissenberg, that would like to see my *Regulus* fail. I think they are feeling quite stupid this morning."

"I don't know," she said, grateful for the neutral subject. "It's not roses all the way at rehearsal. There's quite a row going on between Signor Ricci and Mr Fare."

"Oh—rows!" He dismissed it. "Always there is trouble in the production of any work of art. But this is going to be a triumph—world shaking. I have sent out new notices, this morning, to all the major newspapers. Warning them of a surprise debut. They will all be here, Anne, to applaud you. I am making your name, my dear."

"And I am grateful." Strange that it should seem so unimportant. If this was the way he intended to bribe himself into her bed, he was out of luck. But, just the same, she did wish the rooms were not sound-proofed. He was refilling their glasses, and moving his chair a little closer. She tried a diversion. "Have they found Mr Marks yet?"

"Marks! Who cares for him? Dear Anne, do not ask me to play the hypocrite with you. You met my unlamented cousin-in-law. Have you any idea what he meant to do to me—to my country? He was talking..." He paused. "He was threatening..." Another pause. "I will not pretend to care about his..." He hesitated. "His death."

"His murder," said Anne, and breathed a sigh of relief at a low insistent knocking on the door to the hall. "Excuse me, Your Highness?" She moved over to unlock the door and confront young James Frensham.

"Damnation," said the Hereditary Prince, looking with something very like hatred at the new caller.

"Miss Paget." Frensham, too, carried flowers, but his was a small, carefully chosen bouquet of spring blooms. "They told me at the desk that you were entertaining, so I made bold to come up."

"I am delighted to see you," she said with truth. "Do sit down and have a glass of champagne. Oh—" She looked at the two glasses on the tray.

"No, thanks," he said. "I never touch it. But I'll have a few of your snacks. Dinner at that hotel of yours gets worse and worse, Cousin Rudolf. As if last night's near disaster wasn't bad enough, they upset the flavour bottles into the food tonight."

"We do season highly in Lissenberg," said the Prince stiffly.

"You certainly do. I just hope you can restrain your chef before the international set start dropping in, or they'll drop out again pretty damn quick."

"Which, of course, is precisely what you want." The Prince was bristling with anger, and Anne felt increasingly alarmed. Both men, she thought, had drunk well with their dinner; their natural antipathy was increased to danger point by this unlucky meeting. They were glowering at each other now, the elderly, red-faced, furious Prince, and the elegant young Englishman, who looked in his controlled rage more like an aristocratic Italian brigand than ever.

"You must let me order you something to drink." She rose, hoping to break the tension, and moved over to the telephone, only to pause at yet another knock at the door. Before she could call a relieved "Come in," a pass-key turned in the lock and Michael appeared, a tray expertly balanced on his right hand as he closed the door behind him.

"Martini for Mr Frensham." He moved a small table to Frensham's elbow and put down the tray. "And an urgent telephone call from the palace, Your Highness."

"Impossible. They don't know I'm here."

"They had tried everywhere else." Michael put a plate of canapés on Frensham's table. "They want you quite badly, sir. They've got Mr Marks."

Anne, who had expected the Prince to vent his accumulated wrath on Michael, was amazed and relieved to see him make a visible effort at control. "That's good news. We don't tolerate murder here in Lissenberg." He turned with an attempt at courtesy to young Frensham. "You will be glad to know that your father is on the way to being avenged."

"I'll be glad to have a word with Marks," growled Frensham. "A very odd business altogether, and you need not think that Marks' arrest is the end of the matter."

"Well, of course not," said the Prince. "There will be the trial. I am afraid we abolished capital punishment a few years ago, so I cannot promise you an execution, but I should think a life sentence..." He turned back to Michael. "Where is he?"

"At police headquarters. I took the liberty of sending for your car from the garage. It should be waiting."

Now the Prince's frown was formidable. "You did, did you? You seem to have taken quite a few liberties. As usual. But no time for that now." He rose ponderously, his movements for once betraying his age. "Forgive me, Miss Paget. You see

106

there is no peace for the head that wears the crown." He kissed her hand gallantly and, straightening up, flashed her a look to suggest that the occasion was only postponed.

Frensham stood up too. "I'll come with you. If I may," he added belatedly. "After all, the man Marks was in my father's employment. He may have some explanation."

"Oh, very well." The Prince accepted it without enthusiasm and led the way to the door, which Michael was holding open.

"Until a happier hour." Frensham, too, kissed her hand, his message conveyed by warm lips.

"So much for that." Michael closed the door behind them and began to collect up glasses. "Which is yours?" he asked. "You look all in."

"Here." The pain was gnawing at her, and she took a steadying sip of champagne. "You're not seeing them out?"

"No need. Fritz can do that. The man at the desk," he explained. "Rudolf's man." He did not elaborate on it. She was afraid he did not need to. "Relax, girl. It's all over. It won't happen again, I promise. Uncle Josef won't let himself be conned away another time."

"Conned?"

"A hoax message." His laugh was forced. "From me. Or rather, for me. I was dying, he was told, up at Uncle Hans' pub."

"Dying?" Her lips trembled against the champagne glass.

"Beaten up." He shrugged it off. "Only, he got thinking. No fool, Uncle Josef. Stopped in town, rang Hans, found it was all nonsense. Got hold of me, and here I am. In time, thank goodness." Again his laugh did not ring true. "And thank the lord for young Frensham. Old Rudolf's a fast worker. I was..." He paused. "Worried." And then, "Why did you let him in?"

"I didn't!" Indignantly. "He was here when I came up from dinner."

"Of course. Fritz and the master key. Are you OK now? Because I really ought to be on my way. There's going to be hell to pay at police headquarters."

"Oh?" It was surprising how much she disliked the idea of his going. "But why?" And then, belatedly: "I can't tell you how grateful I am. You came on purpose? I hadn't realised... I just thought..."

He laughed. "I was on the staff here now? I wish I was." He picked up the telephone. "Josef? You're back. Good. Did you get them?" He listened for a moment. "Fine. I'll tell Anne to expect you." Another pause. "Yes, she's OK. Bit shaken. Shall I tell her you'll be right up?" He listened again. "Right—five minutes. I'll wait, I think. What did you do with Fritz?" The answer seemed to amuse him. He replaced the receiver and turned to Anne. "Uncle Josef has got a couple of chains for your doors. He'll be up with them in a minute. I thought perhaps I'd wait and let him in? If you don't mind?"

"*Mind*! I'd be grateful. I don't much like these sound-proofed rooms. But, Michael, chains? Isn't that over-reacting a bit?"

"Maybe. But better safe than sorry. Someone really doesn't mean *Regulus* to be a success. Or the peace conference. Or both. That was a strong dose of ipecac last night. There wouldn't have been much rehearsing today if it hadn't been spotted. And you're such an obvious target."

"But surely, tonight was just..." She paused, embarrassed.

"Just wicked old Rudolf? Well, yes and no. Someone went to a lot of trouble to get Uncle Josef off the scene. That doesn't sound like our Rudolf to me. He's an opportunist, not a plotter. I think someone must have told him you were alone here, with your guard down, as it were. Someone who wanted you"—he paused—"upset."

"To put it mildly." She was beginning to feel better. "I do *thank* you, Michael. I hope you're not going to get into trouble."

"Nothing I'm not used to, or can't handle."

"Thank goodness for that. But—" Calmer now, she had been thinking about what he had done. "I don't understand. Why the martini *and* the message?"

"Not stupid, are you? The message was a brilliant afterthought. Well, once Fritz told me they were both up here, I knew things weren't as bad as I had feared." He looked at her soberly. "And, by God I *had* feared. I suppose that made me slow, or I'd have thought of the message in the first place."

"How do you mean, thought?" And then, understanding. "You mean, you made up the message?"

"Well, of course."

"But, Michael, you'll be in the most frightful trouble. Oh, I am *sorry*..."

His smile was warming. "Thanks. But no need to worry. I may have made up the message, but it was true enough. The police were looking for our Rudolf."

"You mean they *have* caught Mr Marks?"

"Well, not exactly caught. Got was the word I used. Something must have delayed poor Marks. He turned up this afternoon on the riverbank where they found Bland yesterday." Now his smile was mischievous. "*Aren't* those two going to be angry when they find they've left you to go and interview a dead man."

"Dead!" She put down her glass, spilling champagne. "But, Michael, all three of them? Frensham senior...Bland... *And* Marks...Then..." She paused, working it out.

"There has to be someone else," he said soberly. "That's right. That's dead right. We're not out of the wood yet. But try not to worry about it. Your job is to sing for all you're worth and try to put some heart into the rest of the cast, who sound as if they need it. This opera has just got to be a success. For the world's sake, for Lissenberg's...Did you know our Rudolf has sent out a new lot of publicity, promising a miracle debut?"

"Yes, he told me." The pain was back, making it hard to think clearly. Frensham and his two assistants all dead. All murdered. They had threatened the opera, and Michael wanted it to succeed. They had threatened Lissenberg, Michael's home. What had Hilde Bernz said about him? Always there when there's trouble. It was true—but what did it mean? She looked up at a sound from the door. "Here's Josef," she said with relief.

Josef was full of apologies. "I'll never be such a fool again," he said.

"Only half a fool," Michael comforted him. "After all, you got on to it quick enough."

"Thank God." He moved through to fix the chain on the bedroom door.

"I'd better be off," said Michael. "Or they'll have the thumbscrews out down at police headquarters. Take care of yourself, for all our sakes."

"You're going back to headquarters now?" She looked at her watch and saw that in fact it was only ten o'clock.

"I certainly am. Be good, dear Anne, and let the rest of us be clever."

"I'll try. And, *thank* you, Michael." His first use of her given name was curiously heart-warming.

"My pleasure. For a smile like that...Take care of her, Josef."

"Trust me. You can." Alone with her, Josef produced a

109

small package. "Dr Hirsch left this for you, Anne. In person. He's an old friend of mine," he explained. "Told me to keep an eye on you, see you rest. I don't seem to be doing too well so far, but at least I can leave you alone now, to get some sleep. Don't forget the chains; and your pill. And rest well, child: feel safe."

"Thank you." Putting up the chains behind him, she was close to tears at his kindness—and Michael's. But...Michael. Now she was alone, the nightmare suspicion was back. Michael knew everything, he must have known about that rare mineral under the opera house, but had never mentioned it to her. Ever since Dr Hirsch had told her about it, this doubt had been gnawing at her. Had Michael kept quiet about it because it was his motive for murder? For some curious reason, it seemed easier to imagine Michael killing all three men—Frensham senior, Bland, and Marks—than hiring Marks to do it.

How could she believe such a thing? And yet, she had been wrong before, as her anxious dreams had reminded her. She had thought Robin her faithful husband. She thought Michael an engaging young dropout. Or—did she? What did he conceal behind that mask of cheerful fecklessness? She was more and more convinced that he was older than his shaggy hair and untidy clothes made him seem. Dr Hirsch had parried her question, referring her back to Michael himself. But did she dare ask him? Carl had warned her...Hilde had warned her...She would not believe them. She would ask him next time they met. And, at last—restlessly—she slept, and dreamed once again her nightmare dream where Michael had Robin's face. Or was it the other way round?

"Anne?" The telephone woke her. "Your breakfast is just coming," Josef went on. "And I've got good news. They've found out who tried to sabotage the dinner the other night—and the electricity."

"Thank God. Who was it?"

"You remember one of the hotel taxis crossed the frontier just before it was closed that night?"

"Yes?"

"It got the police thinking. They came down hard on old Brech, who runs those taxis, and he finally confessed. He'd had an anonymous letter offering him a vast bribe to see that the opera was a failure. He's a stupid man, Brech. The hotel trade would have been a goldmine to him."

Anne's sleepy brain moved slowly. "Anonymous? But who? Why?"

"There are plenty of people, here in Lissenberg, who would like to go back to our old, quiet ways. Frankly, I sympathise with them—up to a point. We were happier before. Every man his own goat and his own vineyard—and none of them interested in tourism and high finance. I can think of a lot of people who would like to turn the clock back."

"I see." She remembered what Michael had said about tourism and plastic souvenirs. "But not murder. Brech would never have done that, just for pay, for an anonymous letter. Besides, the first time, it was his car."

"That's right. No, the murders are another story, and one we'd best leave to Herr Winkler. He'll cope." Josef's laugh came reassuringly down the line. "He's sent Brech straight home to Germany. Sensible man. No prosecution . . . no publicity." Then, "Your breakfast is on its way."

"Thanks." She got out of bed and padded over to unchain the door and let Lisel in with the tray. The programme that lay on it was a simple one. *Ten o'clock: rehearsal. One to one thirty: break for sandwiches. Afternoon: rehearsal.*

A long day. She took the second of Dr Hirsch's pills and got out of bed to move over to the window and admire the beginning of a fine day she would be too busy to see. A knock on the door reminded her that she had not put the chain back after Lisel. "Come in," she called, deciding she was not prepared to live in a fortress all day.

Lisel reappeared with her usual brilliant smile. "These for you." She held out a plastic-swathed coat-hanger. "Frau Riley says very cold today."

"Oh, thank you. And you can take the tray, thanks, Lisel."

Mrs Riley, the wardrobe mistress, had excelled herself. The elegantly tailored dark red trousers had a contrasting top and a long, warm, matching tunic. And, in a separate plastic bag, was a soft, mink-type fur jacket—the best imitation Anne had ever seen. It was no surprise to find that they all fitted perfectly. Anne smiled at herself in the glass and thought how surprised her friends at the plastics workshop would be if they could see her now. One wore trousers, of course, at the workshop, but they were not trousers like these. How long ago? It seemed an eternity. And she would never go back. Even if the opera should be a disaster, she was safe in her certainty of death.

But she remembered Dr Hirsch: that was no way to think.

111

She picked up the newspaper Josef had sent up on her breakfast tray. It was yesterday's *International Herald Tribune*, and someone had marked a lead piece on the front page. "Hopes Rise for Peace Conference" read the headline of a long article describing the encouragingly positive attitudes of the powers that were sending delegates. Down at the bottom, Josef's pencil had been at work again. "Opera a Good Omen?" was the heading of a brief last paragraph describing the plans for *Regulus*.

Clever Josef. She put down the paper, ashamed of herself. He was reminding her, as Dr Hirsch had done, of the wider implications of the opera, of the duty they all had to make it succeed, and give a rousing, positive start to the peace conference. But where did that lead her? So far she had thought of Frensham's death only in relation to Lissenberg and that sinister mineral under the opera house. But suppose Frensham and Bland and Marks had been behind the sabotage. Suppose they had wanted the opera to fail not only because that would make it easier to pull down the opera house, but also for the adverse effect its failure would have on the peace conference. Frensham, she knew, had been in the armaments business. He might well have had a stake in the failure of a peace conference. And here—sudden and horrible—was a convincing motive for Michael. Had she suspected him, instinctively, and with justice, but for the wrong reasons? Had Frensham been behind the sabotage and had Michael, discovering this, killed him? She did not believe it. She would not believe it. She must talk to him, must ask him...Could you ask a man if he was a murderer? But talking to him would help. Help her to prove herself wrong? With all her heart she hoped so.

But the long, hard-working days ground past, and there was no sign of Michael. Workmen, thronging in the arcade and in and out of the opera house, were hard at it undoing the effects of Brech's sabotage, and Anne looked eagerly at each jean-clad figure, hoping it would be Michael's, but it never was. After haunting her, a friendly spirit, for her first days in Lissenberg, he had simply vanished, without word or message, and she missed him more than she liked to admit. One sight of him, she began to think, would automatically clear the miasma of suspicion from her brain, but in the meantime she dreamed, and sweated, and suffered.

9

Herr Brech had been all too efficient as a saboteur. Even after his confession, it took several days to get the lights in the opera house working again. The belated move there, on a Monday morning just a week before opening night, brought instant chaos. Hilde Bernz summed it up gloomily as they moved up to the artists' bar for their lunch break. "No one's going to need to sabotage this opera. I knew the stage would be difficult, but dear God..."

"And poor Carl," said Anne. "If only we'd been able to work here sooner he would have seen what a problem the entrances and exits were going to be."

"Pure hell," agreed Hilde. "Much, much worse than Salzburg. I'm going to insist on a pair of flat-heeled shoes. If I've got to run several miles on and off in the dark every time, I'm not doing it in heels. You're lucky to be wearing those elegant Roman sandals."

"It's the chorus I'm worried about," said Anne. "I don't see how they are going to shove their way through those two side exits. It's crazy. I mean, in the dark...suppose one of them stumbled; it would be mayhem." Just the kind of disaster, she thought, that might wreck a first night. "Excuse me?" She moved over, glass and sandwich in hand, to the corner of the bar where Carl was standing alone with a drink but no sandwich, staring gloomily into space. "Carl, dear." She put a gentle hand on his arm, and then wished she had not done so. His behaviour had continued to puzzle her, varying from day to day, even from one meeting to the next, between the professional and the romantic.

But for the moment, he was all professional. "Anne! Dear Anne, I am so sorry. It was to be your big chance. Instead— disaster. I should never have agreed to direct. But it seemed so simple, so straightforward. *Opera seria.* Nothing fancy. Just beautiful, pure singing. Just letting Beethoven speak. And now, look at it! A shambles! Adolf Stern singing Regulus as if he were Siegfried! You can almost see him looking round for his anvil. He doesn't like to have to stand still and let great music unfold itself. I've told him and told him, Annchen. He won't listen!"

"He knows best," said Anne. "That type always does. Why

113

don't you ask Princess Alix to speak to him, Carl? He might take it from her?"

"Anne! You're my good genius. I'll do it tonight—if I get the chance. What with him and young Frensham, there's no getting near the Princess these days."

Anne laughed. "So I hear." According to Hilde Bernz, Alix joined the opera group in the hotel bar most nights and was being assiduously courted by both Stern and Frensham. It explained Frensham's failure to repeat that one visit to her, but Anne had been both surprised and relieved to hear nothing further from Prince Rudolf. "Which one are you backing?" she asked now.

"Oh, Frensham of course," said Carl. "Alix would never throw herself away on Stern." He reached out, took a sandwich and bit into it. "These are good. I'm sure you're right: she'll make him see reason. Now tell me, wise Anne, what in the world I should do about the chorus? Falinieri's in despair about them. He says he can hear them shuffling off right through your first solo."

"Well, of course he can," said Anne. "That's really what I came to talk to you about. It's a devil of a stage, Carl."

"Couldn't be helped," he said gloomily. "Something about the rock formation."

"I see. Well, there it is, and we have to make the best of it. Hilde's asking for flat heels, sensible woman, so she won't trip getting on and off stage in the dark. I'm sure we principals will manage, but, Carl, what I was thinking—why not keep the chorus on stage all through? Just let them move aside when they're not singing? I don't see how else you're going to manage. Beethoven just didn't write for a stage this size—or a chorus so big, for that matter. I'm so afraid one of them might trip, and they'd go down like the cards in *Alice*."

"Disaster." He used the familiar word with complete conviction. "That's a good idea, Anne. I'll think about it." He looked at her gloomily and lowered his voice. "Let's face it. It would only take one of them, bribed, like Brech, to stumble, and that's it."

"You feel that way, too? But isn't it odd? After all, Brech's been safe out of the country since last week. And there's been no trouble since he left."

"No," said Carl. "But they haven't arrested anyone for those three murders either. I'd feel a hell of a lot safer if they had. After all, what Brech was doing was schoolboy stuff

114

really—nuisance value, that's all. It wouldn't have thrown us so if it hadn't been for the murders."

"That's true. And we are in a twitch aren't we? All of us. It's beginning to show. Fare and Ricci are at each other's throats again, have you noticed? And Gertrud's in an odd state. She seems angry with me for some reason; I wish I knew why. Oh, Carl, I do hope this afternoon's rehearsal goes well, for a change. We could do with a bit of encouragement, the whole lot of us."

"You, too, Annchen?" He put a friendly arm round her shoulders. "My tower of strength."

"Thanks!" She moved away a little, casually, to put her glass down on the bar and escape his grasp. "As for the chorus, why don't you leave things as they are till the dress rehearsal on Saturday. Let them struggle on and off. If Brech has left someone behind to go on with the sabotage, that's the obvious way. Fuss at them, lecture them, but don't suggest keeping them onstage until the very last minute. The lighting's no problem, because the sides of the stage are blacked out anyway. That's what makes it so damned difficult to get on and off. All you have to do is tell them at the last moment, and the saboteur, if there is one, will have to do some quick rethinking."

"You're a genius, Anne. I'll do it. But—sooner, don't you think? They must have time to get used to the new positions. Friday, maybe? The day before the dress rehearsal?"

"Only four days off. Carl, are we going to make it?"

"We must," he said. "Let's just hope the rehearsal goes better this afternoon."

It went disastrously worse. At four o'clock Falinieri stopped them and shouted. "Enough! Stop! Too much! I can bear no more. You," to Gertrud, "go and sulk somewhere else. As for you," to John Fare, "if I could replace you, I would."

"But you can't," said Fare. "This opera's jinxed. Everyone knows that. It's into the gossip columns now. Maybe Beethoven knew what he was doing when he suppressed it in the first place."

"Nonsense," said Falinieri. "It was not suppressed, it was lost—as you well know, Mr Fare. And if there *is* anything in the gossip columns, I wonder who gave them their lead. Ah." He had spotted the flicker of apprehension on Fare's face. "Now I have you, Mr Fare. Any more trouble from you, and I will accuse you publicly of trying to damage the opera you are appearing in. You know what that would do to your

115

career. Now, go away, all of you—and, Holy Mary, come back more cheerful in the morning."

Anne looked about for Carl, but he had already vanished, and she could hardly blame him. Hilde Bernz was talking to Gertrud, and Anne did not much feel like joining them. Gertrud's inexplicable hostility was something she could do without, right now. The endless evening stretched before her. Usually they worked much later than this, but even so the solitary evenings in her elegant, empty suite had begun to seem interminable. The chains on her doors were ridiculous— no one came near her. The rest of the cast went up to the hotel every night, and sometimes the principals even dined there now that the restaurant was in full working order and a dance band functioning. It would be good to dance, Anne thought, to get some exercise after all the day's endless standing and sitting. But it was entirely taken for granted now that no one suggest she go too.

Had she hoped that Michael would come and cheer the solitude he had helped to impose on her? If so, she had been deluding herself. There had been no word from him since the night he had rescued her from the Prince and young James Frensham. Rescued? Absurd. She had probably imagined the whole thing—turned a couple of courtesy calls into some kind of threat, made, in fact, a public fool of herself. No wonder Michael kept away. He had doubtless got some absorbing new job by now and, indeed, Gertrud had once or twice mentioned seeing him at the hotel, and would, probably have said more if Anne had not been too proud to question her.

Proud. What was there to be proud about? She looked at her watch. Time at last for a drink before dinner. She found Gertrud and Hilde in the bar, both in evening dress, and felt suddenly shabby in her short skirt. She bought a glass of sherry and joined them. "You're going out?"

"Yes." Hilde sounded embarrassed. "Gertrud knows a pub up in the mountains. The Wild Man, or something. She says we'll ruin our figures on dumplings, but it sounds worth trying."

"Pity you can't come." It was very far from being an invitation. Gertrud rose to her feet. "Time to go, Hilde. Mustn't keep them waiting!" And then, over her shoulder. "Your regards to Michael?"

"If you see him." It was as near a question as she would go, and got her merely a quick, speculative backwards glance from Gertrud as the two of them left the bar.

116

It was nearly empty now. Most of the cast must have decided on a change after the day's depressing rehearsal, and she did not blame them. She should have brought down a book to read over her dinner. She would go and fetch one. As she rose to do so John Fare entered the bar. "All alone, our prima donna?" His voice was slurred as if he had been drinking already in his room. "Let me buy you a drink, since the others have chosen to abandon us."

"Abandon—?"

"Some party up the mountains. Very carefully arranged, *sotto voce*, behind our backs. Damn their eyes. What'll you have?" Then, "Tell you what—better idea; come to the Golden Cross with me." He swayed on his feet as he spoke and his breath was strong with whiskey.

She smiled at him placatingly. "What a nice idea. But—you know my problem. I'm just on my way to ask Josef for a tray in my room." It was the only thing to do. Swearing, he lurched away towards the bar while she retreated into the lobby and went straight to Josef at the desk.

"Yes?" He looked tired tonight.

"I wish you'd have a word with the man in the bar. Mr Fare's had quite as much as is good for him already. We don't want another disaster of a rehearsal tomorrow." And then, the words almost speaking themselves, "What in the world's become of Michael? We're all in the dumps. We could do with a bit of cheering up."

"I'm sorry to hear it." Josef did not seem particularly surprised. "As to Michael." He smiled and shrugged. "He's still working with the police, so far as I know. And not a clue in sight, I believe."

"They're keeping very quiet about those murders."

"We don't like crime in Lissenberg. So—we don't talk about it, Miss Paget."

The use of her surname was like a door closed in her face. "Thanks for the warning," she said with some bitterness and moved away from him to the lift. Then, turning back, "But if you should happen to see Michael you might tell him his conspiracy of silence is playing hell with the cast. Could I have a tray in my room please? I'm tired tonight."

Tired of living. And that was absurd, when she had so little of it left. She had thought of her room as sanctuary, but when she got there, it had never seemed so unwelcoming. Rain, sheeting down, cut off her view of mountains and castle. She had finished *The Birds Fall Down* and was reduced to

117

a diet of thrillers from the paperback stand in the hotel. This is despair, she thought, dropping her fur jacket on a chair, stepping out of her shoes and kicking them, suddenly, one this way, one that. I can't face it. A whole evening sitting alone here, face to face with death. Well: death? A solution? She still had the pain-killers the doctor back in England had given her. How many would it take?

Nonsense. She remembered what Falinieri had said to Fare. *Regulus* was jinxed enough without a suicide. But Alix would sing her part, and sing it well. She thought of the headlines: "Princess Takes Part at Last Moment." Doubtless Michael and the police would hush up her suicide as capably as they had the three murders. Josef would help. "We don't talk about it, Miss Paget." The snub direct. If she knew his surname, or Michael's, she would use them. Write them a note? Miss Paget regrets...

She shivered. Poison in the air. She could not, actually, be considering suicide? Impossible. Unthinkable. Imagine poor Lisel finding her. On the impulse, she hurried into the bedroom, found the pain-killers and flushed them down the lavatory. Then, to the mirror, to comb her hair, put on lipstick and smile wryly at herself, thinking of that other night, when she had had to fend off the advances of both Prince Rudolf and James Frensham. I could just do with that tonight, she told herself. If either of them were to ask me out, I'd go like a shot.

And, on the thought, the telephone rang. She picked it up. "Yes?"

"Josef here." Had he the grace to sound slightly embarrassed? "Dr Hirsch called to say he was passing this way and would like to drop in and see you."

"Oh, how nice! Thank you." She put the receiver down but the bell rang again at once.

"Anne?" This time it was Alix, the deep voice unmistakable. "Good. Dear Anne, I'm having a short-notice dinner party tomorrow night. For the cast...The principals, that is. Do come. It won't seem right without you. I know you're supposed to rest, but enough is enough, surely?"

"So far as I am concerned, enough is a great deal too much," said Anne. "Thanks, Alix. I'd love to come. I've got Dr Hirsch turning up any minute. I'll tell him I'm coming."

"That's right." Alix's warm laugh was approving. "So—eight o'clock tomorrow. And, Anne, the others are coming by car, but Winkler wants you to take the walkway."

"Walkway?"

"It's a well-kept secret. Father's idea. Well, there's always been a lift down from the palace to the town—to a private room in the Golden Cross. Very handy for incognito dinners. In the old days, that is; when diplomatic guests always stayed there. When they planned the conference centre and the hotel, Father insisted he must still have his private way in. It took some engineering, I can tell you: a kind of moving stairway up sideways through the rock. But useful for tomorrow; we don't much want our prima donna out on the roads. Herr Winkler said he'd send someone to escort you up. He didn't really want you to come at all, but he agrees it would seem odd if you didn't. There will be a couple of journalists at dinner, by the way, friends of Mother's who've turned up early."

"Not so small a party as all that," said Anne.

Alix laughed. "Small in palace terms. And I promise you the food will be good. No ipecac. You sound as if you could do with an outing. What's the matter, Anne? Aren't you feeling well?"

"Just bored," said Anne. "We're all a bit overtired and edgy. A night out will be lovely. Thanks, Alix." Replacing the receiver, she felt slightly sick. If the Prince had invited her out to the Golden Cross again, she had meant to go. And there was a lift up from there to the palace. Melodrama? But here in Lissenberg anything was possible.

A knock at the door heralded Dr Hirsch, and, letting him in, she cast a regretful glance at the untidy room.

"A bad day, I hear?" After the first greetings, he put his hat and raincoat tidily on a chair as she swiftly gathered up her abandoned fur coat and shoes. "I've just given John Fare an injection," he told her. "Good thing you warned Josef or there would have been trouble tomorrow. I think he'll do as it is. I thought I might just drop in and thank you." His glance was friendly, enquiring.

"I'm glad you did." Curiously enough, the pain—absent when she was thinking those mad thoughts of suicide—was back now, full strength. And—she had thrown away her pain-killers. Absurd. Just part of the general melodrama. "Dr Hirsch." He was taking her pulse, and she got it in fast before he could silence her with the thermometer. "I've done something stupid."

"Yes?" He sat down comfortably beside her on the sofa.

"I threw away my pain-killers."

"Oh you did, did you?" He turned to give her a very sharp look. "Not, I take it, because there was no more pain."

"Well...no." She could not meet his eyes.

"A very bad day," he summed it up. "I think perhaps I am a little proud of you, Miss Paget. But you would never have done it, you know. Not with Marcus to sing. Not with Carl Meyer and the others depending on you."

"I...I suppose not." She blessed him for his quick comprehension.

"I know not. So—how wasteful to throw away the good pain-killers." He opened his black bag. "Which I will replace. Only—too many of these would make you very sick indeed, my child. So..."

"Thank you. But you're right, I don't think it will happen again. Or, anyway, not till after...not till I'm off your hands. I suppose, at the end, one might have the right..."

He was shaking his head at her. "I do not propose to let you 'off my hands' as you put it. You are my patient, child. I have taken, as a doctor, a great responsibility in letting you sing in this opera. Do you think, when it is over, I will send in a fat bill, kiss your hand, and say goodbye?"

"Do you know, I hadn't really thought."

"That is good. Then go on not thinking, and let me do it for you. If all goes well, when *Regulus* closes, you will be Lissenberg's new star. I do not think it will be difficult to find somewhere pleasant for you to stay."

"You mean, to die. Will they give me a state funeral, do you think?"

"That's no way to think—or to talk. But I will forgive you this time, because I can see it has been a very bad day. I only wish it was the Princess's party tonight. You are going, of course."

She looked at him in surprise. "I said I would. I thought you'd be cross."

"Like the ogre in the fairy story? Lock you up in this palatial suite of yours to bore yourself into morbid thoughts. No, no. You will put on your best dress and go to the ball, Cinderella. Only—go carefully. Who is taking you?"

"The Princess is making arrangements. So—you think there is still danger?"

"With three murders unexplained? What do you think?"

"I think they have been most scandalously hushed up. Dr Hirsch, who owns the *Lissenberger Zeitung?*"

"I thought you didn't read German."

120

"I don't. But Frau Bernz mentioned that it had said nothing about the murders for days."

"So." He said thoughtfully. "Yes, it's true; they have kept remarkably quiet. But as to who owns it, which could be the explanation, I'm afraid I cannot tell you."

"Cannot?"

"Just so. It's about the best-kept secret in Lissenberg. It could be Prince Rudolf; it could be the Frensham empire. Or, of course—" he finally produced the thermometer—"it could be both of them. It's one of the questions one doesn't ask, by the way. Don't go discussing it at the castle, if you want a pleasant evening. The pain has gone again?" he asked as he rose to his feet.

"Why, yes. So it has. But thank you for the pain-killers just the same."

"Pain is a strange thing. If we only understood...But one thing I do know: the less you think about it the better. Now, Miss Paget, before I go, who do you think is spreading the poison through the opera cast?"

"Poison? Funny, it does feel like that. And—dangerous. But the answer is, I absolutely don't know. John Fare is the obvious person to pick on, but he...he's not strong enough, somehow."

"Think about it, Miss Paget, and watch, and if you get an idea, come to me, fast. I don't like it."

"No more do I." She thought of her own desperate moments earlier on, of John Fare's injection. "At least it can't be Michael," she said on an impulse. "He's not been near us."

"And why in the name of madness should it be Michael?"

"There's something very odd about that young man."

"Of course there is," said Dr Hirsch heartily. "And now, forgive me, I'm late at the hospital. Have a good party, Cinderella."

10

Next day's rehearsal went almost too quietly. Everyone seemed subdued, listless...It was a stage Anne recognised, when they were beginning to know their parts but were not yet quite into them, but also, she thought, everyone was tired. Gertrud and Hilde both had dark circles under their eyes, while John Fare was white as a sheet and shook a little. Even Carl, who had so far managed to seem a tower of confident strength, looked tired and anxious, and Anne wondered all over again at the change in him. She thought she preferred the shaggy Bohemian she remembered, so sure of himself and his music. It was that confidence that had infuriated poor Robin. And since when had she been thinking of her dead husband as poor Robin?

It was a relief when the rehearsal ended without disaster and they separated to dress for the Princess' dinner. Twisting her Woolworth chain in the neck of the green velvet dress Mrs Riley had made for her, Anne thought for a moment of Prince Rudolf and his jeweller's box. Did she actually regret not having looked inside? Ashamed of herself, she reached for the telephone to call Hilde and suggest a drink, but as she did so it rang.

It was Josef. "Your escort is here."

"He's early," said Anne.

"He suggests a drink." Michael's voice.

"Lovely. Oh, I am so glad it's you, Michael!" But how absurd. Picking up her coat to hurry down and join him, she felt all her old doubts creeping back. While he had been so mysteriously absent, she had simply missed him. Now that he had returned, she could not help wondering what he had been doing. Helping the police—or hindering them? Searching, perhaps, or pretending to search, for himself? Because—she made herself face it, now she was thinking again—his complicity might help to explain the curious cover up of the murders. He had friends, powerful friends, in Lissenberg. Might they not be trying to protect him? She shook the doubts out of her mind and hurried downstairs.

"Stunning!" He was waiting at the lift door and led the way into Josef's office. "I thought we'd hide peacefully in here." He pulled out a chair for her and poured slivovitz. And then, drinking to her, "I've missed you."

"You've kept very quiet about it." It came out more sharply than she had intended.

"I've been...busy." He paused for a moment, as if that was all he was going to say, then went on. "Away part of the time. An errand for Winkler."

"About which you don't intend to tell me." But then, think of all the things she probably would not ask him.

"Quite right." His smile was teasing. "Anyway, I achieved nothing."

"But you're still working for the police?" Surely, if Winkler trusted him, so could she.

"Off and on. Here and there. Escort duty tonight. We're taking no chances with our prima donna. Hence the trip through Rudolf's folly."

"Rudolf's—"

"—Folly. You've no idea what it added to the expense of the whole opera project. But he would have it, and, then, he was boss. God knows it's convenient enough tonight. They're using the hotel taxis to take the guests up to the palace, and you know how I feel about them, even without Herr Brech."

"Is there any news of him?"

"Not a word, I'm glad to say, since he was politely seen to the frontier and urged not to come back. Above all things, we are trying to avoid a scandal—the wrong kind of news story."

"Cover up," said Anne. "I don't like it. It's all wrong when it's murder."

"You and Winkler both. But 'don't like' is a bit mild for the state he's in. Cheer up, it's not long now."

"No. Only six days until we open. Michael, it terrifies me. It's not together yet, that opera. I'm...worried." And then, almost regretting having admitted it—even to him—she changed the subject. "What are you tonight?" He had discarded his jeans for a remarkably well-cut corduroy suit and turned, in the process, from shaggy student into—well, what? Professor? Poet? And—she had been right, he was older than he seemed.

"What am I?" He repeated her question. "Oh, I see." He smoothed back unusually tidy hair and smiled at her. "Devil of a time with my tie. I'm clean out of practice, but, you see, tonight I'm a guest." The smile melted into a laugh. "Don't look so horrified, Anne! We're democrats here in Lissenberg, and besides, think how useful I'll be if anything goes wrong with the service."

"Or the lights," said Anne. "Or practically anything else, so far as I can see. What can't you do, Michael?" Perhaps, this way, she could work round to her questions.

"Oh, lots of things." He looked suddenly harassed. "Drink up. It's time we started." He helped her into her coat and opened an inconspicuous door in the corner of the room to

123

reveal a flight of dusty stairs, going steeply down. "Watch how you go." He switched on a light and started down.

"It's cold." She was glad of her fur jacket.

"Yes. We're right at the back of the building. These stairs are against the rock." He pushed open a door at the bottom. "I came up this way," he explained. "Left it unlocked." He flicked a light switch and a series of naked, low-powered bulbs came on and revealed a long, drab passage stretching away to the left. "You could say this was the complex's life line," he told her. "It runs under the whole thing."

"You mean you could get to the hotel this way?"

"That's right. Or the conference centre, if you could get in. The locks on these doors are pretty special."

"I should hope so! Where's the entrance from the opera house?"

"That *was* a problem. As the corridor is at the back of all the buildings, it runs clear under the stage. We're about there now." He pointed to a door. "If you could get through there, which you most certainly cannot, it would take you up to the opera house."

"It's a bigger door than the others."

"And a wider stair. Did you ever stop to think of what would happen if there was a fire in that opera house?"

"My God." She thought of the chorus, stumbling off through the two narrow exits.

"The fire-proof curtain would come down," Michael said, "and the cast would be trapped. That stair's the answer. It leads from a concealed entrance, centre-back of the stage. The falling of the fire-proof curtain releases the locks on the doors at the top and bottom of the stairs so they can be opened by hand."

"Pity we can't use it for the opera," said Anne. "The central exit. We could just do with it."

"I know. But what it would have cost...Maybe one day when you've made our fortune for us, we'll do something about it. Here we are." They had reached another door. "Be a love and look the other way while I open it. What you don't know—"

"Won't hurt me." She turned to look back down the long, bleak corridor and heard a noise like a telephone being dialled.

"There. You can turn round now."

This door led not to a stair but to another corridor. "They

certainly trust you," she said, as Michael closed the door behind them.

"Which is more than you do. Right? You've been looking at me like Little Red Riding Hood and the wolf ever since I turned up. What's the matter?"

"Oh, nothing...Everything. I've got the horrors tonight, that's all."

"Horrors general or horrors particular?"

"Oh, I don't know. The rehearsals seem to go worse and worse. And nobody says anything about the murders. Michael, what would it do to the peace conference if the opera was a disaster?"

"Well, it would hardly be the best of omens, would it? Don't fret, though; it's always darkest before the dawn. As for the murders, the less said, surely, the better?"

"From the murderer's point of view, certainly."

His hard hand caught her elbow and pulled her to a standstill facing him. "Now I begin to understand. You think I—" He stopped.

"Michael, I don't know what to think." She was shivering now. With cold, with fear, with misery? "If you'd only explain..."

"How I wrecked Brech's taxi while I was driving you just behind? How I killed James Frensham? But—why?"

"I don't know." It came out slowly, more of an admission than she had intended. She pulled her arm away. "Oh, please, Michael, let's stop. I hate this."

"Not a bit more than I do. But you're right. We'd better stop. You're shivering. And we can't afford to risk that voice of yours. Not in idle chatter in a cold cellar." He crossed the passage and pressed what looked like a rough lump in the wall. "Your magic carpet, my lady."

"Good God." For a moment she forgot the misery of their misunderstanding as the fake cement rolled back to uncover a sleek, modern lift door. Michael pressed a button at the side and it slid open, revealing the bottom of a moving stairway that sloped very gently away into the darkness.

Michael flicked a couple of levers and a string of lights came on, while one side of the stairway purred smoothly into life. "Miracle of modern technology." He steadied her with a casual hand as she grasped the moving rail. Was it her imagination, or was the hand less friendly than before? Well, no wonder. Stepping on behind her, he let go her arm.

125

"Damned expensive, the whole thing." His tone was impersonal. "Do you begin to see why this opera has to pay?"

"My goodness, yes. But Michael, was it really necessary?"

"Of course, not. But have you ever tried to persuade our Rudolf that something he wants is not necessary? Well, don't!" The cold rage in his voice made him suddenly formidable. "And that's something I've been wanting a chance to say to you. Don't you kid yourself that he cares so much about the opera that he won't do anything to upset its star. Because Rudolf doesn't work that way. What Rudolf wants, he gets. Regardless. So, if he says, at dinner tonight, just suppose he says: 'Come on, beautiful diva, one last drink at the Golden Cross, just with me.' Don't you go, Anne Paget. Don't you be fool enough to go. There's a lift from the Golden Cross to the castle."

"I know. Alix told me. But, Michael, he wouldn't!"

"Want to bet?" said Michael.

Since Princess Gloria was still in full mourning for her cousin, Alix was acting as hostess, and the party was held in her suite of apartments. Plainly, even austerely decorated, they were in remarkable contrast to the rest of the palace, and Anne liked them much better. The other guests were already assembled and she noticed a glance or two of surprise when Michael followed her into the room.

"Your bodyguard, I take it," said Hilde, *sotto voce.*

"I suppose so."

"You'd have thought they might have run to evening dress for him." The other men were all in formal black and white. "Michael." She summoned him over with an imperious gesture borrowed from the stage. "Fix my lighter for me, would you?" It was more command than request.

"Gladly." He took it and returned to a window embrasure.

Hilde turned back to Anne. "Ghastly rehearsal, wasn't it?"

"We are not talking of the opera tonight. Or—not in that tone." Carl appeared from behind her and took an arm of each. "Come and meet the press and, for all our sakes, be cheerful. We've a great success on our hands, remember."

"Who says?" But Hilde went with him willingly enough.

Princess Gloria's journalist friends were an American and an Englishman, who explained that they had come early in order to write "in-depth" pieces on Lissenberg. "And a fascinating place it is," said the American, Jarrold. "Medieval

126

law of succession—Salic, do they call it? No trades unions, no votes for women, three murders and no publicity."

"Marvellous landscape," said the Englishman with heavy tact.

"Stupendous," agreed his colleague. "I want to see the secret path the refugees used in World War II, but no one seems to know just where it runs. Quite a gang they are here in little Lissenberg. What they don't want you to know, you sure as hell don't find out." He turned to Anne. "Miss Paget, I've been wanting a word with you. We know all about that voice of yours. What I want to know is, what have you been doing with it all your life? Where have you been?"

"Married," said Anne.

"Oh?" He looked around the room. "Your husband is here, perhaps?"

"My husband is dead."

If she had hoped to silence him, she was disappointed. "I'm sorry." It was perfunctory. "A musician too, perhaps?"

Michael appeared between them. "The Princess would like a word with you, Anne."

Moving away by his side, Anne heard the journalist's question to Hilde. "Who is that?" And her answer, "The hired help."

It did not improve her temper. "Thanks for the rescue," she said.

"A pleasure." If he had heard Hilde's description of him, he gave no sign of it. "Sorry I couldn't stand by you, but Frau Bernz must be obeyed."

"You don't like her?" asked Anne, surprised.

"Do you?"

"Why, of course." But did she? She thought of last night, of the ruthless way Hilde and Gertrud had abandoned her to go off to the Wild Man. Ruthless? How odd to think of it like that. "Michael—" She was going to ask him if he had met them at the Wild Man as Gertrud had implied.

But he was looking past her into the room. "I have the strongest feeling that Frau Bernz is telling those newshawks *Regulus* is going to be a disaster."

"But Carl told us..."

"Precisely." He was gone.

Left alone, Anne made her way across the room to where Alix was standing between Adolf Stern and James Frensham. "You wanted to speak to me?" She felt foolish intruding on their conversation, but Alix greeted her with relief.

127

"No," she said, "but I'm delighted to."

"Oh." Anne felt more foolish than ever. "Michael said..."

"That Michael!" said Adolf Stern. "What in the world is he doing here, ma'am?"

"He is my guest, Herr Stern, just as you are."

"Only more so," said James Frensham. "I hope you've warned your father, Alix. He's not going to be exactly pleased." He sounded as if he rather enjoyed the prospect. "I cannot imagine why you insist on standing up for that young troublemaker."

"Can't you?" Alix gave him a very straight look, and Anne felt a sudden, horrible pang of jealousy. Alix and Michael? Michael and Alix? Impossible. Absurd. And yet...She must pull herself together. Frensham had turned impatiently from Alix to speak to her.

"I'm glad to see that the doctor has let you off the leash at last," he said.

Anne laughed. "You sound as if he had had me in purdah."

"Well, hasn't he?" He had contrived to isolate her from Alix and Stern. "We have missed you at the hotel this last week."

"Why, thank you."

"Can I hope that you will join us later tonight? They have a new late show that I am sure you would enjoy."

"*I* am hoping to have the pleasure of seeing Miss Paget home." Anne turned in surprise at Prince Rudolf's voice. "I am late." He bowed elaborately over her hand and she thought for a moment that he was going to kiss it. "As guest of honour, you must forgive me, Miss Paget, but I have a million things on my mind just now."

"I am sure you have. I do hope everything is going smoothly."

He laughed. "You hope for a miracle, then. But if miracles fail us, it is remarkable what hard work will do. You will let me tell you something of my labours over a drink at the Golden Cross on your way home?" It was hardly a question.

"Why, thank you." She looked from one to the other, thinking of all those long, lonely nights in her suite at the hostel. "But I have promised the doctor I will go straight home. I am only out on leave, you know."

"But you have to get home," protested the Prince.

"I think Herr Winkler has made arrangements," she began, but the Prince was not listening. A furious gesture had summoned Michael over to join them.

"What the hell do you think you are doing here?" Naked rage flared in the normally cold blue eyes.

"Herr Winkler sent me. And—" he paused. "Alix asked me."

"Alix!" He turned furiously away and moved over to where his daughter was still talking to Stern.

"Oh, Michael." Anne was appalled. "I'm so sorry..."

"No need to be. It's OK."

"But you'll be in terrible trouble!"

"Nothing I can't handle. These are Alix's apartments, remember. And here she comes."

"Time to go into dinner, I think." Alix had a wry smile for them both. "If you would let my father take you, Anne?" It was part plea, part request.

"Yes, of course. Thank you." Moving reluctantly away to join the Prince, Anne was aware of a quick, intimate exchange between Alix and Michael.

"Young cub." The Prince's angry eyes were still on Michael as he held out his arm to Anne. "If these weren't Alix's apartments..." He left an ominous silence, then shrugged and said a strange thing. "But after all, he does not exist. Shall we go, Miss Paget?"

To Anne's relief the conversation round the oval table was general, with the Princess keeping it skilfully clear of dangerous topics. She was sitting between the two journalists, and Anne was full of admiration at the way she kept them harmlessly in play. When Tom Jarrold asked her how she felt about women's lack of the vote in Lissenberg, she countered with a question about Watergate that kept him floundering for five minutes. When his English colleague, Bob Chapel, asked about the murders, she made big eyes at him, saying only, "We can hardly talk about that, Mr Chapel, with my poor cousin across the table."

Unfortunately, James Frensham heard this, and leaned over to her. "Your poor cousin," he said, "would be only too glad to talk about the murders. Or, rather, to hear someone talk about them. What is this conspiracy of silence anyway?" His voice was rising. "My father is dead. Murdered. And no one does anything. No one says anything."

"Not even the local paper." Michael spoke up from what passed as the bottom of the oval table.

"And what do you mean by that?" The handsome face closed into a formidable frown.

"What I say. It takes a great many people to make a conspiracy. Of silence, or of anything else."

"Time for us ladies to leave the gentlemen to their talk." Alix put down her coffee cup and spoke into a little, uncomfortable hush. "Anne?"

"Yes." Rising, Anne was aware of both the Prince and James Frensham trying to speak to her, but ignored them. "Alix," she said as they left the room together, liveried servants bowing to right and left. "Would you think me intolerably rude if I asked to go home early?"

"I'd think you very sensible." Alix laughed. "Between my father and my passionate suitor, I'm afraid you've had a hard time of it, but how else could I arrange the table?" She raised her voice as the other women followed them into her drawing room. "I am so sorry you don't feel well, Miss Paget but, of course, tomorrow's rehearsal must come first. Fritz!"

"Yes, Your Highness?" The man at the door moved forward and Anne saw, without pleasure, that he was the one who had taken Josef's place at the hostel desk the week before. Alix gave him her orders in rapid Liss, then turned back to her. "I've asked him to fetch Michael," she said. "He'll see you home."

"Thanks." What had begun as an excuse had swiftly become the truth. The difficult dinner on top of a hard day's rehearsal had left her exhausted, and, with exhaustion, inevitably came the first twinge of pain.

"You *do* look tired, poor love. " Hilde Bernz joined her, all solicitude. "I hope Michael has at least been provided with a comfortable car for you."

"Oh, I think so," Anne said vaguely, and got a sharp, enquiring look.

"You didn't notice, coming?" asked Frau Bernz. "Michael must be more entertaining than I thought. Telling you about his time at Oxford, was he?" Her tone made it clear that she did not believe he had ever been there. "Fascinating story, I have no doubt." She turned as Michael reappeared. "What was your subject at college?"

"Philosophy." He gave her his most charming smile. "And now, if you will excuse us, I must snatch away our Cinderella." He opened a door masked by tapestry.

"But I haven't said goodbye to the Princess."

"Can't help that. The men are just moving, and if there's one thing we can do without right now it's a stand-up row between our Rudolf and young Frensham about who takes

130

you home. And those two journalists watching all agog and asking casual, clever questions on the side." He took her fur coat from a servant, helped her into it, and gave her shoulders a quick, approving squeeze. "Sensible girl, aren't you, to see trouble coming and get the hell out. But—" His glance seemed to sum her up. "You're really tired?"

"A little. It wasn't exactly an easy evening. I feel bad about Alix."

"She can cope. She's trained to it. And, mind you, it could be a little awkward for Frensham to make too much of a row in front of her."

"I should say." Anne laughed. "Extraordinary man. She'll never have him, will she, Michael?"

"It would be tidy," he said, as they started down a long flight of stairs. "Dynastic, you know. If the opera's not a success, he looks like ending up pretty well owning Lissenberg."

"Yes, but she'd never, surely? Besides, I don't quite understand. Michael, is she the heiress? It's the oddest thing, but nobody talks about that. And—what's Salic law? I thought it was something in Shakespeare."

"Full marks." Cheerfully. "It is. And clever Mr Jarrold's been given the wrong end of the stick by someone. We don't go much on answering impertinent questions here in Lissenberg, as he seems to be learning."

"May I ask one?"

"It won't be impertinent."

"What is the law of succession here, if it's not Salic?"

"Pretty modern, I'd say. And why not? Late eighteenth century enlightenment, and all that. When the original Prince took over, his eldest son was already established as a rich plantation owner in the States. Then came twins. I don't know whether that had anything to do with it, or whether the Prince was just progressive, but he and his Diet drew up a constitution that said the succession should be always elective among the direct heirs of the dead Prince."

"Goodness. Elected by whom?"

"Oh, the Diet, of course. The comic thing was, they forgot to say heirs male. The opposite of Salic law in fact."

"So Alix could succeed?"

"No reason in the world why not. Here we are." They had reached the bottom of the stairs and two footmen threw open double doors and ushered them out into a courtyard where one of the familiar green police cars stood waiting. "I thought we'd go back the other way," he explained, helping her in. "Do you know your Kipling?"

"Yes, but I'm surprised you do."

"It wasn't all philosophy at Oxford." He slid under the steering wheel. "I'm really quite educated. Or—" he switched on the ignition—"Did you catch Frau Bernz's slight case of doubt? To add to your other problems." His tone took her back to their conversation in the underground passage.

"I don't understamd a thing about you," she said almost angrily. "What in the world did the Prince mean by saying you don't exist?"

"He said that, did he?" Michael sounded amused. "How about coming up to the Wild Man with me and letting me prove I do?"

"Oh, Michael, I really am tired. I'm sorry..."

"So am I." He swung the car off the main road on to the one that led to the opera complex. "When this opera's over you and I are going to go dancing together and keep it up all night."

"Lovely." But the pain was savage by now, and she knew it did not sound convincing.

"You certainly do think I'm up to the elbows in blood and thunder." His tone was dry. "Pity. I'd hoped you might trust me a little."

"Oh, Michael, I *want* to." So many questions she wanted to ask, but he would only parry them as he had the one about the Prince. Anyway, he was now driving too fast for speech. When he pulled up at last with a scream of brakes outside the hostel, she put out a pleading hand to hold him for a moment, to try to say something.

He did not notice. "What's up?" He was looking away from her, to where someone was hurrying towards them down the hostel steps, a dark figure against the light from the open doors, revealing himself finally as Josef as he came round to Anne's side of the car.

He opened her door. "In, quick!" he said. "Run, child!"

Anne obediently lifted velvet skirts and ran up the steps to where the big hostel doors stood wide. Herr Winkler was waiting there, grim-faced, something under his arm. "Good." He hardly moved to let her pass and she realised that he was covering the steps with some kind of gun. She watched anxiously as Michael and Josef raced up the steps together.

Once they were in, Winkler slammed the big doors behind them and turned at once to Michael. "No trouble?" he asked.

"None. What's going on?" Michael's quick glance took in the crowded foyer, where members of the chorus stood huddled in groups, whispering to each other.

"We've had a flood," said Josef, and Anne saw that the bottoms of his trousers were soaking wet.

"A flood?" Michael looked from Josef to Winkler.

"I always said it was crazy." Josef ran a hand through untidy white hair. "Moving the stream for the opera complex. I seem to have been right. Something gave, tonight. Just a little while ago. The stream broke through and flooded the lower tunnel."

Michael and Anne exchanged one quick glance. "How deep was the tunnel flooded?" he asked.

"Totally. At the lowest point. Lucky you didn't come back that way." The telephone rang and he crossed to the desk to answer it. "Ah—" He handed the receiver to Winkler. "They've found where the stream was blocked. They're clearing it now."

"Good." Winkler spoke briefly and put the receiver down, then picked it up as the bell rang again. "Winkler here." And then, "No, safe here, thank God. No, stay where you are. Tomorrow will be time enough." He put the receiver down and looked at Michael. "That was Hans. Were you thinking of going up to the Wild Man?"

"Yes. But Anne was too tired."

"Thank God. There's been a landslide across the road. Ten minutes ago. I think perhaps you had better spend the night here."

"I propose to," said Michael. "I take it we all will. There must be plenty to do in the opera house."

"It's not the opera house," said Winkler. "That's our one bit of luck. The water came through the rehearsal room, not the opera house itself. It's that little bit lower, of course. But let's go and see how bad it is."

"Yes, indeed," agreed Josef. "But first—" he turned to Anne—"bed for you, there's a good child. Tomorrow's another day."

"She ought to have something," said Michael. "Hot milk?"

"It's waiting in her room. Lisel is there seeing to things."

"Oh, thank you, Josef." Anne turned to him, tears in her eyes. "You think of everything."

"Dear child, for you, who would not?" He bent down—why had she never realised how tall he was?—and kissed her, very gently, on the forehead. "Now, sleep well, and be ready

133

to work in the morning. We'll have somewhere for a rehearsal if we work all night."

"You'll be careful? You and Michael? You won't go exploring the tunnel before the water is out?"

"We have to check the locks," he told her. "But yes, we'll be careful."

"Michael!" She must explain, say something—tell him she could not help trusting him—before he went down to risk his life in that dark, flooded tunnel.

"Be good!" He turned, raised a mocking hand in salute, then followed Josef into his office, whence the stair led down to the tunnel. Choking back tears of frustration, Anne was suddenly aware of Gertrud at the back of the lobby watching her speculatively. With hostility? Why?

It was suddenly the last straw. With hasty goodnights all round, she fled for the safety of her room and the comfort of Lisel's friendly presence. All the time Michael's last, mocking words rang in her head: Be good. She had suspected him, shown that she suspected him, and he had done nothing to explain, to help her to understand; he had merely accused her of lack of trust. But how could she trust him?

"Lisel?"

"*Ja, mein Fräulein?*" the reply, in Lisel's Liss-accented German, was in itself a reminder of how useless it would be to ask her about Michael. Besides, more and more she was aware of a curious conspiracy, a kind of web of silence woven round him. "He does not exist," the Prince had said. "Poison," Carl had called him. "Where he is, there's trouble." Who had said that? But tonight's threat had surely been against him. Or her? When Lisel said goodnight and left, she did not need to remind Anne to put up the chains on her doors.

Next morning the note on Anne's breakfast tray told her that rehearsal would start half an hour later than usual. "To give time for repairs in the theatre." Nothing else. If anything more had happened, any new disaster, surely she would have been told?

She dressed quickly, resisting the temptation to telephone Josef, who must have enough on his hands as it was. Downstairs, the entire cast of *Regulus* seemed to be assembled in the foyer of the hostel, all talking at once and some of them reading copies of the *Lissenberger Zeitung*.

"We made the paper at last." Adolf Stern showed her his copy of the paper, with its huge black heading.

"Opera what?" she asked. "I don't read German script, bother it."

"You could call it 'jinxed', I suppose. Now they are talking about it at last, they've put a lot of things together and left the reader to draw his own conclusions. It makes a fairly melodramatic story," he went on in his precise English. "Perhaps you are fortunate not to be able to read it. The world press is bound to pick it up. Exactly the kind of publicity we do not wish. By the time the scandal press has finished with us, it will sound as if the audience were liable to be drowned."

"As well they may be," said Hilde Bernz. "Have you seen the rehearsal room?"

"No?"

"It's a disaster area. They won't have it ready for the opening, however they try."

"No," Stern agreed. "A pity about the conducted tours, but think how much worse if it had been the opera house itself."

"Which was doubtless what was intended," said Hilde Bernz darkly. "How do we know that there will not be another flood, during the performance, and this time on to us? I've always said that stage was a death trap. If we had any sense, we would throw up our parts *en masse*."

"You don't mean it," said Anne.

"No." Shrugging. "I suppose I don't." She looked at her watch. "Time for rehearsal, God help us."

The opera house smelled strongly of damp and paint, since water had seeped down around the huge skylight that lay between the helicopter launching pad and the cliff, and workmen had been busy all night repairing the damage. Carl Meyer, waiting on the stage, made a short, vigorous speech. There had been an attempt at sabotage, he told them. The stream had been deliberately blocked. "Someone does not wish our opera to succeed. I promise you, my friends, that every precaution has been taken. Herr Winkler has asked for reinforcements from our friends the Italians. His police and their assistants will be on duty above and around the whole complex from now until when the season is safely over. There is not the slightest danger to anyone, except that of losing our nerve. My friends, this had made me very angry, and I hope it has you, too. It is not just the threat to Beethoven's great opera. Think, for a moment, I beg you, of what a failure here would do to the peace conference. You are all young; you do not remember war, but there are those of us here who do. Is it asking too much to ask that you, the young

135

ones, who have the chance to help, will throw your hearts into making this opera something the world will remember, with blessings? Now, no more talk. We begin."

"My God," said Anne to Hilde Bernz later that afternoon. "It's working...it's coming."

"At last," said Hilde. "With—what is that English phrase of yours?—with blood, and sweat, and tears. Well." She shrugged. "The eyes of the world are upon us now. I'm worried about young Gertrud, though."

"Yes." Gertrud had inexplicably burst into tears over a slight rebuke from Falinieri. "She's singing marvellously, but there's something wrong, just the same," Anne went on. "It's curious how one can feel it, in a small cast like this. I wish you'd try and find out what's the matter, Hilde. She doesn't seem to like me much anymore."

"Jealous," said Hilde. "She's seen Prince Rudolf's press release, too. Pity, really. Are you looking forward to being the great new star, Anne?"

"Don't," said Anne. "For God's sake don't. We're jinxed enough as it is."

"*Bitte*?"

For once, Hilde's English failed her, but they were interrupted by Carl, announcing that their brief rest was over. "We will now take the last scene, ladies and gentlemen, and you will imagine your audience reaching for its pocket-handkerchief."

11

Thursday's rehearsal went even better, and at the end of Friday's Falinieri thanked them with tears in his eyes. "It will do, I think." He held out a hand to Carl.

"I think so too." Carl looked both exhausted and jubilant as he turned to face the cast, still grouped onstage in their final positions. "I thank you all, from my heart. This has been a day to remember. Tomorrow: the dress rehearsal. And today—I should warn you—while you have been at work here, the world has come to Lissenberg. We are news, my friends, which is good or bad as you make it. I do beg you to be careful what you do or say from now on. Imagine that everyone you meet is a journalist, and you won't be far wrong. We want a real success, not a scandalous one."

Since a light lunch had been provided in the greenroom, the cast had not been out in the cloisters all day. The difference, now, was extraordinary. Down to the left, lights blazed from the hotel—fully open at last, with conference delegates and journalists pouring in. Cars were drawing up outside it all the time, letting down their passengers, then swinging round, past the steps of the opera house and so down by the hostel and away.

Hilde and Anne paused for a moment, looking down the valley. "They were right to turn it into a one-way system," said Hilde. "I thought it was crazy, but just look..."

Adolf Stern joined them to stare gloomily at the crowded road. "We aren't going to get a lot of sleep tonight. Those of us whose rooms look out this way." This with a reproachful glance for Anne, whose bedroom faced away from the valley.

"Sleep?" Dark circles had carved themselves deep under Gertrud's eyes. "What's that?"

Reaching the hostel, Anne paused at the desk. "Josef."

"Yes?" He turned to her with a harassed backwards glance at the switchboard where lights flickered angrily.

"I wish you'd ask Dr Hirsch to come over. No, not for me, though I'd be glad to see him. But—" she looked quickly over her shoulder, but no one was within earshot— "I think he ought to see Fräulein Stock. Maybe a kind of check-up on the cast? We've been at it pretty hard these last few days."

"Who hasn't! But, yes, I'll see if I can fix something. I'll say it's for you, if you don't mind." He turned away to the switchboard, leaving her both disappointed and puzzled. She had hoped for a chance at a casual question about Michael, from whom she had heard nothing since the night of the flood. It was horrible to have the cloud of suspicion still heavy between them—but, looking back, she could not tell herself that he had said anything to clear it. All very well to ask her to trust him. She longed to, if he would only help her, explain, come to see her...

"I'm glad you sent for me," Dr Hirsch told her as he went through the familiar routine of pulse, blood pressure, temperature. "I've given Fräulein Stock something to help her sleep. She should have asked for it sooner. This has been a hard time for everyone, but I'm glad to say you seem to be thriving on it. How's the pain?"

137

"Do you know, I seem to have been too busy to notice it. It scares me a bit. Once or twice before, it has happened like this—disappeared for a while, then back worse than ever. Suppose that were to happen tomorrow? Or on the first night?"

"Why should it? Don't expect it; don't think of it. And, if it should come, you've got the pills I gave you. Take two if necessary, but not more. They're a new blend of mine. I'm not too sure about side effects."

"Side effects?"

"Very unlikely. And nothing that would affect your singing." A shadow crossed the still face. "Of course there is a risk that they might be habit-forming."

She was actually laughing. "Dear Dr Hirsch, how many habits can one form in six months? All I ask is that I get through the next two weeks without disaster. After that, who cares?" And yet, was that true now? In London it certainly had been. Looking back, there was nothing about that life that could not have been left, with—what was the phrase?— *a gay goodnight and swiftly turn away.* But now—now everything was different. She was amazed, and ashamed, to find her eyes full of tears. "Dr Hirsch, I don't want to die."

"I should think not indeed. Frankly, that's the most encouraging thing you've said to me yet. You didn't much care, did you, when you got here? That's why you were—tempted, the other night."

"That's just it." As always, his quick understanding warmed her heart.

"Good." He was repacking his bag. "Do you sleep?"

"Mostly. I'm so *tired.* I don't think I've ever been so tired in my life. And, besides, the air here's so delicious."

"Long may it remain so."

"What do you mean?"

"Have you thought what would happen if Lissenberg went bankrupt and young Frensham took over? I don't know whether he'd have all these buildings down, or just dig his mine under them, or what—but of one thing I'm sure—he'd have that szilenite out and up for sale. Oh, he's been keeping quiet, while the excitement of the opera and the conference lasts, but afterwards, when it's all over...that's going to be another story. I just hope *Regulus* has the resounding success it deserves—otherwise...Well, old Frensham came here to foreclose, you know. Of course, it will take some time to settle his estate, but once that's done, I can see his son turning

Lissenberg into one big industrial site. A rural slum, with all its sounds and smells."

"Horrible. This entrancing valley, these kind people. Tell me it won't happen."

"Sing like an angel at the dress rehearsal tomorrow—not to mention the first night—and maybe it won't. It will be harder for young Frensham with the world's eyes focussed on Lissenberg. Did you know the dress rehearsal had turned into a kind of preview?"

"Gracious, no. Why?"

"Because of all the publicity. You could say Prince Rudolf has been too successful. Twice as many journalists have come as were expected—gossip columnists as well as critics—and most of the foreign delegates are bringing extra staff members. Naturally, they all expect seats for the opera. So—chaos at the box office."

"I thought it was sold out already. The first night."

"So it was. They began by going through the lists, asking locals to give way to visitors. It's caused quite a bit of hard feeling. And wasn't nearly enough anyway. So—be prepared for a crowded theatre tomorrow."

"Full?"

"Packed. Well, you wouldn't want it half full, would you?"

"No. Do the others know?"

"Carl Meyer made an announcement over dinner. And asked them all to stay home tonight. Relieved to do it, I think. The hotel's a madhouse, with the conference delegates arriving and all the extra guests. They've had to reopen a couple of hotels in the town that had closed because of the new one. They've put the orchestra down there. So—chaos there too. You can't get a table in a restaurant without bribery and corruption, and tempers are rising all over. Lissenberg's just not equipped to cope, and people don't like it."

"People?"

"The old guard. The natives who liked Lissenberg the way it was." He sighed and rose to his feet. "Frankly, dear child, I hardly know what to wish for. It begins to look as if the Lissenberg I love was doomed either way. If the opera succeeds, we're going to drown in tourism and Prince Rudolf's plastic gimcrackery; if it fails, we'll be one giant factory, and a threat to the world as well."

"Then it had better succeed." Anne had a sudden, vivid sense of the plastics workshop with all its sounds and smells.

"You're right. So—no worrying, sleep well; good luck for

139

tomorrow. I shall be there, by the way, both tomorrow and Monday, in my professional capacity."

"I'm glad. But I hope you won't be needed."

"So do I." He smiled his painful smile. "You're feeling better."

"Yes. I don't think this is a time to be feeling anything else."

"Then to bed with you. A good book and an early night. I'll tell Josef not to let them put calls through, shall I?"

"Yes, please. Unless it's urgent. Or—" Angrily, she felt herself blush. "Or Michael," she longed to say, but could not—would not let herself.

Next morning's note was short and to the point. "Costume call, eleven a.m.," it read. "The dress rehearsal at five is now a preview. Good luck to us all." Anne smiled to herself and poured coffee. Dr Hirsch had done her good. Despite the gnawing misery of her misunderstanding with Michael, she had slept soundly and felt, amazingly, well this morning—ready for anything. I shall enjoy my two weeks of hard work and glory, she thought. Make the most of them while they last. After all, what else mattered?

A tap at the door announced Lisel, with her arms full of flowers and a reproachful shake of her head over the chain that Anne had not replaced.

Anne smiled at her. "Goodness, what beautiful flowers." Lisel was depositing them, carefully, spray after spray, on the bed.

"*Schön.*" Lisel nodded. "I come back with"—her hands sketched the shape of a vase. "And, Herr Josef say"—she wrinkled her brow, trying to remember the message—"stay here, *bitte*?" She broke into Liss and was obviously describing a state of confusion downstairs. Much, much *Menschen*, she concluded. And then with a wry face, "*Journalisten. Tchah.*" Bringing the vase a few minutes later, she indicated firmly that Anne should chain the door after her.

The flowers were an orgy. An immense, ornate florist's extravagance with Prince Rudolf's card, "To our prima donna," and the bold signature "Rudolf, P." A rival bouquet from James Frensham; red roses from Alix, white from Carl, and, finally, hidden by the others, a tiny nosegay of sweet-scented violets, which she knew at once were from Michael. She would have known his handwriting anywhere. And that

140

was odd, as she had never seen it. And all it said, was "Anne." The least he could do?

At five to eleven the telephone rang. "Good morning." Josef sounded harassed, as well he might. "The cast are assembling now, to go up to the opera house together. If you would join them downstairs?"

"At once." Anne swung on her fur jacket, tucked the violets in its buttonhole and hurried downstairs, meeting Adolf Stern on the way.

He looked angry. "One might as well be back at boarding school. Do you know they actually refused to let me go out last night? That Josef! I'm going to make a complaint about him today. Anyone would think he was a hereditary prince himself. Or a twopenny-halfpenny local Führer."

"Your English is very good," said Anne.

"I should hope so. Look at that!" They had rounded the bend of the stairs to see the rest of the cast assembled in the lobby. "A Sunday-school outing."

"Well, there have been three murders, remember. And that flood wasn't exactly funny."

He snorted with angry laughter. "Awkward to lose a principal now. But, ask me, it's more that they don't want us talking to the press. Telling of the treatment we've had. Confined to the hostel indeed! I shall have a thing or two to say when I do get interviewed. *And* I want my contract changed. Yours should be, too—mind you see it is. This dress rehearsal must be paid as a performance, since they've turned it into a preview without even consulting us. Good morning." He turned his anger on Josef, who was waiting for them at the foot of the stairs. "Have we your gracious permission to proceed?"

"Now you are all here." Josef was consulting a typed list. "Yes. Thank you for your cooperation, Herr Stern, Miss Paget." His smile was warm for her. "If you will please to keep with the others, and hurry? I am afraid there is a crowd out there, waiting for you. They got inside this morning; we had some trouble clearing the lobby, and I'm afraid we're not very popular as a result."

"*Quatsch!*" Stern broke into basic German. "So stupid," he concluded. "They're only journalists trying to do their job, Herr—" But Josef had hurried away to marshal the front of the procession. Stern turned angrily to Anne. "What the hell *is* his other name?"

"Do you know," she told him, "I've never heard it."

141

Or Michael's either, she thought, following the rather subdued procession out of the big bronze doors into a soft, spring morning, and the flashing of dozens of cameras. Police had cordoned off the far side of the arcade, but behind them was a milling crowd of journalists and photographers. She turned to Stern. "I don't know about you, but I think I'm glad of some protection. I feel a bit like a Christian sacrifice as it is."

"Nonsense," he said. "If you're going to be a star, you've got to learn how to cope." He threw out his chest, enjoying every moment of it, and took her arm to escort her up the cloister, thus effectively interposing himself between her and the photographers.

The wardrobe mistress, Mrs Riley herself, was awaiting Anne in her dressing-room. "I noticed yesterday that you'd lost some weight," she said abruptly. "I've had the tunic taken in a little. I'd just like to see ... I wish to God we'd had more costume rehearsals." She was helping Anne out of her fur jacket. "Crazy to have so few. You'll be all right; your tunic's short, but the chorus! And shuffling about in the dark, the way they have to. All the Prince's doing, of course, making me cut costs on their togas. Was it my fault that they crumpled and marked every time they wore them?"

"Of course not." Anne pulled her own tunic over her head and adjusted its folds. Like the other Romans, she was dressed in white, while the Carthaginians wore deep crimson. It had become obvious, the first time they rehearsed in costume, that the Roman white was going to be a problem, since it showed every mark and crease. As the whole production was planned in terms of contrasting blocks of crimson and white, Mrs Riley's suggestion that she dye the costumes had been met with contumely, and the solution had been to keep dress rehearsals to a dangerous minimum.

"And now look at us." Mrs Riley went on grumbling as she adjusted Anne's tunic. "Half the world press here this afternoon, and I bet you one of the Roman matrons falls over her own skirts. Oh well, you're perfect, thank God." She handed Anne the breastplate and helmet she wore for her first entrance, with Regulus, just home from Carthage. "I took in the straps of the breastplate too," she said. "Don't lose any more weight, there's a dear, or I'll have to get you a new one, and I'm way over my budget already. *And* all the seats today are complimentary ones, so that will be no help! If you ask me"—she lowered her voice—"Prince Rudolf is off

142

is head. We've not paid a bill for the past two weeks, and all the local ones have come in for the second time. They were to be pacified, the local tradesmen, with first night tickets. Now they've been switched to this afternoon. I do hope they'll make a decent audience for you, Miss Paget. Oh!" she put her hand to her mouth, "I wasn't supposed to say, about the bills—you won't mention it, will you? Only, if there was trouble this afternoon, I wouldn't want you thinking it was your fault."

"Trouble?"

"There've been some pretty tough letters coming with the final demands. *And* talk downtown—I'm staying in Lissenberg, you know—" She stopped. "I oughtn't to be telling you this."

"I think you should. But—quickly."

"A demonstration of some kind. They've put most of the shopkeepers in those side-galleries almost over the stage. If they chose to throw things...unpaid bills, they said, but it might be worse."

"Oh, my God," said Anne.

"I *shouldn't* have told you!"

"Oh, yes, you should." She took the wall telephone off its hook. "*Herr Meyer, bitte.*" And then, "Carl, I know you're busy, but could you come to my dressing-room for two minutes? Thanks." She turned back to Mrs Riley. "And thank *you*. Now, off with you, and I won't say who told me."

"We *can't* search the audience," Carl protested.

"Why not? Remember the peace conference, Carl. I don't think you can *not*!"

"Oh, routine, of course. Metal detectors. Naturally that's been laid on. But—that won't spot rotten eggs or soft tomatoes—or unpaid bills, for the matter of that."

"I could wring Prince Rudolf's neck," said Anne.

"Yes, but it's a bit late in the day." He glanced anxiously around as if he thought the dressing-room might be bugged—and, really, Anne thought, by now anything seemed possible.

"When do I get paid?" she asked. So far, it had not been important that the advance promised under her contract had not been forthcoming. Now, suddenly, it was.

Carl looked at her with something approaching dislike. "That's just what Herr Stern has been asking," he told her. "*And* he wants extra for today."

"Well, dear Carl, of course. Look, we need Michael. He

knows everyone in Lissenberg, doesn't he? Would be able to get in touch with the angriest of the tradesmen? The ones who might really demonstrate."

"I suppose so. But what could he tell them?"

"That I care so much for Lissenberg, and"—she smiled at him—"for Beethoven, that I would like their bills to be paid before I get anything."

"But, Anne—"

"No buts." What an amazing advantage it was to have only six months to live. Perhaps she would die in less comfort as a result of what she was doing, but what comfort is there, anyway, about dying? "I mean it, Carl. Now, please, go and get working on it. I will not have this opera, and the peace conference, wrecked on Prince Rudolf's idiotic meanness." Suddenly furious, she remembered that vast bouquet he had sent her. "He doesn't deserve to rule," she said. Her telephone rang and she picked the receiver off its hook. "Yes?"

"All cast onstage, Miss Paget. And"—anxiously—"is Herr Meyer there, perhaps?"

"Yes. We'll be right there." She heard the audible sigh of relief and thought: we're all tense to breaking point. "You must do it, Carl. Straight after the costume call."

"But Annchen, can you afford it?"

"I must. Anyway, think what a difference the success or failure of this opera will make to me. Carl, I've made up my mind. You'll do it?"

"Oh, yes, I'll do it, and God bless you." But he looked miserable. "I only wish I could afford..."

"Nonsense." She suddenly thought how oddly they had played this scene. Usually, when they were together, he made some pretence—she never felt it as more than that—at being devoted to her. This time he had entirely forgotten to do so. She reached out impulsively and took his hand. "Dear Carl, you're a good friend to me. Now, how about this costume call?"

It went better than she had feared. She suspected, correctly, as it turned out, that Mrs Riley had taken a couple of inches off the chorus' togas without consulting anyone, and this made a great difference when it came to climbing the shelving flights of steps that rose from each side of the main stage. Carl had simplified their movements as much as possible at Friday's rehearsal, when he had announced they would stay onstage throughout the opera, but from time to time either crimson Carthaginians or white Romans had to come down the steps to make a dramatic background for a scene between contrasting soloists, and then get back into position as the stage was blacked out. He took them through these movements now and it all went smoothly. At last, satisfied, he looked at his watch.

"Time to go and rest," he said. "A light lunch is being served in the hostel at one. I do beg you will all go straight back there and stay. Herr Winkler has made a particular point of this. His men have all they can cope with on their hands already. I believe he has had to beg even more help from the Italians. So, if you will very kindly go back down the arcade in a body as you came, it will be a help to everyone."

There were a few grumbles, but when they did emerge, *en masse*, the good sense of the arrangement was obvious. The green meadow that lay between the two wings of the opera complex was now black with people. The crowd had been concentrating on the arrivals of conference delegates at the hotel, but it changed direction when the cast appeared under the great portico of the opera house, and surged forward across trampled grass to give them a friendly cheer. The morning's foot policemen had been replaced by mounted ones, who seemed to be on amicable terms with the crowd. It was a pleasant scene, in the kind spring sunshine, with here and there a family contentedly picnicking beside the stream that ran down the middle of the valley.

"If it's like this now, what about later on!" grumbled Adolf Stern. "Ask me, this place is about a badly designed as you could get. Lunatic that we have to come outside at all between the hostel and the opera house."

"I suppose no one expected such crowds." Anne was thinking of the sinister corridor that ran under the buildings. Would they be reduced to using it? She very much hoped not. Not after that flood.

She felt a coward, but had her lunch sent up to her room, hoping against reason that Michael might telephone, to wish her luck, to say he understood, to explain ... Absurd hope. He was doubtless fully occupied trying to pacify the angry tradesmen of Lissenberg. What a fool Prince Rudolf was, she thought, settling herself on her bed, to put so much work into his project and then risk it all for a few unpaid bills.

And yet the morning crowd had seemed cheerful and friendly enough. So did the still thicker one that greeted them when they emerged after lunch to go up for the long,

145

careful business of costume and makeup. There was no room now for picnickers; the crowd was packed solid, standing, on either side of the stream. Anne turned to Hilde Bernz. "I wouldn't have thought there were this many people in Lissenberg."

"There aren't," said Frau Bernz. "Buses have been bringing them in all morning. From God knows where. We're news."

"And this is only the preview." Anne looked anxiously across the crowded valley. "What will it be like on Monday?"

"I hate to think." Adolf Stern joined them. "And I wish I knew where all these people were going to spend the night. If they're meaning to camp, I shan't get a moment's sleep. You're lucky to be in the guest's suite, Miss Paget."

"Yes, I do hope they go home when the dress rehearsal is over."

"Why should they?" Stern was determined to make the worst of things. "Weather like this, they can sleep out well enough. And God knows there's not room for a midget in town. A friend of mine telephoned a while ago to ask for help. His paper sent him here at the last minute, and of course he's got nowhere to stay. And would that Josef let him come and sleep in my room? No, sir, he would not."

"Well," said Anne reasonably. "It would be a bit of a thing to have a journalist right here in our midst. Ah, here we go." She was glad that the general move gave her the chance to move away from Stern and his grumbling.

In her dressing-room she found a scribbled note from Carl. "I talked to Michael. He sends his thanks." No word from Michael himself, and his violets were beginning to wilt.

Would he be in the audience, she wondered, starting to change. During the costume call that morning she had looked up at the galleries to left and right of the stage, and thought how very unpleasant people in them could make it for the actors, if they should want to. She was almost beginning to agree with Stern about the design of the opera house. But then, who could have expected all this offstage drama?

At least, she thought, costumed and made up at last, the general tension had left little room for individual stagefright. She herself ought to be down in the greenroom now, sharing this time of tension with the rest of the cast. Marcus, page to Regulus. The chance of a lifetime. A deathtime. *Don't think of that.* She adjusted her helmet, smiled at herself in the encouraging glass, and went down to join the others.

Since the vast stage had no curtain, there were various vantage points from which the auditorium could be seen. "It's packed already," reported Carl Meyer, ten minutes before the last call. "And Michael says, don't worry. He is in the right-hand gallery, and Josef on the left, just in case, but he seems to think all's well. We're a romantic lot here in Lissenberg; a gesture like yours is bound to have a great effect. He said to tell you you'd never regret it."

"I know I won't." She would not have long in which to do so. Nor want it, if all Michael had for her was gratitude. And yet, she made herself face it at last, she should be glad of this. Michael would be sorry when she died. That would be all. That must be enough.

"You're feeling all right?" Something in her tone had made Carl anxious.

"Stage-fright. Naturally. I'll be fine when we get started."

"That's what they all say. There, the orchestra are tuning up. God, Annchen, I wish I had something to do!"

"You'd better get round to the front of the house," she said. "There must be someone you ought to be welcoming."

"They're all here! No one was chancing being late today. Not with the battle for seats, and the crowd outside. Listen to them." He opened the greenroom door a crack, and behind the tuning of the orchestra she could hear the good-humoured roar of the audience.

"They don't sound as if they were going to throw things," she said.

"Of course they're not. Don't even think about it. You're right, though. I must go round to the front. Annchen, I'm counting on you."

She laughed. "Carl, dear, sound a little more certain when you speak to the press, or you might find you did more harm than good."

"Does it show so? It's my great chance, Anne!"

"I know. But there's always Monday. After all, too good a dress rehearsal is supposed to be unlucky."

"Not when it's a preview with half the world's press present."

"As many as that? Ah, there's the five-minute call," she said with relief. "Good luck to us all, Carl dear."

"Dear Anne, you're a miracle." He took both her hands, kissed them warmly and left.

She must forget Michael, forget everything. She was an idealistic young Roman, doomed to death. And that at least

147

was true. A roar of applause from the audience told her that Falinieri had taken his place on the podium, and then came the miraculous hush as the last, tuning instruments fell silent one by one. As audience, it was almost her favourite moment, the pure anticipation of what was to come. As performer, it left her shivering with a mixture of fear and excitement. She settled her helmet firmly on her head and moved out into the corridor to hear the overture better. The chorus were already in place, offstage, but ready to file on when the opera began; first white-clad Romans from the right, eagerly expecting the return of their hero, Regulus, then, massed against them, the threatening crimson of the Carthaginians, to form a background for her own entry with Regulus.

No need to go down yet, and it was quiet here. Mrs Riley and her assistants were down there checking the chorus for last-minute adjustments. She could listen to the overture in peace. But she must not let it make her cry as it had once or twice when the theme of her last duet with Regulus was introduced, then modulated into her farewell to his daughter Livia. Extraordinary and rather eerie to be so totally alone in the backstage rabbit warren. Or rather sidestage, she thought, remembering that the Roman chorus had had to take their places on the far side of the stage before the theatre had been opened to the audience.

The overture was rising to its climax and she had forgotten even to think of shedding a dangerous tear. Time to go down and join Adolf Stern for their entrance. A whisper from the audience, like wind over a cornfield, greeted the end of the overture and then came the slow, throbbing notes to which the Roman chorus would be beginning to file onstage. She took a deep breath, a diver about to take the plunge, and went down to where Adolf Stern was awaiting her.

12

"Colossal!" Carl had hurried round behind the scenes for the opera's one, long interval. "They're drunk with it. I love you all."

"We love ourselves," said Anne. "It *is* going well, isn't it?"

"Better than I've ever heard you. And not a movement wrong, so far."

"'So far.'" Stern took him up on it. "Why should there be a movement wrong, pray? Are you looking for trouble, Herr Meyer?"

"Of course not. My unlucky turn of speech. I just wanted to say, it's tremendous. You're tremendous. All of you. Beyond anything I had imagined...hoped for. And—one other thing. The press have asked for a photo call after this performance. The stage hands are willing. Well, it suits them. Much more convenient now than after Monday's late show. If you don't mind?" It was addressed to the principals, but the chorus too were all there in the crowded greenroom, since the Romans had filed quietly across the open stage when the auditorium lights went up and the audience turned away at last to push towards the bar.

"My contract only calls for one photo call." Adolf Stern answered the general question.

"This is it," said Carl. "Anything else will be separately negotiated. I do beg you, Herr Stern."

"Disorganisation," said Stern. "We should have been notified sooner. But"—he set his helmet at a jauntier angle—"since you ask it, I think we should agree."

"Yes, indeed," said Anne, and the others joined in.

"*Thank you.*" Carl was sweating with anxiety. "And, then, as you know, there is the reception Prince Rudolf is giving for press and cast after the performance. The valley outside is as crowded as ever. It looks as if people are settling down for the night, and the police do not want to create a disturbance by removing them. So—His Highness asks that you will be so kind as to come straight to the hotel, all together, in costume, so that the police can protect your walk up the arcade."

"We can't go back to the hostel and change?" asked Gertrud.

"I'm afraid not. Your day clothes will be taken back there, and your costumes collected first thing tomorrow. The Prince apologises deeply for any inconvenience, and begs you will recognise that it is entirely due to the brilliance of your performance, on which he congratulates you."

"And no doubt he plans to squeeze some more publicity out of our being in costume," said Adolf Stern, but his voice was drowned by the ringing of a warning bell.

If possible, the second half of the opera went even better than the first. The audience had had time to compare notes, and approve, over drinks in the luxurious foyer. When they filed back into the house, Anne could hear the higher note of expectancy, and knew that, barring disaster, they were safe.

So far there had been no moment when she could even think of looking up at those dangerous side-galleries, but halfway through the last act, Regulus caught her and his daughter Livia in each other's arms—a scene that Anne oddly disliked playing with Gertrud. It was a relief to stand back while Regulus rebuked his daughter. And, since the audience's attention was focussed on Regulus and Livia, it gave her a chance to look quickly up to right and left. The central section of the audience was blacked out, but the two galleries of cut-price seats were dimly illuminated by the stage lights and she could just see their occupants, sitting still as death, apparently riveted by the performance. Impossible to recognise faces, but at least she knew that Michael was there.

The music called her attention back to the stage. Frau Bernz, Regulus' wife, had just made her entrance, and it was time for Anne to join the three others in the quartet that she thought the high point of the opera. Regulus' wife and daughter had recognised at last that nothing would turn him from his resolve to keep his word and go back to Carthage, torture, and certain death. Finally accepting this, his daughter turned to Anne, to Marcus, her lover, and urged that he at least take the path of wisdom and stay in Rome, with her.

"Never." Anne could feel the impact of her cry on the audience. From then on, as the opera rose, stage by triumphant stage, to her final exit with Regulus, and the blood-red Carthaginian chorus closing in behind them, Anne knew that nothing could touch them. The opera was where it should always have been, safe in the eternal canon of music.

Only, at last, taking the first of the many curtain calls Carl had planned, "in case," she found herself thinking again of those side-galleries full of dissatisfied tradesmen, and became, on the thought, aware that they were indeed throwing something. But it was rose petals, crimson and white, not unpaid bills, that came gently fluttering down onto the stage. Smiling, bowing; bowing, smiling, she looked in vain for Michael as the house lights went up at last. Had he not waited for the end?

Even with the house lights on, it began to seem as if the

applause would never stop, but finally the audience began to drift away, and the exhausted, euphoric cast assembled on stage for the long business of picture-taking. By the time the last photographer was satisfied, or rather, when the stage hands and electricians proclaimed that they had had enough and began to leave, it was after eight o'clock—the time when the Prince's reception began. "Lucky we don't have to go back and change," Anne said to Hilde Bernz as they hurried to their dressing-rooms.

"I'll say. Are you going just as you are?"

"I think so. Just pick up my watch and purse. A bit absurd, with the costume, but I can't help it."

"And leave the makeup? It will look pretty frightful close to."

"You're right." Anne sighed. "Besides, I haven't got any theatrical remover back at the hostel. Oh, well, I'll see you."

The dressing-room was full of flowers, and she looked quickly through the cards so as to thank any of the senders who would be at the reception, then began the slow task of removing the expertly applied makeup that turned her from young woman to younger man. She was interrupted by the telephone. "Yes?" she picked it off its hook.

Silence. "Yes?" she said again, and heard breathing— quiet, steady. "What is it?" And then, trying for a German phrase, "*Was ist*?"

Still nothing but that heavy, regular breathing. A crank, of course. She replaced the receiver, and went back to work on her face, only to have the bell ring again. She picked the receiver up, heard the same breathing, replaced and lifted it at once to call the operator. But the connection had not been severed; she got the breathing again. A practical joke, merely. She would ignore it. Her hands had been sticky with makeup remover when she lifted the receiver and as a result it had come off black on them. She washed them quickly in the small basin in the corner of the room and went back to work, ignoring the phone, which had been silent for a while, but now rang again. This was all taking too long. The others would be waiting for her; she was making them all late for the Prince's reception. Her hands were beginning to shake from the long strain of the day. She washed her face, quickly and ruthlessly, then went to the cupboard for her purse and the bag with her own makeup.

Odd. She thought she had left them on the top shelf, above the hanger with her fur jacket. No sign of them there. Des-

151

perate now, she looked quickly on the cupboard floor behind her shoes, but the two bags were not there either. On the chair, then, under her clothes? She could see they were not. Absurd. She could not possibly have lost them in this tiny, bare room. Fighting panic, she looked on the shelf above the basin, knowing all the time that they were not there. The telephone rang again and she picked it up automatically, still looking wildly round the room. "Found your bag yet?" asked the croaking, whispering voice. "Now, listen, you murderess..."

"Murder?" It startled her into a reply, which she knew at once was a mistake.

"How did you do it? Tamper with the steering? Fix the brakes? Or drug their drinks? My little sister never drank. Nor did that husband of yours."

"Robin!" She was shocked into silence. What horror from the past was this?

"Yes, Robin. Your fine husband who seduced my sister; carried her off to England; promised her marriage. I don't care about what you did to him. He deserved everything he got. But my sister; you killed my sister, you..."

She listened, horrified, to the whispered string of obscenities, then slammed down the receiver, pulled her fur jacket from its hanger and hurried out of the room—anywhere to get away from that odious voice from the past and its unspeakable suggestions. In the corridor, she paused. It was all too quiet. Held by that horrible voice, she must have taken longer than she had realised, and the others had all gone on down and would be awaiting her impatiently in the greenroom. She had thought of borrowing makeup from Hilde, but now this seemed a trivial waste of time; she merely longed for the comfort of the company. She hurried along the empty, echoing corridor, past the half open doors of other dressing rooms, and down the steep flight of stairs that led to the greenroom, her apologies ready on her lips.

At the bottom of the stair she stopped dead. Not a sound from the greenroom. Impossible. But it was empty. She hurried across it to the door that led through to the front of the house. Locked. Impossible again. How could they have gone without her? Locked her in? Another way out? From the stage down into the orchestra pit? A climb, but not a difficult one. All some absurd muddle; the result of the long, exhausting day. She almost ran back and through to the huge stage, then stopped at sight of the heavy asbestos safety curtain

152

which was normally only lowered once, during the interval. Now it effectively blocked her escape that way.

Escape? On the thought, the lights went out. She drew in her breath to shout to the one remaining electrician for help, then held it. The electrician's box commanded a total view of the stage. Impossible that whoever was up there was not aware of her presence. He must have blacked her out on purpose. A practical joke? No. She made herself let her breath out quietly . . . steadily. Someone wanted very much to frighten her, and someone was succeeding. Frighten? Hurt? Kill?

"Murderess," the voice had called her. Was the speaker up there now, in the electrician's box, gloating in anticipation of revenge? It was a thought to chill the blood. Almost instinctively, she began to move, in the total darkness—not back towards the greenroom, but out on to the huge stage. The electrician's box was reached by a stair and long corridor from the greenroom. Whoever had been up there would have to come down that way, and in the dark. It gave her a little time.

Now she was moving, foot by cautious foot, down the shelving steps that led to the centre stage. To trip and fall would be fatal. But at last her groping foot found flat boards. She must be standing almost where she had been when she and Regulus sang their final duet. It seemed a million years ago. But she had noticed something, out of the corner of her eye, while they were singing. A tiny shift in the position of the backdrop that suggested the Roman forum if you looked at it from the front of the house. From where she stood, onstage, it was merely a striking mass of colour, but this afternoon she had seen it as different—as faintly out of true. It had made her think, swiftly, while Adolf Stern was singing, of what Michael had told her about the door there leading down to that sinister underground corridor.

Locked? Unlocked? But Michael had told her. The falling of the safety curtain released the lock. She did not at all want to face that grim subterranean corridor alone, and in the dark, but still less did she want to stay here, waiting for . . . For whom? As she asked herself the question, she heard the smallest possible noise from the direction of the greenroom. Someone was coming. Someone in the dark, like her. Coming slowly therefore, not wishing, presumably, to betray himself by using a flashlight. But . . . coming.

They might or might not know about the backstage corridor. Not many people did. And, even if it had a second lock,

153

or a bolt, there might be a recess, somewhere that she could hide. If she could only find it. She had made herself stand still, while these thoughts tumbled through her mind, and now, miraculously, she had her reward. From above, a faint gleam of light. Impossible? No, it was there and, with it, she felt a stirring in the air. Of course. When the performance was over, the skylight between landing pad and stage was usually opened to air the auditorium. There was someone on duty all the time, to close it at the least threat of rain. On duty, unfortunately, outside and above the theatre. No use to her. Except for this blessed hint of light. Moonlight, she thought, shafting in as it rose, and not for long. It made it possible to place herself. She had been a little nearer the centre of the stage than she thought. If she moved straight towards the darker loom in the darkness that had to be the backdrop, she should reach it at about dead centre.

Her sandals—Marcus' sandals—were made of blessedly silent plastic. As she took her first, careful step forwards, she heard another noise, and what sounded like a smothered oath from the direction of the greenroom. Her pursuer did not seem to know the opera house as well as she did. It was an advantage—not much of one, but an advantage just the same. Nor, she began to hope, was he aware that she knew he was there. He? It could be a woman just as well.

Her questing hands found the heavy canvas of the backdrop. She bent down to feel its bottom. Yes, as she had hoped, it hung loose to the stage. She lowered herself, silent as death, to the cold floor and rolled gently underneath.

Behind it, the blackness was absolute, but her groping hand felt the cold rock face. There was just room to stand up between it and the curtain, and she did so, very quietly, and began to feel along the rock, searching for the door. It must be camouflaged to look like rock from the auditorium when no backdrop was used, so she should find it more easily with hands than eyes. Feeling her way, she wished she could remember how Michael had opened the door from Josef's little office. The lower ones had been worked by some kind of dialled device, but not, she thought, that first one on this level. What kind of a lock could be controlled, remotely, by the falling of a safety curtain? And would it be the only one?

She went on silently searching, then stopped, rigid, at a shout from somewhere onstage. "Fräulein Paget?" A man's voice. A stranger's? No, she thought she had heard it, but where...when? "I am so sorry," the voice went on in careful
154

English. "I did not know you were here still. Did I frighten you, turning out the lights?" A thin edge of light showed under the backdrop. He was onstage, then, using a flashlight. "Where are you, Fräulein? We will be very late for His Highness's reception."

At last, when he spoke of His Highness, she recognised the voice. Fritz, the palace servant. So—not the obscene, whispering threatener? How could she be sure? Every instinct kept her quiet. He shouted again, beginning to sound angry. "This is stupid, Fräulein. You are locked in. I can let you out. Where are you hiding?" His voice sounded farther off, as if he was moving away, back towards the greenroom, having swept the stage with his flashlight and seen nothing. Crazy to let him go. No, crazy to trust him. There had been something very dubious about his previous behaviour. And, she remembered suddenly, he had pretended to speak no English. Whether or not his was the threatening voice, he was no friend...And now, at last, her questing hand felt a change in the texture of the wall. Here it was warmer; rugged like rock, but not clammy. Feeling carefully up and down, she found the dividing line, but no hint of a hinge. How would one fit a door into solid rock? If only she had asked Michael more about it.

"Fräulein Paget, this is ridiculous!" Fritz's voice came from farther off still. "I go to turn the lights on. Then I shall find you."

A promise? No, a threat. She traced the width of the door with trembling hands. When the lights went on again, would her feet show below the backdrop? Ah, she could feel hinges this side of the door. So—back to the other, where there must be a fastening of some kind. Up and down, quietly searching in the dark. Nothing at the usual height for a door-knob, but this was no usual door. She made herself pause and think. Imagine the stage without the backdrop. There was no upper circle in the opera house. She did not think many of the audience would be able to see the bottom of the rock wall. So, if one wanted to conceal a fastening, one would set it low.

She knelt down, very carefully not touching the backdrop. How long would it take Fritz to find his way back to the electrician's box in the dark? Not long, since he was now using his flashlight. Anyway, when the lights did come on, there must be no tell-tale bulge in the backdrop.

The wood was rougher at the bottom of the door. She sat back on her heels and went over it desperately pressing,

155

pushing, twisting anything that could be pressed or pulled or twisted. And thought, as she did so, of Prince Rudolf, who had planned the whole tunnel complex. It would be like him to have something at once very simple and very tricky. Press, pull, twist...Had something shifted? No. And in the excitement of thinking it had, she had taken her hands off the door, and must start all over again from the bottom.

And as she did so, the lights came on. A band of light showed under the backdrop and made the darkness of the back wall more absolute. A dim glow, showing through the canvas, suggested it would make a fairly adequate screen—until Fritz looked behind it. "Now I see you," came his voice, triumphant from the electrician's box. "Come out, Fräulein Paget, the game is over. His Highness will be displeased. Let us waste no more time."

He was not triumphant; he was in a cold rage. She resisted the temptation to crawl out from under the backdrop. Besides, how undignified...She would rather die here. Die? And on the thought a shot rang out, appallingly loud in the sensitive opera house. "Just to suggest you hurry," came Fritz's voice. "Next time, Fräulein, I might aim true."

Bluffing, she thought. He did not know where she was. But he had given up all pretence of friendliness. She could hear his footsteps clattering down the iron ladder from the electrician's box. Then, one by one, dressing-room doors slammed. He was carrying out a systematic search now. He would find her soon enough.

All this time she had been continuing the frantic search, both hands moving steadily up the side of the door, feeling, pulling, twisting. She did not even know what right and left hand had been doing, when the door suddenly gave and she almost fell through it. Blackness absolute. There would be stairs down. She must be very careful. But first, she must shut that betraying door. Safe on the other side, breathing fast but quietly, she felt about and found herself on a small platform, walls on either side of the door—rock, of course—and the expected stair going down dangerously soon. Small wonder no-one had ever considered this for theatrical exits and entrances.

There was just room to get behind the door and shut it without falling down the stairs. It shut neatly, and she heard the latch click home. With a bit of luck Fritz would not realise she had got through, even if he did know about the door. Was it soundproofed, she wondered. Probably. And ridiculous to waste time on such imaginings when she ought to be climbing down that dark stair and hoping she could get out at the bottom. Hoping? She remembered how Michael had made her turn her back while he dialled. Had he said that the falling of the curtain unlocked both doors? Anyway, to hope is better than to despair. She moved forward, very cautious in the jet blackness, soft sandals careful on the rough floor, a guiding hand on the wall. And, as she moved, heard, from behind the closed door, the unmistakable, muffled thud of another shot.

Step by careful step, she inched her way down the stair, trying, as she went, to remember how far down Michael had taken her from Josef's office. But those steps had been made of wood, and regular, these were carved from the rock and varied both in height and depth. And it was cold, cold and damp, so that she could feel her own breath damp on her cheek. If she had to stay here long, it would probably kill her. Well, she thought to herself, taking another careful step, one way or another, I do seem due to die.

And do not want to. Not down here, half buried already. Not with Michael still alienated. And not with the ecstatic applause of that last curtain call ringing in her ears. With all the opportunity of *Regulus*, two weeks of pure, hard-working happiness, stretching before her. It was not just for her own safety, her own life that she must fight, but for the opera, for the peace conference, even, which seemed so strangely linked with the opera's success. For Lissenberg and its future. Worth fighting for—all of it—as Dr Hirsch had said. She moved steadily forward, and at last her right foot, feeling for the next step, found floor instead, and her hand, instinctively reaching out to steady her, felt the smooth surface of a door, and felt it, miraculously, shift a little. It opened away from her, showing a glimmer of light. She was looking down the corridor, which stretched away to right and left, faintly illuminated by widely separated lights. Had it been lighted when she first entered it with Michael? She thought not; thought she remembered him switching on the lights, but could not be sure.

Pushing the door shut behind her, she saw with dismay that it had no other form of catch but the curious dial that Michael had known how to use. She must hope that if Fritz should find the door at the top of the stair, the lock on it would hold him, at least for a while. So—she must waste no time. Which way? To the hostel, or to the hotel? Or, perhaps better still—if she could only open the door that masked the

157

walkway—to the castle? Anyway, not the hostel. No one would be there. She turned to the left and moved quickly down the corridor.

And here was a surprise. The next door—the one that led to the castle corridor—was open. Fritz was a palace servant. Had he come down this way? Left it open? If he had, he would be coming after her any minute now. Hurry...hurry...No time to wonder whether it would have been wiser to go on down the corridor and hope to get through the door to the hotel.

And here was the masking door that concealed the entrance to the moving stairway, also standing open. That settled it. Something very odd indeed was going on, and they ought to be told at the palace. She pressed the button and the inner doors slid smoothly open. The walkway lay dark and silent in front of her, and she looked desperately at the levers Michael had used to start it, trying vainly to remember his complicated, swift movements. And, as she did so, the lights went on and the down side of the walkway sprang smoothly into life. Someone must have switched it on from the other end, be coming down from the palace. Who? Friend or enemy? Why was she so sure that this was merely another danger?

Hide. She must hide. There was no possible cover in the corridor. Of that she was certain. So, where? She could hear voices now; two men, words still indistinguishable, but approaching steadily and fast. Only the downward stairway was moving. Swiftly inspecting the other one, she saw that there was a gap between its mechanism and the solid rock underneath. If she lay there, quite flat, quite still? And if someone turned it on? No knowing what would happen. She was on her knees, peering into the dark gap, trying to weigh the chances, when she recognised a voice, much nearer now, James Frensham. "You're sure about the timing? I don't want any more mistakes like that idiotic flood."

A low laugh from the other man. "*And* you'll be at the hotel. No, the timing's safe enough. And the position. *I'm* not the one's been making mistakes, Your Highness."

"Don't call me that!" The raw fury in Frensham's voice sent Anne without further thought into her dark, narrow hiding place. It felt like a grave. Might well be one.

"Set to go off at midnight tomorrow." This was the second voice again, placating. "It seems a pity, really. I enjoyed the

158

show today. Thanks for the ticket." They were very close now, almost overhead.

"It was the only way to get you in." Frensham's voice was almost a growl. "You saw enough? You're sure you can get the explosion localised? Remember, you'll be staying in the hotel too. And I don't want the hostel touched."

"They'll get a bit of shaking. So will we, I expect. No more. I promise you. You hired the best; you've got it. You say the door's dead centre; back of the stage. Perfect." It sounded as if the two men were standing still for a moment. "I know my way now, if this door's open. Are you going back up?"

There was a pause, while Anne lay ice-cold, yet sweating, gazing up at the mechanism above her, wondering what would happen if James Frensham switched it on to go back to the castle.

"No," came his voice at last. "I'd best put in an appearance at Cousin Rudolf's last party." They laughed together and Anne heard the sound of the doors opening and closing again behind them.

She lay where she was, sweating, listening to the silence for a few moments, then made herself crawl out. All well; all silent; the other stairway motionless now, the two men on their different ways down that sinister corridor, Frensham to put in an appearance at "Cousin Rudolf's last party," the other man... Was going to plant a time bomb in the opera house. Set for midnight tomorrow night. A bomb that would destroy the opera house, or at least render it unusable, without affecting the hostel or the hotel. If she could give warning swiftly enough, he might be caught in the act. She bent desperately over the mechanism that worked the stairway. There were instructions, in German, incomprehensible. This lever? That switch? Some combination of the two? Useless.... Desperate, she set herself at last to the long climb, wondering as she did so whether she should not rather have chanced the corridor, the risk of meeting either Frensham or his accomplice...

Too late now to worry about that, or about how she would get into the castle. The door might be open, she must hope, for Frensham's return. But he was staying at the hotel... It was tiring, walking on this unyielding surface that should have been moving under her. She was aware of the endless length of the day, stretching behind her; of exhaustion, and fear. A new fear now. She had lost her pills with her bag. *Don't think of them. Don't start expecting pain.* No time for

159

that, under the twin threats of Fritz's hatred and James Frensham's plot. No wonder she had felt that the opera was threatened from all sides. And why was she so suddenly and blessedly certain that Michael had had nothing to do with it? It might be irrational, but it was a flash of happiness just the same, and brought an upsurge of strength and hope.

She almost tripped. The stairway had begun to move under her feet. Someone had switched it on at the bottom; someone was coming up behind her. She began to run, as silently as she could, remembering how conversation had echoed down the long tunnel. How far had she come? Would whoever was behind her be hurrying? Fritz? Frensham coming back? The explosives expert—his job already finished? She had been tired already; now, running, she fought exhaustion. A stitch in her side hinted at pain, terrifying. Her breath came in gasps, racking, surely audible to her pursuer.

Was she hearing footsteps now, through her own labouring breath, or merely imagining them? But, at last, she saw doors ahead; the other end, the castle—help. Suppose they were locked? She would suppose no such thing. They opened smoothly at her touch. She was in the remembered lower lobby of the castle, two men in uniform starting forward to challenge her. Not castle footmen; two of Herr Winkler's borrowed Italian policemen.

"Thank God," she said, and then, with an effort, in Italian, "You must help me; there is danger."

They had recognised her by now, her costume unmistakable. Their first expression was one of amazement. Then they exchanged one strange, satisfied smile and advanced on her.

13

Pain and cold. Cold and pain. Anne opened her eyes and added a new dimension to the grim catalogue. Cold, and pain, and darkness. She was lying on cold rock; not tied in any way, but stiff in every limb. Establishing this, by moving slightly, brought a blinding climax of pain. Not the old, familiar kind at all, but simple, straightforward pain in the back of her head, where, presumably, one of the "policemen" had hit her.

How long ago? She had no idea. Very carefully, very gently, she lifted her left wrist to her ear and heard her watch still ticking. Pity the dial was not illuminated, but at least, since it ran twenty-four hours and she always wound it in the morning, there must be some time to go before Sunday midnight, when the bomb was timed to go off. And, thinking that, she realised that she must be somewhere behind the stage, tidily put away to be disposed of in the explosion. Since they had not bothered to tie her up, it was a safe assumption that she was helpless here, but she made herself get groggily to her feet just the same, to make sure. After all, they might have thought they had killed her. From the flashing pain that accompanied each movement, they must have got pretty near to doing so. Oddly, she found herself almost welcoming the pain. Why? As, somehow, a sign of life rather than the other, familiar threat of death? Leaning against the wall for support, she felt it cold and rough behind her and made herself go on a slow, staggering exploration of her prison. Movement made her feel deathly sick, and she had to stand still again, fighting it down, refusing to let it happen. If she was to spend her last hours a prisoner in this hole, it should not be in the stink of her own vomit. Breathe . . . hold; breathe . . . hold. That was better.

It was a very small cell. Standing on tiptoe, which hurt, and reaching up, which hurt almost unbearably, she could just feel the roof. The door, wooden and immovable, had what felt like a small grille in it. So, she would not die for lack of air. It might have been comforting if she had anything to eat or drink; if she did not remember, constantly, that midnight bomb. Tears. What a waste of time. And she had none to waste. She brushed them away with an angry wrist and noticed that movement was hurting her less. So—keep moving. There was a pile of something in one corner of the cell, and she made herself investigate it. Odd bits of wood and metal; unrecognisable, and then, a new, unexpected bite of pain as she cut her hand on a sharp edge. It was too much. She almost gave way to the kind of wild sobs that would turn into hysteria; instead, she let herself sink down on the floor and suck the warm blood from the wound.

My only nourishment, she thought, and stiffened at the sound of voices.

"Cold down here." German, a voice she did not know.

161

Coming to rescue her? Coming to kill her? She made herself lie down on the cold rock, slumped as she had found herself. On her back; the bruise on the back of her head agonised against the rock.

More talk; in Liss now, incomprehensible. Then the original voice, apparently in explanation. "The others don't lock."

A gleam of light, filtering through the grille on the door, warned her to close her eyes and lie as inert as possible. She heard a key turn heavily, the door creak open, feet shuffling.

"Finish him off?" asked the German voice.

"Waste of time."

"Suppose the girl comes to?"

"She won't." A casual hand grasped Anne's hair, lifted her head and let it fall back onto the hard rock. As she thought, I must not utter a sound, pain crashed through her, and she plunged into merciful unconsciousness.

"Anne? Are you there? Is it you? Anne?" A trickle of sound reaching her through the black mist of pain. A dream, of course. Wish fulfilment. Michael's voice. "Anne? Are you there: Can you hear me? Anne? It has to be you."

"Why?" asked Anne, with an enormous effort.

And, "Thank God," said Michael.

"I don't know what for." But she did.

"For being together." He said it for her. "Have they hurt you badly?"

"I don't think so. A touch of concussion, perhaps. But pain's—just pain. But you—what have they done to you, Michael?"

"Not too much." His voice belied the words. "But tied me up very efficiently."

"Michael, forgive me?" She could not move yet, but lay, in the heavy darkness, fighting a new wave of nausea.

"Forgive you?"

"For suspecting you . . ."

"Oh, that. Very reasonable. Intelligent girl. Logical. Saw the facts; drew all the right conclusions in all the wrong directions. I was proud of you."

"Thanks." But her eyes were full of tears. "Oh, Michael, I feel better now. I don't mind so much . . ."

"Mind?"

"Dying. Not with you."

"I'd rather live," said Michael. "If it's all the same to you. Are you tied?"

"No. But it hurts to move."

162

"I expect it hurts to die," said Michael.

"It will be quick," she told him. "There's a bomb, going off in the opera house, at midnight on Sunday. Michael! What time is it?"

"So that's it. Clever young Frensham. Unknown saboteur. Trying to wreck the peace conference. How sad for poor little Lissenberg. All that."

"His man called him 'Your Highness.' Michael," she said again, "what time is it? My watch is going but the hands don't illuminate."

"If you want to know that, you'll have to come over here and look at my watch. I'm not just in a position to do so."

"Oh, Michael, are you tied very tight?" She had begun, through the haze of her own pain, to recognise something wrong with his voice.

"You could call it tight," he said. "You don't happen to have a razor on you, I suppose."

She actually found herself laughing a little, painfully. "I'm in costume."

"Dagger?"

"Plastic."

"Pity."

"But, Michael." Feeling the plastic dagger, she had touched the cut on her right hand. "There's something sharp...in a pile of junk in the corner. I cut myself on it."

"Good girl," he said. "Not just lying there. Doing something. Find it again? Without cutting yourself."

"Of course I can." Pain screamed as she pulled herself slowly up the wall to her feet. "I wish it wasn't so dark."

"If it hadn't been," he told her, "they might have noticed you weren't the corpse you seemed. The corpse you sound. Are you sure you're OK?"

"Now you're here." She had been fighting a new spasm of nausea, but this time with far more incentive. She moved towards the sound of his voice, feeling for him in the darkness. "There you are." Keeping her head upright, she crouched down, very slowly, very carefully, fighting the pain, found his forehead and put a loving, gentle hand on it. "Cold," she said. "You're cold."

"I don't know how you tell. So are you. So...let's not waste time. That sharp instrument, if you can find it."

"Yes." The pile had been in the corner near where he was lying. She went through it very carefully this time, moving one unidentifiable object aside before she began cautiously

163

to feel the shape of the next. "Ah," she said at last. "Here it is. But what on earth?" She was pulling the sharp-edged piece of metal out from among the rest of the odd-shaped rubbish.

"Something I forgot to tell you." Michael sounded exhausted now, strength audibly draining from him. "We're in the old torture chanbers. Anything's possible. Now, if you've found it, get cutting. I don't reckon they meant me to last till midnight."

"Michael!" She had thought him lying awkwardly on his side. Now, feeling carefully, she understood why. His hands and feet had been tied together behind him, so that he lay like a tightly strung bow. "Wicked!" she said, and got a low, strained laugh.

"Convenient for carrying," he told her. "But it pulled the rope a bit. You might be able to get at it. Careful, though."

Careful! It was devilish work, there in the cold darkness, pain screaming in her head as she felt for the inch or so of slack rope between the knots that bound his hands to each other and to his feet. Her sharp instrument was conveniently short, but had only a rudimentary sort of handle, so that she cut herself as well as the rope, but Michael had become quiet now, breathing heavily. How long had he been tied like this?

When the rope gave at last, it did so suddenly, and she fell backwards as the tight bow that had been Michael unstrung itself. She lay for a moment, dizzy with the new pain of her head, but his voice revived her.

"That's better," he said. "Thanks. I was really afraid I was going to disgrace myself by fainting. Nice little friends James Frensham has. Did you hurt yourself?" Suddenly anxious.

"A little. I seem to have a genius for hitting my head." She made herself sit up. "What next, Michael?"

"My hands and feet, I'm afraid. They're still tied together. You do my hands, I'll do my feet. Fair division of labour." She heard him moving in the darkness. "Damn them, they've broken my watch, dropping me. We'd best get working if you're up to it."

Impossible to gauge time as she struggled with the thick rope and awkward tool. "Shall I wind my watch?" she paused to ask. "If I don't, and it stops, we'll know it's about eleven in the morning."

"But suppose you don't notice when it stops? Wind it, I think. And good to know we've got over twelve hours to get out of here and give the alarm." His breathing sounded easier and his voice less strained now that the most savage of his bonds had been loosed.

"You sound as if we were going to be able to." She had been refusing to think further than the immediate need to free him.

"Well of course. We've got to, haven't we? Ouch!" Her blade had slipped. "Not to worry, you're doing fine."

"Oh, Michael, I'm sorry. It's just—I'm so cold." She was shivering uncontrollably now, her hands shaking as she worked.

"Then we must certainly get you out of here before you catch your death. Relax a moment, and let's see what I can do." She could feel him straining at the rope. "No, sorry. A bit more...Don't mind cutting me; it's in a good cause." And then, "Are you bleeding too?"

"A bit." She laughed shakily. "A fine mess we'd be in if we could see ourselves."

"Just as well we can't. It might discourage us. Ah!" They had both felt a strand of the taut rope part. "Now let me have a go."

She sat back on her heels, letting the cold and pain have their way with her, then sighed with relief as she heard the rope break. "That's better," he said. "Pass me the blunt instrument, and I'll get to work on my feet." And when he took it: "Good God, no wonder your hands are bleeding."

"It *is* awkward," she agreed. "But it's a bad workman blames his tools."

"Job's comforter, aren't you?"

She could hear the fret of blade against rope as she sat back on her heels, glad to rest for a moment and feel the waves of pain begin to settle. "Michael?"

"Yes?"

"Before we die, I wish you'd explain."

"Explain?"

"About yourself—about what's been going on. How could I help suspecting you when nobody would explain, nobody would answer my questions?"

"They weren't allowed to," he told her. "And, to tell you the truth, I said no, too. Much safer for you not to know."

She surprised herself with a little ghost of a laugh. "Safer? I don't feel just that right now. Except for being with you."

"I'm glad you feel that way too. Ah!" He gave a gasp of triumph as the rope finally snapped. His hand groped to find hers in the darkness. "Anne, I've not dared before; it was too

165

dangerous for you. But you do know, don't you, how much I love you?"

"Do I, Michael? You're such a mystery."

"Oh, that!" Impatiently. "Time enough for that when we *have* some time." His other hand had travelled up to stroke her cheek, very gently. "Dear Anne, don't torment me. If you can, just say you love me."

"I can't help it!"

He laughed and pulled her closer. "Resisting every inch of the way! Then, my darling, give an inch more and say you'll marry me?"

"But, Michael..." Now, at last, tears streamed down her face. She ought to tell him... she must tell him she was dying.

"No buts." His gentle hands held her as his lips found hers. Ecstasy. Despair. But they were doomed anyway; what did it matter? *Gather ye rosebuds while ye may...*

"Rose petals," she said at last. "Red and white. Your idea."

"Naturally. There were some unpaid bills, too, but the chances seemed good no one would notice."

"Oh, Michael, I do love you."

"Then that's settled." He was taking off his jacket, his hands lingering for a moment at the back of her tunic where the blood had clotted. "You're a brave girl," he said.

"Oh, brave... But, Michael, you keep talking as if we could get out."

"Well, of course we can. Do you think I'd have put you to all that trouble for nothing?" He stood up, slowly, shakily, and she realised he had needed the time of that ecstatic kiss to get the circulation moving again in his legs. Should that make her angry? In fact, it warmed her heart.

"Highly programmed, aren't you?" she said.

"I aim to be." His laugh was almost back to normal. "I need to be, if we're to get out of here. It's a long time since I last went this way." He gave the hand he was still holding a little, loving shake, let it go and moved away from her, apparently feeling his way along the wall, away from the door near which he had been so ruthlessly dumped.

"A long time?"

"I used to play here when I was a boy. Foolish of Frensham not to think of that, but then, I don't suppose for a moment that he knows... By the way—"

"Yes?"

"Who attacked you? Brought you here?"

"Police!" She shivered at the memory. "Michael, it was

166

horrible. I thought I was safe. I'd got away—thought I'd got away—from the opera house, up to the castle. The way you took me. And then, in the lobby, two of the Italian policemen..."

"Not policemen," he told her. "Frensham's men. Some kind of Mafia, for a bet. It took me too long to realise. I just hope Winkler has by now. If not..." His voice came from further away as he went on exploring the cell.

"If not?"

"It won't be only the opera house," he said grimly. "Frensham has plans for Lissenberg. You did say, didn't you, back a while, that one of his people called him 'Your Highness'?"

"Yes. He was angry. Frensham."

"Too soon," said Michael. "But it shows what he's planning. We must get moving."

"Moving! But, Michael, how?"

"Ever heard of an *oubliette*? I wish I could remember." And then, moving back towards her. "Of course, stupid of me. Come and help me?" She could hear him shifting the pile of junk in its corner.

"*Oubliette*? Why, yes." She felt her way over and joined him. "*Dove in the Eagle's Nest*. You fell down it."

"Right. Lissenberg had its own line in robber barons in the middle ages. Their castle was above here; handy for the pass and the old ford. There used to be a straight drop from the *oubliette* into the river. Handy if anyone came enquiring too solicitously for one of your guests. I just wish I knew what the opera house architect did about it when he changed the course of the river."

"Did he know it was there?"

"That's another of the things I don't know," he told her cheerfully. "Probably not, or Frensham might have heard of it. He took a great interest in the building of the opera house."

"We're behind the scenes somewhere, aren't we?"

"Yes. Oh, we'd go up with the explosion all right, if we stayed around. There; feel." He took her hand and guided it through the diminished pile of rubbish to what felt like a wooden bit of the floor. "There's a terrible lot of stuff on top still. Careful, now, just the same. The catch that held it shut wasn't all that strong when I was a boy. I don't want you going through before we're ready. Feel the shape of it, there's a good girl, and work from the other side."

It was possible, now, to feel the curve of the trap-door, and she moved obediently away, and went on dragging increasingly heavy pieces of wood and metal off the wooden surface. It was surprising how one forgot pain and cold thus occupied.

"There, I thought so." His voice was triumphant. "Someone else wasn't too sure about the catch. The bottom bits of metal run clear across the trap-door. They've been holding the rest up. They're heavy, too. Leave the rest to me. You deserve a breather. Relax."

"I'd rather be working."

"I know. And I know what you *can* be doing. Find the bits of rope we got off me, and see if you can unknot them. They might come in useful."

Obeying him, she found the rope where he had been lying by the door. "There's quite a lot of it," she said, surprised.

"They hung me up by it for a while," he told her. "That's why I was in rather poor shape when I arrived. There was something they wanted to know."

"Oh, Michael. Did you tell them?"

"A very convincing lie. But to make it so I had to hold out as long as possible. I rather hoped they hadn't bothered to cut away the rope. There!" She heard his strenuous breathing and the grating of metal on rock. "That's the last piece. I wonder what on earth it was. Bit of an iron maiden, perhaps. It's heavy enough for anything. And spiky! Now, let's see. Stay still, I don't like the feel of these hinges." And then, "God Almighty!" A tearing sound; a great gust of air; and then, far below, a series of reverberating crashes. "That was the *oubliette*, that was," said Michael. "I am so glad neither of us was on top of it at the time."

"Yes." She was trembling with more than cold now. "Michael, do you think anyone will have heard?"

"I doubt it. But we won't hang around to find out. Pity," he said regretfully. "I'd meant to try and get the lid back on, just in case anyone comes looking for us, but we'll just have to hope they don't. Now, let's see. That was the hinge side, so . . . Would you say it was any lighter in here?"

"No."

"That's what I thought. Never mind. Bring me the rope and we'd best get going."

"Michael! But how?"

"There's a way." As she crept towards him, a comforting hand reached out and found her shoulder. "I don't know why. In case they dropped someone through too impulsively with his valuables still on him, perhaps. The main thing is, there *is* a way."

168

"Was a way," she said. "How do you know..."

"Defeatist thinking never got you anywhere. We've a job to do, remember. A warning to give. So, like it or not, we have to get out of here."

"Yes," she said meekly. "Besides. I've an opera to sing in." And then, on a desperate, indrawn breath. "Michael!"

"Yes?"

"I've just remembered. When I was changing into my costume yesterday...I suppose it was yesterday? Michael, I wound my watch. I do it sometimes when I'm nervous."

"Wound it full?"

"Yes. I remember..."

"And that was yesterday afternoon. Saturday."

"About four. When I took it off. Oh, Michael, I'm sorry."

"Not to worry. It could happen to anyone. But it does leave us maybe a little short of time. So, pass me that rope." She could feel him measuring its length. "Not enough to rope us together," he said regretfully, "but I'll take it along, just for luck. Round my waist. Then I think I'd better have my jacket back; it might hamper you, going down. It's an easy climb, I promise; I used to do it all the time when I was a boy. Hand and footholds cut in the rock all the way."

"But we don't know what's happened to it since!"

"We're going to find out, aren't we? With an opera house and a peace conference at stake. Not to mention Lissenberg and our lives. Kiss me, my darling, before we go, and don't forget we're going to be married just as soon as we can find a priest."

"Priest?" She *could* not tell him, now about her overriding date with death.

"Family custom. D'you mind?" His lips, finding hers, made answer impossible and she was glad to let it go. They might so easily die, together, on the way down. Why trouble him with talk of another death?

The kiss was long, shaking, demanding, reassuring. "There's a conversation for you," he said, letting her go at last. "And now, having discussed everything that's important, let's go. You'll do precisely what I tell you, when I tell you?"

"Yes."

"Good." She felt him sit up and swing his legs over the edge of that gaping, sinister hole. "Then, here we go. There. The first foothold. Thank God the rock here is sound. Now, the handhold." She felt him moving away from her, downwards. "Right. Now it's your turn. Turn round, get a grasp on the ridge at the edge of the hole, put your right foot over, and I'll guide it. What a good thing Mrs Riley kept your tunic short." A loving hand found her right foot and placed it in a niche in the rock. "Now the left foot. It'll be a bit of a stretch for you, I'm afraid. It was for Alix, and she's taller than you."

"Alix?"

"We used to play together." His hand was guiding her left foot. "As kids."

Jealousy. Absurd. But, "I can't." He was still guiding her left foot downwards, but her hands were stretched almost beyond bearing where they clung to the rim of the hole.

"You must." The pull on her foot slackened. "Let go with your left hand, then, and hang on for dear life with your right. It will only be for a moment."

The moment seemed endless, and so did the downward climb that followed, but it was, as Michael had promised, fairly straightforward, a mere matter of putting hands and feet obediently where he guided them, hanging on for dear life, and not thinking about the drop below, and the unknown ahead. In a way, Anne thought, the darkness actually helped. And so did an increasing freshness in the air.

"There's a draft from somewhere." Michael's low voice confirmed this. "We're going to get out, I think, but God knows just where. Or what into. I think we'd best keep pretty quiet from now on. Don't drop anything, for God's shake."

"Nothing to drop," she whispered back. And followed in obedient silence, as his hands guided her, movement by movement, still downwards.

"It was always a long way." And then, "Shhh..."

Below and to the left had come an unbelievable, unmistakable sound. The revving of a car's engine. "I thought so." It was only a thread of a whisper. "The underground car park. Ah. We're down. Quiet as you come." Instead of a foothold, her reaching right foot found solid rock. No, not rock. Concrete? Standing, she swayed, and his arms went round her, steadying. "Look," he breathed, but she had just seen that in one direction the darkness became less absolute. And now, from that way, came the sound of another car starting up.

"If we only knew what time it was." His hand touched hers. "Stay here, stay very quiet, while I take a look."

"You'll be careful."

"I always am." He lowered her gently to the hard ground,

her back against the wall down which they had come. "Don't stir from there," he whispered. "Not an inch."

"I won't." She sat where he had placed her, letting exhaustion have its way with her, refusing to think about that bomb, far above them now, ticking its way towards midnight. The car park that served the whole complex was underneath the opera house, dug deep into the head of the valley. She did not know much about blast, but it seemed grimly logical that in this enclosed end of the valley the force of the explosion would be as violent downwards as upwards. The cheerful ticking of her watch maddened her. Ticking towards what? And how long had Michael been gone? She heard another car start up, then another. So—argue from that. If cars were driving away, it could mean that it was late at night, the opening reception of the peace conference already over. Coming up towards midnight?

A whisper of movement beside her. Michael's voice a thread. "This way, quiet as you can. We've not much time, I think."

The sound of more cars, the noise echoing strangely in the enclosed space. "The reception's over." His voice was almost drowned by the revving of engines. "They're all in evening dress. Going home. It's late, I'm afraid."

Too late? Useless and dangerous to ask. From the way the noise was increasing, they must be close to the car park now. "This way." As they groped their way forwards, the light at the end of the tunnel increased as well as the noise. Now, Michael guided her round a corner of rock and she found herself looking down on to the huge car park. Dimly lighted, it was still about a quarter full of cars, many of them moving and manoeuvring their way towards the exit, which was at the far side from where they stood.

"Damnation." Michael's hand was on her arm. "Just too late," he said quietly, pointing, and at the same time holding her back in the shadow at the back of the ledge on which they were standing.

Straining her eyes, she saw the reason for the delay at the exit. Uniformed attendants were checking each car as it left. Uniformed. The "police" who had knocked her out. Frensham's men.

"I could steal a car easily enough," Michael told her. "That's what I'd planned. But we'd never get past that check-up. They've just started it. I wonder why. Pity we didn't get here ten minutes ago. How's your strength?"

171

"Good," she said.

"Bless you for a gallant liar." He guided her back round the corner of the rock, light and sound diminishing together.

"Not back up?" She did not think she could face it.

"No, not that, but I'm afraid it's almost as bad. If nothing has changed, this tunnel should take us along to where the river goes under. You can swim, can't you?"

"Oh, yes. But, Michael, you don't mean..." They were talking a little louder now, their voices reassuringly masked by the reverberation of engines.

"It's the only way," he said. "And not much time either, I'm afraid. The reception was due to end at eleven. Less than an hour to go. I hope to God they get all the cars out in time. Stupid of Frensham to slow them up with that search. But like him. What are a few extra deaths to him? Because we've got to face it. There's a strong chance that we're going to be too late to give the alarm. We may have to say goodbye to that opera house, and just pray to God there's no one in it. We'll build another one, I promise you; smaller; the right size for Lissenberg."

"We?"

"We Lissenbergers." As they talked, he had been guiding her along the smooth concrete floor of the tunnel. "Look." He paused for a moment to point upwards at a darker patch in the general gloom. "That's the way we came down. No wonder I never noticed it from down here. I don't suppose anyone else has, except maybe the workmen who built the garage. They would have had light."

"I wish we had." It had been hard to move away from the dim light of the big garage, back to feeling their way in the cold darkness.

"Not long now," he told her. "And just as well. I want you right away from here before it goes up." And then, "Don't mind too much about the opera house. It's people matter, not things. And just think what a surprise we're going to give James Frensham. Ah!" His guiding arm tightened on hers. "Listen!"

The sound of water, ahead and below. Water rushing fast. A waterfall? "Michael, I can't!"

"Oh, yes you can. You want to live, don't you? To sing again. To marry me? Well, that's our way, down there." He was holding her close, the sound of water below them somewhere. "You'll have to go first," he told her. "You dive in, not too deep, and a deep breath first. Then hold it, just as

172

long as you can. Stay under till you're bursting, till you can't stand it a moment longer, then up to the surface and let yourself go with the current. You should be about halfway down the valley, more or less level with the hostel. I'll come right in after you. Tread water, if you can, and wait for me. The current shouldn't be too strong. Then all we have to do is get safe under the road bridge, and we're home and dry."

"Home and wet," she said.

14

So many questions, and no time to ask any of them. Obediently, she kicked off her light sandals. Her cloak and dagger she had left behind in the torture chamber, but she baulked momentarily when he told her to take off her tunic. "It might just make the difference."

He was right, of course. Shivering in bra and pants, she thought it impossible to be colder. He had stripped to his jeans, now put a chilly arm round her shoulders in a quick gesture of love and encouragement. "I'll be right behind," he said. "I love you dearly. You're a good breather. Breathe, and dive, not too deep, remember—and God speed you. Now, quick!"

She obeyed him, marvelling at herself. A long breath, a plunge that seemed endless before she met the icy shock of the water, and then the current had her. She had dived in sideways to it, but the very force of it turned her round. Hold your breath...She was counting to herself...Twelve, thirteen, fourteen...Something scraped against her side; the icy water surged savagely round her...Twenty, twenty-one, twenty-two...What was the longest she had ever held her breath for? Twenty-nine, thirty...The water felt easier round her...Could she be out in the valley already? Michael had not told her how the stream emerged...Best not to know?...Thirty-three, thirty-four...Or had she lost count?

It made no difference. Could make none. Her lungs were bursting, and her legs, as she kicked out for the surface, so cold that they only just obeyed her. Air. An enormous shuddering breath...Her mind began to steady. Forty, she said

173

to herself, and opened her eyes. An amazing jumble of light and sound. Not daylight. The water around her dark as it was cold. Shadows to right and left must be the banks of the stream. But above them glowed light, and from beyond she could hear the sound of voices, laughter, shouts...Almost too cold to think. Tread water, Michael had said, wait for him. But if she did not make herself swim, the cold would kill her. And starting to swim, was aware of movement behind her in the water.

"Anne?" Just audible above the rush of the water.

"Yes."

"Quick. Can you? It's not safe here. I'd forgotten the crowds." The words came out in breathless gasps as he swam beside and a little behind her.

He was right. At any moment someone might look down into the stream and see them. And it was Frensham's "police" who were in control of the crowded valley. Suppose they had been told to keep an eye on the river. But why should they? How far was it to the bridge at the bottom of the valley? Too far, she thought. As far as from here to doomsday.

"Anne." He had read her thoughts. "You've got to make it. I can't leave you. But I'd have to."

He was right. There was still a slim chance of saving the opera house. And she had no breath to waste on speech. Struggling to keep her icy limbs at work, she was aware of him treading water to look ahead. Then, he was beside her again, urging her towards the left bank of the stream, holding her against it. "Lights," he whispered. "At the bridge. Checking cars, I think. Here, too. God knows how we'll get by. The river's as light as day there. Anne, my darling, I'm sorry."

"Not your fault," she said. "We did try." And then, "Dear God!"

Midnight. The end of the world. Thunder and lightning. Screams from the valley above them. Chaos is come again. In the sudden, blinding flash of the explosion, Anne could see the guards on the bridge, heads turned in amazement towards the head of the valley. Even the water seeemed to shake around them, where they clung to the bank.

"Now," said Michael. "It's our chance. Now! I love you, Anne."

As they moved out into the middle of the stream, Anne felt the water roughen. How long before debris from the explosion started to come down? She had thought she was too exhausted, too cold, to swim another stroke; and yet found

174

herself striking out strongly at Michael's side. The bridge loomed ahead, dark and low over the water. Lights flashed above; she must keep her head down, for fear that her white face betray her. They were under the main span of the bridge, safe for the moment, then out into the air below the bridge. Don't turn round. No shouts. No shots. She was still swimming, but only just. She missed a breath, swallowed water, felt herself struggling, began to sink.

"I've got you." Hands firm round her ears, holding her. "Don't struggle."

But not to struggle was to die of cold. She had not imagined cold like this. I am being refrigerated, she thought. I am in the deep freeze. I shall die...I am death...

Something was happening. Voices, not just Michael's. Capture after all? She was plucked out of the water. Exclamations. Something warm around her. Hands. Friendly hands, surely? A boat, a small, unsteady boat. She was among knees. "Hoped you might turn up this way," said a voice.

"Hans!" exclaimed Anne, and fainted at last.

Warmth. Why had she never understood the sybaritic delight of just being warm? "Quite a girl." A voice she knew. Hands—clever, familiar hands—studied the bump at the back of her head.

She was lying on her side. With an enormous effort she opened her eyes and saw a familiar pair of dark, well-creased trousers, a gold watch-chain. "Dr Hirsch," she said.

"My favourite patient." His voice was warm. "I'm proud of you, Anne. Move a little for me, would you. Just to set an old man's heart at rest."

"You're not old." With a great effort, she moved her head, just a little. "It hurts."

"Well, of course. Cold water's recommended for concussion, but only in moderation. Now, the rest of you, there's a good girl. Right hand? Good." She had managed the slightest possible clenching of the fingers. "Left hand? Yes. Right foot?"

"It doesn't seem to be there," said Anne.

"Don't worry. You *were* cold. More hot water bottles, Lisel, and another blanket, please."

"Lisel? I'm at the hostel?"

"No, ma'am. We've got you safe in Lissenberg, where you belong."

Belong? "Michael?" she asked.

175

"No need to fret about him. Very tough young man, our Michael. He's out seeing to things."

"Oh." Forlorn not to have found him at her bedside. "Things?"

"All kinds. But not till you're better."

"I *am* better." With an immense effort she pulled herself up on her elbows, dragging her non-existent feet with her.

"Good girl." Dr Hirsch had been ready with a pillow for her head. "And here's Lisel with the hot water bottles. And your breakfast—lunch. You must be famished. Don't fret about those feet of yours. It's the shock, of course, and the cold."

"Cold!" She dipped bread in hot soup and thought it the best food she had ever tasted. "I thought I was dying of it. But, Dr Hirsch, I have to know." Her mind was seething with questions. "The explosion; the opera house. The opera?"

"Cancelled, I'm afraid. The opera house is—just gone. They thought of using the rehearsal room, as a kind of makeshift, but with you gone missing, and the damage from the floods..."

"Someone really didn't mean that opera to happen," she said sadly.

"But it did," he told her. "Don't forget that stupendous preview of yours. When you're a little better, you shall see the newspaper reports..."

"Newspaper? Dr Hirsch, what day is it?"

"Only Tuesday," he told her. "You opted out of Monday, and who can blame you? It was a bad day, Monday."

"What happened?" She knew he wanted her to ask it.

"The explosion," he reminded her. "You didn't ask if anyone was hurt."

"I think I was afraid to. Who, Dr Hirsch?"

"Prince Rudolf. No one knows what he was doing there. Or if they do, they're not saying. The blast got him. He was in the underground tunnel; terrible in that enclosed space. He must have been on his way from the hotel to the opera house, judging by the way his body was lying. Dead at once. Don't look so grieved, child. He was in dead trouble, whatever happened, poor man."

"He was good to me," she said, tears slowly forming in her eyes.

"In his fashion. I'm glad someone is crying for him."

"But—what's happening?" The full implications of it were gradually unfolding themselves in her tired mind. "The peace conference? Dr Hirsch, what about that? Is it wrecked? Has it all been for nothing?"

"Not a bit of it. People are odd. You might have thought— I imagine someone did—that the delegates would have packed their bags and gone home after such a disaster on their very doorstep. But not at all; they're hard at work. It was a highly localised explosion," he explained. "An immense force behind it, but driven down rather than sideways. Lucky for you and young Michael you didn't stay around underneath there. There's a hole right through to the car park. Full of water, of course, from the stream. But, amazingly, the hotel is hardly damaged; a few broken windows, a cracked wall or two. They built well, Prince Rudolf's architects. And the conference centre's untouched. So...the conference has sent out an official message of condolence and got down to work."

"Condolence...Poor Princess Gloria." She knew it did not ring true. What would Princess Gloria care, so long as her cocktails arrived on time. "Alix?" she asked. "How is she, and the children?"

"We don't really know," he told her. "They're incommunicado, up at the castle."

"Incommunicado! But, Dr Hirsch, why?"

He was taking her pulse, a familiar friendly gesture. "You'll do," he told her. "I'm afraid you haven't heard the half of it yet. We're under military rule. Those 'Italian policemen' who came in so timely to help Herr Winkler turn out to be a kind of private army of James Frensham's. Scum of the earth."

"I know," she said. "They attacked me...And what they did to Michael...Where *is* Michael." She pulled herself further up in bed, her legs still frighteningly inert.

"Out trying to get in touch with Winkler. Not easy, the way things are. Frensham's men have confined Winkler and his twelve men to police headquarters, 'for their own safety'. As if anyone would hurt them."

"But why? I don't understand."

"There was rioting after the explosion. In the valley. Started by *agents provocateurs*, I'm sure. *The Red Flag*...shouts of 'People's power,' all that kind of thing. My God, I'm glad you and Michael got safe through there. Otherwise you would be really dead, not just officially!"

"Officially dead? But, why?"

"To keep you alive. Luckily, the explosion was so total up at the level where you were to be shut up, that there is no

177

way anyone can tell whether you were there or not. Of course, it's difficult for them. They can hardly say they know you're dead because they left you there to die, but they've put out rather a clever story. Someone played a nasty trick on you after the opera. You got trapped, somehow, by the safety curtain coming down. Michael realised what had happened, and went to look for you, and got trapped too. You were both caught by the explosion, and that was that. One of these days, when we've time on our hands, you must tell me how you did happen to get trapped behind there. A bright girl like you. How did they manage it?"

"Really, just like that. A nasty trick. But—Dr Hirsch, who is 'they'?"

"Basically, James Frensham. He's in the process of taking over the country. He's got Alix and Princess Gloria and the children sewn up tight in the castle. 'For their safety.' And, of course, his private army disposed of the 'rioters' with no trouble at all. Not surprising when you consider that the whole thing was a put-up job together."

"But why?"

"To give him his excuse to put the country under martial law. 'To protect the delegates at the peace conference.' He's doing a whole lot of protecting, is young Frensham. Not a native soul in Lissenberg lifted a finger during the riot, so far as I know, but we're under tight curfew. Armed patrols— the lot. You haven't asked where you are."

"So long as you're here, it hardly matters. I suppose I thought it was your house." But, looking round the sparsely furnished, windowless room with its naked electric light bulbs, she realised how unlikely this was.

"One of the first places they'd look, if they should suspect you had survived," he told her. "No, you're in the cellar of a disused warehouse down by the river. Michael used to play here when he was a boy. I suppose you could call it his pad now. There are about five ways into it, all of them inconspicuous. And the river handy for a quick getaway down to the Rhine if necessary."

"I don't understand." She was getting tired. Her head ached, and the numb nonexistence of her legs was increasingly frightening.

"No wonder, child. You need sleep. But first let me explain. We've known for a long time that young Frensham had plans for Lissenberg. That's why Winkler asked Michael to come home and help keep a quiet eye on things. Because we had

178

no idea what form they were going to take. Now we know. Half his blasting has been done for him by that explosion. All he needs is to drain off the river and he can start mining for szilenite. Once he has the authority."

"Authority?"

"As elected Prince of Lissenberg. He announced his engagement to Princess Alix this morning. Poor girl, I thought she would have held out longer, but since he's got her mother and the children it's understandable enough. So, tomorrow, when the Diet meets to decide on Prince Rudolf's successor, Frensham can expect to have it all his own way. No ban on women here in Lissenberg. As the eldest child, Alix should succeed, if ratified by the Diet."

"Will they?"

"Ah, that's asking. But he's got a lot going for him, has James Frensham. Prince Rudolf left a desperate load of local debt. Well, you know . . ."

"I do indeed." She remembemed those crimson and white rose petals with their concealed final demands.

"And the one thing Frensham has, is money. That's what got him where he is. That, and his ruthlessness."

She shivered. "Yes, that's the word." And then, "Dr Hirsch, I heard him. On the walkway, coming down from the castle. Talking to the man who was going to plant the bomb. If I told the Diet?"

"Good girl. You do remember. Michael told me you'd heard something. But I didn't want to lead you. *Now* do dou see why we are keeping you hidden? You're to be our surprise witness when the Diet meets tomorrow. It's public, you see. The twelve members up on the platform, debating. Then, when they have come to their decision—which is usually at once—there's a moment like the one in the marriage service. The leader of the Diet rises and comes forward to the edge of the platform and makes a short speech in Liss. 'Speak now, or forever after hold your peace,' is the gist of it. That's when you'll get up and make your accusation."

"Get up?" She looked down at the lifeless lump of bed-clothes where her legs were.

"Don't worry, child. The worst thing you can do. Now, relax. I'm going to give you an injection to help you sleep. You'll be fine in the morning."

"Michael?" she asked.

"I doubt if he'll be back before it's time to get you to the

Rathaus. He's got a lot to do." She hardly felt him give the injection, but sleep came warmly rolling over her.

She was waked, what felt like several centuries later, by Dr Hirsch, frantically shaking her shoulder. "Anne, get up! Quick. They've caught Michael. There's not a moment to lose if we're to save him."

"Michael!" She pushed away the duvet and swung her legs out of bed. "Oh!" she swayed, but she was standing.

"Just so," said Dr Hirsch with satisfaction. He helped her to a chair and wrapped the duvet snugly round her. "That's earned you your breakfast."

"But—Michael?"

"Nothing wrong with him that I know of. I just thought that would blast you to your feet. I'm a wicked old man." He sounded thoroughly pleased with himself. "How do you feel?"

"Shaky...but better. My head's stopped aching." She stretched out first one foot, then the other, from under the duvet. "Look!"

"That's good. That's wonderful. I'll send Lisel in with your breakfast. Then you'd best get yourself dressed. Lord knows what time Michael will want you to start for the Rathaus."

"But what about Frensham's men?"

"That's what Michael's working on. Security's tighter than ever in town this morning. 'Police' at every corner, checking identification, and a special guard round the Rathaus."

"It sounds hopeless."

"It isn't. Remember the weakness of Frensham's position. He's got a whole conference of international diplomats sitting up in the valley watching everything that goes on down here. *And* the international press buzzing round harder than ever after that explosion. Naturally, they have asked to watch the quaint old-fashioned custom of electing the Hereditary Prince, and naturally, he has had to agree. We're hoping the delegates will take time off and come too. So, it's all got to *seem* open and above board and democratically sound. James Frensham protecting the good citizens of Lissenberg from the Red Terror—that kind of thing. He's on the side of sweetness and light, and got to act the part. He'll have to have Alix there, too, and my bet is she may surprise him. Now eat your breakfast, and save your strength. You'll need it all before the day is over."

Coffee and croissants and two boiled eggs. "Lord, I feel better," she told Lisel and then tried again, haltingly, in the Liss she had begun to pick up.

Lisel beamed her approval and produced Anne's bra and pants, good as new, a shabby pair of well-patched jeans and a teeshirt with a message: *I love Lissenberg. "Und hier—"* With a smile of pure mischief she handed over a polythene bag containing the shaggiest wig Anne had ever seen. *"Studenten,"* she explained.

Anne had worn her own hair, cut short and straight, as Marcus. The transformation wrought by the outfit and wig was quite extraordinary. "I don't recognise myself," she told Dr Hirsch when he appeared.

"I don't believe even Michael would know you. You'll have to choose your moment to take off the wig and be known. Not too soon, for God's sake."

"No. But, Dr Hirsch, I'll have to speak English."

"No problem. There will be enough people who understand. It's the first language in our schools." He laughed. "James Frensham speaks bad German and no Liss. It's one of his disadvantages."

"Will you teach me a couple of Liss phrases? You know, something like, 'It's God's truth, believe me.'"

"Of course I will. You're not stupid, Anne."

"I may not be stupid, but I'm frightened to death." She slashed the scarlet lipstick Lisel had brought onto pale lips and marvelled all over again at the transformation.

"Wow," said Michael, at the door. Or at least it was Michael's voice.

"Oh, Michael!" She did not know whether to laugh or cry. "Your poor hair! And what's happened to your face?"

"Purely temporary, I promise you." He ran a hand over the bristling crew-cut. "It'll grow again. And as for my face, that's Dr Hirsch's work, and he promises I can undo it as fast as he put it together." He pushed a finger into one of the soft, plump cheeks that effectively took away all character from his face. "We've not much time, I'm afraid." A quick look at his watch. "It's all taken a bit of organising. You know what to say, Anne? When I give you your cue, just tell it exactly as you heard it. Right?"

"Right." If it went wrong, this might be their last meeting.

As so often, he read her thoughts. "We're going to win this one," he said. "Word of a Liss. Then there'll be time to talk. And you'll forgive me." It was more statement than question. "Ah. There they are." They could all hear a curious, familiar grinding sound from above.

"What on earth?" asked Anne.

"Garbage day." He produced a peaked cap from the back pocket of his jeans and put it on at a jaunty angle. "We're meeting the others in the Rathaus square," he explained. "The problem was getting you there. I never did get to see Uncle Winkler," he told Dr Hirsch. "So—no papers. But we picked the cleanest garbage can for you. Come in." He opened the door and two brawny garbagemen walked in, dressed, like him, in jeans and the official-looking cap, and carrying a huge, battered garbage can.

"We did the best we could," said one of them, in Liss, his look of apology as he removed the lid explaining the words to Anne.

"Phew!" said Anne.

"Sorry, love." Michael grinned at her, the familiar smile strange in the fat face. "It won't be long, I promise. We'll have to do a couple of other pickups for the benefit of the men on duty in this street. Then straight to the Rathaus square, and you're out of it."

"I've got to *ride* in it?"

"I'm afraid so. They hang on the back, see? You did strengthen the handle?" To the men.

"Yes, sir. It'll hold all right."

Sir? thought Anne. But Michael was speaking. "In you go. Lucky you're such a little thing."

"Thanks!" She held her nose ostentatiously and climbed in.

The ride was a nightmare. The crouching position that had seemed reasonable enough when she first got in was soon slow torture, the smell, once the lid was on, appalling, and the swaying movement of the trash can, hung from its one hook, combined with it to bring on wave after wave of nausea. The garbage truck stopped twice. She heard the other cans crash off their hooks, felt the whole truck shake as they were emptied in. Not long now. A couple of other pickups, Michael had said. But they were stopping again; shouts, orders, and then a great roar of laughter as the truck moved slowly forward. They must be in the Rathaus square now, and it was obviously full of people. She could hear the buzz of many voices, cheerful, expectant...Lissenberg seemed to be taking martial law in its stride. But the slower swaying as the truck weaved its way through the crowd was worse than anything. I will not be sick. I WILL NOT BE SICK.

They had stopped. Her trash can was lifted off its hook,

carried a little way, set down. Michael lifted the lid. "Oh, my poor Anne!" She was so stiff he had to help her out.

They were in a little courtyard opening off the square, invisible from it. The other two men were unconcernedly filling their trash cans with plastic sacks of rubbish. "Quick," said Michael. "The others are just outside. Keep close, and don't say a word until I tell you. That voice of yours is too well known." He took her hand and led her through the archway into the square, casually, as if they had just paused to peer in. "You're American," he explained. "No languages."

The square was packed with people, apparently waiting for the Rathaus to open. A cordon of Frensham's police guarded the steps that led up to its big doors. Anne saw this momentarily from the higher level of the archway, then Michael led her forward to be swallowed by a crowd of young, jeans-clad figures like themselves. Friendly voices greeted them. "Thought they were going to stop you," said one.

Michael laughed. "So did they."

"What did you say to them? That made everyone laugh? We couldn't hear over here."

"Threatened to go on strike, of course. The hand that rocks the trashcan, rules the world. Ah, here we go." As the crowd began to move slowly forward, Anne marvelled at the split-second precision of his timing. And she was amazed, as she had often been before, at the civilised behaviour of the Lissenbergers. There was no pushing or shoving in this crowd. What nice people they are, she thought. Intolerable to think of James Frensham taking them over, turning them into industrial plebs. Well, if she could do anything to help stop him, she would.

They were nearly at the foot of the steps, now, and she saw that people were being let through the Rathaus doors in groups. "We go in by trades," Michael turned to tell her. "It used to be guilds, of course." And, anticipating the question she knew she must not ask. "We're the student body. Our leader vouches for us." One of the shaggy young men had moved forward to hand a sheaf of papers to the man on guard at the Rathaus door. There was a sharp, inaudible exchange as the man leafed swiftly but efficiently through the papers.

"They want to search us," said Michael. "Sensible enough. No worse than catching a plane."

But it was. Evidently worse. One of the girls in front of them let out a little protesting yelp, and Anne felt Michael's hand tighten on hers. "We bear it," he said. She nodded. One

183

of the men just in front of them had had his pocket knife confiscated. Anne thought he was about to protest; thought the searchers hoped he would do just that; but he merely shrugged and went on in. It was her turn. Hands, insulting, intimate hands, and what was obviously a coarse remark in Italian. "American," said Michael behind her, "*Versteht nichts.*"

American, like Princess Gloria. Clever Michael. The hands finished their task more respectfully; she received a dismissive, unpleasant pat on the seat of her jeans and was inside the hall. It was crowded already, but their party were filing round the back to a position in a side-gallery that commanded a good view of the dais, with its long, heavy table running parallel to the audience. Counting the twelve big chairs behind the table, with the one in the centre larger than the rest, Anne was aware of carefully controlled movement in what seemed their casual group of students. They were settling themselves, obviously, in prearranged positions. She and Michael were side by side, in the second row of the gallery, right in the middle of their crowd of allies. The man in front of her was short, strong, and broad-shouldered. He turned and grinned hugely at her, holding out a hand.

"He's your shield," said Michael, *sotto voce*, as she returned the warm grasp.

Shield? They were all unarmed. She looked round the big hall. Frensham's men were acting as marshals, truncheons at their belts, but apparently otherwise unarmed. She looked up to the gallery at the back of the hall. "Press up there," said Michael, as if he had been following her thoughts. "The eyes of the world are upon us, remember." His eyes seemed to lead hers to the red velvet curtain that hung behind the table on the dais. That must be where Frensham's real strength was. But would he dare use it?

"Ah." A sigh of pure relief from Michael. "Here comes the diplomatic corps. The conference has taken time off for the election. Thank God for human curiosity." As the little group of formally dressed elder statesmen were politely guided down to the front rows, he pointed them out to Anne. America... France... England... Russia... "Top men all of them, and a top woman or two. There'll be no indiscriminate shooting in here today." No indiscriminate shooting. The group around them was talking louder, suddenly, as if he had somehow ordered a rise in pitch. "If anything should start happening," he said, very quietly, "down between the rows of seats, and stay there. You're our witness, remember. We need you. Here they come."

A string quartet, crowded together on the left of the dais, was playing what Anne had learned to recognise as the Lissenberg national anthem. The crowd rose to its feet, suddenly silent, as the twelve members of the Diet filed in. Twelve elderly men in crimson robes who bore the burden of deciding what should happen to Lissenberg. Or thought they did. Behind the velvet curtain that matched their robes, Anne thought she saw movement.

Two flunkeys in the familiar palace uniform had followed them in, carrying two more chairs, which they placed on the left of the dais, one broad step lower than the table. One of the violinists played a false note, and Anne, probably the only person to notice, looked quickly and was amazed to recognise Carl Meyer. What in the world was he doing? But the rousing Hadyn march chosen by the first "Hereditary Prince" had come to its crashing climax. Everyone was sitting down. And the man in the larger, central chair, was rising to his feet, to open the proceedings.

"Good God," whispered Anne. "Josef?"

"Shh—" said Michael.

15

Josef was speaking in Liss. Inevitable—maddening. She would have no idea of what was going on. His short speech was greeted by a roar of approval. And then a microphonic voice took over in English. "Ladies and gentlemen, friends and honoured guests, since the eyes of the world are upon us in this day of our crisis, I have taken it upon myself to arrange that each speech shall be translated, for the benefit of our guests, after it has been made. For this, as for every decision made in this house, I must have your approval."

Josef spoke again, more briefly still. Unless anyone objected, the interpreter's voice explained, Josef would take the first shout of approval as his authority. Total silence. Obviously, Anne thought, the English translation would suit

James Frensham as well as it did her. But how in the world did Josef come to be chairman of the Diet? She must not ask Michael—not now. The hall was hushed for Josef to speak again.

His next proposal was greeted with another approving shout, and as the interpreter began to translate it, Anne saw James Frensham usher Princess Alix on to the dais. Dead pale, in a long, plain white dress, Alix wore a glittering diadem in the hair that was the only note of colour about her. Frensham, holding her arm protectively, had obviously planned for this occasion, Anne thought, and felt yet another chill of apprehension. His impeccably tailored black velvet lounge suit was at once daytime casual and yet formal enough for anything. For accepting a crown?

At sight of Alix, the twelve members of the Diet had risen, and the crowd now followed their example, an excited babble of talk breaking out. Frensham inclined his head, slightly, graciously, as it were in acknowledgement, but Alix held herself rigid, looking at nothing. Her father's funeral was to take place next day, Anne remembered, the question of the succession having, by precedent, to be settled first. No wonder she looked tormented, hag-ridden.

Frensham seated her formally, and Anne noticed that Josef contrived to sit down immediately after her, just before Frensham could gracefully do so. She rather thought Frensham noticed it too. He bit that sculptured Florentine lip of his and flashed a dark, speculative glance at Josef, who had risen again, now the audience were seated and silent, and begun to speak. Surprisingly, this time he began in English. "I have had a request," he said, "from Mr Frensham, that since our transactions concern him closely, and he unfortunately understands no Liss, they should be conducted in English. It is a grave breach of Lissenberg custom." He kept his tone extraordinarily neutral. "But, situated as we are"—a courteous glance travelled from the diplomatic corps in the front rows to the gallery full of journalists—"it might be good manners to use a language all will understand. I therefore propose that we use English, and will put the question to a show of hands, in the hope that we can settle it swiftly and get to business. Yes?" One of the Diet members had leaned forward to speak to him. "Quite right, thank you. This speech of mine must, of course, be translated into Liss. Then, when you have had time to consider the merits of the proposal, I will put it to a show of hands."

186

Once again the interpreter's voice came over the microphone, this time unintelligible in Liss. And unnecessary, Anne thought, watching the quick whispering that was going on throughout the hall. Practically everyone present obviously did understand English. When the interpretation was over, a man at the back of the hall rose to his feet. Herr Winkler. "Permission to put a question, Your Excellency?"

"Granted."

"This establishes no precedent? We act, now, out of courtesy to our foreign guests. Future meetings will, of course, be conducted in our native Liss."

Hardly a question, thought Anne, but it was greeted by a growl of approval.

"Agreed." Josef did not pause to consult his fellow Diet members. "I will phrase the question as follows: For this one occasion, as an exception, out of courtesy to our foreign guests—and for no other reason—I put it that we conduct our deliberations in English. Those in favour please raise your hands."

On the platform, James Frensham, frowning more heavily than ever, muttered something to Alix, who shook her head. Anne felt Michael nudge her, and raised her hand among the forest of others around her. The diplomats and journalists were abstaining, she saw, but in the body of the house most hands were raised. A courteous people, the Lissenbergers. It was a considerable concession, she thought, and wondered if it would have been made if Winkler and Josef had not made it so crystal clear that although James Frensham had asked for it, it was not in fact to him that it was being made.

"Thank you." Josef was on his feet again. "The question is carried unanimously. I will only ask that if something should be said that any member of the audience cannot understand they say so at once and we will translate. This is a day of grave crisis for us here in Lissenberg, and there must be no shadow of doubt about the validity of any decision to which we may come."

He paused for a moment, then went on: "We are now opening our proceedings as the legitimately constituted Diet of Lissenberg. It is our sad duty, today, to name the heir to the princedom, according to the laws and traditions of our country. Our foreign guests are welcome to listen, but they will understand and respect my request that they take no part in these proceedings." He took a deep breath and Anne wondered what had happened to the inconspicuous Josef who

187

looked after the hostel. This was a man of power, someone who knew how to control an audience. "Two days ago," he told them, "the worst disaster of our history happened here in Lissenberg. A mysterious explosion destroyed our new opera house, the successful enterprise of our beloved Prince Rudolf, and he himself was found, just as mysteriously, dead in its ruins. Despite the help so generously given from outside, our police have so far found no clue as to the criminals, for, my friends, let there be no misunderstanding—this was no accident. It was a criminal plot. We do not yet know the perpetrators, nor what, precisely, they intended, but the results are all too evident. Our Prince is dead, our opera house destroyed. When the culprits are discovered they can expect the full rigour of our law. In the meantime, the succession must be established. We all know what the late Prince's intention was. When he sent his eldest son into exile, and wiped his name from the history and records of our country, he stated it clearly. Princess Alix was the eldest of his children. Nothing in the written law of our country prohibits female succession. Princess Alix it should be." He raised a hand to still a growing murmur—Applause? Dissent? A little of both?—and turned to address his fellow Diet members directly. "Yours is the decision," he told them. "But there is more. This morning, the Princess announced her engagement to her cousin, Mr Frensham, who has done so much for our country. She has asked me to put it to you that he should be joined with her in her high office. That is correct, is it not, Your Highness?" For the first time he looked directly at Alix, and spoke to her alone.

"That is correct." Her low voice sounded frozen, as if the words hurt her. They fell like stones into the absolute silence of the hall.

"Thank you." He turned to look round the table. "There you have it, gentlemen. Princess Alix, heir named by her father, and her husband-to-be, James Frensham. May I have your views?"

"What of the Prince?" asked the man on Josef's left. "The young Prince. We all know his father disinherited him, but did he do it justly, I ask you, and, more important, had he the right? It is we, the Diet of Lissenberg, who must decide this issue, not the wishes of a dead man, and one, if I may speak frankly"—an apologetic glance for Princess Alix, who sat, still as death, ignoring everything—"who did not always act entirely for the best interests of Lissenberg."

"That's just it," put in a grey-headed man from the end of the table. "You have gone to the heart of our trouble, fellow councillor. This is no time to be casting blame, but we all know that our country is on the verge of bankruptcy. And we all know who can save us. I move that we thank our beloved Princess Alix for her wise choice of a husband, and long live Prince James and Princess Alix."

"Not before they are married," protested another member.

"I still say, 'Find the Prince,'" urged the man on Josef's left, and there was a murmur of agreement from some of his colleagues, and an excited buzz throughout the hall.

Josef raised his hand for silence. "Gentlemen—" He spoke low and sadly to his colleagues round the table, and the hall was hushed to listen. "I am afraid you are wasting your time—and ours. I grieve to tell you, but I have it on the authority of Herr Winkler that the Prince is dead."

Now the hush in the hall was absolute. Even the Diet members were silent for a moment, taking it in, and Anne saw Alix raise a hand to brush away tears. What was this about a Prince? She turned towards Michael, but his hand on hers commanded silence. Josef was speaking again. "So the choice that lies before us," he summed it up for them, "is between Princess Alix and her husband, or her younger brother or sister, who are now twelve and ten years old. I put it to you, my friends, that this is no time for a regency."

"You could act," said the man on his right, and once again the hall seemed to hold its breath.

"Not in this crisis." Josef spoke as if the suggestion had been the most natural thing in the world. "We must face the fact that, with the opera house destroyed, bankruptcy is no longer a mere threat. It is upon us. Fortunately for us, Mr Frensham himself, as his father's heir, is the late Prince's and Lissenberg's major creditor." Could there be the faintest hint of irony in his tone? "We have his promise that his first act as Prince of Lissenberg will be to wipe out the debt. Then he proposes to put our affairs in order, and I have no doubt that he can do it. We all know his record."

"Yes," said a councillor who had spoken before, "I agree with all that. But, I say it again, we cannot proclaim him Hereditary Prince until he is actually married to the Princess."

"Who is in deep mourning," said Josef.

James Frensham had been frowning heavily as he listened, now he leaned over and spoke quietly to Alix, who

189

nodded—reluctantly, Anne thought—and rose to her feet. "Your Excellency, may I speak?" Once again that lifeless voice silenced the crowd. "My cousin—my betrothed," she corrected herself, "has suggested a compromise. A marriage contract, formally drawn up, witnessed by you twelve gentlemen, binding on both of us." Beside her, Anne felt Michael stiffen, almost thought for a moment that he was going to leap up and protest, but all he did was to take her hand again and hold it tight.

Alix sat down, graceful, composed, an automaton, while the members of the Diet discussed this new proposal. It seemed to satisfy them. "With the wedding date named?" asked one, and received a curt nod from James Frensham, who was beginning, increasingly, to dominate the scene, as power seemed to slide from Josef to him. He was getting visibly impatient too, a hand beating a tattoo on the side of his leg as the discussion continued.

"Gentlemen." Josef was on his feet again. "I think the time has come to take a first vote. I put it to you that in its hour of need, Lissenberg should invite Princess Alix and her husband-to-be to take office as Hereditary Princess and Prince." He looked up and down the table. "Those in favour?"

Six hands went up.

"Those against?"

Five hands. Every eye in the hall was fixed on Josef, who stood there, for a moment, apparently thinking, then exchanged one long, undecipherable glance with Alix. "I shall not vote," he said at last. "The proposal is carried six votes to five." He raised a hand for silence. "But before we greet our new Prince and Princess, there is one last formality to be gone through." He moved slowly round the table and came forward. "This must be in both English and Liss," he told the hushed crowd. He spoke in Liss first, then in English: "Mark and listen, people of Lissenberg. I, chairman of your Diet, do now proclaim to you its decision. By majority vote, we have approved the accession, as Hereditary Princess and Prince of Lissenberg, of our beloved Princess Alix, and her husband-to-be, James Frensham." His voice rose in challenge. "And if any of you know any reason why these two people should not succeed to the government of our country, you are now to declare it, or forever after be silent." His eyes roved round the hall. Hopefully? Impossible to tell, and Michael was twitching her hand. This was the hardest thing she had ever done. She rose to her feet, and knew she was shaking all

190

over. But her voice, when she forced it out, came resonant with long practice. "Your Excellency." As heads turned towards her she was aware of the man in front, her shield, tense in his seat, watching the hall like a hawk.

"Speak." Josef was looking at her without a hint of recognition.

It was a timely reminder. She put up her hand and pulled off her wig as she began to speak the words she had rehearsed. "I, Anne Paget, a foreigner who loves Lissenberg, must tell you that James Frensham is unfit to govern here." The hush in the hall was absolute. No time to see what Frensham was doing. She must go on, quickly, before something—a bullet?—stopped her. "I myself heard him plan the explosion that destroyed the opera house. Before I could give warning, his men, the 'police' he has so kindly provided for Lissenberg, assaulted me, captured me, left me where the explosion must kill me. Look at him, my friends"—now she was improvising—"and see his surprise. He thought me dead."

It was true. For one crucial moment, James Frensham had sat still, completely taken aback. Now, as the hall seethed into life, he was on his feet, about to give a signal? To precipitate a holocaust from behind that ominous curtain? But as he rose, a figure threw itself up onto the dais from the corner where the musicians had sat quiet all this time. Carl Meyer had Frensham by the throat. "One sign of violence," he spoke towards the curtain at the back of the dais, "and I kill him."

"Not if you can avoid it." Herr Winkler was making a determined way forward down the silent hall, his policemen massed behind him. For all his bulk, he jumped lightly onto the dais and faced James Frensham. "I suggest, Mr Frensham, that you tell your gang to come out from behind that curtain, and lay down their arms. You do not want your trial bedevilled by international complications."

"Trial? What nonsense is this about trials?" Frensham had got himself together. "The woman's crazy! Well, opera singers! Must I tell you that she made advances to me which I naturally rejected? This is her idea of revenge, to hide, and then come here with these lies. A totally uncorroborated story of something she pretends to have heard, and you speak of trials!" He turned, with great dignity, to Josef. "Your Excellency, I suggest that the poor woman be removed and looked after as her state demands. You cannot, for a moment, take her seriously. A woman. No Lissenberger. Unhinged,

191

no doubt, by the disaster at the opera house, the blow to her career. Her story alone!" He spread out his hands in a gesture of dismissal.

"Not alone," Anne protested, and felt Michael rise to his feet beside her. But what in the world was he doing? "Say something," he muttered to her. "Give me a moment." Of course, he was removing Dr Hirsch's padding from his cheeks.

"No." She said again. "Not alone. My friend Michael, whom you all must know, was with me. He saved my life; both our lives. Hear him!"

Tumult in the hall. What in the world was happening? "Michael!" they were shouting, and, "Michael of Liss!"

"Thanks, Anne." He had the pads out now, and was recognisable again, his grin rueful. "And forgive me?" He looked down into the seething, shouting hall, and raised both hands for silence. "Herr Winkler, who told you I was dead?"

A great many things happened at once, and Anne was never quite sure of their order. Alix swayed where she sat and was falling from her chair when Carl Meyer sprang to catch her. Freed for a moment, James Frensham hesitated, his eyes fixed on the row of diplomats, who must be the first targets of any violence, and as he did so, one of Winkler's policemen seized him, while another found the cord of the curtain at the back of the dais. It rose slowly, revealing a group of Frensham's police, armed with light machine guns, a study in desperate indecision. For a long moment the tableau held, the weapons still threatening the crowded hall, then Winkler spoke to Frensham.

"Tell them to lay down their arms," he said. "If you want to live to stand trial."

The hall held its breath, then Frensham turned and spat an order at his men. For a moment, Anne thought they might ignore it, take the situation into their own hands, begin to fire into the helpless crowd. One scream, one sign of panic might start it. But the Lissenbergers did not go in for panic. Instead, a number of men had risen silently in their seats and were filing down to the dais. They must be unarmed, but they moved with the confidence of training. Two of them for each one of Frensham's men, they climbed silently onto the dais, moved round to the back and accepted the machine guns that were as silently handed over.

The crowd was going to go mad again. No, it was not. Josef was in charge. As Winkler's men removed James Frensham, Josef raised his hand for silence, and got it. Even the journalists, who had risen to stampede from the hall with their story, paused where they stood to see what would happen next.

"Gentlemen." Josef addressed not the audience but the Diet. "Our meeting is not over. An objection has been made to our first choice and, in my view, sustained. Do you agree?" There was a mixture of *Jas* and yesses and a strange little ripple round the big table as the Diet members adjusted to the new situation, and the six men who had voted for Frensham whispered uneasily among themselves. "Thank you," said Josef. "Now, more than ever, Lissenberg needs a ruler. Prince Rudolf is still unburied. We are faced with conspiracy, scandal and bankruptcy. Princess Alix"—his voice was gentle—"are you able to speak to us?"

"Yes." With Carl's help she got slowly to her feet. "Gentlemen, you must forgive me. What I said before, I said under duress. My mother, my young brother and sister were hostages for my behaviour. Herr Meyer tells me they are safe, thank God. Perhaps a braver woman would have acted otherwise. I can only beg your indulgence, withdraw all claims to the principality of Lissenberg and name my brother Michael as the obvious heir."

The audience was on its feet now, stamping, clapping, shouting. Michael took Anne's hand. "We'd better get down there and say our piece."

"But, Michael—" She still could not believe it, and yet, in a way, had it not been obvious all the time? Michael...Michael...everywhere...The friendly conspiracy around him...A dropout, he had called himself. "But, Michael!—" she started again.

"Buts later." He was pulling her forward through the friendly crowd of "students" who had made a passage for them to the aisle. Hands reached out to touch her. She caught one vast, amiable wink from the man who had acted as her shield, returned it without thinking, and was with Michael at the exit.

"This way. There's a door, and, remember, I did ask you to forgive me."

Forgive! It was he who had so much to forgive. Would have when he knew the truth. Through the wild confusion of the last few minutes, one thing rang true and clear. Michael was hereditary Prince of Lissenberg. In a moment, he was going to be acclaimed by the Diet, by the crowded hall. And—he was going to name her as his bride. His dying bride. She should have told him. But when? There had been no point in doing so when they both seemed doomed to die anyway, and since then there had been no chance.

"Cheer up. They won't eat you." He was laughing at her, lovingly, as he urged her up the steps of the dais. "Stagefright now, of all things?" He took her hand and led her forward to where Josef stood to receive them.

"Michael!" Josef kissed him, very formally, on both cheeks, and Anne was aware of the great listening silence of the hall. "And Anne." His smile was immensely kind. "No time now for explanations." Michael was kissing Alix, one hand held out to Meyer. Then Alix took Michael's hand and led him formally up to the table where the members of the Diet still sat frozen, watching. "Gentlemen," she said. "Allow me to present my brother Michael!" She was herself again, her cheeks faintly pink, her eyes sparkling with amusement as she took in Michael's shorn hair and shabby jeans. She raised her voice so that the whole hall could hear. "Our father disinherited him. Unjustly, as one of you rightly said just now. May I, whom you have honoured beyond my deserts with your choice, present him as the heir to Lissenberg."

Now the audience went mad. In all her experience, Anne had never heard anything like it. Josef's appeals for silence were simply ignored, and at last, with a sigh and a shrug he moved back to his place at the big table and went through the ceremony of naming Michael in dumb show. This time, when eleven other hands went up in approval, his joined them. Now, at last, as he moved forward again to the front of the dais, the audience began to settle down. There were cries of "Hush!" and "Hear him!" and he was able to repeat the formal request for any objections to Michael as Hereditary Prince, ending, as before, "Or forever after be silent."

A long hush, and then, from the gallery where Anne and Michael had been sitting, one voice. "What about her?" it cried. "She spoke up for us all, didn't she, at risk of her life. I say, Long live Prince Michael and Princess Anne."

"That saves trouble," said Michael cheerfully, took Anne's hand and led her forward. "Don't look so bashful, my darling. It's no worse than taking a curtain call."

No worse! Bowing, smiling, bowing again, letting herself be solemnly kissed—first by Michael, then by Alix, then by Josef—she thought that if she could have died, there and then, as she stood, by wishing it, she would have done so.

16

Would she ever be alone with Michael, and, if she was, how would she tell him? It was all confusion, chaos, explanation, happiness. For them. For everyone but her. And, somehow, at some point, she had decided that, for today, she would not spoil it. Tomorrow would be time enough. For today, she would be still, listen to the explanations, try to understand. They were all up at the castle now, where Princess Gloria, sober for once, had thrown her arms round her son Michael and burst into floods of hysterical tears. She and her two younger children had been held incommunicado by Frensham's men since they had taken over the castle on the night of the explosion, ostensibly to protect her. They had been rescued, she explained, after Frensham and Alix had left for the Rathaus. "I should have known it was your doing, Michael! Who else knows the way in by the great vine? I couldn't believe my eyes when the first one came in at my bedroom window. Who are they, Michael? They've been so kind...But I don't seem to know them."

He laughed. "School friends of mine, Mother. The best thing Father ever did for me was to let me go to the Liss Academy. And I know whose doing that was." He smiled across the room at Josef. "We were a romantic lot. Formed ourselves into the Lissenberg Volunteers. All for one; one for all. That kind of thing. And—when I came home, they remembered. Now we're the United Workers of Lissenberg— its first trade union. How soon will I be able to legalise us, Uncle Josef?"

"If you can solve Lissenberg's financial problems, you can do anything," said Josef. "But the situation's bad, Michael. We have to face it. If James Frensham chooses to call in the money Lissenberg owes him, the country will collapse."

"Will it, I wonder? What makes a country collapse?"

"Lack of money and lack of confidence. If you can't pay people's wages, at a time like this, what's going to happen?"

"I'll tell you what will happen here in Lissenberg. They'll go right on working. That's what the United Workers of Lissenberg, my mad trade union, is all about. We've been saving for a day like this. Union funds. We'll keep going, don't you worry, and without your pay, either, bless you." He turned with a loving smile to Anne. "It's only until Frensham's trial's over, and then, you know, our problems will be solved."

"What do you mean?" asked Josef.

"Don't tell me you've forgotten Lissenberg's legal code? A traitor to the state forfeits all his possessions. To the state. He can choose execution if he prefers, but I doubt if Frensham would do that."

"But he's not a citizen."

"Oh yes he is. Under Lissenberg law he became one automatically when he allowed himself to be elected Prince. Well, you could hardly have a foreigner, could you? The first Prince and his advisors were a methodical lot. They thought of everything."

"Good God," said Josef. "As simple as that."

"Well," said Michael. "First he's got to be proved guilty. But I doubt if that will be a problem, not with Anne's evidence. It will just take a little time. Herr Winkler is hoping also to get evidence to implicate him in his father's death, but of course that's a private matter, nothing to do with the state."

"He had his own father killed?" Anne was appalled.

"I'm afraid so," Josef told her. "They'd never been on good terms. Old Frensham kept him right out of the business, so— young James had him watched. Michael found the evidence when Winkler sent him down to Sicily. When he heard about the discovery of szilenite, James decided it was time to get rid of his father. It was his hired killer, of course, who crossed the border in Brech's taxi just before it was closed that night."

"Brech's taxis," said Alix. "How did they fit in? And that odd business on Anne's journey here. Who was behind all that?"

"Young James too, Winkler thinks. Working by remote control, through Brech, which explains the general atmosphere of muddle. It looks as if he began by simply planning to make the opera fail. What with that, and his father's death, I don't think there's any question but that Lissenberg would have been bankrupt in a few weeks. Then he would have moved in at leisure, in his strong position as his father's heir, got the opera complex condemned on one pretext or another and opened up his killer mine. Brech was his mistake—a small-time muddler, if ever there was one. Not in his league at all. I think he saw that as soon as he got here, and started changing his plans. Of course he'd never been in direct touch with Brech. The nearest we've got to a connection is his man's use of that taxi, which put us on to Brech in the first place. Your Herr Schann was Brech's cousin, by the way." He turned to Anne. "That was the first try. And the thing that threw us off for a long time was the 'accident' that happened to Brech himself when he was driving Falinieri back from Schennen. The comic thing about that was that it really was an accident. We found the truck driver who lost his load just the other day, and he admitted it readily enough. It must have scared Brech at the time, but it didn't stop him. He went right on with his sabotage, and Hilde Bernz went on spreading gloom among the cast."

"Hilde!" exclaimed Anne. "She was the one? But why?"

"Blackmail, I'm afraid, by Brech. She confessed to Winkler after we got on to Brech. But of course she had no idea who was behind him. You must have noticed things started going better in the later rehearsals. So when young James got here after his father's death, which had been so cleverly patterned on the original accident, he found *Regulus* still showing obstinate signs of survival. I think he must have made up his mind and sent for his explosives expert after that night at the hotel when he saw what a success you were going to be, Anne."

"I remember," Anne said. "I was scared, suddenly."

"Right to be," said Alix. "I always knew he was a horror. I think I'd have killed myself rather than marry him. But what could I do, with Mother and the children in his hands?"

"All over now." Michael turned to smile at Anne. "You've been very quiet."

Anne had been thinking that she had a duty to stay alive until Frensham's trial was over. Her testimony was vital. Tomorrow she must tell Michael. For today, she would pretend, and smile, and smile, and pretend. She smiled. "I'm trying so hard to work it all out," she said. "I mean." She turned to Josef. "You're the Prince the Diet threw out, years ago, aren't you?"

"Happiest day of my life," he told her. "You and Michael have no idea what you're getting into. But you'll be all right. There are two of you. It's no job for an anxious bachelor, and that's the truth. Anyway"—he smiled contentedly—"civilised lot, we Lissenbergers. As you can see, they didn't throw me very far. Just into a snug corner that suited me. I'm sorry about the opera house, Anne dear."

"We're going to build another one," said Michael. "A little one, Glyndebourne size, say. Something Lissenberg can afford, and something that won't weigh us down with too many visitors. And we'll open it with Anne in *Regulus*." He turned to Carl Meyer, who was sitting beside Alix. "You've got the production rights sewn up tight, I do hope."

"The opera belongs to the Principality of Lissenberg," Carl told him. "Having been found here. I think, judging by the dress rehearsal, that it should help to solve your financial problem. I've had some interesting approaches about recordings." He smiled at Anne. "You're going to be a very busy Princess."

Smile and pretend. This was their happy evening. She smiled at Carl. "I never did have a chance to tell you how well I thought it went. I'd give anything to sing in it again." My life? "But, Carl, you and Alix?" They were sitting hand in hand, and she had suddenly understood Carl's baffling behaviour to herself.

"Time we came to that. Thanks, Anne." Carl raised Alix's hand to his lips, then turned to Michael. "We've been engaged for a year. I wanted to tell you, but Alix wouldn't let me."

"Quite right, too," Michael told him. "I didn't exist, remember, and Father had thought up some quite nasty punishments for people who insisted on pretending that I did. The funny thing was, it rebounded on him in a way. Since he had announced that I didn't exist, there wasn't much he could do when I came back with my United Nations passport as plain Michael Liss, except pretend I wasn't there and insist everyone else do so too. I must say, I found it remarkably liberating." He turned to Anne. "I hated not telling you, my darling, but it really was much safer for you."

"Yes," she agreed reluctantly. "I suppose I can see that." And she could understand, too, how he had found his strange state of non-existence liberating, as she had her sentence of death. She shivered. Smile and pretend...

Michael was grinning wickedly at his sister. "So all that flirting with Adolf Stern and James Frensham was just camouflage? I did think they weren't quite your line. To hell with Frensham, but hard on Stern, maybe?"

"Stern!" Carl interrupted explosively. "Nothing's too bad for him. If Alix was pretending, so was he. He and Lotte Moser are marrred. Kept it quiet because they thought it better for their careers. There was going to be a dramatic announcement when they had got rid of Anne, and Lotte took over the part of Marcus. Stern broke down and told me all about it after the explosion; when we thought you two dead.

198

They hadn't meant it to go as far as that. That's what they say now. That they hired Fritz just to give you a fright, Anne, and leave you shut in the opera house all night. Quite a fright they must have been planning, since they obviously didn't expect you to be able to sing on Monday night. Stern insists he left it all to Fritz."

"Who was undoubtedly in Frensham's pay already," put in Michael, "and told him all about it. Frensham just took over control. It was Fritz who telephoned and told me you were locked in the opera house, Anne. A nasty trick by Stern, he said. Idiotic to have believed him and gone alone. Of course Frensham's men were waiting for me."

"Well, you'd heard Stern telling me Anne had gone on ahead to the hotel," said Meyer. "And then, when we got there, she wasn't there. It all fitted together . . . God, that was a terrible evening. I'll never forget that pretence at a party. And the next twenty-four hours, with no sign of you, Anne, or Michael. Alix's sore throat worse and Lotte Moser turning up, all smiles, ready to take over Marcus and 'save' us. I'm not sure the explosion wasn't a relief, in a way." He turned to Anne. "Don't look so sad, Annchen. It will be even better next time." And, back to Alix: "How's your throat now?"

"Better again. Good God!" She put her hand to it.

"Yes?"

"I've just realised. When it first started bothering me, Adolf Stern said he had the very thing for it . . . throat pastilles. He gave me his. I finished them the other day, and it began to get better. Then, just the other day, he offered me one, 'to be on the safe side.' And I took it to be polite. And it got worse again."

"I should imagine so," said Carl dryly. "So, with you and Anne both unable to sing, Lotte could step gallantly forward and take over. She got herself thrown out of the job at the hotel on purpose. Didn't think nightclub singing was just the right image. But she's been waiting her time just across the border. Came in with the first of the crowds, according to Adolf Stern, so he and she and Fritz were able to play their little trick on you in the opera house, Anne. What exactly did they do?"

Anne shuddered. "I'd rather not talk about it," she said. "Fritz hated me . . . thought he had reason to. He was a little mad, I think. What's happened to him?" she asked.

"We think he must have lost his nerve," Josef told her. "Heard something, perhaps. Realised he was out of his depth.

He tried to get in touch with Winkler on Sunday, but couldn't, finally he telephoned Hans at the Wild Man, told him he was afraid for Michael; thought he was in danger; behind the opera house somewhere. He was scared rigid; wouldn't stop to say more. Didn't seem to care about you, I'm afraid, Anne. But it was thanks to him that Hans and his friends were looking for you two on Sunday night."

"Poor man," said Michael. "Yes. It must have been for him Frensham's men were checking cars that night, Anne. Inconvenient for us; worse for him."

"They found him?"

"Must have. His body washed up in the river this morning."

"Another death for Frensham to answer for," said Josef.

It was odd, Anne thought, to see how naturally he had retaken his place as head of the family. Perhaps she would tell him first. But that was the coward's way ... Michael had the right to know. Tomorrow she would tell him.

"It's been a long day," said Josef. "And tomorrow Herr Winkler wants statements from everyone concerned. Time for bed, I think. Gloria, my dear, did you arrange about a room for Anne?"

"Room for Anne?" At some point in the evening, Princess Gloria must have been reunited with her champagne cocktails. By now her speech was slurred. "Moving in already, is she? Better have my room, I suppose. Hereditary Princess's." She made an awkward mouthful of the phrase.

"Mother!" Alix began a protest, but Michael intervened. "I believe Anne would rather go back to the hostel, wouldn't you?" He turned to her. "Winkler's put a man there, just to be on the safe side, but Stern and Lotte left this morning. No problems now, and I expect you'll be glad to get back into your own things."

"I certainly will." Here, suddenly, was the chance she had both wanted and feared. The chance to be alone with Michael. She must take it, get it over with, finished. Then she must call Dr Hirsch, ask for stronger pills; something that would keep her going for the duration of James Frensham's trial. And oddly, it was now, thinking this, that she realised for the first time that she had lost the last batch of pills, days ago, when her purse was stolen, and simply been too busy, too frightened, too exhausted to worry about them. Extraordinary.

Goodnights were being said. Josef, too, was returning to

the hostel and for a moment she thought she would be spared the task of telling Michael tonight. But Josef had his own car. A cold finger from Princess Gloria, a warm kiss from Alix and another from Carl. These ought to be her family. Well—she braced herself—Princess Gloria would not mourn her for long.

One of Michael's trade union members was waiting with the little green car in which he had driven her before. "You've been very quiet." Michael held the door for her. "Tired? You've a right to be. You were tremendous, there at the Diet. I was—proud of you. I always am." He climbed in beside her. "Forgiven me yet for what I've bounced you into?"

"Forgiven! Oh, Michael." She turned in her seat to face him. "It's not that. It's what you have to forgive me."

He let in the clutch and they slid gently downhill. "Married already? Ten starving children at home? Who cares? I love you. You love me. There's no arguing about that. We know; you and I. We're lucky."

Lucky! They were at the fork in the road already. She could not do it to him here in the car, with the hostel so close. "Michael, can't we go up to the Wild Man? I'm hungry." Extraordinary, but it was true.

"Lovely girl. I'd hesitated to suggest it after all you've been through. But yes, indeed we'll go and see old Hans. I could just do with a hunter's breakfast."

As on the first time they had gone there, the Wild Man was in darkness. Michael played a tune on the car horn. Haydn? The Lissenberg national anthem. "Michael!" She was shocked and sounded it.

"Proving a point," he told her. "We love our country; we don't worship it. After what you've done for us, no one's going to care if you have five ex-husbands and a whole hostel full of illegits. Though, frankly, my darling, I find it hard to believe."

"If it was only that." As the lights went on along the front of the Wild Man, she let him help her out of the car. His arm was warm under hers. An electric charge shook through them. He bent and kissed her, lightly, gently, as if they had all the time in the world for passion. "No matter what," he said, "Lissenberg and I are yours till death us do part." And then, feeling the shock of it go through her. "What is it, Anne?"

But Hans was at the door making great roaring noises of

welcome. "Michael and Anne. The people in the world I most wanted to see!"

"We want to see *you*." Anne reached up to brush a kiss against his cheek. "You saved our lives the other night, and I fainted before I could thank you."

"A pleasure." He beamed down on her. And then, mock formal, "Your Hereditary Highnesses, welcome to my poor house."

"Hereditary," said Anne. "It's a funny word for it."

"It's a funny place, Lissenberg," said Michael. "But I like it. Is young Hans home yet?" he asked Hans.

"Not him. Out celebrating with the rest of the union, I reckon." His huge smile embraced Anne. "My son had the honour of sitting in front of you in the Rathaus today."

"My shield." Her eyes filled with tears. "I love you all."

"And she wants a hunter's breakfast." Michael was shepherding her to a secluded table. "We both do. And a bottle from the back of the cellar, Hans. Seems Anne's got a problem. We have to talk."

"Talk away." Hans had swiftly set their table and produced two glasses of slivovitz. "The place is yours. Even I can't produce a hunter's breakfast in under twenty minutes."

Anne sipped burning liquid and faced Michael across the table. "I'm dying," she told him flatly. "I knew it when I took the job. The doctor gave me six months to live. I've got five now. I thought I might as well make the most of my time. Michael"—his face was breaking her heart—"I'm sorry."

"Dear God, so am I." He reached across the table and took her hand. "You're sure? You believed him? Beyond a shadow of doubt?"

"Oh, I believed him. With pain like that...I tell you, Michael, before I came here, found so much that was worth living for, six months seemed too long. Even here, once, on a bad day, I looked at my pain-killers and thought, why not take them all? Have it over with. Michael, when you look like that, I almost wish I had."

"My darling, no!" His hands were chafing her cold one. "There are things you must never forget." He winced at his own unlucky phrase, and she smiled at him.

"My 'never' is a short one. You'll need another Marcus when you have rebuilt the opera house. Oh, Michael, forgive me. I meant it for the best." Idiotic, hopeless words.

"Forgive!—Nonsense. Whatever happens, I wouldn't have missed you for all the world." His hands closed hard on hers.

"We've a ballad, here in Lissenberg, a legend, an old one—older than the country. Called 'The Other Road.' It's about a hunter and his young wife, riding through the forest. They come to a fork in the road, and choose one turning. It's a long ballad, they meet brigands, she's killed and he rides on alone." He hummed it for her, quietly, now holding both her hands:

> "There were two roads through the forest
> And we took the one on the hill.
> If we had taken the other,
> Would you be with me still?

"And then the last verse:

> There were two roads through the forest,
> We chose one, and you are gone,
> But I'd rather have had you, my darling,
> And lost you, and ride alone."

He leaned across the table and kissed her lightly, tenderly, first on one cheek and then the other. "I shall have you for five months, God willing, and then I will miss you for the rest of my life. But at least, I shall have you to miss. Forever. I knew, that first time, when you ran in front of the car; hair in rat's tails, coat soaking, eyes huge, like something frightened in the woods. Frightened! I didn't know you then, did I, but I loved you, that's for sure." They sat quiet for a moment, while she thanked him in her heart for accepting it so swiftly, so absolutely. "We'll be married at once," he said at last. "The Prince Bishop's a friend of mine. He'll see us through."

"But Michael; your Father! We can't."

"I owe him nothing. Everyone in Lissenberg knows that. Less than nothing, you could say. He hated me, Anne—did his best to destroy me. It's not funny to be declared a non-person at twenty. If I hadn't got that Oxford scholarship, I don't know if I'd have survived."

"A non-person? Michael, I wish you'd explain. How could he?"

"I got in his hair," said Michael. "I didn't like what he was doing here in Lissenberg, and, of course, being young, I let it show. So, he announced in full Diet that I no longer

203

existed. Anyone who mentioned me was an enemy of the state, with penalties to match. I'd made him very angry. Oh—I was full of bright ideas."

"Trades unions and such?"

"Exactly. Profit sharing—oh, all kinds of things. Of course"—he smiled at her—"it cut two ways in the end. When Winkler got me into the country on the United Nations passport a college friend helped me get, there wasn't a great deal he could do. Except play along with the conspiracy of silence he had started and go right on hating me."

"Poor man."

"But not a nice one—even if he was my Father. It's all over now, done with, unimportant. And it's most certainly not going to affect our wedding. Mind you, we'll keep it as quiet as we can. It will have to be in the cathedral, though. Do you mind?" And then, "Good God, you haven't really got a couple of divorces round your neck? That *would* be a problem for the Prince Bishop."

Extraordinary how little they knew about each other. "No," she told him. "I had a husband, but he died—in a car smash with another woman. Pregnant. He'd been living with her on the side." How long ago and far away it all seemed. When had she decided not to tell him about Fritz and his obscene, horrible suggestions?

"Poor fool," said Michael. "Well, that's all right then. Father's funeral tomorrow and the wedding next week, just as soon as the Prince Bishop can organise it. It will make a change from bad news. I reckon that's what Lissenberg needs right now. They've had a hard time, you know. Father was a disaster in more ways than I want to tell you. And Mother . . . well, I was meaning to apologise for Mother."

"No need." Her eyes were full of tears. "Oh, Michael, no need."

"That's settled then." He lifted her hand and kissed it. "And here, in good time, come our hunter's breakfasts. You won't believe it, but I'm still hungry."

"Oh, Michael, so am I."

"Now," said Michael, when Hans had put the two heaped platters in front of them and opened a cold, dusty bottle, "we are going to talk about the past. I want to know all about you. It strikes me, looking back, that I've told you a lot about myself, and you've just kept quiet and listened with those big eyes of yours wide open, and said nothing. I know you by heart, and yet I know nothing about you. So, begin. Parents,

204

brothers and sisters, school, the lot...I believe I even want to know about that crazy husband of yours, if you feel like telling me."

"I'll tell you everything...Anything...No parents; no brothers and sisters. Oh, Michael, I've been so lonely..." For a moment she was back in the bleak bed-sitter, looking out at spring flowers, facing—alone—the fact of death.

"You'll never be lonely again. I may not be able to promise much, but that I can. You've a whole country to care for you now, and they do, you know. They did already, before you stood up in the Rathaus today and saved them from tyranny."

"Today. Was it really only today?"

"Hard to believe, isn't it?" He refilled their glasses with the golden wine. "Eat up, my darling. It's late, and you're tired. We've"—he paused—"five months to talk. Five months are a long time."

She smiled, and drank to him. "A lifetime, Michael."

It seemed like a lifetime indeed since she had left the hostel. Only four days ago she had hurried up the arcade to the dress rehearsal, with the crowds seething and shouting in the valley. Now, all was quiet. Frensham's men had cleared the last straggler out of the valley before the Diet met. They too were gone now, most of them allowed just to melt away over the border into the obscurity from which they had come. After all, as Michael had pointed out, it would have been awkward for Herr Winkler and his twenty policemen to try and hold them all in custody, in Lissenberg's apology for a gaol.

"I love you, Michael. Always." Still trembling from their last kiss, Anne turned back to him at the top of the hostel steps. She was tired now, almost beyond speech, beyond thought of all the things she should be saying to him.

"And I you." He kissed her hands, one after the other. "You're asleep on your feet, my darling. To bed with you, and dream of me."

But in her room, Gertrud was waiting for her. "I thought you'd never come." An ashtray loaded with stubs spoke of her long wait. "I have to talk to you, Anne."

"Tonight? It's very late. I thought you'd be gone by now. Can I help you, some way?" How strange suddenly to find herself in a position where she could help people.

"Why should I be gone? Oh, the rats have all left, now the

opera's sunk, but I'm a Lissenberger, remember. That's why I'm here."

"Oh?" Drugged with fatigue, Anne hung her borrowed coat in the closet and sat unwillingly down to listen, to try and keep awake.

"You've got to listen to me." Gertrud lighted another cigarette. "I'm the only person who can tell you the truth. The only person who will."

"The truth? What are you talking about?"

"About this nine-day-wonder between you and Michael, of course. About the friend he bribed to shout for you in the Rathaus. About what they are really saying in the town tonight."

Anne passed a hand across her forehead. "I don't understand."

"Of course you don't. What do you know about Lissenberg? Cooped up in this fake valley of Prince Rudolf's, how should you know? Oh, you're the little heroine today. Naturally. But don't count on it lasting, Anne Paget, because it won't. We care for our own in Lissenberg, and everyone in the place knows I'm engaged to Michael."

"You?" Was she stupid with fatigue? What was this?

Gertrud laughed, not pleasantly. "Never bothered to ask who I was, did you? Just some young local had in to play a minor part in the opera. Passable voice...not bad-looking ...unimportant. Right?"

"Who are you then?" Anne asked into a lengthening, nightmare silence.

"Michael's cousin. A Liss like him. The family voice. You might have guessed. My parents were dead. I grew up at the castle. Cousin Rudolf...liked me. Michael did too." She reached into the low-cut neck of her blouse and brought out a ring on a chain. "That's Michael's signet ring. I've had it since I was sixteen."

"A long time ago." Anne's voice sounded dull to her own ears.

"Would you like to see the letters he wrote me from abroad? I've got them all. Love letters. If you hadn't turned up, with your fancy voice and your pitiful waif's eyes, it would be official by now, and Lissenberg would be wild with joy. Anne, don't you see?" Now her tone changed, became friendly, pleading. "If it was just that, I'd have stepped back, disappeared, left Michael to be happy, returned his ring. But it's not just that, is it? He's not going to be happy; you're a dying woman. Oh, God, even I, who should hate you, have felt sorry for you, have admired you for what you've done, how you've coped...But not this. Don't you see what you'd be doing to Michael? Every minute you keep him in the dark, let him think he's happy, you make it worse for him. Harder for him to find happiness afterwards. How long have you got?"

"Five months. But how did you know?" Now she had moved from mere fatigue into the black tunnel of nightmare.

"Oh, that! I've a friend works for Dr Hirsch. She thought it odd the way he dropped everything and came running when you called. When she found out why, she thought it her duty—as a Lissenberger—to tell me. Don't you see, Anne? Michael must have an heir. Alix is out of it. She renounced her rights today. That settles her. And Lissenberg needs a family, not a mourning Prince."

"His young brother and sister?" But this was a new, a heart-shaking idea.

"Them!" Gertrud's tone was withering. "That just shows how little you know about anything. Everyone here in Lissenberg knows that whoever's children they may be, they're not Rudolf's. He was ill, fifteen years ago. After that there were no more of his little bastards here in Lissenberg. Oh, no, I'm not one of them—in case you were hoping so. I'm the only child of Rudolf and Josef's elder sister. By our law, I've as good a claim as Michael. That's why our marriage will solve everything."

"Nobody mentioned you today."

"I told them not to, of course. It was Michael's day." She fingered her ring lovingly. "I had no idea he was taking this crazy affair with you seriously. Well, romantic stuff, I can see, escaping together and all that. But—a passing fancy, Anne. He'll wake up soon enough and see where his duty lies. Easier for you both if you've seen it for him first. And—more dignified for you. The Prince Bishop would have to get the Diet's approval to marry you—did Michael tell you that? I wouldn't stay quiet then. I couldn't. It would be my duty as a Lissenberger to speak. And Dr Hirsch's. Just think what an unlucky beginning to Michael's reign, whichever way they decide. And what misery for him. Anne, I'm begging you, because I love him. Because you do. Spare him that. He's been through so much—what his father did to him, the public exile. It was done in full Diet, you know. Wicked. And Michael standing there, quiet, taking it, because he would not

207

call his father, his Prince, a liar in public. You couldn't put him through something like that again, Anne. Not if you love him."

"Oh, I love him."

"Then do it for him. For us all. For Lissenberg."

"Do what?" She was so tired... If only she could be quiet, think, face this new disaster. Because it was a disaster. She did not like Gertrud, but she believed her, found it hard not to agree with her. She ought not to have let Michael talk her into marriage. In her heart, surely, she had known it was wrong. Wrong for so many reasons. "What shall I do?" she asked, now, listlessly, defeated.

"Vanish," said Gertrud. "You came into our lives, suddenly, a mysterious, romantic figure. Go out of them the same way, and you'll be remembered forever. With love. Stay, and they'll hate you."

"But it's not possible. How would I get away? And, besides there's Frensham's trial. I have to speak at that."

"You're making difficulties," said Gertrud impatiently. "The Diet heard your evidence today. It will be on the record. As to how you get away, that's easy. I'll help you."

"You?"

"Michael's not the only one with friends in Lissenberg." She looked at her watch. "Josef will be in bed by now. The hostel's closed for the night. I've got a master key and a car outside. And a friend on guard at the frontier. I can have you at Schennen in time to catch the milk train."

"Go? Now?" Her tired brain could not take it in properly. "How can I? I've no money. I lost my purse." But not her passport, she remembered, since it was safe in a drawer.

"Money! That's no problem." Gertrud produced a fat wallet. "Mine's the rich branch of the family, I'm glad to say. Don't worry, I'll get it back from Michael. He'd want you to go in comfort. Now, you'd better get packing, hadn't you, if you're to catch that train."

But I haven't agreed, Anne thought tiredly. Or had she? Gertrud certainly seemed to think so. She had dragged Anne's suitcase out from the closet and was beginning to pack shoes in tidy pairs. The shoes Prince Rudolf had ordered for her.

"No," said Anne. "If I go, I go with what I brought."

"Hardly worth bothering with, as I remember," said Gertrud.

"You're right." Crawl away and die. "I'm too tired," she said. "I'll just go as I am."

"Sensible," said Gertrud. "Makes the travelling so much easier. But you'd better take the fur coat. You don't want to catch cold, in your state."

Why not? An everlasting cold, and have it over with. But she had no pills.

"My friend said you were on pain-killers." Had Gertrud plucked the thought from her mind? "Thought you might be running low." She produced a chemist's bottle. "A new supply, just in case."

"Thank you." She should have said. "Get thee behind me, Satan." But she was so tired...So tired...Michael, she thought, oh, Michael, my darling.

"Time to go," said Gertrud.

17

It began to rain as Gertrud's friend passed them through the control at the bridge over the Liss and rained steadily all the way to Schennen. A kind of nightmare reprise of her arrival, Anne thought tiredly. "What time is it?" she asked. Her watch, like everything else, was left behind, broken, useless...

"Late." Gertrud was concentrating on the black, wet road shining under her headlights. The swish of windshield wipers soothed Anne towards sleep. Incredible. She jerked upright. She was leaving everything in the world she loved, and all she could do was sleep. "I'll need your address," said Gertrud. "For your pay from the opera."

"Yes." Not for Michael. Oh, never for Michael. She could trust Gertrud for that. "I'll write it down for you at the station." She would go back to Mrs Briggs, to the glum bed-sitter. She had always known it was her place for dying. With money to ease things, Mrs Briggs would be kind, would nurse her, so long as nursing at home sufficed. After that, the un-tender mercies of the Health Service. But, what difference...

Unless...She had fought off the idea ever since Gertrud had produced the bottle of pain killers. A tempter? A solution.

A final solution. Five months with Michael...That was one thing. A selfish thing. One to be forgotten. As the wet miles lengthened between her and Lissenberg, as she felt her heartstrings stretch and bleed, she knew that Gertrud was right, for however many wrong reasons. How could she have imagined inflicting her death on Michael? Michael who had been through so much, and now would have so much on his mind: the whole future of Lissenberg. So—five months of dying alone. Without Michael. With nothing but a hole to hide in. Must she? If she had taken that overdose, early on in Lissenberg, Michael would be a happier man tonight, and she would be out of it all.

Would he? Would she? Who could ever tell what would happen if they had taken the other road? What was that song Michael had sung to her at the Wild Man? Tonight? Last night? A million light-years ago, in another life. "There were two roads through the forest..." Oh, my beloved Michael, will you ever understand why I had to take the other?

"Christ! The train's in." Gertrud put her foot on the accelerator as they came in sight of the station. "Be ready to run for it. And best of luck."

The car stopped and Gertrud reached over to open Anne's door as she fumbled with her safety harness. "That's it. Hurry!"

Rain sluiced down. The door slammed behind Anne as the car pulled off. And, as it did, so did the train, grinding and groaning its way off into the darkness. Dark. The station, too, was dark. Only, here and there, a feeble light illuminated the platform. Surely Gertrud must have seen what had happened. Would come back? Indeed she would not. Nor had she taken that vital address. If she had, she would not have passed it on. But Michael would find her. Carl would find her. If she was there to be found.

Better not to be? No guard had been there to see the train on its way. The station was closed and dark, but Anne remembered the bus shelter, at the end of the platform, with its convenient water supply. She could sit there. It would be cold, and her coat was wet, but she could sit there. If she wanted to, she could die there. Thoughtful of Gertrud to provide those pills. Thoughtful? Too thoughtful by half.

All planned? All of this planned? The missed train, the dark station, the pills...It would be so easy, so logical. So right? How long would it take? If she took all the pills, now, at once? What time? She did not know, but there was no hint of light in the sky. Dark...dark...As exhausted as she was, the pills should work quickly. Easier for Michael this way?

She had reached the shelter now, where it stood, faintly illuminated by the last light on the platform. She could just see the standpipe outside, with its chained, communal mug. Had Gertrud thought even of this? All planned...all subtly organised? If I do it, she thought, if I kill myself, here in the cold darkness, it will be murder. Gertrud will have killed me, and I shall have let her. What a shameful end. What a sordid story to begin Michael's reign. No. I shall die in my own way, and my own time. She opened her handbag, felt for the bottle of pills and threw it with all her force into the darkness across the tracks. Then she moved tiredly into the shelter and sat down to wait for the next train.

Too cold to sleep, too cold to think, and that was a mercy. Crazy to have thrown those pills away; melodramatic... absurd. Any moment now the pain would strike. She was listening for it, waiting for it...Her head ached from the blow Frensham's men had struck her. It had done so off and on ever since. Four days...And suddenly, like a lightning flash, it struck her that during those four days there had been no trace of the other pain. Extraordinary...It was the longest remission she could remember. Oh well, she thought wryly, perhaps I should make a habit of living dangerously. But now it would come, now it was bound to come. She braced herself, waiting, and thought about Michael.

She ought to have left him a note, a message. Incredible, brutal to have come away like this. But Gertrud would have destroyed a note, suppressed a message. Michael would understand...Michael would forgive her...Perhaps, one day, he might even be grateful to her. He would never marry Gertrud. Strange to be so sure of that. Strange, and comforting. But, after a while, after she died, he would marry and be happy. Have heirs for Lissenberg...children for himself...Call one of them Anne? Oh, Michael...She let herself think of him, of the goodbye they had not known was forever. The kiss on the hostel steps. "I shall love you always..." Tears tasted salt in her mouth...What would he say, in the morning? What would he do? Gertrud would say nothing. She saw that, suddenly. I can't bear it, she thought, and yet, it was right. I was right to come away, even if Gertrud was wrong to make me. Right...wrong...Michael...cold. She slipped down on the hard bench and, mercifully, slept.

Cold. Starting awake, aware of the noise that had roused

her, she thought, the train. Must not miss another one. Up, staggering, to her feet and out in a rush into dawn light. Rush of wheels; scream of brakes; Michael, flinging himself out of the big car. "Anne!" He gathered her up as she swayed towards him. "Anne?"

"Tired." She opened her eyes. Had she said it aloud?

"Well, I should think so." Dr Hirsch was sitting by the bed. Hospital bed; nurse, highly starched, at its foot. "Running off like that. I ought to scold you, young woman, but I can't. I've got to apologise instead."

"Apologise? Why? Where am I?" She looked at the door, half hoping that it would open and reveal Michael.

"In my clinic. We rushed you here, Michael and I. Never been driven so fast in my life. Pumped out your stomach straight away. Hence the apology. But we didn't know, do you see? Whether you'd taken them or not."

"Taken—"

"The pills Gertrud Stock gave you. No time to wait and see. Better safe than sorry. And Michael almost off his head. You shouldn't have done it, Anne, not that way. Run off like that."

"I'm sorry." And then, "But how did you know?"

"By a miracle. Well, by luck, if you like. Michael rang me when he got home, told me his good news ... and his bad. He wanted to know just how things stood. About your health. I thought he had the right."

"Of course he had the right."

"So I fetched your notes. And found that something had been added. In my assistant's hand. Emergency supply of painkillers, yesterday's date. Idiotic creature. Doing a scandalous thing like that, and then making a note of it. Characteristic. Scared me rigid. And as for Michael ... We met at the hostel; woke Josef; found you and Gertrud were both missing. How did she get to you, Anne?"

"She was in my room when I got back. Had been there a long time. She had a master key, must have got in while Josef was at the castle. Were she and Michael really engaged, Dr Hirsch?"

"That's what she told you! Years ago. Boy-and-girl. I was always against it. First cousins, and in that family. She'd never have got him, even if she had succeeded in murdering you."

"Murder?" But it was what she had thought.

212

"I don't know what else you'd call it. Leaving you alone there, with what you faced, and an overdose at hand. I'm proud of you, Anne."

She smiled shakily up at him. "Don't be too proud. I nearly did."

"Tell me." He had taken her pulse, but kept hold of her hand as if to go on monitoring it. "How's the pain been, through all these excitements?" There was a little rustle, as if the starched nurse at the foot of the bed had moved suddenly.

"Funny you should ask that." Anne's smile came stronger this time. "I suddenly thought...waiting for that train...I haven't had it since...since..." She stopped, puzzled. "Friday? I'm not sure. When I realised that, I thought it was bound to start. I fell asleep instead. I was so *tired*, Dr Hirsch. Does Michael understand...Will he? When can I see him? I've got to explain, do you see. Quickly. Because Gertrud was quite right. Not in what she did...What I let her make me do. But she was right. We can't marry, Michael and I. You'll help me to make him see?"

"I'll do anything you want. Ah!" A tap at the door. Michael? No. The nurse opened it, spoke to someone, turned to Dr Hirsch. "They're ready, doctor."

"Thanks. Excuse me a minute, Anne?"

Tension in the air. Unmistakable. "There's nothing wrong, is there? Michael?" Suppose he had found Gertrud. A murderess....

"Nothing in the world. Relax, child. Rest. Don't fret."

Absurd advice. She had told him she would not marry Michael and he had made no attempt to dissuade her. He might at least have thanked me, she thought, and felt tears of self-pity forming. Not that, never that. I shall die in some comfort after all, she told herself, in Dr Hirsch's clinic. And I still have a little pride. "Nurse." She pulled herself up in the bed. "Could I have my bag? I'd like to put some lipstick on."

The nurse's hands, passing her the bag, were shaking.

"Something *is* going on," Anne said. "If it's Michael, and you're not telling me...I'll...I'll..."

"It's not Michael. I promise it's not. The Prince, I should say. We've all got so used to calling him Michael. He's with the Diet. Emergency arrangements." She was talking almost wildly, infected by the general tension.

"Anne!" Dr Hirsch was carrying a sheaf of papers. He

213

gave a little nod to the nurse, and she moved round to the other side of the bed as he sat down on the chair by Anne. "You're a good, strong girl, aren't you?"

Ridiculous question, to a dying woman. "You mean, am I going to have hysterics if you tell me I've only got a month after all? No, Dr Hirsch, I won't. I promise. I'll thank you; truly I will. It's a...a solution, isn't it?"

"Not that. No, not that at all." Something had shaken him deeply. "Anne, you remember I asked your permission to write your English doctor and ask for your notes?"

"Of course. And I remember last time we talked about it, they hadn't come."

"Just so. When Hans hauled you two out of the river and I saw how things were between you, I sent for them."

"Sent?"

"A messenger. I had my duty, as a Lissenberger. Had to know just where I stood. Before I said anything. My man had a bit of trouble persuading your doctor to part with the file. He had to invoke our ambassador in the end. He's come back with a healthy respect for your British red tape. He only got here last night. With the lot. Your notes: X rays, everything. By which time you'd vanished. We didn't only pump out your stomach when we got you back here. We X rayed you, Anne." He was holding her hand again, and the nurse had moved a little nearer. "You're absolutely not going to faint, or have hysterics? But this is as sure as I'm a doctor, and a happy man. Whatever it was, child, and whether your doctor was right or wrong in his reading of the first X rays, we'll never know. But the new ones are clear. There's nothing wrong with you, Anne, except a little fatigue and a bump on the head. You're well. You've just been too busy to notice. The sal volatile, nurse. Old-fashioned, but it works."

"Whew!" The strong spirits settled the swaying of her mind. She lay for a moment, quiet, looking at him, trying to believe him. "It can't be true," she said at last. "And yet— you wouldn't tell me if you didn't believe it yourself. Would you?"

"Of course not. You must believe me, Anne. I promise you, you can. I'd show you the X rays, but they wouldn't mean anything to you. They mean your future, Michael's, the future of Lissenberg, to me."

"It's impossible."

"Nothing's impossible. Mind you, it's easier for me to be-

214

lieve than for you, because I had been nourishing a few unmedical hopes for some time."

"You had?"

"Yes, indeed. Flying in the face of the facts. But, Anne, think. Would a dying woman have survived what you and Michael went through the other night? In fact, I'd been hoping before that. You looked different; you seemed different. Of course you wouldn't notice. I was watching you. I did. Despair breeds illness, and happiness is sometimes the best cure there is. Happiness and occupation."

"Happy?" She thought about it. "Do you know, I think I'd forgotten what it tastes like." She looked back, across a great gulf, to the plastics workshop; the sad little room; Mrs Briggs. I must do something for Mrs Briggs, she thought. She smiled at Dr Hirsch. "If it's really true," she said. "I wonder if it didn't begin to happen when my voice came back."

"Came back? Had you lost it?"

"Oh, yes, didn't I tell you? When Robin— when my husband was killed and I found out about the woman he'd been living with, it just went. It was the last straw. Everything gone."

"I can imagine. And when did it come back?"

"When I got Carl's letter, offering me the part of Marcus. I suddenly found myself singing." She laughed and told him about Mrs Briggs, who had thought she was a gramophone record. "Goodness, what I owe to Carl," she said.

"Lucky you feel like that. Poor man, he's close to a nervous breakdown. He feels it's all his fault. Getting you here and telling you so little about the setup. He did it for the best, he said. Didn't want to distract you. But it was all our faults really. We none of us took Gertrud seriously enough. Except Michael. He tried not to let her see how he felt about you. He told me he was really glad when Winkler sent him off to Sicily, so he wouldn't be tempted."

"He might have explained." But of course there was no way he could have. "And there was I imagining all kinds of things. I was even jealous of Alix at one point." She stretched luxuriously in the high bed. "Do you know, Dr Hirsch, I am beginning to believe you. I actually feel well. I've just been too busy to notice. Please, can I get up for breakfast?"

"You can do anything in the world you want to." He smiled his stiff smile. "And lord knows you've a right to be hungry after the job we did on you. I do apologise, Anne."

"No, no." This time she reached out to take his hand. "You

were absolutely right." Her voice trembled a little. "You have no idea how close I came to it."

"I can imagine," he said. "And, frankly, we might not have been in time. If you'd taken the lot, it would have been touch and go. They were different ones, you see, stronger. Michael was frantic. Do you remember the speed we arrived at?"

"Do I not!" Now she was laughing. "He keeps trying to run me over. But, doctor, where *is* Michael?" Now, more than anything in the world, she wanted to share their happiness with him.

Dr Hirsch looked at his watch. "He's late," he said. "Something must have come up at the Diet. Well, there's a lot to do."

"What will happen to Gertrud?"

"Exile. Michael wrote her a note, when we knew you were all right, telling her to go at once, and be thankful."

"I wonder... That's a very desperate woman, doctor. I think I had better get dressed. It just might be her that's keeping Michael at the Diet. Could I have my clothes please, nurse?"

"They're not very suitable, I'm afraid, your—" Extraordinary, the woman had actually been about to say "Your Highness." "We sent to the hostel for some, but they haven't come yet."

"Never mind." Anne could laugh at it now. "Those dreadful jeans were good enough for the Diet yesterday. They'll have to do for today too. Quickly, please. I have the strangest feeling I ought to be at the Rathaus."

"But you're not strong enough. Not after..." Dr Hirsch dwindled into silence as she got out of bed.

"You've told me I'm well, doctor. I'm grateful, and about to prove it. What's a little thing like a stomach pumping to a hearty woman like me? As for being hungry, that can wait. Michael can buy me a hunter's breakfast when there's time. Pass me my underclothes, nurse. Oh, and, doctor, would you be a darling and drive me down?"

"I'll certainly not let you go alone." Routed by her evident determination to get dressed whether he was there or not, he turned and fled.

"We dried the jeans," said the nurse apologetically, "but they're pretty awful."

"Never mind. My fake fur will cover the worst of them."

"Fake?" The nurse handed it over lovingly. "My father was a furrier, ma'am. If that's not real mink, I'm not a nurse."

216

"Good God." said Anne, a whole new light opening upon Prince Rudolf and his expensive habits. "Oh, well." She wrapped herself in the light warmth. "So much the better." Lipstick, comb; odd to have this feeling of urgency, of Michael needing her. She was probably lightheaded with hunger, but she was going to respect the feeling just the same. "Glucose tablets," she said. "Please?"

"Yes, ma'am."

This time Anne recognised the form of address. "Not your Princess yet." She accepted the tablets with a smile of thanks. "Just wish me luck."

Dr Hirsch had his Jaguar ticking over at the clinic's opulent door. "You're very anxious, aren't you?" He helped Anne quickly in. "I respect your instincts. We'll make the best time we can, but it's a twenty minute drive."

"Make it fifteen." Anne fastened her safety harness.

Just outside the town, a police car passed them, siren screaming. Not surprising, thought Anne, glancing at the speedometer. She leaned forward as the policeman jumped out of his car and came back to them. One of Herr Winkler's men, thank God, the one who had passed Michael and her across the bridge when she first came. His name? Of course: "Herr Weigel," she spoke before either of the men could. "Can you help us? I need to get to the Rathaus?"

"Your—" Once again that pause. "Of course," he said. "Follow me."

As it had been yesterday—yesterday? Impossible—the Rathaus square was crowded, but this time, instead of arriving by the garbage truck, Anne swept in behind the screaming police car. Weigel was there to open her door before Hirsch could get round to do it. "Quick," he said. "I think the Prince needs you. I've been getting it on the closed circuit. Trouble in the Diet."

"I thought so."

"I'll see you in."

"Thanks." She followed him round to a side entrance, and as they went the crowd in the square recognised her. "Anne!" they shouted. "Princess Anne!"

She turned, briefly, to smile and wave her thanks, then followed Herr Weigel in at a small side door that gave directly onto a dark corner of the dais. For a moment, standing there side by side, they listened, unobserved, to the uproar in the hall. If possible, it was even more packed than it had been yesterday—that faroff, hard-to-imagine yesterday when she

217

had been a dying woman. But though the press were here, the conference delegates were absent, presumubly back at work.

"Order!" Josef's voice. "I must ask for order in the hall. Gertrud of Lissenberg has the right to speak." Now Anne saw that Gertrud and Michael were standing downstage of the big table where the Diet members sat, facing away from the audience and towards the Diet members.

"Hush." Anne put a hand on Herr Weigel's arm as she whispered. "We'll hear her first." There was little chance of their being seen where they stood in the shadows. All attention was concentrated on Michael and Gertrud.

"As I was saying." Gertrud must have been interrupted by the crowd, but went on as coolly as if nothing had happened. "We must think of the future of Lissenberg. We all know and love Michael, but we must recognise him for what he is, young, full of wild ideas, an enthusiast. Trade unions, he wants, and a tiny opera house that will make us a laughing stock. He has not told you, I notice, that underneath the ruins of the old opera house lies a fortune for us all. A fortune which I propose we exploit to make Lissenberg one of the world's richest countries."

"A fortune of death," said Michael. "For us. For the world. Are there not problems enough, between the great powers, without our producing a substance that makes the neutron bomb seem like a child's toy? We are men of peace, here in Lissenberg. How can we take a selfish decision that will make a mockery of everything the peace conference stands for? Gentlemen, I put it to you, once again, that work be started as soon as possible on a new, smaller opera house. In the meantime, no-one to be allowed into the ruins of the old one."

"No!" Gertrud's protest came as Josef rose to put the vote. "Before the vote is taken, I must be allowed my chance to question Michael's right to ask for it. Only the Hereditary Prince has that right on a question of this importance. Yesterday, you acclaimed Michael and his fiancée as your Prince and Princess. A romantic gesture, gentleman, but a mistake. You should have asked a few more questions. If we are really going to put our heads in the sand and bury a fortune in the mountains, then Lissenberg faces the worst financial crisis of its history. And do you think my cousin Michael is the man to cope with that? Yesterday you were carried away by a kind of romantic madness. Today I urge you for all our sakes, for the sake of Lissenberg, to think again. My cousin

Michael is young, a dreamer, an enthusiast. But Lissenberg is facing financial disaster. We need hard business heads, my friends—not romantic dreams. Oh, Michael is a glamorous figure; we all know and love him. He has played out his little drama as Prince Incognito, waiting at table, meddling with the police, riding on garbage trucks, making trouble...trouble everywhere. His father sent him into exile, and it begins to look as if his father was wise. Just think what has happened since he came back. Nothing but death and disaster for Lissenberg. And as for the woman he brought with him: have you noticed, my friends, that she is not here today? Your new Princess, whom you so generously acclaimed yesterday, is absent because she tried to kill herself last night. Dr Hirsch has her in his clinic now, fighting to save her life. Why did she do it?" Gertrud paused expressively, and Anne, who had been listening in a kind of frozen horror, felt Herr Weigel's urgent hand on hers.

He was right. This must not go on. She stepped forward, between Michael and Gertrud. "Let me answer that," she said. "It is my right. As you can see, the story that I am dying is"—she paused, and the audience waited, breathless—"exaggerated," she finished, and got a little sigh that was almost laughter. What rumours had Gertrud's friends been circulating? "I don't know what stories have been told you," she went on now, seeing her way clear. "If I may, I will tell you the truth. Yesterday, my friends, I thought I was a dying woman. And, so thinking, let Fräulein Stock persuade me it was my duty to leave Lissenberg, to leave the man I love. I am sorry to disappoint you, Fräulein Stock." She turned to face Gertrud. "But I did not take the lethal pills you so kindly made available. That is why I am here today, very much alive, and, thanks to Dr Hirsch, and, I think, to Lissenberg, a well woman." And, speaking again to the hushed audience: "If Michael will forgive me, and you still want me, it will be great happiness to be your Princess." She held out a hand to Michael. "There are worse things in life than romantic ideals."

It brought the crowd to their feet with a great roar, and it took her straight into Michael's arms. When she emerged, laughing, blushing, shaken from his kiss, they were still shouting tumultuously. "How very public," she said.

"Just demonstrating your fitness to be our Princess. Anne, it's really true? I know it is, I feel it is, but just say so, for me alone?"

"It's true. God bless Dr Hirsch. Michael, I can't believe it either."

"We'll just have to do our best, but I agree it may take a little time. When I think of last night...No time for that now. Chin up, Your Highness, we've a job to do." He eased her out of the fur jacket and the crowd gave a warm, delighted laugh at sight of her teeshirt with its message: *I love Lissenberg*. Meanwhile the Diet members had conferred briefly, then risen to their feet and were filing round the table, led by Josef.

"Children," Josef kissed first Anne and then Michael warmly on both cheeks. "I am so very happy for you."

"Thank you. We're quite happy for ourselves." Michael turned to shake hands with the next Diet member, while the crowd burst spontaneously into the Lissenberg national anthem.

"What happened to Gertrud?" asked Anne, when the handshaking was over but the singing still continued.

"She ran for it," said Michael. "Best thing she could do for all of us. I hope Winkler has the sense to let her across the border. If you don't mind, love? She did try to kill you. And—I don't like to think what lies she was going to tell when you interrupted her, God bless you."

"No." But in fact Anne thought she did know. Had Gertrud perhaps talked to Fritz, heard his mad, slanderous suggestion that she had been involved in the deaths of Robin and his mistress? She shivered. That was the past, to be forgotten. "I'm glad I got here," she said.

"I should say! Talk about the nick of time! I was scared rigid she would come out with the name of szilenite and then we really would have been in trouble. As it is"—he turned to Josef—"we must get the motion about the opera house through. Too many people know there's something under there by now. We've got to get it sealed up tight, and quickly. Do you know"—he turned back to Anne as Josef moved to the front of the dais to ask for silence—"James Frensham made a kind of boasting confession last night. He's dead proud of himself. Thinks he's going to get a medal or something. That bomb was really intended for mid-day Monday at the conference centre. It was organised by a gang of high-powered international crooks who prefer expensive swords to ploughshares. I don't know which great power would have been blamed for the outrage, but you can imagine what it would have been like, with all those front-rank diplomats killed and everyone blaming each other."

"And Lissenberg in the middle of it."

"Yes. We really do owe a debt of thanks to James Frensham. A very able man. He infiltrated the gang and quietly arranged for the bomb to be used when and where it suited him. Then he had most of the other conspirators rounded up in that car check that caught poor Fritz and nearly did for us the other night, but he's a pretty frightened man now the story is out. I've promised him we'll keep him safe in gaol here, just as long as he likes."

"The rest of his life, I should think. We'll have to build him a special one."

"That's my Princess! Your first royal we. Dear God, Anne, but I love you."

That was the moment at which Josef finally got silence, and Michael's last three words echoed out across the hall.

"What a lot of conspiracies," said Anne, under cover of a new outburst of friendly laughter.

"All over now, my darling. Let's just get this vote done with, and I'll buy you a hunter's breakfast."

ABOUT THE AUTHOR

Jane Aiken Hodge was born in Boston, Massachusetts, and educated at Oxford and Harvard. She is the daughter of the distinguished poet and critic Conrad Aiken. Her recent novels, popular successes here and internationally, include *Strangers in Company, Shadow of a Lady, One Way to Venice, Rebel Heiress, Judas Flowering* and *Red Sky at Night— Lovers' Delight.*

Get Your
Coventry Romances
Home Subscription NOW

And Get These
4 Best-Selling Novels
FREE:

LACEY
by Claudette Williams

THE ROMANTIC WIDOW
by Mollie Chappell

HELENE
by Leonora Blythe

THE HEARTBREAK TRIANGLE
by Nora Hampton

A Home Subscription! It's the easiest and most convenient way to get every one of the exciting Coventry Romance Novels! ...And you get 4 of them FREE!

You pay nothing extra for this convenience: there are no additional charges...you don't even pay for postage! Fill out and send us the handy coupon now, and we'll send you 4 exciting Coventry Romance novels absolutely FREE!

SEND NO MONEY, GET THESE
FOUR BOOKS
FREE!

- - - - - - - - - - -

F0381